OF GODS AND GLOBES
III
TRIGGER WARNINGS AND THE ABYSS

LANCELOT SCHAUBERT

WITH

EMILY MUNRO

INTRODUCTION BY

DR. ANTHONY CIRILLA

Contents

Schaubert, Lancelot

Of Gods and Globes III / Lancelot Schaubert

ISBN: 978-1-949547-14-6

FICTION / Fantasy / Dragons & Mythical Creatures

FICTION / Anthologies (multiple authors)

FICTION / Science Fiction / Space Exploration

Printed in the United States of America

For Kendall Bates:

memento mori, frater.

INTRODUCTION

A Dialog Between Editor Lancelot Schaubert and Three-Time Contributor Dr. Anthony Cirilla:

Ed. Lancelot Schaubert: So this *Of Gods and Globes* series isn't astrology, or isn't supposed to be, so what the heck are we doing here — enough for a *third* volume?

Dr. Anthony Cirilla: As with most complicated concepts in history, we have to start with, "What do we mean by astrology?" The etymology of it is difficult to distinguish from astronomy: the study of the stars. And the development of studying the stars, like many branches of science, were tangled up with what we might call magic today. Isidore of Seville introduced the distinction between astronomy and astrology in the seventh century, though their separation wouldn't be completed until the scientific revolution.

But as C.S. Lewis wrote about in the Discarded Image, the relationship between astronomy and astrology was deeply influential on the poetic vision of the universe. In other words, studying how the stars worked was involved in studying the meaning of human life. So if Chaucer tells you that the planet Venus was shining brightly, that meant something more profound than mere symbolic ornamentation. It signalled a connection between the man as microcosm and the macrocosm of creation.

Lancelot: In a way, it's about the influence of the non-physical mind has over matter? Or of larger bodies on smaller bodies and vice versa?

Anthony: Yes, and I think this series of volumes is working in an area of literary symbolism that extends the work C.S. Lewis was attempting in the Space Trilogy, to restore the power of the Discarded Image. Not that we should return to medieval science, but to a medieval recognition that not only does the mind influence matter, but that matter is infused with mind. We talk about Enlightenment, for example, but that mental state has behind it the physical effect light has not only on the eyes but on the mind. Who hasn't felt better after taking a walk in the sun?

That is partly due to things science can explain, but also because the sun rising as metaphor for a soul coming out of darkness into non-physical light (whether emotional, spiritual, or what have you) is in some sense *the* metaphor, the correct metaphor if I may say so, because it grasps at a real symbolic potential for the mind that the sun actually possesses. We use light to discuss the mind's brightening because light actually does brighten the psyche, and so partakes actually in the process it represents symbolically. The celestial bodies are not the only part of our physical environment that have this potential, but again, that they are perceptually *above us* matters for their symbolic reality for our condition. They lift up our eyes, and so they lift up our minds, too.

Lancelot: Do you think the tidal realities of the planets have actual influence on our planet, though the pseudoscience of modern astrology gets this wrong?

Anthony: I suspect you are more qualified to answer this question than I am, but given that we know that the moon holds sway over the ocean tides, and the almost universal testimony of the effect of a full moon on people, it seems plausible that there are planetary effects that are more mysterious than we have discovered. It's possible that a bias towards our seeming superstitious or appearing to descend to horoscope folly has caused the scientific community to leave such questions less explored than they should be.

After all, our words "influence" and "lunacy," not to mention the names of the days of our week, remind us that this belief has a strange staying power. Science has a very different view of energy than when astrology was rejected, so maybe it is possible to study our relationship to the cosmos in a way that avoids the pseudoscience but answers our lingering questions, like the impact of the moon on hospitals. What I don't know about such things could and does fill many books. But even Disney continues to invite us to wish upon a star. What there is to it scientifically I don't know, but anthropologically there's something profound at work in any case. Maybe we need a branch of psychology devoted to the symphony of the spheres? Do you have thoughts you'd like to add on that subject?

Lancelot: Well if black holes warp time, as illustrated in films like Interstellar, and if our planet is delicately balanced between the orbits of multiple comets, the planets, and the sun, then it seems to me that it might have an effect on a place like Turnagin Arm -- whose tidal realities combine a strong east wind with the moon's influence upon a perfectly shaped series of mudflats: the water matches the resonant frequency of that mudflat inlet, drawing still more water out, ending with forty foot tides.

If that's what mountains and moons and winds can do, what of Saturn? What of Jupiter?

It's said that Titan could host life from tidal realities alone. Yes. I think it's woefully unexplored because of the social pressure associated with astrology.

The theories of Milankovitch cycles point to apsidal precession as a place where planets like Saturn and Jupiter can irregularly shift the orbital ellipse of the Earth, completing a full cycle every 112,000 years. That means about 66,000 years from now, the eclipse of our current orbit will be facing the opposite direction, the entire thing over the course of time spinning like an egg. That's what planets do to our orbit. And that can even effect our climate, which of course effects our diet and disease and interactions, etc.

That in mind...

How might stars share spirits with angels, demons, and fae?

Anthony: As before, my thoughts on this subject begin with my background in the Middle Ages. The geocentric cosmology of Ptolemy was seen by medievals as mapping on to the heavenly structure of angels, which all formed a ladder of the great chain of being pointing to God as the only fully realized being whose existence was pure actuality — no potential, because only creatures have potential. The cosmos was filled with God's glory. Medievals called this the principle of plenitude – in his infinite nature.

Lancelot: Mindful of all this, what borders do you believe science fiction and fantasy share?

Anthony: I think science fiction and fantasy are to some extent a spectrum, with "purer" versions of both, but they enhance each other. Fantasy allows us to ask, What if the world were fundamentally different than how we know it to be? What would remain? Fantasy does not imagine the invention of dragons but asks us to see who we would be if we had to fight dragons. Then it reminds us that we do fight them already and so have to rise to the heroic image we saw in the dragonslayer.

Science fiction deals with how a scientist might create a creature that we could call a dragon, and in so doing invites us to consider how technology and scientific innovation is already a dragon we must tame if we are to incorporate it into life in a healthy manner. One emphasizes externalizing the symbolic power of the mind; the other emphasizes the need for the symbolic power of the mind to wrestle with how our scientific innovations impact the poetic structure of our existence. Like the ancients, we are looking to the sky, but we are closer to the heavens physically than they could have imagined. But we are also further from the heavens than the rich philosophical tradition which makes its way into medieval poetry. I believe that literature is at least in part a way a society digests social change for mental health, and we need to think through stories about how our ever growing access to outer space changes our intuitive symbolic response to life. Fantasy and science fiction are, maybe, something like taking in and pushing out a deep, steadying breath to help us undertake that process.

Lancelot: Fantasy and science fiction as mindfulness for a space faring civilization. I like that a lot.

Anthony: After three volumes, what do you think the Of Gods and Globes anthologies have achieved? How have your hopes been met and what surprises has the process had for you? What have you learned?

Lancelot: As with all of my projects, I tend to take the idea very seriously and myself as the joke. If the anthology's the set-up, my clownish existence is the punchline. If I — as a person — am comedic relief, the project itself is the tragic catharsis. So I always try to get collaborators stick to the form, the logic, of the vision. And then I satirize myself in the process: after all, I'm a nobody and probably deserve to do things like this anthology the least of anyone participating, the least of any other anthologizers. Anthologists? Editorial anthropoids?

Originally, I wanted to riff on the Discarded Image ideas in a way that illuminated the longlævi. I pitched that to four philosophers, and you were the only one that took me up on it, Anthony.

The funny thing is that pretty well renowned authors in the science fiction and fantasy field took up the vision and ran with it. So there in the first volume, here I am with my 1980s style cheeseball back cover featuring the brilliant Juliet Marillier's headshot and her wonderful rescue dogs as well as as well as the faces of many other significant voices. Again: I took the vision and the world and the contributors so very seriously, but not so for myself.

Only recently have I realized that there are instances in which the court jester only services the King and, as a result, makes the rest of the high court look foolish. So I've invested in a few more pairs of dress pants and high thread count shirts for the likes of Juliet and others. (i.e. — I invested in a cover this time around that was better than our last guy, which is to say better than me and some Creative Commons images).

So I think right off the jump, more or less we achieved our goals with the first. It helps to have small achievable goals nested with inside a larger goal, and even my own stories in the volumes lie nested inside my larger, long-term goals. (Unlike other editors, since this was a very vision-forward anthology, I decided to practice what I preach and try my own hand at it, putting my story at the back of each volume under the assumption that I'm the lowest and least fictioneer in every book). Personally, I think I learned that I'm not a very good editor or curator. I'm a pretty good producer because of my capacity to network and because of my experience in several different creative fields (music, film, photonovels, design, performance arts, art galleries, etc.). I'm really better at creating a vision, letting other people run with it, and contributing my own creative work. I'm pretty terrible as an editor, to be perfectly honest. Without Emily, I doubt I would have even pulled the trigger on a third. She kept me in line, straight and narrow.

And, frankly, listing on Duotrope and Submission Grinder was... well it wasn't exactly a mistake, per se, because we *accepted* some amazing stories from those sources. But we were also inundated with submissions and I don't have the team nor the time that Neil Clarke has. But hey, we survived — better late than never.

As far as the project goes, I think I learned that this is a near infinite theme (though I will ban Greco Roman deities if there are any future volumes) because it deals with consciousness. It deals with cosmic phenomena. And it also deals with the spiritual forces of the cosmos (whether one universe or an infinite number, I here refer to the physical actuality contingent on spiritual actuality and spiritual possibility). I mean, we probably received three submissions on Venus alone this time around and have already published two on her. And all three *new* submissions are all different and they're all different from the past two stories, even though it's the same demiurge, same planet.

But as regarding other fields, I think it shows the ripe field for science, ripe field for philosophical inquiry, as well as literary symbolism and poetry.

I think if anything, if we could rescue this idea from modern astrologers and horoscopes in the grocery aisle, we would have come a long, long way in advancing the human heart and thought deeper into cosmological phenomenon. And isn't moving further up and further into the great mystery of being what this is all about?

I'm certainly surprised at the submissions, we have received: some of them make me weep, some make me laugh uncontrollably, most of all they humble me.

Last question: whether science, fiction or fantasy,

we're talking about the music of the spheres: where does that come from? And what does it mean?

Anthony: The music of the spheres is an old idea, older than Christianity, older than Platonism. It goes right back to Pythagoras, though I imagine even he was not the first to formulate the initial thought. Essentially the music of the spheres is a consideration of what music fundamentally is and what it means for the nature of the cosmos. Music is a manifestation of order from the potential chaos of sound. Why can music be made in this universe? Why can random objects be shaped a certain way, and indeed why are our voices shaped, to produce this cocktail of audio vibrations that seem capable of working magic on us?

Ancients and medievals broke music into three categories: the music of the spheres, the music of virtuous living, and the instrumental music (including singing) that we normally think of with the word. As they understood it, the joining of spiritual and physical capacity in producing music was what you could call a sacramental manifestation of the human desire to experience order with the cosmos. If one were the sort of being that could step outside of the universe and hear the sounds of the planets spinning, the stars burning, the asteroids crashing, the rivers running, the wind in the trees — if one could hear all of it, what would it sound like? Would it sound chaotic and random?

But classical theism, including but not only in Christianity (it was also found in Socratic and Platonic thought, Vedantic Hinduism, Judaism, Islam, and so forth), believed that God — the grounds of all Being — was a God of order, not of chaos, and that a

God of order would produce a universe which had, at a maximal vantage point, a sound of harmony.

In essence, a music of the spheres.

Chaotic sounds would be akin to hearing snatches of a symphony from another room and thinking it was badly composed because we weren't able to hear the whole thing. The symphony of the spheres was a richly intuitive answer to the problem of evil, but also a richly powerful notion for the problem of human vice. Musical training requires that you discipline your time, your body, your attention — it participates in virtues necessary for a good life, which is why it's considered either the final or second to final liberal art — in competition, of course, with astronomy. Because music is number studied through time and astronomy is number studied through time and space. This means that when you learn music, you are practicing virtue, but you are also learning how to manifest the same principle of bringing harmony out of chaos. It is a way of experiencing the Imago Dei. But it is also a humbling process because the master musician is submitted to his craft, and we learn to be audiences of the symphony of the spheres through the order the liberal arts help us perceive.

And like the musician, the storyteller celebrates a related power to music: the word. Choosing just the right word, just the right story, to catch a gleam from the celestial light of imagination, puts us each time just a little more in touch with the harmony that is love of God, love of neighbor, and love of the cosmos which is the stage for the drama and the symphony of light's ultimate victory over darkness.

Thank you for the opportunity to have this discussion, Lance. It was fun.

Lancelot: Oh I NEED it, otherwise you're stuck with the universe's court jester to ramble on with lame jokes about why we need these stories, so thank you. Helps to have something like this rather than my cap and bells when all music goes silent.

But if that music goes silent in a world of nonentity and decaying art, my cap and bells will be heard.

Even in the abyss, even long after my death, you'll hear that little tintinnabulation of my jester's cap.

> *Do you hear the ringing of the bell tower?*
> *Counting off the days you can't replace?*

— *DENISON WITMER*

TWINS

BY JULIET MARILLIER

Someone needs to set this story down. Cass can't do it now. Mum and Dad would like it to fade away like some not-quite-believable myth. That leaves me to be the storyteller.

Cass and I shared birthdays, being twins, and it was on or close to our birthday that Z used to pay his annual visit. If I could leave him out of the story, I would. But without Z we wouldn't be where we are now.

We were a classic nuclear family: Dad, Tim, financial analyst; Mum, Leda, helped run a wildlife rescue group. Me, Paul. My brother, Cass. You might see Z as a sort of fairy godfather.

Our parents waited until our twelfth birthday to tell us the truth. We weren't quite what we seemed.

OUR ELEVENTH WAS the best birthday ever, thanks to Z. Our family was comfortably well off by most standards, but compared with him we were poor. Z was mega-wealthy. He was the smartest--some said craziest--entrepreneur in the world. Just about everyone had heard of him, but nobody knew his real name, or if they did, they were sworn to secrecy.

Z was a big man, built like a fighter. When he looked at you it was like he could see right inside you. As if he knew you better than you knew yourself. He'd been visiting us for as long as I could remember, and he gave us the most amazing presents. On my eleventh birthday I became the owner of a purebred Arabian mare. Before that, my riding had been confined to weekend sessions on a hired mount from Templeton's Equestrian Centre, paid for by my parents in return for my getting at least B grades at school. Stardust came complete with stabling at Templeton's, which was close enough for me to reach on my bike, and a new arrangement: at weekends I mucked out stables and did other manual work for the owner, Sue Templeton, in return for Stardust's accommodation. I was big for my age. Strong enough to be useful.

For his eleventh, Cass got a prototype of the not-yet-released ZStream virtual reality setup. He asked Z a million questions about how it worked and what ZCorp was doing to develop it further. After Z left, my brother talked about the ZStream project non-stop until I thought up an urgent need to be somewhere else. I was happier cleaning up horse shit than trying to understand.

I loved Stardust, I loved riding, I loved helping out at Templeton's. I'd never liked Z much but after that I felt as if I owed him something.

COMING up to our twelfth birthday, I was a head taller than Cass and still growing fast. I was on my school's junior football team and aiming to try out for State Juniors when I was fourteen. Thursdays after school I did Aikido.

Cass looked a lot like Dad: quirky mouth, dimples, sticking-out ears. He and I both had the same wavy fair hair as our mother. But apart from that we looked so different you'd hardly have thought we were brothers, let alone twins. When I caught my face in the mirror, I sometimes had the odd feeling that it wasn't really mine. *Where have I seen you before?* Weird.

That was the year Cass won the big science award. He got a medal and a lot of attention, some of it the wrong kind. One day I walked into a bad scene at school: three boys had my brother bailed up in a corner under the stairs. Cass was cringing back, white as a ghost, with his ZLink clutched to his chest. The kids were laying into him, trying to take it off him.

'Hit me, go on, show some guts!' one of them taunted. 'Let's see what you've got!'

'Think you're some kind of genius, huh?' another boy sneered, jabbing with a fist. 'Wimp! Runt!'

If they'd seen me coming they'd have backed off.

But they didn't, and it was all blood and bruises for a while. No broken bones; working with horses gives a man some self-control, even if that man has not yet reached his twelfth birthday. The attackers hobbled away, so scared none of them threatened to tell on me. Not even Robbie Tyler, who was a big blabbermouth.

Cass and I walked home. He wasn't hurt, but he was shaken. I got it out of him that this wasn't the first time. And these weren't the only kids to bother him. I said we should tell our folks, and he said no, if there was a fuss things would only get worse.

"Paul? When will I get big and strong like you?" He was hating himself for asking, I knew it. "We're twins, aren't we? And don't tell me playing football would give me muscles. I'd sooner die."

"You could come and help me muck out on Saturday mornings. That'd build you up."

Cass walked on, looking at the ground. "Ha, ha," he said after a while.

"Serious suggestion. I could use some help. Or you could come riding. The Templetons would lend you a horse."

No response.

"Anyway, you're sure to have a growth spurt soon."

Two days before our birthday we went to the beach house for a long weekend. The beach house was my favourite place: all the swimming and surfing I wanted. If the weather was right, Dad and I would hire a boat and go sailing. That was the best, just the two of us and the ocean. Sometimes we saw dolphins up close, leaping out of the water, diving back down, free as free. Mum liked to sit under a beach umbrella and read. Cass didn't love the place like I did: the Wi Fi coverage wasn't the best. But he brought books with him, stuff like *Exploring the Boundaries of Science*. When he wasn't buried in a book he'd walk on the beach and study creatures in the rock pools, or sit on the sand alone, staring out to sea.

On Sunday Dad took me and Cass for an epic walk up to the lighthouse on the clifftop. Waves were crashing in on the rocks far below, like they wanted to break things to pieces. The cliff face had hundreds of nests on it and birds were flying all around us. I imagined spreading my wings and launching myself off, trusting the air to hold me.

Mum and Dad had been kind of tense all weekend, as if they were holding in bad news. That got me worried. My friend Dave's parents had split up not long before, causing a lot of grief, and I wondered if mine were heading the same way. I couldn't remember them being like that before. But what with school and footy practice and weekends at the stables, perhaps I'd missed something.

When we got back from the walk Mum was packing up. We were going home early, she announced, not staying for a birthday barbecue as planned. I wasn't happy. Why couldn't we go home on the Monday public holiday as planned? But I didn't say anything, because I could see Mum was upset. On the drive home she told us Z was coming to visit us in the morning.

"Birthday presents?" Cass had been so deep in his science book that he most likely hadn't picked up the odd vibe.

"A talk," Dad said. "With all of us." There was something in his voice that shut down any further questions.

Cass and I discussed it later that night, in his bedroom. Were they getting divorced? Had they made a bad business deal and lost all their money? Did one of them have cancer or something? Cass suggested we might be moving house, going to a new town, a new school, even a new country. He was starting to look sad so I tried to cheer him up.

"Maybe we're getting a dog and they're arguing about what kind. I'd choose a rescue Greyhound."

"Standard Poodle," was Cass's instant response. "High on intelligence."

"Border Collie."

"Belgian Malinois."

That would keep the bullies away, I thought but didn't say. It occurred to me that a dog would actually be a good idea. If whatever was on Mum's and Dad's minds turned out to be not too serious, I might suggest it. I tried to imagine my brother with a Belgian Malinois, which is like a police dog on steroids, but I couldn't quite see it. On the other hand, if Cass got as obsessive about dog training as he was about strange byways of science, he and his dog might make a great team. I could sell the idea to Mum and Dad by pointing out how much fresh air and exercise Cass would get with all those dog walks.

A knock on the door. Dad. "Time for sleep, you two. Cass, do you want a chapter of the book?"

I headed off to my own room. A bit later, Mum came in to say goodnight. She looked washed-out, as if she might cry.

"Mum? Please tell me what's wrong. Are you sick? Is Dad?"

She sat down on the edge of the bed. Took my hand. "Nobody's sick, Paul. It's ... it's something from the past, something you need to know. I should wait till tomorrow so we can tell you and Cass together." But she didn't say goodnight and leave it at that. She sat there looking at me. A tear trickled down her cheek. She scrubbed it away and attempted a smile. It wasn't convincing.

"Tell me now, Mum. Please."

"Z won't be here until tomorrow."

This was getting weird. Unless they really were bankrupt and were planning to ask Z for a loan. But why would Cass and I need to be told that? Would we need to work for ZCorp for the rest of our lives to pay it all back? "Mum. Tell me. Whatever it is. If I'm supposed to keep it secret I will, I promise."

Mum gave me a strange look, as if she was sizing me up. "Wait for your father, then."

We waited in silence. I could feel my heart beating. After he'd finished reading Cass a chapter of his current bedtime book--a nightly ritual for the two of them--Dad came in.

"Shut the door, Tim." Mum's voice was deathly quiet. "Paul knows there's something bothering us. He wants us to tell him now, not tomorrow. I think we should. Without Z here."

"Cass is just dropping off to sleep," Dad said.

"We'll tell Cass in the morning. It's better this way." Mum's voice was shaky. What on earth could this be?

It came out, haltingly. And it was so strange I couldn't get my head around it. At first I thought Mum was telling me I was adopted, only that couldn't be right because I'd seen the family photos of Cass and me as newborns in the maternity hospital, with our proud parents beaming at their two pink-faced bundles. Then Dad chimed in with something scientific, using words I'd never heard of. Cass would have been diving for a search engine.

"Wait, what?"

Dad sighed. "It means twins with the same mother but different fathers, Paul." Now his voice was as wobbly as Mum's.

My mind went into a tailspin. I must have looked as stupid as I felt. "But ... but how ...?" I mean, I was twelve years old, give or take a few hours. I knew the facts of life. But this sounded impossible.

Dad explained that it could happen if a woman's body released two eggs and each of them was fertilised by a different man. That was possible if a woman had sex with two men during the short period while the eggs were viable.

There were a million questions in my head but I couldn't find a thing to say. I looked from Dad to Mum to the floor.

After a while Dad cleared his throat and said, 'You're my son in every way that matters, Paul. You're a son any dad would be proud of.'

My voice was all choked up, not with tears but with impossible words. I forced them out. "You said, *tell him now, without Z.* Are you saying Z is my father?" The birthday presents were a sort of guilt offering? I couldn't make myself ask what had happened back then, or how it happened. My mother. My own mother. Willing? Unwilling? Some kind of scientific experiment? Something more mystifying?

"He's your biological father, yes." Dad's quiet words felt like a curse. This was what the mirror had been telling me, but I'd been too stupid to work it out.

We didn't talk much that night. They made me promise to keep it secret. Nobody outside the immediate family — which now, incredibly, included Z — could know. Not now, not ever. Dad said, "We've made our peace, the three of us." Mum said, "The details don't matter now." It was clear that they weren't intending to share the full story.

After they'd said good night and left the room I thought about it for hours, while everyone else was sleeping. It didn't add up. If the true story had to be so secret, it must be something terrible. So how could they have made their peace about it? Not knowing meant I might think up far worse things than whatever actually happened. Was I supposed to face them at breakfast time as if nothing had changed? And what about Z, who'd be here tomorrow? I imagined opening the door to him and saying *Hi, Dad.* It was like the worst nightmare you could ever have. Only I wasn't dreaming, I was lying on my bed staring up at the ceiling, wide awake.

Cass took the news well. As soon as the parents had finished telling him, he rushed off to research heteropaternal superfecundation. Z arrived in time for lunch. I couldn't think of a thing to say to him. I knew if I opened my mouth what came out wouldn't be words, it would be a punch in the gut, a kick where it hurt most, a bullet straight to the heart. He'd done this. He'd shattered our family. We'd never be the same again.

Cass had no problem with Z. After lunch the two of them sat on the back porch in intense conversation about Z's plans to venture into space travel. The European Space Agency was developing plans to establish a manned Moon base, serviced via the orbiting space station, and Z was keen to be a partner. It was clear this would be Cass's new obsession.

CASS ROCKETED THROUGH HIGH SCHOOL. They gave him masses of extension work so he was way ahead of me even though technically we were in the same year. Me? I was so screwed up by the whole parents-and-Z thing that I tried whatever I could to take my mind off it. Alcohol, cigarettes, pills. Wagging school. Getting into various kinds of trouble, including some fights that went right against all the principles I'd learned at Aikido. Cass still had enemies, kids who didn't understand that being super-smart didn't make him good at reading people's expressions or listening attentively if they were talking about something that didn't interest him. They hadn't picked up that his occasional meltdowns weren't temper tantrums but signs of a need to slow down, tune out, be on his own for a bit. I think there was so much going on in his mind that sometimes it felt like it might self-combust.

And I couldn't always be there to stand up for him. Once or twice I did, and once or twice I hurt people. Robbie Tyler was the worst offender--Cass was terrified of him--and things came to a head when I broke Robbie's jaw. I was hauled up before the principal and suspended for two weeks. If I got in trouble again it would mean expulsion. I said the right things. Managed to hold myself together, apologised to everyone including that bastard Robbie who had said some unspeakable things to my brother. Inside I was an explosion waiting to happen.

Dad understood. He took time off work while I was suspended. We did things together: going for a run every morning, digging a vegetable garden, experimental baking. We went riding. We cleaned the car. And we talked about ordinary things. Without a single angry word, Dad let me know he was sad I'd got in trouble and that he'd love to see me working hard at school, looking after myself, thinking of others. And I told him how much I enjoyed doing stuff with him, same as I always had. Towards the end of the two weeks, Mum helped me make a study plan. I had no idea what I wanted to do when I left school. If I didn't improve my grades, working as a stable hand might be the only choice. But, much as I loved horses, I didn't want that. I knew I'd have to get away from home if I wanted to escape the shadow of Z.

Funny, how things work out sometimes. I'd been remembering that long-ago weekend at the beach house, and how I'd felt standing on the cliff top watching the birds. That feeling made my choice for me.

CASS WAS ACCEPTED into his university course two years early. By his twenty-first birthday he was starting a postgrad degree in astrophysics. I worked my butt off during those last years at school and won myself a place at the Australian Defence Force Academy, where a person can do higher education while training to be an officer in the armed forces – in my case, the Air

Force. It meant a move to Canberra, far from my family, to study aeronautical engineering. I knew I'd miss Mum and Dad and Cass and my friend Dave. But it was the perfect solution to my problems. I'd get away from home. I'd have a place to live, an income, and a great career ahead of me. I would fly.

The last time I saw Z before I moved away, he took me aside. "Where you're going, Paul, you'll be asked from time to time if you and I are related. The older you get, the more often that's likely to happen."

I couldn't argue with that.

"It will be easier for you to say there's a distant connection," Z said, surprising me. Wasn't this breaking the family rules? "That's fine with me, and with Leda and Tim," he added.

Really? They'd talked about it and made a decision without even consulting me? I wasn't a kid of twelve any more. "Fair enough," I said, though there wasn't anything fair about any of it. I took a deep breath. Steeled myself. "Z. Listen. You've been generous to us, to Cass and me, in the past. I'll always be grateful for Stardust." My one great regret about moving away was having to leave my horse, though she'd be fine. Sue Templeton's daughter was going to look after her and ride her. "But I want no favors in the future. No gifts. I want to make my own way. To be quite honest, father or no father, I'd be happier if I never saw you again."

Z seemed lost for words, which was surely a first. His face was impassive; his eyes told me nothing. After a few moments, his mouth twitched in a grimace, or perhaps a half-smile.

"You're more like me than you'll ever know, Son," he said.

THE ACADEMY SUITED ME. The degree course was hard, but I got interested quickly and that made things easier. As for the Defence Force training, that had its own set of challenges. I learned to control my temper; I learned to play a different sort of game. To read people. To harness my strength. To take calculated risks. I was told I had leadership qualities. I made new friends, but I was careful. The temptation to play as hard as we worked was always there, especially when we were feeling homesick or things went wrong. But I knew how much was at stake now. I couldn't afford to mess up again.

Cass and I talked on the phone pretty often. Shared our triumphs and failures. He had a circle of university friends, mostly D&D enthusiasts, and he seemed happy with his life.

They all flew over for my graduation: Mum, Dad and Cass. I showed them around, introduced them to my friends, and got all the news from home. I didn't ask about Z, though nobody could miss what he was up to these days – it was all over the media, plus it was a hot topic at the Academy. ZCorp had reached an agreement with ESA to jointly fund the establishment of Camp Athena, a group of habitat modules made viable with the discovery of a water source on the Moon's surface. Z's billions, or trillions, or whatever the extent of his wealth actually was, would lighten the expense for the participating countries. What I didn't already know about this mission, Cass told me whenever we got time on our own during that short visit.

At one point Cass said he'd expected Z to be there for my graduation, and Mum said, "Too public. He wouldn't have wanted to draw attention. This is Paul's day." I hadn't told her or Dad about my farewell words to Z. Besides, chances were he'd stayed out of contact for his own reasons, the Athena mission being a really big thing. He probably didn't give a stuff about what I'd said.

THINGS SAILED ALONG PRETTY WELL for a few years. Cass moved out of home at last, to share a flat with friends. He had a permanent research job at the university, unusual for someone still in his twenties, but then, my brother was not your average person. Me? I had a few different postings, improved my skills, and was promoted. I completed two deployments to the Middle East. When I got leave I mostly went home to see the family, and that was how I met Sara. I'd caught up with my old friend Dave, now a married man with two kids, and we were down at the local pub for a catch-up. The place was heaving – there'd just been a football match and people were celebrating the win over a visiting team.

I spotted Sara over by the bar, and I liked the way she held herself, proud and self-contained, as if she didn't care what anyone thought of her. She was tall, athletic-looking, with gorgeous red hair. Dave knew her; said he'd introduce us. We hit it off straight away. Sara had moved to the area a year earlier to teach English at the local high school. We had a few beers. When the crowd started to dance, we joined in. I wished I had more time to get to know her. Two more weeks of leave and I'd be gone. Drawback of life in the military. Still, we fitted a lot into the time we had: movies, dinners, walks. We were happy and easy together. I'd seen how content Dave was as a family man, and I allowed myself to imagine a future that included a wife and kids, a home of our own, days at the beach like the ones we'd enjoyed growing up, before the dreaded twelfth birthday. When I had to return to base, Sara came to see me off. The farewell kiss was memorable.

THERE WAS ANOTHER DEPLOYMENT, and things didn't go well. When we got back I was offered counseling, along with the rest of my crew, but all I wanted was to see the folks, see Sara, try to deal with my own messed-up mind. They gave all of us extra leave, and I came home.

At the time I couldn't appreciate what people were doing for me, Dad in particular. He gently persuaded me to get up and go outside, he made sure I ate properly and stayed off the booze and got enough sleep. He was still the good father he'd been when I was a mixed-up teenager.

That was what got me thinking--once I'd climbed far enough out of the black hole of depression for my mind to start functioning again--that the way to honour the man who'd fathered me since I was a newborn was to be like him. To follow his example. Sara had been patient with me too, offering love and warmth and no judgement. She knew when to step back and when to step in. It had been hard for her while I was away. What happened to us over there was all over the media back home, at least a version of it was. They called me a hero. Some hero. I saved Pete, yes. Brought him home to his family, a ruin of the man he'd been. But I couldn't save them all. Over and over I saw them suffering, dying, I saw the blood and the burning. Some things stay with you forever.

Sara still believed in me. It was a gift. I knew I wanted to spend the rest of my life with her. But there was the promise never to tell the truth about Z. Sara hadn't asked, not even once, though by that stage I'd used the "distantly connected" explanation with a lot of people. She'd never commented on how different Cass and I looked. I couldn't propose to her without telling her the truth. If we had children, they'd need to know it too. A marriage should be built on trust, not lies.

I could have asked Dad for advice. But I knew Mum was the one I had to talk to, and I couldn't quite bring myself to do it. She'd been badly wounded by whatever happened nine months before our birth, and although she and Dad were good together now, my gut feeling was that she would freak out at any suggestion the secret might be shared more widely. I waited for the right moment.

Sara coaxed me out one evening during that leave. We didn't go far, just to the pub with Dave and his wife. We sat in a quiet corner, me with my back to the wall so I could see all the doors. The plan was to have one drink, maybe two, then call it a night and head home – Dave and Susannah only had a babysitter until nine. Besides, they all knew the outing wasn't easy for me.

When I was only halfway through my first drink, my phone rang. It was Cass, bursting with news.

There was no way I could interrupt the flow, ask him to wait.

"He says I can go, he says he can get me a place on the research team! It's true, Paul, it's real! I do some training, pass the fitness tests, and I'm in!"

He was telling me, basically, that Z could get him onto the Athena team as a researcher. My brother would be going into space.

"Excuse me," I murmured to the others, getting up from the table.

"Are you okay?" asked Sara.

"Fine, fine. I'll only be a minute." I edged my way out of the noisy bar into the hallway, phone to my ear. "Wow, Cass, that's big news. Congratulations! I'm out with friends at the moment, I'll talk to you more tomorrow if that's okay. What physical training do you have to do? The standard must be pretty high." I knew for a fact that without me to push him, Cass got very little exercise. We never did have that childhood dog.

Cass was saying something about gravity and space suits; if he'd answered the question about fitness, I'd missed it.

"Cass." Now I did stop the flow. "I'll call you tomorrow, okay? Listen, I'm on leave for a few more weeks. If you like, I'll work out an exercise program for you. We can do it together while I'm in town."

"Thanks, Paul. Sorry if I interrupted your date."

"Don't mention it, Bro. Talk to you tomorrow."

I disconnected. Turned around. And there was Robbie Tyler with his back against the door to the bar, his arms folded, and his expression making it clear his opinion of me hadn't changed since we were kids. Cold sweat broke out on my skin. Things that weren't real started to close in on me. *Stay calm,*

Paul. Breathe. "Robbie." My voice came out as a croak.

"Paul."

Out of the corner of my eye I glimpsed someone else further down the hallway, just standing there. And what was that silent shadow up by the door to the toilets? An ambush. My heart skipped a beat. "Excuse me," I said, gesturing toward the door to the bar.

"Who the f--- do you think you are? Big shot pilot, hero of the day, huh? Snuggling up with Sara Mackay, as if she wasn't mine first? You took her, you bastard! You stole my girl!"

This was so ridiculous a laugh burst out of me, only it came out as a weird braying sound. "You? With Sara? Bullshit! She's way out of your league."

"Are you looking for a fight? Come on, try me, come on." His fists went up. He took a step toward me.

I felt the rush of adrenaline. My head filled with screaming. *Charge the bastard, shut his foul mouth for good! One punch, that's all it'll take ...* "Dave!" I yelled at the top of my voice. "Security!"

Robbie rushed me. We were on the floor in seconds, wrestling, punching. He was the worse for wear, smelled of drink, and I was close to doing him some real damage when the door crashed open. There was Dave, six foot three and solid with it, and behind him came the bouncer. Robbie's shadowy offsiders had disappeared.

I released my grip as the security man moved in. Got to my feet, unsteady, breathing hard.

Dave put his hand on my shoulder. "It's all right, Paul," he said quietly.

"Tyler, did you forget you're banned?" The security man had Robbie in a hold that made any attempt at escape pointless. That didn't stop Robbie from letting out a barrage of foul curses, some of them directed at Sara, who was now hovering in the doorway. "Off the premises right now, and don't let me see you again!" ordered the bouncer. "If there's a next time, I'll call the cops and you'll be spending the night in the lockup." With that it was over.

I'd been staying at Sara's most nights, and she drove me back there now. She made us both tea. Put a box of tissues beside me on the table. Sat close but not too close.

"He said you were his girlfriend before." That had hurt far worse than the few punches Robbie had got in. "Accused me of stealing you." *Have you been keeping a secret too?* I didn't ask the question.

"My friend Trudy and I went out with his group a few times, when I first moved here. Trudy was keen on one of Robbie's mates. But Robbie and I were never an item. The girlfriend thing is all in his mind. Creepy." A pause. "You do believe me, I hope?"

I nodded. Squeezed her hand. "Of course I believe you. You and him? It's laughable."

"He really hates you, doesn't he? Why?"

"I hurt him once. Years ago. I'll tell you the story some time." I was suddenly worn out, ready for a long sleep, though I might need pills if I wanted that – the bad dreams would be crowding in tonight. If scum like Robbie Tyler could reduce me to a quivering mess, what good would I ever be to a woman like Sara?

One thing I could do, and that was keep my promise to Cass. That way, he got the fitness training he needed and I didn't spend too much of my precious leave trapped in my own mind, fighting ghosts. Cass and I worked out at the local gym. Swam laps together. And spent time at Templeton's, riding – for a beginner, Cass was not bad. By then Stardust was enjoying a well-deserved retirement, and I didn't have the same bond with the hired horses. That brought back the dream, the one where I was a family man with a wife and kids and a dog, only now the scenario included a property with a few acres and some horses. While Cass and I were riding, I focused my thoughts on that. I could leave the Air Force, I could get a civilian job, I could ... but no. Not without telling Sara the truth I was forbidden to share.

Dad told me I was doing a great job with Cass. That got me thinking that one day I might really be like him. A good father. A good husband. The Paul of the good dream.

We were out riding. I was on a bay mare, Aurora, and Cass was trying out Murphy, a grey gelding, since his usual mount, the placid Brian, was unavailable.

The weather was glorious that morning, sunny with a light breeze, and Cass coped well with the challenge of a new and livelier horse. It was as we were heading back, not talking much, just enjoying each other's company, that a gunshot rang out, loud and close. I flinched, then steadied Aurora. But Murphy shied in panic and Cass was thrown. The sound he made as he hit the ground will be with me forever. Murphy sprinted back toward the stable, spooked. My brother lay unmoving. I was down in a flash, leaving Aurora to her own devices. I knelt beside Cass. Breathing. Alive. But not looking good. Broken bones? Head trauma? Spinal injury? I couldn't move him without risking more damage. Phone. My fingers were clumsy on the keys. Templeton's. Ambulance. A wait that felt endless. I murmured words of comfort that Cass surely couldn't hear, and I scanned the fields around us for any sign of a fool with a shotgun. Nobody in sight. Only the one shot. Maybe someone after rabbits. But only an idiot would shoot so close to the riding area. Cass and I had been here at the same time, on the same days, for a couple of weeks now. It wouldn't have been hard for someone to track us down.

"Breathe, Bro. Breathe. Help's on the way." I looked up toward the row of tall eucalypts on the rise, and over toward the road into town, and down to the creek where reeds and bushes would provide good cover for anyone not wanting to be spotted. "You're going to be okay, Cass. I promise. Hang in there. Just a bit longer."

A vehicle went past on the road, a flash of blue, someone gunning the motor. No more shots. Every instinct urged me to gather Cass up, to run, to get him to help before he died right here where he'd fallen. I held myself still. Then Sue Templeton and one of the grooms came in the Jeep, and not long after that we heard the welcome sound of the ambulance siren. My brother was oh-so-carefully loaded onto a gurney. I heard the paramedics on the radio to the hospital, saying Priority One. And he was gone.

Bad became worse. Cass had a ruptured spleen and needed surgery. We camped out in the waiting area: Mum, Dad, me, Sara. Took turns to fetch tea and coffee, go to the toilet, make phone calls. It was hours before the surgeon came out. She looked exhausted, drained. And she gave us the news. She'd had to remove part of the pancreas as well as the spleen, because they'd found a growth. A tumour. They'd know more later, after biopsy results came through.

Cass couldn't have known he had cancer, surely. He'd never said a thing. The surgeon explained further, but I couldn't concentrate, could hardly hear her through the white noise of guilt and regret and fury that was filling my mind. I did pick up one part at the end: it was possible the cancer had spread more widely. The location, close to several vital organs, would make further surgery extremely high risk. We didn't ask the questions we wanted to, not then. How long did Cass have? Was there anyone, anywhere in the world, who could save his life?

A social worker came to talk to us. Told us to go home; we wouldn't be able to see Cass for a long while yet. But we couldn't leave him on his own in the hospital. We made a roster; we'd take six or eight hour shifts in turn. That night, I ended up sleeping on a bench in the waiting area. Around midnight a nurse brought me a pillow, a blanket, and a cup of tea. That simple act of kindness made me cry.

I slept little. Woke early. And did something I'd promised myself I'd never do. I called Z and asked for help.

Z HAD a word in the right ears, and as soon as Cass could be moved, he was airlifted to the major teaching hospital in Sydney, where the top abdominal surgeon in Australia had agreed to assess him. Mum, Dad and I were installed in a luxury hotel a stone's throw away, all expenses paid. Sara couldn't get leave and stayed behind. We were all hoping for a miracle.

Z had been keeping a low profile; dodging public attention. He'd travelled a long way by private jet to be near the hospital, but we didn't see him. Then we got more news, news he couldn't be told by phone. I let him know I wanted to meet. Two large, silent men in a car with darkened windows collected me and conveyed me to the place of his choice, via an underground carpark and a lift labelled Private Use Only.

We met in a room cleared of anything that might identify the location. The blinds were drawn. One of the large men was stationed by the door, the other out in the hallway. Z was wearing his standard collarless silk shirt and light-coloured suit, garments that reeked of exclusive design. I thanked him for his support—it was only appropriate—but he dismissed my words with a wave of the hand.

"You look ten years older, Paul," he said. "Bad news? Tell me."

"Doctor Chen won't operate. It's terminal. Chemotherapy might delay things, but not for more than a few months, and there would be adverse side effects."

Z stared into space. His silence spoke worlds. I

worked on keeping control of myself. I wouldn't show him how close I was to falling apart.

"The drugs mean he's barely conscious most of the time," I said. "But he has lucid periods." I paused for breath. "He doesn't know yet. They want me to tell him. And it needs to be soon. He'll be moved to a palliative care unit."

Z's hands curled into fists on the table. Still he said nothing.

"The Athena mission." I cleared my throat, steadied my voice. "It's his whole world. When he's aware, that's the first thing he asks about: *I will be better in time to go, won't I? How soon can I start training again?* I think he'd accept death willingly if he could travel into space first. I don't know how I'm going to break the news that it won't be happening."

Another lengthy silence. Then Z said, "You could go, Paul. Take his place. Let him follow your journey. You're as well qualified as anyone on the team. Perhaps better."

Shock robbed me of breath. I considered a dark scenario: that this whole thing had somehow been set up so that I, the biological son, would be the one to fulfil Z's ambitions. That the gunshot, the accident, the way Robbie Tyler kept popping up in my life like a bad smell, were all part of some mad plot to make that happen. Briefly, I considered an even wilder idea: that Z might be something like a god, manipulating the lives of others. He took decisions as if there were only one way: his. If he was a god, what did that make me?

"Paul? It makes complete sense. The Chief of Defence would love it. The prestige ... I could have a word."

Perhaps I should have thought of this. After all,

I was the brother who'd wanted to fly. But this was Cass's dream, not mine. Mine was Sara, our kids, the dog. It was a mutually agreed departure from the Air Force after a respectable twelve years' service. In that future my loved ones were close and there was time to breathe. When I found my voice again, what came out was, "I'm a mess, Z. If there's a psych test, I'd fail. I'm supposed to be seeing a counselor; I just haven't done it yet." The truth being that I couldn't face talking about what had happened on that last deployment. Which made me think of Mum and Dad and Z, and how there was something they wouldn't talk about even after thirty years.

"Ask your parents," said Z. "Ask your girlfriend. Ask Cass. It's their trust you need, Son, not mine. But get back to me quickly. It sounds as if the clock's ticking."

"So," I forced the words out, "we're forgetting about secrecy now? The whole world knows you're a partner in the Athena project. The astronauts will have their pictures all over the media. I look like you. You look like me. The tabloids would lap this up. *Entrepreneur's Secret Son.*"

"The media can be controlled. First steps first. Talk to your family. Make a decision. And get started on the counselling, if only to maintain your excellent record with the Air Force." There was a pause, then he turned that penetrating gaze straight on me. "You can do it. You and I, we're not like others. Aim high, Son. You're destined to be a star."

I had no response to this. I wouldn't ask what he meant by *not like others*. Was he deluded enough to believe we were more than human?

Z rose; held out a hand and grasped mine in

farewell. "I hope to hear from you soon, Paul." The meeting was over.

I had to call Sara. We needed to talk. The Z issue was only part of it. If I agreed to take Cass's place, I'd be away for many months – Cass was supposed to spend time at Camp Athena as part of the research team. Then there were the health risks of space travel: dangerous levels of radiation, the effects on the body of changes in gravity, not to speak of the psychological impact on even the sanest of people. What would that feel like for the partner left behind to wait? How could I ask that of her?

I was still working up the courage to call Sara when I went to visit Cass that evening. I walked into the waiting room and there she was, deep in conversation with my mother. They were both wiping away tears. Sara jumped up and threw herself into my arms. For the space of a few breaths the dark cloud lifted, and I was happy. "When ...how ..." I mumbled into her hair. Then I stepped back. "Has something happened? Is he okay?"

"No change since yesterday," Mum said. "He's sleeping just now. Sara got a week's special leave."

"Sit down, Paul." Sara sounded serious; whatever this was, it couldn't be good. Had she come all this way to break things off with me? "Leda has something to tell you. I'll just pop out and get us some tea."

Nobody else was in the waiting room. All was quiet. Just the occasional rattle of trolley wheels, a soft voice out in the hallway, nothing more. "Mum?"

"I have a question first." Mum dabbed her eyes with a tissue. "Why haven't you proposed to Sara yet?" A silence. "You love each other. Anyone can see that."

It had never been harder to find the right words.

"I've got a few answers, Mum. I won't base a marriage on a lie. What if we have children?"

"She knows the truth now." For all the tears, there was a new note in my mother's voice. She sounded resolute. Like a warrior. "I could see how this was eating you up. I've just told her the whole story." When I failed to respond--I couldn't get any words out--she said, "What did you mean, a few answers?"

I sat down beside her. "It's too much all at once. Tell me your part first."

Sara returned as if on cue, carrying a cardboard tray with three cups. She handed us one each, then settled on my other side. And Mum told the story from the very beginning.

"It was an assault. It happened at work, at River Rescue. He'd been there earlier in the day to look around; I was friendly then, hoping he might make a donation. He came back as I was closing up, when the other staff had all gone home. Brought a bottle of wine, sat down with me to talk about fundraising and poured me a glass. I think he must have spiked my drink. I...I didn't consent to what happened after that. But I was helpless to stop him. Later on he apologized, called it a misunderstanding, and offered to drive me home. I said no and he left. Tim came to pick me up. I told him the truth."

That bastard. That slimy scum. And now he was trying to tell me how to live my life. With an effort I slowed my breathing; unclenched my hands. "And you didn't report it?"

"Paul, the justice system in this country is weighted against women who report sexual assault. Few cases result in conviction. A woman can expect to be cross-examined mercilessly, have every possible detail of her life put on show, with the slightest inconsistency in her testimony taken as an indication that she's a liar. Should she break down under questioning it's suggested she's mentally unstable, unreliable. If the accused happens to be a high-profile, fabulously wealthy man, she's got next to no chance. He'd have hired the top barristers. I wasn't prepared to go through that. What he'd done to me was enough trauma."

I swore under my breath. "And that was what Dad wanted too?"

"It was my decision to make. He supported me as he always has. At that point, of course, we didn't know I would be pregnant. Or that the result would be our wonderful twins." Mum reached out and took my hand; squeezed it gently. "It was the right decision at the time."

"What about Z? He should have been punished for what he did."

"But he wouldn't have been," Mum said quietly. "Imagine your life if this had gone to trial. Imagine all our lives. As it is, Z has supported the family generously over the years. That's his choice. It makes him sad that he can't acknowledge you publicly as his son. He's told us so many times."

The door to the waiting room opened. It was the ward sister. "Cass is awake. You can go in and see him now. One at a time, please, and it needs to be brief."

Mum had been brave. She'd told her story at last, not for her own benefit but for mine and Sara's. Sara had flown back here, she'd been a listening ear for Mum, she'd stood by me when I was at my lowest. It was time for me to find my courage. "I'll go in first," I said.

Cass was hooked up to various machines. There was a drip in his arm. It was only a day since I'd seen him, but he looked thinner. His skin seemed to be tightening over the bones of his face, and his eyes were sunken and shadowed. "Bro." He gave a ghost of a smile.

I sat down on the bedside chair. Tried to find the words. But Cass beat me to it.

"I'm dying, aren't I?" His voice was a wisp of silk, tenuous and fragile. "Tell me. How long do I have?"

I told him. The cancer had spread. He couldn't have more surgery. Chemo might delay the end but not halt the progression. He'd be moving out of the ward and into Gabriel House, the palliative care unit. "They won't say how long. Depends on the chemo. But ..."

"But I won't be going on the Athena mission."

"I'm sorry, Cass. I'm so sorry, Bro."

"Not your fault."

I knew my brother well. I shouldn't have been surprised that a brain like his could put together the snippets of information, the half-heard conversations, the body language of staff and visitors, and reach the truth.

"You should go," Cass said. "On the mission. You'd be great."

So here I am, on my way to Camp Athena, in a high-tech shell hurtling through space at unthinkable speed. Behind me I leave my family: the one that is and the one that will be, for Sara and I had fertilised eggs frozen. They wait in an IVF facility, future children conceived before the radiation hazard of this venture can threaten my capacity to become a father. I make those children a solemn vow: if I survive this, if I have a future, I will not let Z meddle in your lives.

The Chief of Defence said I would be an asset to the mission. It must be true. If it were not so, surely even Z's wealth and influence could not have won me this place. So I thank my parents for guiding me when I was lost; I thank my wife for her love and her steadfast belief in me.

Cass was never going to cling on long enough to watch me do this. He was gone well before the mission became reality. But he has come with me, in the form of a diamond created from his ashes. I wear him around my neck on a cord; he is always close to my heart. The rest of him, we scattered from the cliff top near the lighthouse. He flies with the gulls, high over the waves, whole and free. The diamond, I will leave on the Moon.

When I am home, when this is over, I will see you in the sky, Brother. Shining bright, a beacon of hope and joy. I will tell my children the story.

Author's note:

TWINS is based on the Greek myth of Castor and Pollux and the related tale of Leda and the Swan. Re-casting these stories in a contemporary setting proved to be a challenge, but themes emerged that are entirely relevant to today's society: wealth and power going hand in hand; the impact of military PTSD; the way the legal system treats women who speak up about sexual abuse; the varied nature of families. Above all, TWINS is a story about real people facing tough choices.

DEATH IN VENUS

BY CHRIS EDWARDS

Madame Eichenfluss arrived at the orbital with her customary lack of fuss. One of the attendants at the gate recognised her and commented favourably upon her latest novel, but aside from that minor social entanglement she managed to slip onto the station gratifyingly unnoticed. Or perhaps not unnoticed, but the Morningstar received many wealthy visitors and consequently enforced rather draconian rules regarding press and privacy.

The orbital itself seemed pleasant, a little ornate and behind the times, but well-tended and clean. Generous "windows" (clearly electronic screens, but designed to give the fiction of a few centimetres of glass between one and the void) gave a handsome view of the planet below, glowing with reflected sunlight. It was a striking vista, and one that she spent several minutes admiring before continuing her stroll. None of the staff seemed inclined to pay the slightest attention to the screens — perhaps they had seen it often enough for it to lose its magic.

Madame Eichenfluss was relieved to feel that Morningstar observed usual earth gravity in its rotation. She had been expecting the lower gravity so often favoured by the idle rich, but she was too old and too prim to go bobbing around like a cork. It was a wonder to her contemporaries that she didn't simply juvenate rather than allow herself to fall into the decrepitude of age at scarcely a century old. Even had she not had considerable personal resources to call upon then her own government would have gladly provided the service for such an esteemed national treasure.

She had observed the juvenated, in fact even now one was before her on the debarkation ring; physically perfect, eternally youthful, bodies constructed for strength, health and pleasure. They carried no outward sign of their age, and yet the steps were those of an older person. The unneeded hand on the handrail, the slight pause before pushing off into the press of people in the corridor — these were not the traits of true, heedless youth. Once one has learned to live with caution, it is a very hard lesson to forget.

Of course, she missed her own youth, but that coin had been spent as it should be — foolish decisions, loud conversations in the small hours of the night, risky activities that worried her parents, passionate affairs and heartbreaks. All of these had faded over time to a sober stoicism as she found and dedicated herself to her craft, the process only accelerating after Gustav's death. Juvenation seemed to her something of an insult to the young, a facade which mocked that which it tried to replicate.

This, then, was the meat and drink of her thoughts as she promenaded along the corridor, when suddenly her attention was drawn to the view. From the dark crescent of the night side of Venus, there came a flicker of light. Rippling waves of energy raced and coiled lazily across the atmosphere, luminescing the clouds with their touch. She felt a sense of deja-vu, as if this bizarre sight was somehow familiar to her. Then there was the unaccustomed quickening of her own pulse, a flush of excitement as her breathing sped up. Her mind flit through old memories, even as her eyes remained transfixed. One of her fingers absently ran along the papery skin of her jaw, tracing the path of a lover's touch from decades ago.

"Ashen light, they call it."

Madame Eichenfluss turned, suddenly very aware of what a strange sight she must have looked, a centenarian dowager practically panting with excitement! Beside her was a young lady — yes, truly young, not juvenated — who seemed to be in her early twenties. Amusingly, she was dressed in much the same style as Madame Eichenfluss had enjoyed as a girl, culottes and a blouse so thin it was practically a wisp. The same rebellious fashion that had scandalised her own parents, but then it always cycles around in the end, doesn't it?

"I do beg your pardon," Madame Eichenfluss recovered herself, "I was quite caught up in the... display."

"The ashen light. They don't understand what causes it, you know. There's all kinds of theories, of course, but that's just because they don't like to admit they have no idea what it is." The girl leaned over and put her head on the glass.

For a moment Madame Eichenfluss was struck

with a sense of longing. She seemed so perfect; that combination of self-assurance and insecurity, of healthy growth and artless sculpting that only the young can achieve. "It is certainly very beautiful." But the truth was that she had lost interest in the lights from the moment she had seen the young lady.

The girl looked around at her and smirked, "Maybe you should write a book about it?"

For some reason that she couldn't fathom, Made Eichenfluss felt embarrassed by this. Usually she took pride in her craft, but the girl's attitude made it seem as if words were chains she was hanging around experiences meant to be lived. Awkwardly, she tried to shift the conversation into more familiar territory, inquiring after the girl's name and conditions of travel. Her gambits bought her little, though, except to learn that the girl was traveling with her grandmother, whose chaperoning eye she had managed to escape. It was not long before the girl became bored of the conversation and drifted away.

For the rest of the afternoon Madame Eichenfluss felt quite out of sorts. By turns she felt invigorated, embarrassed and excited; a giddy rush of sensations that she hadn't experienced with such force for almost half a century. As she bathed in preparation for dinner, she found herself in one of her increasingly rare moods to enjoy some self-pleasure, and was surprised at the intensity of her own response. She smiled at the idea of a famous elderly author being found dead in a bathtub after over-exerting herself in this fashion. Presumably the Morningstar would cover it up, the death certificate would read nothing but "heart failure", but the story would get out — it always did.

The dining room of the Morningstar was a grand affair, the ceiling showing a massive view of the darkened planet below. Real human waiting-staff went gliding to and fro across the carpeted floor in crisp uniforms. It was a showy tribute to a gilded age of the past, but on a certain level it worked.

Madame Eichenfluss dined alone, but she was used to that. From the corner of her eye she kept a lookout for the girl, trying not to be too obvious. Perhaps she took her meals in her cabin?

As the soup course was being cleared away, she asked her waiter if he knew anything about the ashen light phenomenon.

His brow creased, "It's a side effect from the collection of eighth-state cold plasma. Just a little atmospheric discharge."

Madame Eichenfluss was a good enough judge of human character to see that he was skittish around the subject. Presumably the girl was right; in this age of scientific wonders it must be troubling to find anything that humanity could not understand.

Between the soup and the main course, she was surprised and gratified to find the girl sitting herself down at the other side of her personal table. Politely she enquired if the girl's grandmother was perhaps taking dinner here as well?

The girl shrugged, "She's around."

It seemed that neither of them was inclined to talk, but the silence didn't feel awkward. As Madame Eichenfluss sipped her wine, she realised it felt more like that delicious tension of a tryst; that stage of an assignation where unspoken promises have already been made, and all else is simply anticipation of what is to come. Above them the night-side of Venus rolled across the heavens. Ancient goddess of love and lust, seemingly casting her spell over the old woman.

But what could she possibly offer to somebody as

young and vital as this creature? No matter how well maintained, her body was ancient by comparison. And yet the girl did not recoil as their hands brushed across each other on the table.

"My dear, what is your name?" Madame Eichenfluss had to know at least that much.

"What's your name?" The girl retorted.

"Madame Eich...that is to say, ... Ulrike. My name is Ulrike"

"Then that's my name too," replied the girl, smirking.

Madame Eichenfluss was casting about for another avenue of interaction when suddenly the girl rose and sauntered away with a simple "See you later." Somewhat dumbfounded, the author downed the remainder of her wine to slow her pounding heart, and then ordered another. She picked at her main course, but found that she had little appetite. Instead she ordered and drank two more glasses of the heavy, fragrant house red, and retired to her room.

Drunk for the first time in a long time, she disrobed entirely and looked at herself in the mirror. Although she would not partake of juvenat, she had no desire to inhabit a broken body, even she had taken the basic regimen to hold infirmity at bay. She looked no more than perhaps sixty in natural years. But then, so few people aged naturally these days, who really knew?

Caught by a whim, she opened the curtains to show the face of Venus staring down. Perhaps there was a reverse viewer on the outside of the hull, and some passing space-hand would suddenly look down to see a naked old woman staring up? The image made her laugh.

Suddenly there was a knock at the door. Madame

Eichenfluss turned, almost falling over, and steadied herself with one hand on the bed. Somehow, she knew who it would be before she even reached the door. When the image showed the girl standing outside, she opened it without even thinking to put on clothes.

The girl prowled into the room, looking about. Behind her Madame Eichenfluss closed the door, her hand already trembling with excitement. Gustav had been dead a long time, and heaven knows, they'd shared their bed with plenty of others before that. When had she become so closed-off to physical pleasure? The girl was so like her, so like the way she had been when she was young. It was almost painful to look at her.

Madame Eichenfluss put her hands on the girl's shoulders as they both looked out at Venus. She could feel the beating of her own heart, the perfume of the heavy wine on her breath, the feeling of young, strong muscles under healthy skin beneath her hands. The girl turned her head to look into Madame Eichenfluss's eyes, now with seeming approval, "There you are!"

The kiss was like a river running through her body, sweeping away everything that had calcified around who she had once been. And then suddenly she was helping the girl to shimmy off her clothes and throwing her down onto the bed and losing herself to passions she thought long forgotten. In the throes of ecstasy, she looked up to see those white waves rushing across the surface of Venus, cresting in time with the beat of their bodies.

For a moment she was pulled back to herself. What was she *doing*? Suddenly, and just for a split second, Madame Eichenfluss caught sight of the mirror. Her ancient body bucking on the bed, but wrapped around her was not a girl but a spidery figure wrapped in pulsing white light. Combined with the alcohol and the exertion, it was too much and she suddenly felt a clamp fasten around her chest, pain raced up her jaw and arm. The girl's face looked down at her sadly as darkness swam up to embrace her, but made no move to summon help.

The captain brushed her white glove across the filigreed wall and inspected the tip of one finger for dust as she waited for the medical team to finish. As always with these matters, discretion was best, but she needed to know what to tell the board. Eventually the medic stepped out into the hallway, looking somber.

"Another one, then?" she asked.

He nodded in confirmation, "It'll be written up as heart failure, of course."

The captain chewed her lip, "She didn't fit the usual profile. Bit old?"

The medic shrugged, "Hardly an exact science, Captain."

She sighed. Probably best not to start a panic over a statistical outlier, "Very good, then. I'll let head office know."

She turned and began to walk back to her office, mentally composing the message in her head. Like all of the permanent staff, she was very careful never to look directly at the image of Venus hanging in the viewing ports along the wall as she went...

Searching for the Door into Death

by Michaele Jordan

She was so young she still believed in true love, complete with dancing and roses and fireworks. When she first met him, it was just like Romeo and Juliet. Their eyes had met across a crowded dance floor. (It was her big brother's senior prom. He'd begged her to come as his geek buddy's date.) She'd stopped breathing for an eternal moment, and then started walking toward him, drawn as if hypnotized, or maybe like a moth diving into the flame of her own burning heart.

"My name's Jesse," he had whispered. "And I think I love you."

"My name is May," she'd answered. "And I love you, too." They'd leaned in toward each other and kissed, softly, slowly, tenderly. She could have hung on his mouth forever.

Then, suddenly: a hand on her arm—her brother snarling, "What do you think you're doing?"—a cold place where love is no longer sheltered. They'd been torn apart.

For a while her world had been empty. Empty streets, empty school, empty house, empty heart. Some people had said it was the pandemic. She'd shrugged, not knowing or caring. Time probably passed. Maybe not.

Then a knock on the door. Outside: the Beatles singing, "You Say It's Your Birthday." Birthday? Her mother had been nattering something, chocolate cake, maybe? So she'd looked out the sidelight, but . . . it was Jesse. He was wearing a mask, but how could she not know his wonderful eyes? She'd flung open the door.

"Do you still love me? Because if we leave right now, we can get to Indianapolis in time to get married today." She'd grabbed her purse and jumped into his car without a thought, her mother's voice drifting behind, asking, "Who's that at the door, Sweetie?"

Later on, they had laughed at all the crazy adventures of that day. Getting lost on the way to Indianapolis—*how can you get lost on a freeway?*—and why Indianapolis?—*'cos you can't get married same day in Chicago*—the JP stuttering interminably—*I was afraid he'd screw up so bad it wouldn't be legal*—the mysteries—*You came to prom in Chicago, but you live in Indianapolis?*—and the discoveries—*No, but my Auntie does, and she claims me as a dependent, in case my father shows up.*

All the glorious revelations, with every adorable detail deepening their love, leading to a wedding night that was not crass and ugly like what the boys talked about at school, but mystical and life changing. It had lasted three days, as they discovered when his Auntie came home and banged on their door. "What? You two still at it? You better get up and moving. The cops in Chicago are looking for her." She'd made them breakfast and kissed them. "You two just never forget you love each other, and everything else will work out as best it can."

And they never had. Each morning had started with "I love you." Each night ended the same way. Their parents had been furious, but there'd been nothing they could do. They were both of age, so it was legal.

And also like Romeo and Juliet, the world had crashed brutally down around them, leaving him dead. A stupid car crash. Rich boy driving drunk. He paid her a lot of money. He said he was sorry. She didn't believe him.

She'd thought the world was empty when they were apart. But at least he'd been alive somewhere. Now he was dead, the world ceased to exist. She sat in her chair, staring at the wall, until the landlord threw her out. Her mother came and led her home, where she sat in another chair and stared at the wall. Or lay in bed, staring at the ceiling. She ate only when her mother insisted. "You can't go on like this," her mother wailed, but she wasn't listening.

Or maybe she was, because that night, when she was lying in bed, trying to sleep, she heard her mother cry again, "You can't go on like this!" And then again, "You can't go on like this!"

And then again. And again. Over and over in a crazy sing-song, until she sat up in bed, and screamed, "Shut up, will you? Just shut up!" Only it turned out, she wasn't in her room. She was perched on a ledge on a mountain top under a vast sky, overlooking half the world. Fields and forests, and a distant city. Her mother wasn't there. I must be dreaming, she said to herself.

"She's right, you know," purred a soft, husky baritone. Definitely nobody she knew. "You really can't go on like this. It's time to fish or cut bait. Either give up or get over it."

"I can't," she answered. She thought about turning around to see who was talking but . . . she didn't. "You think I wouldn't like to get over it? You think I'm having fun here? My heart's been torn out of my body. You don't just get over that."

"You really believe that? Then give up. Stop taking up space and let the people around you get on with their lives."

"You mean . . .?"

"You know what I mean." He meant dying, of course, her murdering herself.

She almost liked the idea. No more pain. No more hungering for what wasn't there. An end to it. And if there was an afterlife, Jesse would be there. Her whole body flushed with the sweetness of that prospect. Except . . . if there was an afterlife? That was a pretty big if. And she couldn't just die, any more than she could just get over it. She'd have to pick up the knife and do it to herself.

That was a very scary thought. She wouldn't have thought she was capable of being scared, what with the aching blanket of emptiness all around her. But the thought of doing it to herself frightened her into more wakefulness than she had felt since . . . well, since. She shuddered.

"So you're not giving up?" There was that voice again. "That brings us back to getting over it."

"But how?" She turned her head, as if expecting to see him. Nobody there, just a night sky. Hadn't it been daylight, looking down from the mountain? But now she was looking up at all the stars in the universe. They were lovely, glorious, overwhelming. They made her feel too small to live.

"You tell me," he answered. "What would make you feel better?"

"Having him back." Her mouth answered without her troubling to open it.

"Then go get him."

The conversation was over. The voice was gone. The stars were gone. The fields and forest—the whole mountain—all gone. She dropped back down into a deep, dreamless sleep.

When she woke, she remembered the dream as perfectly as yesterday. Better than yesterday, actually—better than anything since . . . She made herself think the thought through. Since the funeral. She went downstairs, and her mother jumped up from the kitchen table. "You're up! You've been out so long I wondered if I should call a doctor, in case . . ." In case she'd taken something, her mother didn't say aloud.

May looked at her mother. Her face was drawn, her hair unkempt. As if she'd aged ten years. "Oh, Mom, I'm so sorry. You've been worried sick, haven't you? I'll try to do better. Get a job, help around the house." Her mother stared at her, open mouthed. Then her face crumpled and she started to cry. May sat down and wrapped her arms around her, and rocked her, whispering, "I'm sorry. I'll do better."

She got a job as a telemarketer. Only part time, but better paid than she'd hoped. And it left enough spare time for research. She looked up 'life after death' on the internet. She got several million hits referencing dozens of variant afterlife beliefs. Well, dumb. What had she expected?

She tried rephrasing it to 'restoring life to the dead'. That brought in a bizarre collection of zombie fiction and scientific studies about pig brains. Distinctions were made between clinical death and biological death. There were incidents of artificial respiration working hours after drowning. There was a radical procedure for replacing the blood of the recently deceased with cold saltwater. There were cautionary tales of persons technically revived but brain dead. Some pious cant about finding your lost ones within dreams and inside yourself.

More zombie fiction.

The internet was boring. She decided to check out some churches, and see if any of them could raise the dead. She started with the Christians, since they had a history of it. Yes, everybody was going to be resurrected in the end, they said, but it wasn't the end yet. She'd have to wait. Yes, Jesus had resurrected Lazarus, but that was Jesus. Did she think she was as good as Jesus?

Short form: the churches couldn't do it, wouldn't even if they thought they could. Evil. Flagrant disobedience of God's will. Mutinous on a satanic scale. You'd be damned if you even tried. No, there weren't any secret cults, based on exorcist rites. Just no. Get out of here. One priest even sprinkled her with holy water.

The Jews were more accommodating. Not that they were any more help—but they were happy to talk about it. In fact, it was such a wonderful question that several rabbis came together to discuss it. They mostly figured it wasn't possible in the here and now—probably. Even setting aside Ezekiel in the valley of dry bones, which was an extremely special case, performed only on the specific command of HaShem (which meant God), had not Saul resurrected Samuel successfully?

But Saul's experience was neither typical nor encouraging. He'd done it, yes. But the Samuel that Saul had raised was an angry spirit under compulsion, not a corporeal human being, free to pursue his life normally. (Although, we don't know he wasn't corporeal, one of them pointed out. The text doesn't say he wasn't. And the messenger/angels were generally corporeal.)

Anyway, they all agreed that Saul paid a heavy price, although his unhappy fate wasn't really the result of this particular sin. The whole reason he'd summoned Samuel in the first place was because he was already in deep shit with HaShem.

May intervened before they could debate Samuel's unhappy fate further. She was grateful for their time, she assured them. She'd enjoyed the visit, and the rabbi's wife made the best schnitzel she'd ever tasted, just to die for. (They insisted she take the recipe.) But she was out of time, she had to go. Really. Her mother was waiting. But thanks again.

She got lost three times, looking for the local mosque and decided to give up on Islam. The Buddhists just shrugged. How long had he been dead? If he had already reincarnated, she'd have to murder a baby just to get his soul back out, let alone restore him to his past incarnation. Did she really want that?

So much for mainstream religion. She went back to the computer and typed in 'necromancers'. That was when her memory got fuzzy.

She kept forgetting the names of all the useful websites. (The scams or scumbags, she remembered just fine.) She left the site windows open, but somehow, they always timed out. She jotted down written notes. And lost the notes. It was like the good stuff didn't want to be found.

"Gawdammit!" she snarled at the voice from her dream. Stupid, of course, but remembered that dream better than yesterday. "You told me to go get him. So where do I go?" She said it aloud so she heard herself say, "Where?" How could there be a 'where'?

All the legends spoke of the land of death, the place where the dead went. Christian heaven was a place where the streets were paved with gold, and hell had residential circles and fiery pits. In the Jewish world to come, scholars sat around and discussed the Talmud. As if it were a coffee shop or a flame war in a social medium's comment thread. (Maybe if you weren't a scholar you went to a disco?) Even the Buddhists had a murky place where the soul scrubbed off its last life and prepared for rebirth.

The Greeks, in particular, had thought there was a place so real that it was located on earth, or at least partly located on earth. There was an actual door. Not generally used by people who were still alive, but still, a door. Orpheus had used it to go get his wife back. So where was this door?

"You gotta tell me," she muttered, still talking to the voice she knew perfectly well wasn't real. "At least give me a hint."

THAT NIGHT SHE DREAMED AGAIN. She knew instantly, before she even opened her eyes, that she wasn't in bed and she wasn't awake. "Am I on top of the mountain again?" she wondered. "Or under the starry sky?"

Neither. She was standing in the middle of the ocean, as if she'd walked out there. She turned all the way around—she had no trouble with the footing—but there didn't seem to be much difference between one direction and another.

Endless water, undulating away, leaving a sparkling, rippled surface behind. Occasionally, a roll capped and turned into a tiny wave. Whenever a wave washed over her feet and fell back, she felt a pull, slow but inexorable, as if the sea meant to take her with it. She could sense depths below her as infinite as the starry sky had been. She was just a molecule drifting above the undertow.

"Wow, you are one stubborn little creature." Even knowing where she was, the instinct to turn and look was overwhelming. Of course, there was no one there. Just more shimmering water. Thousands of shades of blue and gray, green and brown. "Really, I'm impressed. Most humans would have given up by now."

"I thought we'd agreed, I'm not giving up," she snapped. The voice laughed and laughed. "You told me to go get him. That means there's somewhere I can go, right? So where's the door?"

"Wherever you want it to be."

She would have screamed at him, but a wave washed over her feet, and she felt the drag of the sea from miles below. Beneath the sea was the earth, holding her fast, pulling her forward as it turned. She was too small and helpless to scream at anyone. She could barely breathe enough to whisper, "What does that mean?"

Again, the voice laughed and laughed. "You're asking an oracle to tell you what a prophecy means?

That's delicious. Humans—so small and silly you wonder how they can live. But, you know what? I like you. I'll give you a hint. The door is behind you."

"What?!?" She spun round again, even though she knew there was nothing behind her. And while she was spinning, she started to sink. The earth was claiming her, drawing her down. She was consumed by gravity, and the waters closed over her head.

Down, down, down. Past glowing coral reefs and impossible looking sea-beasts, until she came to rest on a sludge covered surface littered with skeletons. One raised itself up.

"My darling." Its teeth chattered and clacked, but somehow the noise came out as words. "You should not have come here when you are still alive. But Gawd, it's wonderful to see you! Come give me a kiss." It reached out for her with bones that only faintly resembled arms.

A skeleton wanted to kiss her? Ew! And it couldn't possibly be Jesse. He was buried at Wunder's Cemetery, not far from the lilacs. But this was not the real world, anything could happen here, she could even breathe underwater. What if it were Jesse . . . She couldn't reject him just because he was an ugly skeleton. But she still wasn't going to kiss it, unless she was sure. "When's my birthday?"

It drew back, and managed to look offended. "You're kidding, right?" She crossed her arms and tapped a foot, waiting. "Don't you think you're being kind of petty? I mean, I'm dead, and you're worried I'll forget your birthday?"

"So you don't know?"

"So I forgot! I'll bet you don't remember mine, either."

"Who are you, really? Or maybe I should ask, what are you really?"

The voice started to laugh again, and the skeleton dissolved into sparks. (Sparks, underwater?)

She woke up shaking and drenched in cold, cold sweat. But the voice had played fair. The hint was solid, and she figured it out. "The door is behind you." And then a skeleton in front of her. The door was in between behind her and in front of her. That would be inside her.

Every human carries their own death inside them, the place they retreat into at the end. Most people won't go there—maybe can't go there— until their mortal flesh has nowhere left to flee, and can endure no more. But there were shamans who taught that you had to pass through death to find the path to enlightenment, and mystics who preached that you had to hit rock bottom before your soul could rise.

So the door was anywhere she happened to be when she looked inward, all the way into the darkness she tried to disown.

Deep breath. She called down to her mother that she was starting a big project, and not to disturb her, please. Or hold dinner—she'd make a sandwich later. She pulled her desk chair over to the closet door. Maybe she didn't need a real door. But then, maybe she did. There was a mirror hanging on the back of the door. Fine, she was supposed to look inside herself. Maybe she didn't need to literally look in a mirror. Or then again, maybe she did.

She sat down and stared into the mirror, into her own eyes, looking for that horrible place, where a skeleton had tried to kiss her. It looked just like her closet door. Except it wasn't. The only hard part was making herself stand up and grasp the door knob.

There was nothing on the other side. Literally

nothing. No floor, no ceiling, no earth or sky showing through where the floor and ceiling should have been. No light, and yet no real darkness either. Just nothing. So completely empty that she started to dissolve into the void, because it wasn't possible to exist in nothingness—it wouldn't be empty nothingness if she were in it.

She could just barely remember where she was going and why, and that apparently gave her momentum enough to drift forward (if you could call it forward) until she came to a . . . a . . . call it a memory of existence. There was . . . a presence? Or maybe not, because there was still nothing there. A different flavor of emptiness then, a sentience that didn't need to exist to be there. She stood before it, feeling her own reality drip away until, finally—because she had to do it soon, while she still could—she said, "Give me back Jesse."

The voice laughed and laughed. "You are the toughest little critter I've seen in centuries. This is not habitable. How can you even stand up in here?" She wanted to answer that she couldn't, but her brain lacked the strength to think of the words, and her lungs lacked the breath to speak them. The voice went right on laughing. "I guess I'd better give you a hand, here. I really want to hear this."

The air that didn't exist shimmered and rippled around her. She found herself in a sort of bubble. She became a little bit real again. She could breathe. There was still nothing around her, not even light, but somehow there was a glowing void that pulsed with twisting, incomprehensible images whenever she tried to look at it. "Better now?" purred the voice. "So you want me to give back Jesse. You got a reason why I should?"

"He had his whole life to live!" she burst out. "He had brains and dreams and possibilities! He had true love! And some stupid drunken frat boy ran him down like a dog. It wasn't fair!"

It laughed again, harder than she'd ever heard it before, and it had spent most of their relationship laughing at her. "Fair? You adorable little cockroach. Of course it's fair. Everybody comes to me sooner or later. Everybody. Doesn't really matter much when. Unfair would be if I let somebody snivel out of it."

"But . . ."

"But what? You want something, so should I just give it to you? That's your idea of fair?"

"But you told me to come get him! And now I'm here, turns out you were just jerking me around? That's what's not fair!"

It stopped laughing. "That's true, I said that. I didn't promise, but I did encourage you. Let me think." The glow that was the closest thing it had to a visible presence died down. She was alone in darkness. She wondered if maybe she had died.

Time didn't pass. But she supposed it was later. The glow burst forth into a pillar of fire, so gigantic and glorious that maybe it was going to lead the Israelites out of Egypt again. "Okay, I can make a special case."

It chuckled. "That's a good one. A case, it's a case. Because I let you hope. Not just you hoping because you're stupid. You were hoping because I was having so much fun messing with you that I got careless. So maybe we can make a deal."

She was suddenly alive enough again to shriek with joy, and start babbling, "Thank you, thank you, thank you! I'll do anything you. . . "

"Shut up," it snarled. "I'm talking here." She shut

up, shut down. When she regained consciousness, it was still talking.

"I'm gonna get Jesse back in a little bit anyway," it continued. "So it's not really a reversal of entropy if I let him take a little longer getting here. He's not fully lodged in the deadlands yet. He's still in training—hasn't even gotten past the memory wipe. In fact, it's taken so long to erase his love for you that he hasn't forgotten anything else yet. So if I let him turn and run, he could still function in the dirt world."

"He's forgotten me?" That stung.

"I seem to recall you babbling something about, 'Anything.' You don't get this offer for free, you know. The price is that you belong to me now. For the rest of your life, you're my personal handmaiden. Jesse forgets all about you. Everybody else forgets he got married and died."

She had a sudden flash, plain as a movie clip, of Jesse's Auntie laughing with him and saying, "Whatever happened to that girl you used to go on about?"

And he answered, "Wow, I haven't thought of her in years! I was so sure I'd found true love, and now I can't even remember her name. But I only met her the once, you know, at some dance."

The clip ended abruptly, looped and started to replay. She covered her eyes with her hands. But the words, 'I only met her the once' echoed over and over, slashing a path of pain and ruin through her heart. "Please stop," she whispered.

"So what's it gonna be? You want to save him? Say the word, and he forgets all about you and gets on with his life, and I get a new minion. Or he can stay dead, with your name on his lips at the end. To be fair, there's some who would say that true love is worth dying for, because it's so rare. A lot of people blabber about how they've got it. They're full of shit. And even after you forget about your life, it brightens you, down here in the deadlands. So what's it going to be? Choice is yours."

How was she supposed to choose with the words, 'I only met her the once,' lacerating her brain? His love was the only thing that made her life worth living. Without it, she might as well give up and die.

But so what? She'd said a thousand times she would die for him. Was she just 'blabbering on, but full of shit?' If she loved Jesse more than life, then what was best for him? Life, of course, except . . . she was starting to see that life was a pretty small thing. It always ended up in the deadlands.

"If I take the deal," she said slowly, "and he forgets all about me, will he still get to keep his brightness in the deadlands?"

There was something sort of like a pause. "Wow," it said. "What a wonderful question! Nobody has ever asked that before. I knew there had to be a reason I liked you. But I think he probably would. Well, maybe. I'll have to check. Probably. So, does that mean you'll take the deal?"

Did it? "Probably," she admitted, choking back tears. "But one more thing. What do your servants have to do? 'Cos if you're going to turn me into an agent of evil, the deal's off."

Again with the laughing. Didn't he ever stop? "You think I care about all that good and evil crap? Not my department. You suit yourself on that, if you think you're smart enough to make that call. Except for one thing. No lies. Not even polite bullshit.'What a darling baby!' That's gonna piss a lot of people off. Humans are liars. It's what they do. And it's gonna kill their souls when you start throwing the truth in their faces. Especially prophecies."

"Prophecies?"

"Every now and then I'll tell you to say something for me that humans don't know about yet. They'll think you're crazy. But don't worry. Mostly I'll just tell you to run errands. Go here. Do that. Make posts on YouTube, lots of 'em—I just love You Tube. Get an apartment in West Garfield. Let that homeless bum sleep on your couch for a week."

West Garfield? Ew. He must have heard her thinking. "Don't worry. You'll be safe enough. Nobody can hurt you when you belong to me."

She shuddered. "Wow. Sounds just incredibly awful. But Jesse will be okay?"

"Jesse will live to a hundred and three, and die in his own home in Wicker Park, surrounded by his loving grandchildren."

Grandchildren. Meaning he'd marry somebody else? But Wicker Park was nice. He'd like living there. "But I never see him again?" Just saying it aloud hurt so bad, she nearly changed her mind. She didn't think she couldn't survive never seeing him again while he went off and married somebody else.

For once, it didn't laugh. It sounded almost gentle when it replied, "No, never."

That was going to be awful. But her life was already awful, and it was going to get worse, no matter what she did. Suppose she said no? She'd wake up every morning, and Jesse would still be dead. Plus she would always know she could have saved him, and didn't. She really, really couldn't survive that. She'd be picking up the knife within days.

She didn't remember agreeing, but she probably didn't need to say it out loud anyway. She fell down into the darkness, and woke up, weeping, still sitting in her desk chair, with her head flung backwards, and her neck agonizingly stiff. Dawn was breaking outside her window. She could hear Mom puttering around the kitchen. She smelled fresh coffee.

She was struck by a sudden vivid memory: Jesse telling her that he'd made a donation at a sperm bank. She couldn't remember why, but she could almost see him, hunching his shoulders, and cocking his head, saying. "I hope you don't mind." She didn't remember ever having remembered that before. Still couldn't remember when he could have done it—they'd been together every minute. Her new boss must be making sure she had something to live for.

Downstairs, her mother started to talk as soon as she walked into the kitchen. "Listen, I'm sorry. I know I shouldn't open your mail, but I started doing it when you were depressed, just in case it was a bill or something, and it got to be a habit." Mom handed her an envelope. The return address was a company where she'd applied for a job nearly a year earlier. "Would you look at this? They've got a bunch of new openings. It's still only part time, but it's nearly twice what you're making now—and you could work from home!"

So she was already on the clock. Much to her own surprise, she found she was extremely curious about all the things that were going to happen next. Mom handed her a cup of coffee, and darted off. She'd always been that way, tearing around the house at high speed. "Half hummingbird," her dad had always used to say. "Couldn't sit still for a minute if you paid her a million dollars." Alone in the kitchen, May whispered into her coffee, "I love you, Jesse. I always will."

The Mistress of the Labyrinth

by Donna J. W. Munro

"Just say my name," I whispered to him, knowing that the magic in it would strengthen him.

He was afraid of the sun and wind from above since he's never seen it. I wondered if putting out his eyes might've been a kindness. He squeezed them shut and lowed like a cow as I tried to drag him across this invisible final threshold. It was what she woke him for and we didn't have time to wait for night to fall.

The old gods would soon rise .

Grandmother Terra swore the dark sky holds us all in circles spinning around her, though I've seen the pictures of the tiny moon named for me. I'm a distant pile of oblong rock forever circling father Neptune and the scientific center of the galaxy, Sol. But science and myth don't cancel each other out. I shrugged at her inaccuracies. Who am I to say what is true? We are all forever swimming in the sea of space or air or dreams, trapped by the gravity of the original mother, my own true grandmother.

"Ple...aasssseee, Despoina. Sister," my brother begged through his jutting lower teeth, whistling like he did when he was just a big baby trapped with me in the dark.

"Grandmother wants you," I reminded him and tugged again.

It didn't matter that I was a goddess and strong as a mountain, because he was a minotaur–just as strong and way more stubborn than me . He'd have to see the logic or we would be stuck here all day, pawing at the bright line of light marking our only escape.

"Little brother, the old gods are rising soon. They've used you before, right? I'm here because Grandmother knows. Besides, I promised I'd be back when you were well. You kept hold of that promise here in the dark as the rocks pressed against your shattered bones. You clutched it to your broken heart as your body knit back together."

As big as he was, he pressed his muscular body against me and trembled like a fearful calf. Like he used to when they trapped us down in the dark so long ago.

"Do you want to go with Father when he comes?"

He snorted, sending his hot breath rippling through my hair.

"Me neither. We must hide you, sweet. Right now."

He folded his hand into mine and dipped his horned head low. He wanted me to cover him up and I did, though I wondered if I needed to do it. This world is full of people who see monsters as nothing to fear. As something to cosplay for the fun of it. They themselves have become the great enemy of things. Well, that was what they believed. They don't remember what it was like with the old gods in charge.

I hurried him out of the ruin, past tourists who jostled to get close, asking for pictures in a hundred different languages because our costumes were so authentic—him a bull man, me a shining goddess. I smiled and refused. We walked so swiftly, we soon splashed at the edge of the Mediterranean and then climbed on my boat that turned toward the island I'd bought with the gold I called out of Grandmother's dusty folds and stony crevasses. Hours passed with him in the comfortable lower deck eating the raw meat I'd brought, drinking clean water, and bathing away the dust of the past three thousand years.

I was the daughter of the land and sea. He was the punishment sent upon a queen who'd insulted the sea. Neither of us enjoyed traveling across the blue eye of our father, but I knew I wouldn't be able to coax him into some puddle-jumping jet, so here we are.

Hours passed and the sea grew choppier.

The sky clouded and I knew it wouldn't be long.

I didn't have to see the pinpricks of light in the dark night I'd studied through human telescopes for so long to know that they were shifting. Prison walls would crumble and so would the ties that held those celestial prisons in place circling poor pinned Sol.

Once we docked, I pulled my brother out of the hold, whispering that I'd made us a new Labyrinth so high up that the waves couldn't reach it. In front of us was a steel construction, reinforced against earthquakes and fire that might fall from the sky as it had so long ago. It rose on the center of my small island in a tall cone with the white castle I'd built on top. Small and bright and built for two.

I pulled him into the elevator, and we rode up to the top in silence. The doors slid open, letting us out into the wide, modern living space. My sweet bull of a brother crossed to the window that looked out across the greying face of the Mediterranean.

He must remember the waves, even if he'd been in pieces under the palace when they came and washed the palace away. I remembered seeing the tsunami, tall as mountains and louder than any sound I'd ever heard. I'd floated for weeks, daughter of the sea and safe, but my poor brother lay under the silt and tumbled rocks even after the salty destruction retreated from the shores of Konossos's beach, scrubbed bare of the villages and ships and Minoans.

I put a hand on his forearm and leaned against him.

"Will they... come?"

"For us?" I wanted to lie so badly. He'd suffered enough, hadn't he? But he was all muscle and I was... useful in my own way. "Maybe, but not right away."

Pulling him away from the window, I led him to a room with deep pallets piled up in a dark, warm corner. He sighed happily and glanced around at the soft surfaces and the bowls of vegetables.

He went into his room and lay on the pallets, pulling carrots from the pile and biting chunks off as he hummed and purred.

I left him there to check the net.

It doesn't take much to understand what's happening when you have had lifetimes to study it.

Lakes and rivers are drying up. Droughts, high temperatures, and hurricanes all are a part of the hubris of humans left unchecked. Skimming the news of the day, I find the usual deniers locked in battle with the "fix it someday, slowly" conservatives and the pie-in-the-sky progressives who still think they can turn this thing back.

I'm the mistress of the Labyrinth and the depths and the veil. I whisper in the dark to my sleeping grandmother and feel her dreams. I've been singing in caves and dropping flowers into wells for so many years. I've released the hippocampoi in the North Sea as she groaned for their song only to see them die from the lack of ice to breed under.

When Grandmother wakes...

I rode the elevator down into the lowest basement which was more like a deep cleft in the earth. I'd dug out from the rock for sixty years using mining and then drilling equipment as it developed over the years–bringing me closer to Grandmother's ear. It worked. She'd begun murmuring to me as she slowly woke from her long sleep.

Tonight, I'd try to soothe her and keep her in the place between sleep and waking. I'd had her there for over a hundred years now, but... the stars were talking to her too. It wouldn't be long. In the lowest chamber of the cave I'd dug, I stripped off my clothes letting my skin feel the kiss of cold that woke my magic. Like my father, depths sharpened my powers. I lay on the rough floor, spreading out so more of my body touched more of her and I breathed to calm my galloping heart.

"I have him, Grandmother," I whispered. "My brother is finally safe. You can stop worrying about– "

Next, you must find your father and free him.

The stone under my body softened beneath me as she sent up her anger to warm me. Feeling her stir was one thing, but this–

Free them all, Little Despoina.

My name. I hadn't heard it much in all my lifetimes. It was a sacred word, guarded against all save my grandmother and the priestesses I trusted. My name rippled with fire and stone. When Terra said it, I felt the softness I'd cultivated by living among the humans burn away in her demands.

"Jupiter and the Titans?"

The soft stone cradling me constricted against me and I understood. Shame. The last time Terra had given the gods this kind of power was to stop the titans and their abuses. They'd killed her lover and began eating their own children to keep power for themselves.

Jupiter had subdued them and then subdued her.

She still hated him, but the humans were... worse.

I don't have long, Despoina. No matter how many you save, like my sweet grand bull boy, there will be nothing left of me to care for them.

I nodded. I'd come to that conclusion and so had the stars. All of them cried out.

Cried out to be freed.

I'm the Mistress of the Labyrinth. Of the Veil and the Darkness. I'm the handmaiden of the Earth. When I dive into the sea and find the statue of my father, the night sky is clear, and the wind is still like the whole world is holding its breath because this will change everything. This is the beginning of an end. The frigid blue-gray water is just a temperature change for someone like me, built to survive depths and pressures so massive others would liquefy. Cool, cold, colder. I can feel the pull of Thetis and dryads, merfolk, and other beasties that want to be found, released, saved from the habitat loss, from the bridges or nets, but I'm for the one god I can save and he will be the one who starts the rest.

In the deepest trenches, the fish glow. They pulse with an otherworldly light that humans call adaptive phosphorescence.

They are as blind as they are bright.

Just like the vault of the sky they are an endless cast filling the spinning universes that humans map and quantify and name. The sea is another realm they think they are conquering. Containing within the intellect that the gods allowed them, fools that they were. As I swim deeper, the cuttlefish jet past, clouding the water and lighting my path from this place to that. Through to the hidden prison of my lord father.

Grandmother's words grow louder here.

It is with her borrowed voice that the doors all open for me.

"Sea to earth and earth to sky," I say to the pillars of Hercules. What once looked tamed rages from below to above, pulling the sea apart for me.. The people on the surface will see a rogue wave, but here on the skin of the seabed, I see the vaulted sky glittering with the diamond lights the gods hung in tribute. I see the planets that hold them in stasis, colorful stone balls shaped of breath and sand or ice and stone or even liquid fire. They are prisons built of grandmother's anger from so long ago. Punishments.

Back when father had been pressed into the blue-green giant only visible through the magic of telescopes, I was just a girl. Humans were just children then, too.

"Father?" I flow on the breath of the night wind toward his prison and press my hands against the bitter mist encircling him. "Grandmother wants to know if you learned your lesson."

Inside the ball of blue light, I saw him, curled up like a baby in the womb, spinning endlessly in the sea of his own making. Hubris. Dominating the world and sea with his brothers and sisters had led him here.

"Daughter?" The mumble was weak, but he'd heard me over the muttering voices inside the prison. "I have. I've learned. Will she let us come back?"

Ah, if only he knew how much he was needed. The garbage patches. The sea animals gone forever. The slowing currents. No need to lay all that at his feet just yet.

"She needs you now." I dragged together all my strength. I'd been awake for so long without rest, I didn't have much. Just enough for him. He'd have to listen to grandmother and do the rest.

I drew back my arm and plunged it forward, dipping into the thick slurry of water and rage that encased him. I was the Mistress of the depth and with all I had left, I'd save it.

Every straining fiber screamed as I pushed the atoms holding him apart, rending the strands of the casing and casting them out beyond the sphere.

What would the humans be seeing through their telescopes or periscopes?

As the fire of his escape burned away the flesh of my arms, I laughed. What were humans but little gods full of self-idolatry and hubris? Let them explain or innovate their way out of this.

And as his prison shattered, he gathered me up into his arms.

"Thank you, Despoina. I won't forget you when this is done."

He dropped me to fall from the vault of the sky as he turned his power on Jupiter's prison.

I fell, upside-down, right-side-up. Rising in the layers of the sea or falling through the bitter cold of the atmosphere mattered not–Grandmother called me back to her. The false division between heaven and earth fell away as I struck the blue surface of Father's eye as it raged with waves, though none swamped me. I am made for this, after all. Even if it breaks me into a million pieces of oblong stone and casts me adrift forever.

The waves carried my broken body to the shore of my island fortress where my brother waited in the churning gray surf. He carried me up to the elevator, holding me against him as it shot up to my little white castle, and then laid me in my bed to rest.

"I can hear her now, Despoina. She's singing, " he whispered as he pulled the door shut.

Grandmother is singing, once again.

I AM HEALING. Skin is growing over my bones and my nerves don't scream each time I get out of my soft bed to watch the gods paint the sky with the angry colors of their revenge. The internet is gone. Electricity works, but only because I have sources perched on my roof and tangled in the surf that crashes against my island. Sometimes, I see father ride by on a wave or Jupiter herding storm clouds as Grandmother demands.

For now, they do her bidding.

And the humans?

When I go down into my tunnel, I hear them.

They scurry like ants in the bowels of the earth, hiding as the gods remake things.

I whisper to Grandmother, "Wouldn't it be kinder to crush them now? They will come out and restart the whole thing. Gods' hubris, human pride, what is the difference in the end?"

She ignores me, singing praises to her children as they mow down the humans left on the surface with bloody plague after thundering disaster after scorching punishment. It's while I'm laying there with her as they pick her clean of humans that I begin to understand. Maybe only those of us who've had to live under her skin ever will.

None of us are big enough to see how little we matter.

But as I lay there in a deep pore on her surface, thinking as the Mistress of the Veil who understands all mysteries, I hear what has always been tickling the back of my mind all this time. We gods and humans like to think we matter to her and we do—but only when her eyes turn from her larger life, inward.

Only when she feels us as an attack.

No, not an attack.

An illness.

The answer is rooted in humans and their micro studies of blood and cells and things that we don't see or care about as we live larger lives. A cell thinks it is important in its essential activities producing life but is that one little cell *that* important to an organ? Does one drone bee think it is changing the whole hive when it brings home its teaspoon of nectar?

"Grandmother," I whisper, "Do you even know what we are?"

The singing stops as she turns her eye to me. It fills every space in my mind as she rips away the veil. It is fire and ice and pain pressing in from every pore on my body, from every fold in my mind. Her full attention is deafening.

I scream until my voice breaks.

"Despoina," she whispers, though each sound is a lance through my head and my ears bleed. "You are the only one I need to see."

She's deafened me with her voice, but I can hear her within my head like a gong. I was built for this, but it hurts like nothing I've ever felt. My time in the dark, in the wide velvet of a cavern's night made my mind big enough... to understand she's too big, too much to know.

"Grandmother!" I screamed even though my vocal cords were shreds. *Please no more! My mind bleeding thoughts! Help us, goddess!*

Thoughts had to serve me.

Turn from us, Grandmother! Turn and we will never do it again.

It was a lie, I told. I could see it now. Gods are born, imprisoned, killed, humans come, conquer, die, and I'm left in the fire of what she is as they scrub her surface and fade away.

Again.

And again.

Because she's forever.

And I'm the goddess of the deep, of the dark, of the veil.

I WAKE on the smooth floor of my temple with my horned brother at my side. He's not alive yet, but he will be. He's a gift from her. Outside, the sun rises over the bright blue sea.

It's a world reborn.

I pull up my veil to cover my eyes burned to white, then curl up next to my brother to wait for things to begin again.

Thank you, Grandmother.

We Have No Spare Parts

by Andrew Najberg

Sasha sat cross-legged on the deck with the repair drone control pad in her lap, her face half-obscured by the vision shield. Of course, the drone fed directly into the Nano-transmitter embedded in her optic nerve, but the goggles blocked her eyesight because the vision-gating was imperfect and as of late the fail-rate had increased to as much as thirty-seven milliseconds per cycle without physical reinforcement.

Each time a micro-twitch of her thumb fired the drone's air thrusters to adjust its tilt and orientation, Sasha blew a little "pfft" out of the side of her mouth. I asked her once why she did it, and she said, "it made space feel more real."

The thing about space is that when you're in it like we are in it, it's simultaneously the most unreal thing there is and the only thing you ever think of. If you are in a submarine, in theory, you could stick your hand out into the ocean and feel that it is there. If you stick your hand out into space, you feel that nothing is there. It wouldn't even be cold, not in the way we understand cold. Cold is heat transfer, and there isn't anything out there to transfer heat to.

No, decades out into space, there is a very real way in which the material universe ceases to exist. Our minds aren't equipped to 'get' space as something that we are in because we never really are.

So, Sasha goes "pfft." I hold my own joystick, but my vision field is up, the feed off. My drone is tethered, allowing Sasha perspective on the larger scene. No matter how much time you look through the drone's 'eyes,' you never gain full awareness of its size and orientation, and the wrong minor collision can send it or whatever it was touching spiraling off into the black.

Checking off the sequence steps on my tablet as they are completed, I keep most of my focus on the big screen on the bulkhead that displays the feed from the ship's mounted camera. In it, my drone watches Sasha's drone hover a few degrees offset from the last S of our vessel's name, the E.E.V. Theseus. Under Sasha's guidance, the drone installs the transparent graphene-fiber suction bubble onto the hull seam. With the push of the red button on the thumb-stick, the bubble pressurizes, fills with gas, and the drone inserts the welding bit. The lenses all flare before the display algorithms correct for the intensity, reducing the repair to a pinpoint of light.

A moment later, Sasha presses 'auto-dock' and raises her shield.

"Head down to med-bay," she says. "I can handle the other patch by myself."

I sigh and look at my hands. My thumbs and ring

fingers tremble. I'm normally first technician, but I've been suffering from Kali-Hardin syndrome. The artificial gravity system isn't exactly gravity, but rather a tether to a moving locus in quantum space. Much like the drone tethers make the ship's hull a sort of 'ground' that helps us orient while controlling them, our bodies are oriented to a space outside the traditional 'three' dimensions that I've only seen represented with irrational mathematics. It might solve loads of issues with inertia, but it plays hell on molecular bonds and leads to cellular fragmentation. What might look like minor vibrations of my fingers are a symptom of something much more fundamental that's been gaining a foothold in my body the last few weeks.

So, Sasha's been running lead on the patch jobs. She's pretty good, but I want back in the foreground. Dr. Lorenze has yet to stabilize my red-blood cells and believes I need a full flush and replacement. I flex my fingers and try to steady them on the controls. All my body's systems are in danger, but my fine motor dexterity being in the waste vent is my most immediate grief.

"Doc will be there in an hour just like she's there now," I say. "You know it's always two eyes on the prize for exterior repairs ever since—"

Sasha waves me off. On the big screen, we both watch the pair of drones vanish into the docking port to re-pressurize their air tanks. On the screen, they're like insects scurrying into a hole, except that their exoskeletons are mottled from countless patches and minor mends.

"Yeah, it's been hard enough to rig these and keep 'em running," she says. She snatches up her tablet and opens the welding code to adjust the parameters for the next repair. She catches me biting my thumbnail and not really looking at anything at all. "You nervous?"

"No, not exactly," I say, but then shrug. "But yeah, I mean it's my blood. I know you've been 100% synth-o neg for a while now, but in a way, giving it up means I won't be me anymore."

"You've been watching too many vids from the old days," Sasha said. She lets out a playful hiss, baring her teeth like a vampire. "Folk on earth had a hard-on for blood, but it's just fallible tissue and water."

I cross my arms and rub my biceps. A dull ache under the skin radiates into the muscle. I practically feel the individual capillaries as they cry out for the oxygen my red blood cells are failing to properly relinquish. I understand how much better off I'll be if Lorenze orders my blood replaced, but so little we brought from Earth remains in the form that we brought it in that what is left seems precious. I spend the rest of my shift trying to imagine that the nanites in the synthetic blood won't turn my body into some sort of ant farm.

IT IS strange to think that there was a point at which our ship had a mission. That the mission parameters described a discreet objective and duration. That at one point we thought we'd return to Earth. I was still quite young when we strapped into the launch couches with a flight plan for the asteroid Persephone in the main belt, hence the name of our vessel. We'd intended to land on the asteroid and attach a fission engine to the rocky body to adjust its trajectory and propel it into a high lunar orbit so that local rock hoppers could mine it for rare metal deposits.

I suppose one just doesn't bring Persephone back to the world of the living.

The mission planners had been meticulous in charting our navigation. The main belt contains nearly two million large asteroids and tens of millions of smaller ones. In a way, it is a miracle of mathematics that the people on the ground and their computers could generate an algorithm that could account for so much moving debris for the duration of our incursion into the belt.

We were struck by a pebble traveling one hundred twenty thousand kilometers per hour.

The pebble punched straight through the inner and outer hulls, and in that instant the shockwave that coursed through the reinforced composite that stands between us and vacuum damaged our engine hardware, triggering a full burn straight out towards deep space. The shift in velocity, despite the inertial protection the artificial gravity afforded us, rendered the entire crew simultaneously unconscious.

When we awakened, we'd lost a full third of the crew outright to brain bleeds and other hemorrhages and ruptures, and there was damage to every one of the ship's systems. We'd burned nearly our entire supply of fuel. There were hundreds of micro-breaches in the hull; the mainframe had only closed electromagnetically. The surviving damage control sensors fed us an itemized litany that could fill a small database. There were so many fires to put out, it seemed like we were given squirt guns and told to extinguish hell.

Our macro-report was no better. The long burn

had accelerated us to nearly one tenth the speed of light on a trajectory towards the star Alphecca in the Corona Borealis constellation. We had no fuel to turn back, not even enough for a meaningful course correction. A couple of us were sardonically charmed by the flight path and joked that at least we had a light to lead the way, but heading for the Crown of Theseus felt more like we were headed for the largest zero to ever exist. At its closest, our route would take us within four light years of Alphecca itself, but still further than the distance between our solar system and its next closest star. We'd not recognize it among the starfield if it hadn't been labeled in the computer, and, even if it was a destination, we had no way to slow ourselves down so that we'd actually arrive.

Captain Auberdine said we were lucky. The odds of the actual collision were staggeringly improbable, but just as unlikely was our survival. Despite the small size of the arrow that struck us, the impact would have detonated an older vessel as would the acceleration that brought us to our current velocity. She said that if we could manage the repairs, the ship's systems were close enough to zero waste that we might be able to live out our natural lifespans. She told us that our current cruising speed was faster than any human being had ever traveled. That every metric of odds said we should have collided with a second object on our burn out of the belt. Yes, she reiterated. We were miraculously lucky. I seem to remember that for a moment, we agreed.

I'm supposed to head straight to medbay, but after shift-end, I peel off from Sasha who's headed to rec and dally towards quarters. Sasha's footsteps diminish first and then so do their echoes. I wonder fleetingly why she wears boots – she says it's because her feet get cold, but the floors would never allow that – until I notice the blue lights lit along the corridor. Blue means security which has nothing to do with me or my duties and usually means the sensors detected a rock drifting within ten thousand meters. That had struck me as funny the first time we detected one after the Persephone incident, but now it's one of the lonelier things I can think of.

When I arrive at quarters, Tully is suspended in the hammock watching his tablet. The voices of children escape at low volume, and he is crying. Tully had kids, I recall, but I'm pretty sure they were grown when the mission call came. After the impact, we'd immersed ourselves in repairs, cannibalizing many of the parts of out of the drive system we'd intended to deliver to the asteroid, but despite restoring most of our systems to a high level of function, we'd never been able to reestablish comms with Earth. At first, it had seemed the least of our concerns, but it started to eat at the folks like Tully.

Now, it's been so long since our last transmission receipt that there's no telling if anyone still lives there. After all, it's not like we left the planet in stellar working order. The folk on top would never have said it outright, but missions like ours were at the heart of the colonization effort. Left unspoken was that the colonization effort was the heart of the only viable plan to perpetuate the species. I guess knowing his kids could still be back there is enough to keep him with one foot planted in his memories. Does he regret enlistment? If you ask me, enlistment may well be the only reason any of us are still alive.

I didn't have much say in the matter myself. My parents died in the NVL-94 pandemic when I was just a baby. In a technical sense, I'm not government property, but the paperwork that says so is in some government vault since I have no other direct relatives. Not many forks in a life-path if you don't have any generational wealth to give you a handle. Shortly after puberty, I had my genetic material harvested and frozen, and I was "welcomed" into The Department of Deep Space. In a nutshell, I can't say I was born into this – it was more like I was harvested. Unlike Tully who certainly anchored some of himself to memories of building with blocks and reading to his kids when they were toddlers, my formative memories are predominantly in orbital institutional settings which bore little functional difference from the corridors and bulkheads surrounding me now. Me and the other inductees used to have races to tighten bolts in Zero-G and play who can spin the fastest without hitting a bulkhead.

I wash my face while Tully cries, and it strikes me for a moment that we both have liquid running down our cheeks. From a tactile point of view, the only difference is in viscosity, but both his eyes were replaced two or three years ago. In the process, the organ fabricator's design intelligence adapted his tear ducts to secrete an optimized lubricating solution. He insists that it's really an improvement, that he can now see in an expanded wavelength and that the synthetic eyes sync more fluidly with the reality augmentation fed from his neurotransmitters. However, he always looks down and to the left when he talks about it, so I know that he is ashamed.

Moreover, at this moment, I can't say I really know how to comfort him. It's not that I don't cry – sometimes it's the only choice when you recognize that you did not experience a new place this year nor will you experience a new place in the next ten – but he cries for things that were left behind while I cry for things I never had.

I step over and try to see what's happening on his vid, but he's got a privacy protocol activated so my optic nerves won't register the images. I'm surprised he doesn't have the sound filtered, but the kids from a few moments ago are no longer making sound. I think it's kind of like when someone groans in bed when they're sick. The point isn't that they want you to do something for them, only that they want you to know that they're groaning.

Behind me, I hear a rustle. Warrant Officer Bailey is asleep on her couch with her hair wrapped around her face like a scarf. Though the couches basically embrace the body to inhibit its movement in the eventuality of inertial changes, she is writhing with what must be a nightmare. The fabric of her clothes churns and scrapes at the joints. She gasps. Bailey's twin sister was in the contingent of the original crew that didn't survive the impact incident, and Bailey has never been complete since. Sometimes, she requests that the mainframe procedurally generate an interactive scenario with a simulation of her sister, but every time she does so, she ends up emotionally devastated. Dr Lorenz has threatened to block some of her system permissions.

The truth is, none of us are complete. The crew as a whole certainly isn't. Around Bailey, only a couple of the couches are occupied. Granted, some of us are on duty or at rec, but when our voyage began, none of the thirty-two bunks were empty.

I open my mouth to say something, maybe to Tully or maybe to Bailey but in the end, I depart in silence, the last of the moisture drying off my cheeks.

I ARRIVE in medbay where Lorenze is examining a bank of screens displaying concurrent time lapses of the crew's status. Of the thirty-two screens, only twelve display traditional vitals. The rest run non-stop streams of code I can't read because it's written in a language constructed by the ANTEROS mainframe to represent the minutiae of consciousness. I wouldn't say out loud that I don't trust it – after all, those supposed people can undoubtedly hear me through the ship's internal comm system -- but I can't look at those screens and be convinced people exist in that soup of numbers and symbols.

Doctor Lorenze regards me as I enter. Of course, Lorenze is no longer what I would traditionally call human either as her primary material interface is a mobile array on a tether within which her optic nerves are embedded. She's kind of like the opposite of Tully, I think, as her servos adjust the orientation of her focus. Unlike Captain Auberdine and most of our other physically deceased crewmates, however, Doctor Lorenze's brain is still intact and operational, suspended in electrolytic fluid in a circuit vault within the medbay's central processing assembly. I must admit that I respect and appreciate her retention of instrumentality no matter how minimal, because it at least makes me feel like there is a trace of my species in there. Call it bedside manner.

"You're late," the voice modulator mounted underneath her vision assembly tells me.

"Took a moment to freshen up in quarters," I say.

"The treatment is optimal immediately after attentive exertion," Dr. Lorenze says. "Delaying this long from end of shift will cost us five percent efficacy."

I shrug. I may not have wistful Earth memories, but half-assing things and suffering a little consequence is, as I understand it, one of the most human things there is.

With a whir of servos and a pneumatic hiss, the treatment pod door opens and the patient platform extends from the wall. Lorenze's optical array focuses her attention on the platform. "You know my prognosis was that systemic circulatory failure is inevitable."

"Would punctuality be a decisive factor?"

It's always hard to read Dr. Lorenze because the voice modulator always seems one step to the left of the proper inflection and, well, it's not like she has an actual face I can look at. The vision array has recognizable pupils whose servos allow iris-like adjustment of diameter. Unfortunately, software solutions to changing light conditions solved the problem more efficiently, and I'm not sure changing her pupil size would enable her to emote.

I do know the pause is intentional. After all, she is half computer. With that comes all the benefits of computer processing power. Her actual hesitations take place in time fractions so small they don't make sense to me.

Finally, she answers, "No."

"Right then," I say and lay down on the platform.

As my weight settles and the padding conforms to my body curvature, the platform recedes back into the pod, and the door closes. A moment later, three central spheres in the ceiling, each about fifty centimeters apart, emit several hundred thread-thin laser beams. The beams coat my body in a soft green light. From the outside, every reachable part of my body would appear to glow.

I wince as the lasers combine with the pod's ultrasonics to target individual red-blood cells in my body to reshape them. At least, that's what I was told. In truth, it could just be a pretty light show, and sometimes I think that's exactly what it is. After all, I'm the one who doesn't believe half the crew counts as alive anymore.

Midway through the procedure, as my blood burns and everything inside me throbs, Lorenze speaks directly through my audio-implant. "I know you're reticent," she says, "But this would be a convenient time to uplink you to the system."

"Just the tune up today, thanks," I say.

"We can do a partial sync. Conscious and preconscious only, though with an inhibitor routine to ensure you retain bodily autonomy."

"Yeah, when you put it like that, you make it sound so appealing," I say.

"It should," Lorenze says. "It would increase your work efficiency by as much as 60%."

"I don't need to consult with the hive to patch the hull."

"They would be more comfortable," Lorenze says.

I turn off the audio-implant by putting up a privacy flag. As chief medical officer, she can override it, but she would need to offer a justification to the captain. I can't say that is the hugest obstacle; the Captain has, in a physical sense, been dead for twenty years. Can Auberdine's consciousness in ANTEROS threaten to delete Lorenze? Imprison her in a brig-like system partition? The rules themselves lack heft any-ways. Since we lost contact with Earth, there isn't any external force that can hold us accountable. As a re-sult, when Dr. Lorenze doesn't press the matter fur-ther, I appreciate the respect. Another bit of bed-side manner.

When the treatment completes, the lasers shut down. The pod-door opens, and my platform eases out. Dr. Lorenze's visual array hangs motionless from the ceiling. The blue alarm lights are still lit, but they're in pairs now, meaning there is a matter of ship-wide concern. Dr. Lorenze and the rest of the hive will already know what the alarm is about, but for the edi-fication of the remaining meat sacks aboard, the more fundamental, hardware voice of the ship's core sys-tems says, "Security alert. All personnel to conference lounge for briefing."

WHEN I REACH the conference lounge, the other eight corporeal crew members have already arrived, and the other fifteen extant crew consciousnesses were already there to begin with. They were, after all, in every computer system simultaneously in some sort of warped omnipresence.

As to those of us ambulators, I can't say we're at our best. Spalling looks groggy, and her hair is a frizzy mess. Tully's eye sockets are a deep shade of red.

Brickman languidly polishes his mechanical hand while also flexing a complex rhythm between his prosthetic ankles. Oscar is over sixty percent mechanical now without a single original organ in his torso. Cookwell would appear fully human by outward appearance, but when the tumor ravaged her brain, the entire organ was replaced with a synthetic, and her consciousness now steers her body remotely from the mainframe. She's never been the same since.

I look down at my leg. Inside it, I know, there aren't real bones, but an organic polymer. My heart has two printed valves, and several of my organs have dozens of micro-grafts holding them together like they're some weird flesh quilt. Sometimes I wonder why we bother. Given the unlikelihood that enough of our systems -- biological or mechanical – will last long enough to reach any possible destination, it would almost make as much sense to just let the ship cool into an inert mass cruising among the star systems like some remnant of the Big Bang. If nothing else, it would spare us the psychological strain.

Captain Auberdine's avatar is the last to arrive. Her avatar is a holographic projection capable of haptic form through the condensation of light and sound into a pressure surface that can manipulate material reality. The technology was originally designed to project a cartoonish 'helper' that represented the mainframe and reeked of uncanny valley, but, even before our mission launch, it had become standard operating procedure in pretty much all mission flights to kill the holographic system and rely on more old-fashioned interfaces. Nonetheless, once the Captain died, it only made sense to give her something of a physical form, even if it felt like we were being led by her ghost. If anything, it elevated her authority a bit because it made her almost celestial. Otherwise, her organic components have been entirely recycled, and she exists as no more than a neural map within the mainframe, her and the rest of the crew.

For a while, Auberdine shared the projector with the other 'casualties' of our mission's unexpected duration. The ship is capable of operating three or four avatars at a time, but the rest of the uploaders stopped bothering to descend to our level shortly after their assimilation into the system. We used to joke that the ANTEROS AI would kill us all and re-appropriate our organics into automated repair cyborgs, but after a while we noticed that the ones of us who still held onto our bodies played crucial roles in physical maintenance of the ship.

The Avatar maneuvers to the front of the lounge, though she could just as easily pass directly through everything in her path. Old habits die hard, I suppose, or maybe she's just maintaining a pretext for our benefit.

"As you all should be aware, the sensor array detected an object within our safety zone and sounded a blue alarm," Auberdine says. Her voice was smooth water over a little grit. Though she's really observing from cameras, the Avatar pans her gaze around the room.

From the seat closest to the door, WO Bailey clears her throat. "Are we going to be able to visualize it?"

"Yes," Auberdine says. "We already have."

Bailey straightens.

"Can we see the images?"

Auberdine's avatar adjusts her cuffs even though they're not real and therefore can't have become uncomfortable. Again. Old habits.

"In good time," Auberdine says. "As we ran the routine scans, we recognized anomalies."

Heads moved throughout the room now. Everyone except Shacklefort, anyway. He'd suffered a vertebra collapse when his sleeping couch failed to bolster properly during the Persephone incident. The three vertebrae at the base of his skull were fused metal now, incapable of turning.

"What sort of anomalies?" I ask. Auberdine could have already told us, but none of us want to lose the theater. Even if it is just an atypical rock, this is the most interesting thing that's happened in weeks. I'm surprised the upload folk aren't playing along too, but they probably had a little thought party as soon as the information was received.

"It's broadcasting signals on multiple spectrums."

Auberdine's words land like a steel girder.

"Excuse me, Captain," Sasha says. "Broadcasting signals?"

"Radar, Ladar, Electromagnetic, the works."

"But that would mean—"

"It's almost certainly human in origin, yes."

A low murmur fills the room. Auberdine's avatar freezes for a fraction of a second. The image of a craft appears on the screens, and a holographic render materializes in the air in front of her. The craft is needle thin with spindly fins spiraling from nose to thruster. The fins themselves are gossamer and fluid in the image, almost insectile in design. Though I must allow that their hull design principles might have advanced considerably, any crew in that must inhabit one heck of a tight space.

"How certain," I ask.

"ANTEROS indicates the alternative explanations have negligible probability."

"Is that different than the odds of us surviving the Persephone approach impact?" I ask. Auberdine doesn't answer, but I can almost feel the hive-mind equivalent of an eye-roll, so I ask, "How's it possible?"

"I assume we've been out here long enough that tangible strides in propulsion technology allowed a next gen project to outstrip our flight."

Bailey rises to her feet.

"Excuse me," she says with one finger raised. "But are there people in there?"

Auberdine's avatar regards the image.

"Unknown," she says. "Its hull materials resist penetrative scans, but it has adjusted course in response to us. We expect to rendezvous within a few hours. It initiated a contact protocol with our airlock."

Small as our crowd is – it is amazing how loud it can get when everyone speaks at once. I listen to the cacophony for a few seconds before I give a shrill whistle that shuts the noise down. The echo dies and everyone looks at me. I glare straight at the Captain's avatar even though it's not really her and it's not really looking back.

"Is that a rescue mission?"

It doesn't matter that the form is just an approximation of what Captain Auberdine would look like if she were standing here right now; even via hologram, her hesitation conveys the obvious: she has no idea.

The rest of the briefing consists of the recitation of technicals. The data is dry and hollow, and every new frequency and percentage just asks the same question: if the ship is human and has broadcast capability, why aren't they talking to us?

Afterwards, Sasha, Bailey, and I head to the lower deck to prepare as best we can. Auberdine wants us to skim out a couple drones to observe the approach. I caution her that with the number of variables the docking procedure will bring, the drones will be at risk, but she considers it a matter of security. I must admit, I'm pretty interested to get a look at the ship's external tech. The drones can't safely extend more than a dozen meters out from the ship, so we won't exactly get a long view, but those exterior fins were like nothing I've ever seen. Reminded me of butterfly wings crossed with a fungus that grew in spirals I once watched in a time-lapse.

Bailey and Sasha are still speculating on why the craft hasn't identified itself or broadcast its intentions when we arrive at the drone bay. I immediately set to running the drone diagnostics even though Sasha and I just ran them at the end of our welding procedure. Bailey and Sasha linger in the doorway and lean against the bulkhead.

"I'm still thinking comms failure," Sasha suggests.

"But they've initiated docking protocol," Bailey says.

"Yeah, but that's a fixed packet," Sasha says. "They might not be able to complete a more complex interaction."

"Maybe they are attempting contact, and the problem is on our end," Bailey says with a frown. "After all – assuming they're next gen, could be parts of our interface are simply too obsolete for compatibility."

"Do you think the Hive has more information than they've let on?"

"I don't think they'd lie to us," Bailey says.

"They can't go home, can they? They're in charge here. What if they don't want contact to succeed?"

"It would disrupt the order of things I suppose,' Bailey says.

I purge the drone buffers and queue up the flight routine software.

"And we're at the bottom of that order," Sasha presses. "If more of us show up, the whole hive might end up stuffed into a high-density hard drive for the ride home. And then what?"

My status board goes green. All systems go. "If that ship's come for us, they've not come for passengers," I say, vaguely pointing in the direction I'm pretty sure the ship approaches from. "At least not space hogs like us."

"What do you mean?"

"That hull's so small, only thing I figure might go back is exactly that high-density hard drive," I say. "A lot more likely that ship's piloted by a hive of its own. You think our little cocktail party in ANTEROS contains the only folk who got it in mind to obsolete our bodies? If our bunch gets on board a ship that's built for their kind rather than ours, you think they're just going to make room for us?"

"Oh come on," Bailey says. "They'd never—" She trails off. The truth is no matter which way you look at it, us meat bags have a ticking clock of a different kind than ANTEROS. Eventually, we're going to die or be uploaded, and it might just be that deadline came upon us a whole lot faster than we'd expected. Everyone knows that a catastrophic ship failure can end things nearly instantly, but this is different. There'd been a time when we'd all secretly dreamed of rescue, but now that it might be here, I think we all recognize for the first time that rescue and doom have become synonymous. It's certainly impossible that given the computing speed to which they have access that the Hive hasn't reached a similar conclusion. We've long trusted them not to act in a way that would jeopardize our lives, but now more than half the surviving crew talks to the mainframe in ways I don't recognize as speech. Should I assume I'll recognize their values?

A weight falls into the room between us, so we stop talking and finish the drone prep in silence except for a point where Bailey mutters something about running an airlock diagnostic and excuses herself.

AT FORTY-FIVE MINUTES TO INTERCEPT, I head to the galley for a nourishment tube. As I suck thoughtfully at the paste which tastes rather like spicy chocolate, I allow myself to daydream that the approaching ship has actual food. It strikes me that I would love to eat a piece of bread again, maybe with butter, but that seems like pure fantasy. The orbital mess at the station I grew up in kept us mostly on long store rations, but, occasionally, they 'spoiled' us with a special meal. Everyone could be divided between who went nuts for the fruit and who went nuts for the bread. I was camp grain through and through. The initial food store of the Theseus ran out during the first decade, and the items not accurately considered Earth foods were gone by the end of the first year. I'm not even sure my system could handle something like bread. Did I still produce traditional digestive enzymes?

Questions like that are why I can't agree to Lorenze's pressure to join the uplink. My body has changed so much I often consider myself only partially human, but my day-to-day life with its routine tasks like piloting the drones, standard cleaning and maintenance, and recreation still looks like a traditional human life. Little thoughts, little choices, little acts. When we were knocked off course and knew there'd be no restoration of our original flight path, we lost something fundamental. When the concept of a larger destination is gone, it's amazing how amazing it feels when someone needs you to weld something.

How does someone pass time in a collective digital consciousness? Do they have an equivalent to sleep? Are they aware every microsecond? Can they even tell which thoughts are their own? Auberdine insisted that she retained a sense of self once in conversation. Though she may have her classified and mission knowledge partitioned off from the others, I find it hard to conceptualize a meaningful self in that state. It's not like mainframe data storage is an earth-style suburb, and even if I could somehow apply that as a metaphor, what if you don't like your neighbors once you see them for who they really are? At least with a body, I can close my door and expect anyone who comes to knock.

Sometimes I feel that that proverbial knocking is what everything we do is. After all, what was our attempt to retrieve Persephone but a knock on the door of deep space? Even Demeter had limits on her windows with her daughter , and we were fool enough to try to bring her home for good. Are we being punished for our insolence with this voyage into Tartarus?

Entering deep space isn't that different from dying if you consider your relation to everything else that is living.

I find myself deeply agitated that something is now about to come and knock on our door. Our house is a damn wreck.

I sigh and finish my paste. I'm not convinced there is anything aboard to rescue, so I pull out my tablet and open up the drone coding program.

WHEN AUBERDINE ANNOUNCES five minutes to intercept, I amble towards the airlock. As I turn the corner, Bailey comes into view by the inner luck wearing her dress uniform. I supposed, I should have expected it given that she is the highest-ranking officer with a body, but none of us have worn our actual rank in at least twenty years. I'm impressed that the synthetic fabrics survived so well in storage. It still has that crisp maroon luster. For her part, Bailey beams with excitement despite the pessimistic note we'd had in our conversation during the prep routine.

A couple steps later, I stop in my tracks. Waiting in the corridor on the other side of the lock is Dr. Lorenz. Her visual unit has been detached from its medlab mount and fixed to a hovering, gyroscopically stable maintenance cart.

"It's been so long since I've physically left the lab that it feels like I'm traveling through a whole new world," Dr. Lorenze is saying to Bailey when I arrive.

"If you'd like, we can develop a more permanent

mobile solution," Bailey says. Then, she looks at me. "At least we can try."

I look over the cart. It's a ramshackle affair. The motors and wires are all exposed and connected to a central processing unit and receiving node. I spot globs of old mounting paste. The solder and weld aren't the precision jobs one would expect for a rig meant to serve as someone's body, but there wouldn't have been remotely enough time to code a proper fabrication.

"I suppose we could cannibalize some of the circuitry from one of the old ventilation drones and fabricate whatever else we needed," I say.

Dr. Lorenze shifts focus to me. I shiver slightly. I won't lie. It's weird to know that the only part of Dr. Lorenze that left the medlab is her eyeballs. For the longest time, I kept thinking I'd get used to the different striations of hybridity among the crew, but now I don't believe I'm really supposed to.

"That would be nice," Dr. Lorenze says.

Nice. The word leaves me a little agitated. I'm not sure that word covers anything about what we are right now. I don't think it's covered anything since the Persephone incident, even at our best. The truth is, the more I think about it, the more I don't think any of us actually survived the Persephone incident, just that our organic matter kept proceeding on forward. Then, if you take that away, what's left? What we've dumped into the hive? That's yet another step removed from being alive. What human can be slapped onto a hard drive and sent across the galaxy?

"Are you in distress?" Dr. Lorenze asks.

My irritation grows. It's a pointless question. The ship monitors my physiology in real time, down to the cellular level. She knows exactly what my emotions are doing. "You know what I think I'd do if I were them?" I ask, pointing to the airlock and hoping Lorenz understands 'them' to mean the arriving ship. "I'd take one look at his group when that lock opens, pack it up, and head on my way."

"And why would that be?"

"Because they're expecting humans, and I don't know what we are anymore." I cross my arms.

Dr. Lorenze's visual array and the cart to which she is attached are still in the way only something mechanical can grow still. I wish Lorenze could sigh or grimace or roll her eyes. The only thing that betrays her subtext is her pauses, but this time, I don't know what her pause might signify.

I don't get a chance to find out.

A soft metallic thump occurs outside the airlock. The report sends a singular shock through the ship's structure.

Bailey draws a short gasp. "The drones," Bailey whispers.

"It's okay, Sasha should have them out right now," I say. I glance at my tablet. If I turn the screen on, the course code I'd programmed and uploaded will still be visible. No one would have reason to have re-inspected the routine after the pre-flight check. Sasha would have watched them launch and orient themselves along the hull exactly as expected. They would have clipped to the mobile anchor and skimmed half the length of the ship to the lock and fixed tether.

What is she thinking, I wonder, as they then deviate from their observation? Is her brow furrowed? Is she twitching her thumb and going "pfft"? I hope that she recognizes what I've done. She, after all, knows not to trust the others.

There is a slight scrape as metal outcroppings slide

against metal grooves, and I know that the ships docking arms are reaching for the latch insets. In a proper procedure, the next step once latch lock occurs will be umbilical extension. Again, the metal vibrates, some God knocking. I feel the entreaty in the bottoms of my feet.

Then, a second thump sounds, this one dull and resonant, but also harder, almost a clang. The last reverberations I heard before I blanked during the Persephone incident flooded my mind. Red security lights illuminate down the corridor in both directions.

Auberdine's voice bursts over the comm.

"Docking procedure failure," she says. "Unknown detonation outside the lock. We need immediate diagnostics."

I don't know if I've done any damage to us or to them, but I find it unlikely. I just hope they find it sufficiently hostile that they'll break course away. Maybe they'll simply correct course and make a second attempt. Maybe they'll retaliate. No doubt I'll face some sort of retribution from the crew. My decision might have been rash, maybe even useless, but it is my own, and that, in the end, is the most — and the last — human thing I can think to do. Maybe it doesn't matter, in the end, if we have no spare parts or if we have all spare parts: maybe if you replace every part on me, what matters is the mind that thinks and wills apart from that demon who attempts to seduce it by some hallucination or simulation or group upload. Little thoughts, little choices, little acts. That I'm human enough to refuse the hive. I don't need to hear Sasha's voice break into the channel. I don't need to hear her frantic explanation that the drones inserted themselves between the strange vessel and our own. You never gain full awareness of drone size and orientation: the wrong minor collision can send them spiraling off into the black. Or whatever they were touching. They blew their air tanks. Pfft.

Sasha had been right. It *did* make space feel more real, spare parts or no.

WAR ON BRIHASPATI GRAHA

BY SHASHI KADAPA

Princess Sphoorti dragged Traksura to the shrine. *All the conditions for his death were met. She straddled the shrine threshold so that Tārakā- sura was neither indoors nor outdoors. She hefted him on her thighs, and he was neither in the air nor on land. It was dusk, neither day nor night. She opened her talons. They were not weapons. She was not a male or an animal, but a female. She ripped into his guts, tearing out the entrails and ridding the universe of a vile rakshasa.*

PRINCESS SPHOORTI STAGGERED as the cosmic winds and dust shook her, digging into her flesh and making her squirm. Disoriented, she stood in dazed disarray alone on the sandy river bank of a fiery world.

In one instance, she was exercising in her palace, and in the second instance, a whirlwind lifted her and dropped her on this hostile world. There was a deafening thunderclap, and a huge form towered above.

Stunned, she drew her sword and looked at the form. It was an ascetic, a sage from the time of the ancients transformed by their dedication into a powerful being, over a hundred meters tall, towering in front of her. Clad in a tiger skin loincloth, with skulls of ancient demons and animals strung around the waist and neck, the figure had a wild, flowing mane, and tendrils of lightning flew from the locks of its hair.

It roared, "Girl, your destiny has come. I am Kapali, an avatar of Bhagvan Shiva. I will give you the strength and weapons to fight Tārakāsura."

Huge volcanoes spurted molten magma and rocks many miles into the sky and fell in a withering, fiery torrent. Large animals she had never seen wandered around, eating and killing each other. It seemed that she had powers that protected her from the strong, acidic, abrasive environment.

Questions flashed through her mind, "Who, what, were, why?"

PRINCESS SPHOORTI WAS heir to the throne of the Puru Vaunsha dynasty. It was a long line of illustrious kings that began when Kaal, time, and the universe were formed. The kingdom extended across many galaxies and over countless eons, her ancestors had proved their valor and dedication to all the strange and exotic life forms that thrived in strange worlds.

Of unmatched beauty, she could fight with master swordsmen, outshoot the best archers, and had a way with horses and dogs that made even the wildest one come to her. Many paeans were sung about her courage in battle and war strategy. She had mastered the Vedas, learned the scriptures and all the court laws and rules, understood finance, and trade, and her subjects loved her.

Her ancestors had sworn that when evil threatened the universe, one of their scions would lead the battle. This was her destiny. Now she was on a desolate world.

The ascetic roared, "Girl, you are now on Guru Brahaspati Graha, planet Jupiter, the embodiment of Bhagavan Brihaspati, preceptor of all things. You are in a vast universe of nothingness trying to defeat the evil army of Rakshasas. Time is relative here, different from your world and your consciousness. If you fail, the universe will be reduced to shunya, zero, and the evil forces will rule forever over man, beasts, and the five elements, and all the gods will be their slaves. "

Not understanding, Sphoorti asked, "Who is Tārakāsura and why should I kill him?"

"Tārakāsura is the ruler of Patal Loka, the nether world. He prayed to Bhagvan Shiva, who gave him the boon that he could not be killed except when special conditions were met. He infects the cosmos, the stars, all the water, air, ether, living things, and inert entities, and wants to expand his empire. At a celestial time of conjunction, when all the planets are aligned, he will bring together the evil forces and turn the whole universe into a burning sandy morass where all things will be trapped. Many brave kings from distant stars and constellations will fight under your command. The time has come. Are you ready to receive special powers?"

Awed, Sphoorti got down on her knees, and Kapali touched her head. She felt a surge of power rushing through her veins. Kapali placed a trishul, a trident in the sand, a sword, and a bow in her hands.

"Take these weapons. The sand grains will become your soldiers. The trishul represents my states of consciousness—waking, dreaming, and sleeping. The sword is Asi, the god of the gods, and was forged from the first fire in the universe. It will cut through anything. This bow is Pinaka Ājagava, the divine bow of Bhagwan Shiva. No one can intercept or escape an arrow from the bow. It comes with a divine quiver that will always be full. Fight bravely and with valor, and that is the gift I demand. At your extreme moment of bravery, when you cannot win with bravery alone, I shall come to your aid."

The figure struck the ground, the sands opened up, and a parrot flew up and perched on her shoulders.

"This is the wise sage Shuka, one of the ancients, and he will guide you. He has assumed the form of a parrot since it is wise. "

Shuka said, "Greetings, Rajkumari, Bow down low and smear the dust from this plant on your forehead. You pay homage to Bhagvan Brihaspati, the preceptor. Tārakāsura is also his student, and the omnipotent Bhagvan will not take sides in this battle. However, you fight for Dharma, or righteousness. Hence, Bhagvan will not put you at a disadvantage. The rest is up to you. Prove that the reputation of your dynasty still holds true."

Sphoorti, bent down, grabbed a fistful of the dust, and smeared it on her forehead.

"Rajkumari, a portal will open to the vast plains of the river Kaveri, which flows with water and lava. On one side of the bank are the evil armies of Tārakāsura. On your side are the armies of Deva Kapali and all the generals. They wait for you to lead. Are you ready? "

"Yes, Rishi. I am ready."

As Sphoorti walked over to the crest of the hill, vast armies were arrayed over the banks. All the legions of the Senapatis, the captains, and the warriors stretched over the endless horizon.

"Get into the chariot, as it belongs to Bhagvan Indira. The charioteer is Mātali, a renowned warrior, and he protects you."

Sphoorti bowed to the chariot and the charioteer and got in.

"There are seven Akshauhini in your army, each led by a king famed for his courage and victories. Many allies have joined us in this fight against the rākṣasa. These kings rule vast galaxies."

"An akṣauhiṇī is a battle formation with 21,870 chariots, ratha, in which archers and the main captains ride. They are supported by 21,870 war Chatur Dantaih, or four tusk elephants, and 65,610 horses, or turaga. For these, 109,350 infantry, or sainyam, will follow. The ratio for each aksauhini is 1 chariot to 1 elephant, 3 cavalry to 5 infantry soldiers. The rākṣasa are many yojana in height and width (one yojana is 12.8 kilometers). "

"Are you ready?"

As they emerged from the gate, the parrot whispered, "O Rajakumari, request that aged sire meditating on the river bank to be your ati-senapati, commander-in-chief of your army".

"Who is that old man?"

"He is Guru Ati Senapati Atharvana, the greatest warrior. He is the son of the River Ganga, the holy river that flows through the cosmos and floods the Milky Way. His knowledge about war and war formations covers the entire time since creation. If he leads your army, then you will win."

She bowed to Atharvana and made her request. He looked down at her and said, "Yes, Rajkumari. I will lead your army. I do not know who will win. Fighting bravely is in our hands. We cannot control victory or defeat."

IN HIS CAMP, Tārakāsura, glowered in fury and anger at the distant, puny masses that streamed beyond on the other bank of the river. When he was angry, he towered two yojansa in height and one yojana in width. When he stood, his chest was hidden in the clouds.

Tārakāsura shouted orders, and his army started to arrange themselves into formations. Seeing this, Atharvana shouted instructions, and his army arranged themselves into formations. Both armies stood on either bank of the River Kaveri. The battle had begun.

TĀRAKĀSURA and his army of 11 akṣauhiṇī arranged themselves in the Garuda (eagle) formation, while

Atharvana used the Makara (crocodile) formation. The signalers included drum beaters on four-tusk elephants as well as trumpet and conch players, and they sounded out the codes to direct the soldiers into the appropriate positions. The huge formation moved swiftly and agilely, like a shoal of fish.

The formations extended to the horizon and stood on the opposite banks. It was crucial to cross the river and land on the opposite bank, as it would give them an advantage. Many soldiers would die; some would live, some with honor and some with disgrace.

THE GARUDA FORMATION was spread out, with large wings supporting the curved beak. Bhandasura led the right wing, and Ilvala led the left wing. At the beak was Tārakāsura and Kabandha and Prahasta formed the two eyes. Subāhu and Takṣaka were at the tail to prevent attacks from behind. Soldiers on the wings moved in an engulfing wave, dipping and rising, making it difficult to shoot at them.

Foot soldiers and archers marched between the elephants and the generals, forming a buffer. The formation was designed to raid the enemy quickly, and while the beak would kill the leading soldiers, the left and right flanks would sweep away the enemy like a swooping eagle. When the formation was run with perfection, it could move very fast, like an attacking eagle. The formation could succeed only when it was supported by strong flanks. Any breach in the flanks would cause it to collapse like an eagle with a broken wing.

Spies told Atharvana of the activity on the enemy side and the eagle formation they had formed. He spoke to his generals, Kings Puru, Yadu, and Turvasa.

Atharvana said, " Tārakāsura has used the Eagle formation. His army is 11 akṣauhiṇī and it will easily swamp our smaller army. I propose to use the crocodile formation. "

"Yes, general, I have one suggestion to make," said King Yadu. "The weakest point of the eagle formation is the group of enemy soldiers at the wing joins. The jaws of our crocodile should slice away the two wings of the eagle. In the river, the rākṣasa's cannot use their full power."

Atharvana shouted orders to his generals and the signalers to set up the crocodile formation. Atharvana rode at the tip of the snout in his chariot, with King Bharata and Puru leading at the left and right jaws.

Sphoorti was kept near the heart, surrounded by her soldiers, and rode her favorite steed. The rest of the kings and soldiers were arranged along the flanks. Turvasa, Anu, Drhyu, Alina, Paktha, Bhalanas, Siva, Visvanin, and tribal kings were arranged on the left and right flanks, while the kings of Ariana, Chorasmia, and Sogdiana formed the tail tip. The tail tip was to lash out at the flanks in a quick burst, killing the demons and allowing the formation to fight in very close quarters.

ATHARVANA BLEW HIS CONCH, and Tārakāsura did the same from the other side of the river. The ground trembled at the approach of the two armies, dust rising until it blotted out the sun, casting the ground in semi-darkness.

Atharvana and his army moved fast, charging across the sand and into the water. When they clashed, the eagle formation of Tārakāsura plunged forward into the river, and the wings spread out, trying to crowd and kill the enemy soldiers. The waters ran red with blood, and Tārakāsura whipped forward. His tremendous size allowed him to rise above the soldiers massed below his feet. He showered arrows on them, trampling hundreds under his massive feet.

Kabandha and Prahasta, who were the eyes, directed their demons, making small adjustments in their movements. The objective was to allow rākṣasa's Bhandasura and Ilvala, who led the right and left wings, to kill the soldiers on the flank of the crocodile formation.

KING PURU RODE up to Atharvana, who stood in his chariot and continuously shot arrows, killing the demons by the hundreds.

"O Ati-Senapati, our soldiers are being slaughtered with no respite. If this continues, we will be decimated."

"Yes, King Puru. The worst onslaught is coming from the forward right flank, led by Tārakāsura. You have to draw him to the center. Then we can trap him in the jaws of our crocodile formation."

King Bharata said, "My side will move to the extreme end, and you, King Puru, do the same. The two wings of the Garuda formation will be stretched as they move to counter us. Our center formations can then rush in and hit the joints of the wings, separating them. Turvasa and Anu can then hit the center and destroy the formation."

Rakumar Yaudheya, full of energy and eagerness, was ready to make his mark in his first battle. Without asking for permission, he disappeared into the crowd of soldiers to challenge Tārakāsura. They could see the pennant of his chariot as it crept through the masses. King Bharata had a sinking feeling that his son would die.

TĀRAKĀSURA STOOD in his massive chariot, goading his four bulls, which belched fire and snapped at anyone that came their way. He swung his mace, which was bigger than a tree, and swept away scores of warriors. When Yaudheya challenged him to a fight, he roared with laughter.

"What is this? Atharvana sent a fly to fight me."

"Tārakāsura, my arrows will sting like scorpions and make you run."

The young prince pulled his arrow, uttered a mantra holy chant, and fired a zitaka bana, or scorpion arrow. As the arrow rose above, it split into a thousand scorpions that slithered under Tārakāsura's armor and started stinging.

Wild with pain, the demon jumped from his chariot and ran, trying to remove the armor and the stinging scorpions. His charioteer and demons followed behind. Yaudheya continued to fire arrows, releasing the dreaded scorpions and directing the demon to the center, towards his generals.

Tārakāsura kept running into the waiting arms of Atharvana's formation. Atharvana ordered his formations to attack, and the elephants and soldiers plunged in. Archers fired volleys, spears, swords, and knives flashed. Iron met flesh, tearing in, and drawing out entrails, and soldiers died with a grunt or cries of pain. The right and left jaws of the crocodile formation cut through the wings, breaking the formation and throwing the leaderless enemy into disarray.

It took a few minutes for Tārakāsura to overcome the stinging scorpions and marshal his forces. The delay was sufficient for Bhisma's soldiers to cut the enemy formation completely, and the demon stood cursing and growling in anger.

Gesturing at the remaining archers, Bharata and Puru signaled their archers to fire at the far wings of the eagle formation to prevent reinforcements from reaching the center. A blanket of arrows flew towards the wings until the sun was momentarily blotted out. The river waters ran red with blood, and the chariots and elephants trampled over the dead and dying.

The infantry, with spears and swords, ran at the flanks. The wings led by the demons Bhandasura and Ilvala were in disarray, and they ran back over the bank to their side. Tārakāsura had risen to his full height and glared at his routed army.

Sphoorti came forth on her horse, which rose up on its hind legs. They glared at each other, shouting taunts and insults. He rose to his full height, towered above her like a mountain, then quickly decreased his size until he was like a small child.

Notching an arrow, she fired and hit Tārakāsura on his abdomen, drawing blood.

She shouted, "Foolish Tārakāsura, I have Pinaka, the bow of Shiva, and I will cut off your limbs."

He would have continued fighting, but his soldiers were almost gone, and so he rushed back with his generals, Vrikaasura and Uluka, with taunts and insults stinging in his ears.

The demon army was in full retreat. These demons fought as individuals and could kill in a one-to-one fight. However, they had never fought as an army. The forces led by Atharvana, on the other hand, were well trained and fought as a troop.

YAUDHEYA HAD by now ridden over the bank to the other side in his chariot and was still shooting arrows, hurling spears, and killing with his sword. His horses were tired, and he knew he had to turn back.

He turned back and came face-to-face with the three demons, Tārakāsura, Vrikaasura, and Uluka.

"Ah, vile prince, it was because of you that my demons died and we retreated. I will tear your limbs and eat them before you."

Tārakāsura gestured at his demons to capture him alive, and they moved forward.

Yaudheya had almost run out of arrows, and he fired bolts to cut the axles of the chariots of Vrikaasura and Uluka. Before he could fire his last arrow, demons raged in from behind, knocked him from his chariot, and stabbed him with their spears and swords, all the while laughing.

Vrikaasura shouted, "O Prince, throw down your sword, surrender, become our slave, and live."

"Death is more welcome than your foul touch."

He pulled out his sword and rushed at them, swinging and slashing at the demons. They replied by stabbing with their spears, but they realized that he would jump over and reach the generals.

Uluka then circled from behind and shot arrows, skewering the prince. The weight of the arrows as they pierced his chest forced him down to his knees. He still refused to throw down his sword and held it high.

He died like that, with his chest full of arrows and his sword held aloft. The demons would have taken his head as a trophy, but the enemy was near, and they ran.

King Bharata, Atharvana, and others kneeled in front of the boy. Bharata said, "I will not cry now and sully the memory of your bravery. I am truly proud to have been your father."

Atharvana bowed to the boy and said, "Brave prince. Your courage has allowed us to cross the river. You have saved countless lives and fought very bravely. I salute your death."

SHUKA HAD TURNED INTO A PARROT, sat on a tree, and heard Tārakāsura growl at his generals. "We should not have turned from the river. We should have been on the other side."

Tārakāsura looked at Samhasura, their guru, and said, "Great timeless asura king. What formation should we use tomorrow? "

Samhasura answered, "It is best that we use the Mandala (Galaxy) formation tomorrow. It is a defensive formation. Arrange all your Asura generals at the nodes. With our superior forces and strength, we can draw them inside, swamp them, and kill them.

ATHARVANA ADDRESSED HIS GENERALS. "You fought very bravely today. Many soldiers fell, and I pray for them."

He listened to Shuka, who had flown back, and then spoke, "It appears that Tārakāsura has planned the Galaxy formation. This is very dangerous for us."

Sphoorti said, "Please explain this formation and what we can do."

Atharvana said, "In today's fight, the rākṣasa's could not use their full strength and mighty forms. They got caught in a melee in the river. Tomorrow they fight on land."

He paused to drink some Soma and continued, "The galaxy formation will be spread far and wide. The asuras will rise to their full height and use all their demonic strengths. They will even fly and fight. Even if we kill one, others will rise."

"What do we do?"

"We will use the Vajra (diamond) formation and all the celestial weapons. Soldiers, chariots, and elephants will form the outer periphery. The generals will be inside and lead their soldiers."

ATHARVANA'S ARMY set out in a diamond formation with him in the lead. When it moved rapidly, the formation looked like a diamond, indestructible and impossible to penetrate. The phalanx was tight and extended to 4x3 Yojana.

The galaxy formation of Tārakāsura had set off, and they stretched beyond the horizon to more than

7x3 Yojana. It looked like an ocean of huge warriors on the move, and some of them towered into the clouds, undulating like giant waves, ready to smash everything in their way. Tārakāsura rode at the front, and his generals and captains were arrayed in their own defensive positions. Some rode and flew on fire-breathing dragons, while others rode on demonic, massive, twin-headed elephants and lions.

When the two armies met, it sounded as if a thousand volcanoes had exploded. The foot soldiers and infantry clashed first, each soldier trying to hack and cut their way through the enemy.

MUKĀSURA RĀKṢASA ENGAGED VISHOKA, the young prince of the Balanas, in the first pitch. The demon was huge and towered over the puny Vishoka, squashing helpless soldiers under his feet and allowing his underling demons to drink and feed on the bodies. His mouth bristled with fangs, and he would roar in delight as he grabbed them by the fistful and shoved them in his mouth. Vishoka shot a brace of arrows, but these hardly scratched the massive demon.

Mukāsura bent low and grinned at Vishoka, who stood in his chariot. "Puny fly. I can swallow you now. But I will let you live and see how I eat your soldiers. Then I will eat you. "

Fighting the massive rākṣasa directly was not possible. Vishoka prayed to Indira, the king of all gods, from whom he had gained boons after severe penance. "Bhagvan Indira. Grant me your Vajra astra (thunderbolt weapon). I seek this to kill this vile demon that eats my soldiers."

"Valiant Prince, I will give you my thunderbolt weapon, but it will destroy everything within ten Yojana's range, including you and all your soldiers. Do you want it? "

"My life does not matter. I will pretend to flee the battlefield in shame to that hillock on the horizon that is ten yojana away. The enemy will follow me. Give me the weapon, I pray, and let me die a glorious death."

"So be it."

The brave Vishoka acted as if he were frightened and started fleeing the battlefield on his chariot, crying for mercy. Mukāsura laughed and trumpeted loudly, inviting other rākṣasa to join him and enjoy the killing. A thousand rākṣasa captains with ten thousand soldiers each joined the chase as Vishoka raced on his chariot.

The rākṣasa laughed and taunted while Atharvana and his army watched with anger and shame. Atharvana shouted, "Stand, fight, and die like a warrior."

The rākṣasas fired bolts that killed Vishoka's horses and smashed his chariot. They shot arrows to cut off his legs and right arm.

Bleeding, Vishoka stumbled on his amputated legs and crawled to the top of the hillock.

He raised his bow in his left hand and screamed, "Deva Indira, grant me your thunderbolt. Let me die with honor. "

The dying prince drew the string with his teeth, waiting for the weapon.

The rākṣasas realized that something was wrong. The 'coward' prince was turning to fight. The sky was clear; the sun shone brightly in a cloudless sky. Yet there was the sound of thunder.

An arrow that blinded the sun in its brilliance appeared on the bow of the prince. He opened his teeth, and the thunderbolt weapon flew out, hitting the massed rākṣasas. The sound was deafening, the flame of the thunderbolt dimmed the sun and the milled rākṣasas captains and countless demons, and the prince was reduced to ashes.

There was silence on the battlefield. Sphoorti was the first to speak, "O brave prince, your mother was indeed honored to bear a son like you. I salute her. "

TĀRAKĀSURA WAS livid with anger when he came to know that hundreds of his captains and thousands of soldiers had been killed by a crippled prince.

He thundered, "We are rākṣasas. We do not die. We use guile and our great strength to strike fear in our enemies' hearts and kill them. "Go and kill."

THE RĀKṢASAS FELL on the enemies. They grew to their formidable size and swung wildly in anger, killing their own soldiers and those of Bhisma's army.

The generals and soldiers of Atharvana had not broken their position and fought as per the signals from the trumpeters and drummers. They met the charging Asuras, who cut them down, thrusting with their swords, while archers from both sides rained arrows.

Dust flew from the ground, quenched by the blood from the bodies ripped apart with swords and maces. The ground turned slippery, and it became a morass as the soil mixed with blood, making the soldiers slip and fall, and still the flames were not quenched. The sounds of war cries and of the injured and dying blotted out the shrill cry of an elephant trumpeting in rage.

At one stage, Sphoort was unseated from her chariot and was surrounded by the asuras. By feinting and stabbing, she killed Kālanemi. Chekitana and Vriprachitti rushed to her aid, and they killed the other demons, but they died too.

The number of rākṣasa's and Atharvana's soldiers who died was uncountable.

THE FIGHT CONTINUED for the next few days. Different formations were tried, shattered, regrouped, and the fight continued. Yama, the god of death, jackals, and vultures, were the only ones who were sated. Atharvana formed the oormi, or ocean formation, and Tārakāsura formed the sringataka, the horned phalanx, and the fight continued.

Several other formations, such as the Ardha Chandra or Half Crescent formation, Shakata or the Box Cart formation, Sarvatomukhi Dand formation, Suchimukha or the Needle formation, Padma or the Blooming Lotus Formation, and several other formations, were used.

It appeared that this fight would rage on until the last soldier died. Days passed without any result. Both sides were untiring and replenished their sources either through divine means or through demonic power. The carnage was so great that it was not possible to walk without treading on a body or torn limb.

. . .

It was night, and Tārakāsura was very angry and worried. He had expected the war to last a couple of hours, that none of his soldiers would be killed, and that the enemy would flee. He had expected the puny humans to die by the thousands. However, the tiny humans had killed his most able captains and were getting stronger. He was worried that his demons would run away.

In despair, he asked his generals, "What can we do? Whom should I summon to the battle?"

They chorused, "Gajāsura."

"Are you sure? How will we feed him? How will we send him back? If he does not have enough to eat, he will start eating us."

"There are plenty of enemy soldiers. He can eat his fill for one hour, then he will go back to sleep."

Accordingly, Tārakāsura sat for a demonic ritual, and a hundred cows were slaughtered, and their carcasses placed on the ground. Then he began chanting, "O mighty Gajāsura. Rise from your slumber. Pray, come forth, and join the battle."

The chants went on for a long time, and then the ground shuddered and split as in an earthquake. A terrible asura in the form of an elephant emerged. He was taller than a mountain, and his girth extended to many yojanas. His tusks were long and covered with pointed spikes. A thick coat of natural armor covered his body and head.

He blew fire from his trunk and mouth. When he took a step, the earth trembled due to his weight. The force of the wind blew away many chariots when he whisked his ears. When he yelled his war cry, trees in a nearby forest were uprooted, and one had to cover one's ears. The other asuras, who were monstrous, looked like small insects in front of him.

Eyeing the carcasses, he drew them up in his trunk and swallowed them like an elephant drinking water. He trumpeted, "Ah, my brother Tārakāsura, why have you woken me from my sleep? I am hungry."

Tārakāsura replied, "O great Gajāsura. I need your help to fight the puny humans who stand massed over there. There are many and you can eat them."

"Yes. I will."

Gajāsura was not bound by any rule about not fighting in the night. He jumped over and landed in the camp of Sphoorti, trumpeting his battle cry.

The terrified soldiers, tired after days of fighting, ran around in the darkness, not knowing what this terrible demon was. Gajāsura stood in the camp, blowing fire with his trunk, and then sucking in masses of soldiers.

The generals and captain rushed out to rally the troops, and Atharvan shot a fire arrow into the sky, lighting up the area. They looked in horror at this huge elephant that was killing and eating soldiers. They shot arrows and hurled spears, and these bounced off the armor.

Sphoorti came running and asked Shuka, "What is this?"

"That is the dreaded Gajāsura, son of Mahiṣāsura, an asura in the form of an elephant. It cannot be killed, and it has an appetite that cannot be satiated. When it was born, Dev Brahma, the creator, Vishnu, and Shiva approached Mahiṣāsura and told him that his son had such a ravenous appetite that he would eat everything on earth in a day. It is better that he sleeps for 10,000 years, awakens for one hour, and feeds before going back to sleep. Mahiṣāsura agreed and requested that Shiva give Gajāsura the boon of invincibility. Shiva agreed, and Gajāsura was given the boon. However, he will be killed by any weapon that belongs to Shiva."

"Are the 10,000 years over now?"

"I do not think so. I think Tārakāsura summoned him."

"What do we do? In one hour, he will kill all of us."

Atharvan said, "None of us can kill this demon. Sphoorti, you have the trishul that Dev Kapali gave you. You mount that weapon on your bow and shoot Gajāsura in the eye."

Sphoorti drew out the trishul, strung it on her bow, chanted a mantra, aimed at the eye of Gajāsura, and let it go. The trishul flew straight and pierced the eye, moving into the brain and tearing it up.

It died with a terrible roar that sounded through the hills, and the camp of Tārakāsura. The asuras knew that their ally was dead, and a deep gloom descended on the camp.

Tārakāsura sensed this and said, "Our friend Gajāsura was destined to die today. He has killed thousands of enemy soldiers. Victory is ours."

THAT NIGHT, Sphoorti had intense nightmares of being drawn into a vortex and fighting Tārakāsura outside an old temple. Dark suns glinted in the sky, emitting dark sparks that fell as thunderbolts. She dreamt of falling into a huge morass and fighting demons. Then she dreamed of an old crone waiting in the deep darkness. She saw very bad omens: the sun was eclipsed and was then covered by huge back clouds that came from nowhere.

The land was dark, but not yet night, and from the wastelands, an army of huge wolves the size of wild horses started howling in the gloom. Vultures flew overhead, and they circled viciously, waiting and looking at her with gleaming death eyes and sparkling talons.

Burning meteors rained, innumerable funeral pyres burned in the dusk, and the horizon was filled with weeping widows clad in white. Bizarre creatures with misshapen heads and half-burnt faces wandered around.

She cried out and got up from the nightmare. She knew that the next day would be very important, that she would live or die.

A SPY INFORMED Atharvana that Tārakāsura had created the dreaded chakra vyuha, or wheel formation. This is a very insidious and multi-layered defensive formation that works like a rotating wheel. Expert warriors stood in interleaving positions, supported by captains. When the wheel starts moving toward the target, two soldiers are placed on both sides with others behind them, forming a total of seven concentric circles.

The soldiers keep moving in a circular formation, and when the last soldier completes the turn, the whole phalanx turns inward. An enemy soldier who is caught in the vortex is gradually pushed to the center, and it is impossible to find a way out of the maze. There is only one entry and exit point, and only one person can enter at a time before the entrance closes and moves to another point.

Atharvana pondered and then spoke to the assembled generals. "I think Tārakāsura wants to capture Sphoorti. It will be impossible to break out once you are caught. I will go in her place."

Sphoorti said, "Great general, this war has been going on for days with no victory for either side. It will only end when Tārakāsura or I are killed. Only I can kill him. Let me go. I will break into the wheel, and you and the other generals can follow. Let us end this war. Countless have died. "

Very reluctantly, Atharvana agreed, and they set out to meet the formation.

He said, "Sphoorti, hold out your hands." When she held them out, he tapped them with his arrow. She was surprised to see that she now had the talons of a lion that could be retracted.

"You will need these to kill Tārakāsura."

"I will go with her disguised as a parrot and guide her," said Shuka.

TĀRAKĀSURA CALLED all the remaining rākṣasa clan members of the netherworld to form the chakra formation. As Atharvana and his army came up to the spinning formation, they were awed by its power and speed. It was spread over a diameter of 61 yojanas.

As it crept up, it swallowed all those who stood in its way. Atharvana directed his generals and the army to flank the formation. Only he knew the entry and exit paths, but only Sphoorti had to enter first.

He fired a volley of arrows, and demons died by the hundreds, and immediately new ones would come in their place. He and Sphoorti raced around the periphery, and then he spotted the entry spot.

"There. Rush in with your chariot, keep going, I will follow."

Sphoorti lifted her pinaka bow and kept firing arrows, killing anyone who came in her path. The formation opened, and the rākṣasas moved to let her in and then moved back to close the gap. The formation kept moving, and Atharvana waited in vain outside with his generals, but the entry point had vanished. She was alone inside with many of the fiercest demons that infested the universe.

She kept riding in, going deeper and deeper along the maze rings, and lost track of where she was. Towering more than a yojana, the demons did not shoot at her but just kept pushing her in ever tighter circles. Shuka kept whispering and encouraging her to go on.

Soon, Sphoorti could hardly turn her chariot without hitting the demons, and she realized that the eye of the chakra was around the next curve.

Then she saw a number of rākṣasa's standing in their chariots in a line along both sides of a path with their bows and maces.

At the far end stood Tārakāsura in his huge chariot, pulled by large bulls, breathing fire. She skidded to a halt and notched an arrow.

"Evil Tārakāsura. This is your last chance to surrender or die."

Baffled guffaws sounded like thunder as the demons laughed. She looked like a tiny ant in front of them.

She started shooting, and the stream of arrows seemed like a thick torrent of waterfalls. The first set of arrows cut the bow strings of the demons. The next stream shattered the mace and swords that they held. Another set smashed their chariots, and they tumbled to the ground, their crowns flying away and landing at their feet.

The fallen rākṣasa's rushed at her with their spare maces and swords.

"Fight one-to-one, O rākṣasa's. You are many; I am alone."

Screaming in rage, they surrounded her and then rushed in to kill her. Sphoorti fell to the ground under their huge form and weight.

She crawled out, and Shuka asked her to invoke the name of Shiva. She chanted the mantra and raised her arms. The Ekasha Gada, the mace of Shiva, appeared in her hand. It had the power of ten thousand elephants.

She allowed the fallen demons to get up and arm themselves, and then she set about smashing them. The terrible mace pulverized them into a mass of gore and flesh. Then she faced Tārakāsura who rushed forward on his chariot to crush her.

Raising her mace high, she hit the wheels, and the chariot broke into pieces. The bulls, mad with fear, ran into the massed soldiers, trampling many to death. Atharvana, who stood outside, heard their loud bellows and the screams of the dying soldiers.

"Sphoorti is fighting and gaining victory."

They stood in front of each other. Tārakāsura towered above her, with his head reaching the sky, and Sphoorti was so small that she hardly rose above his toes.

"What will you do now? No weapon can kill me. "

He pulled out his long sword belt, spiked and supple like a rope. Bending down, he started sweeping the earth, digging out clumps of rocks, uprooting trees, and leveling hills.

Sphoorti would be caught in the next few sweeps, and she hid behind a rock. The next sweep smashed the rock into pebbles, and Tārakāsura glared at her, ready to kill. As he swept the spiked belt, Sphoorti tumbled, and the mace fell from her hand. She pulled out her sword and knew that she would die in the next few seconds.

Bhagvan Kapali appeared in a flash of thunder. All the demons stared in fear for they knew he could destroy them with one glance. Kapali caught Tārakāsura arm and hit him on the head with his damru.

"You are reduced to her size and are even. Now fight."

Tārakāsura shouted at this outrage and then picked up a sword. "Tiny or huge, I can still slay this girl."

They started fighting.

Shuka warned her, "Do not get too close. He is stronger than you, but you are agile. Make him bleed and weaken him. "

The blows were swift and strong, the sound of steel ringing through the air and deafening the shouts of the rākṣasa's.

Tārakāsura was an expert, but he had relied on his brute strength and size in a fight. He swung at her chest, and she bent low and slashed at his knee, drawing blood. He thrust and slashed; Sphoorti parried the blow and swung up, slashing his chest. Tārakāsura countered with a block from the shield, stepped back, and slashed from the top right down. Sphoorti jumped back, bowed low, and thrust diagonally up at his stomach. The sword moved in a blur, flicking across the armor and seeking out joints.

Tārakāsura leaned back to avoid the blow as it struck his neck, and Sphoorti jumped up and kicked him in the stomach, forcing him back. They rushed at each other, slashing, cutting, and parrying, and the hills resounded to the sound of steel striking steel. Sphoorti was agile and fast with surprising feints and lunges, Tārakāsura struck with heavy strikes, slicing with power and wearing her down. Both bled from wounds on their forearms and chests. Their sweat and blood flew and fell on one another.

He was tiring visibly, and his blows were growing weaker. Sphoorti was also worn out and barely managed to hold the sword.

Their duel had taken them away from the rākṣasa's. Sphoorti glanced around and saw a temple. The nightmare came back to her.

Shuka whispered in her ears, "Princess, the time for his death has come. I will give you one drink of soma. You will get a surge of power. Drag him to the temple, but not inside. Kill him with your talons. Be quick.

Sphoorti smashed the sword out of the Tārakāsura's hand, grabbed him by the neck, and dragged him to the temple. All the conditions for his death were fulfilled.

She straddled the temple threshold so that Tārakāsura was neither indoors nor outdoors. She hefted him on her thighs, and he was neither in the air nor on land. It was dusk, neither day nor night. She opened her talons, and they were not weapons. She was not a male or an animal, but a female.

Shuka screamed, "Kill him now. The boon of Shiva does not protect him now."

Sphoorti dug in with her talons into Tārakāsura's

guts and throat, casting them on the temple's outer area.

Tārakāsura twitched and died with a great roar that was reduced to whimpers and then went silent. The spell was broken, and his great army disappeared in a flash. There was peace in the universe. The fires died down, and a cool, fresh wind started blowing, bringing relief to her soldiers. Her ancestors would be proud that she reinforced their illustrious line.

A Cup of Justice

BY TEEL JAMES GLENN

I suppose most stories that begin 'I was drunk to near coma when the robbery occurred' come to no good end, yet I submit this one exception.

My name is Major Collin Stone-Whytte (retired) of Her Majesty's Horseguard. I was wounded out of service in Afghanistan and so came to have far more leisure time on my hands than was good for me. The demmed wog bullet left an ache in my hip that pained me greatly when the weather was damp and when is it not in England? I was well into my cups on that October night when I staggered home from a gentleman's club in Kensington.

I had stepped to a bush in a hedge-lined road to relieve myself when I heard the sound of voices from just beyond the hedge.

"I say we shouldn't ought ta' trusted Solly," one voice said. "Arlo, he's in there getting the bleedin' lion's share."

"He said he had to put down the guard first, Mickey," a second voice said.

What deviltry I had stumbled onto?

"There's Solly now," I heard Arlo say, "See he's waving us in!"

The two men who had been holding horses left the beasts to head toward a large dark building.

I poked my head through to see a building I recognized as a small private museum for Mediterranean artifacts.

"There was only one warder," Solly said from the door. At his feet was a still form. "No one else around, boys, good pickings!" The three moved into the building.

I admit I was not thinking at my clearest but I felt a certain bravado and gentleman's obligation.

When I reached the door I first bent to check the uniformed watchman and discovered that his skull was bloody. He had clearly been struck down in a cowardly assault.

I looked up to see where the larcenous trio had gone. Their progress through the museum was easy to follow by their bobbing lantern.

There were paintings on the walls and a frieze of mythological figures. The dark shapes that dotted the room I knew were statues of nymphs and heroes.

I leaned on my walking stick and limped after the crooks having to work hard not to bump into the art displays as I tried to keep an even keel. I took a small flask from my tunic pocket and sipped some Dutch courage before I moved forward. I still felt that my English being up was enough to overcome the hooligans.

I was wrong.

As I rounded a corner with my stick raised in preparation I came face to face with one of the thieves.

Arlo cursed when he saw me. "'Ere, who's this?" He was a burly brute, almost as tall as I but broader. He was holding an armful of small statuary and when he saw me he dropped them to reach for a cudgel thrust through his belt.

I swung my walking stick to strike the man on the hand as he reached for the club. He cursed vulgarly and his exclamation summoned his confederates.

The other two thieves spun to face me. The taller of them, a dark haired brute with a long scar on his left cheek, yelled, "Get him, Solly!"

Artifacts scattered as the two men charged me.

"Stop right there you blackguards!" I yelled, "surrender and face justice!"

Their charge was more than my befogged mind could deal with. I barely managed to get in two strikes before the three of them slammed into me. I went arse over teakettle into a display of pottery. A statue of some fellow in a toga holding a cup and an amphora tumbled with me. Shards of crockery flew all around me as it smashed under my weight.

The pain in my leg was nothing next to the beating they gave me. At least, in the heat of the moment, they only laid about me with fists.

I felt the pint of whisky in my jacket shatter under one of the blows and had the most absurd thought that it was a horrible waste. "What a horrid way to end the evening," I thought just before a fist sent me into oblivion.

I woke in considerable pain and confusion. The weak light that seeped into the windows of the museum brought my new circumstances to me as if with a bolt from above.

"The robbery!" I tried to sit up quickly but nauseousness forced me to sit back down.

"I'd stay where you are for a while, old fellow," a soft, sweet voice said from behind me. I turned my head slowly to see who had spoken.

What I beheld was so unexpected a vision that I gasped; before me stood the most beautiful man I had ever seen. I do not use the word lightly, for he was beyond handsome with features that arrested the eye as a sunrise on the Adriatic might. His age was indeterminate for his body was fully formed and manly muscled, but his features were soft in a boyish way. He had curly blond hair, a cherubic face and the most startlingly lambent blue eyes.

Most remarkable was that the fellow who stood before me was dressed not in correct evening clothes but was draped in a flowing white Greek khitan! He smiled down at me and gave a short gentle laugh.

"Don't look so shocked, dear fellow," the stranger said. His voice had a slight accent as I noticed now, one vaguely eastern in nature.

"Oh dear," he said, "I'm not dressed inappropriately, am I? I so hate to be out of style."

I was sure the whisky and the blows had addled my mind but I said, "You seem poorly dressed for the weather, sir, at the very least."

"Oh!" the blond boy-man said. "You are so very correct!" He looked at my own tunic and attire and nodded. There was a flash of light like a photographic explosion and he stood before me in a long coat and scarf, trousers and jackboots in purest white. "Is this better?" He twirled like a ballerina.

"It's less likely to get you picked up for a tart in the East End," I said.

"Those brutes ruined Silenus' amphora!" he shrieked. He started to look around as if he were the one who was suddenly aware of where he was. He began to move among the fragments of the artwork scattered around the room. He touched a frieze of the Corona Borealis on the wall that had been marred. "This was the crown I gave to Princess Ariadne that was set by her in the heavens." He began to sob.

"The Persian monsters!" He wailed as he sifted the bits of the smashed frieze through his fingers. He looked up at me and his glowing blue eyes were the hurt eyes of a child. "They will pay for this outrage!"

He seemed to see me again and the fury disappeared as quickly as it had come. His face was abruptly boyish and sweet again. "Oh you are in sad shape, old fellow; do sit down before you fall down."

I stumbled to a nearby bench and sat with a grunt of pain. "The warder," I said.

"The fellow by the back door?"

"He's hurt," I said.

"I've sent him along to Morpheus," the stranger said, "that sleep is restful and healing but you, my friend, you have slept with me more than with he."

"Slept with you?" I asked. I was sure I had never been so drunk as to forget so smashing a fellow.

"Why the sleep of the intoxicated, old fellow," he said. "The respite from the cares of life afforded by the fruit of grape and grain."

I shot to my feet in indignation at his implication. It was a foolish move for I fell forward when my bad leg gave way beneath me.

The white clothed stranger moved in an eye-blink to catch me in his arms. I was surprised by the strength of his grip, I felt like a child or a blushing bride.

"Careful, Major,' he said. "You shall do yourself more mischief then the brigands did."

It was all so absurd that I found myself saying, "You have the advantage of me, sir."

"Ah, my manners," he said. He looked down into my eyes. Up close his blue eyes were like a Mediterranean sky. I felt drawn in and mesmerized. "I am Dionysus," he said in a tone that was a choral serenade. "Late of Olympus."

That was when I passed out again.

My return to consciousness the second time was a gradual thing and I became aware first of a lovely aroma wafting to my nostrils. Cognac!

I opened my eyes to see the blond man smiling at me and holding a snifter of excellent vintage up to my lips.

"Partake," he said in a silky voice. "Divine madness is the answer for most ills." I sipped and felt warmth course through my limbs.

I became aware that I was seated on a bench across the room from where I had fallen. I could see the guard resting with a blanket over him, his head on a pillow and a smile on his face as he snored.

"Thank you, sir," I said. The Cognac warmed its way through my system. "I am afraid I have been too much in my cups for I thought I heard you say--"

"You can not be too much in my cups," the stranger said. "After all it was I who brought the magick of the grape and grain to mankind."

My head spun again. "Then you did say--"

"Yes, Lord Dionysus." He bowed formally.

"Dionysus?"

"I do thank you for attempting to protect these treasures." He waved around the room. "And for calling me."

"Calling you?"

"You are rather a parrot aren't you, old fellow?" The white clad stranger said. "You called me when you spilled that lovely fifty year old malt on the statue of me." He held up a fragment of a shattered idol that had part of a face still visible: it was the image of the stranger!

My breast still hurt from the shattered bottle. I looked down at the bit of blood spreading on my blazer. I downed the rest of the snifter in one gulp. "You are a Greek God?"

"Well, I think of myself as a pan-Hellenic deity actually," he said, "but I am open to worshipers of all nationalities—except perhaps Persians; bunch of destructive louts!"

I was sure I had been made mad by a blow to my head, but he seemed such a pleasant sort so I said, "I am sorry for all this."

"You are sorry?" His beautiful face transformed into a scowl and I felt an odd sense of disappointment as if a cloud had blotted out the sun.

"Well, you are a visitor here to England, old chap," I said, "host's duties and all that."

He gave a radiant smile. "Why, thank you Major." He set the stone image of his face down and looked around with his hands on his hips. "But now that I am here I am afraid I shall have to intervene very directly in this infuriating invasion of my sanctuary."

"This museum?" I asked.

"Oh, yes. I consider anyplace where I or the fermented fruit are worshiped to be my temple. And it has been violated."

I saw that darkness flash cross his features and suddenly felt very sorry for the three blokes.

"Not very likely we can track them down, uh—your Lordship," I said.

"Why not," he asked. "You know what they look like, do you not?"

"Aye, your lordship," I said, "and heard their first names, but that's a matter for the constables."

He clapped his hands and the sound, so sharp in the hollow space of the gallery, startled me. "Then that is all we need."

"But the authorities--" I began.

"I believe my authority trumps any local police force, sirah," the Mediterranean deity said. Then he smiled at me in a warm way. "And I am drafting you to assist me." He giggled. "Draughting!" he repeated, "I am so droll!"

I did not know what he meant at the time but indeed it was a droll comment as things turned out.

The Greek god waved his hands and I felt compelled to stand.

"I say, sir, what is happening?" I whispered.

"Oh we are going to find and chastise the three individuals who breached the sanctity of my temple-"

"Museum," I corrected.

"Museum," he said with a nod. "And also recover the items they took; one of those things taken was a very nice necklace that my old tutor Chiron gave me." His face clouded again. "I will get that back."

As he spoke my body responded to his gestured commands and I felt I was beginning to change. It was an actual change I speak of, not a philosophical one; that is to say, as my muscles twitched and spasmed my flesh began to warp. "Bloody hell!" I exclaimed. My arms lengthened and my hands turned in on themselves so that I could not open my fingers. "Why not just make a godly gesture and summon them up?"

"Oh please," Dionysus said, "I would love to just go about smiting randomly (which is much more Zeus' sort of thing), but your careless attention to the single malt has manifested me and thus I am somewhat limited in my scope of action on this plane i.e.: I shall need transportation."

"Transportation?"

"That parrot thing again! Yes. I will require a steed who knows the area and who knows our prey: you!"

As he said, my body began to change even more rapidly.

The compulsion of the deity pulled me down on all fours and bending my neck up.

With my head up I looked directly into the eyes of Dionysus who had a serene expression on his face. His smile almost made me feel good about the oddness that was occurring to me.

Almost.

I looked past him to a set of French windows where I could see the gibbous moon reflected and saw the thing he was remaking me as:

I was a dappled draught horse!

"This is not cricket!"

"Oh please," he said in a smarmy tone, "it's not a spider-or-heaven forfend- a swan (Big Z was a real scream with that one) so don't complain. I mean—

you don't expect me to trudge through the dreary rain on foot do you?"

I was taken aback by that, I mean, after all he technically was a lord and all that, albeit a foreign one. Still it was rather presumptuous for him to turn me into a ruddy horse and I said so.

"Of course I presume, old fellow," the God said, "I am an Olympian! Now turn around, I wish to mount you."

II.

All things considered, I was a decent horse. I found my gate quickly as we moved along the silent roads outside the museum.

The roads were deserted at that hour but that worked to the advantage of the deity's quest.

"Methinks the miscreants are abroad in that direction," Lord Dionysus said in an exaggerated posh accent. "I am sure you can detect their spore, can you not trusty steed?"

"I really would appreciate a little better attitude, your lordship," I said in a –uhum–hoarse voice interspersed with whinnies. "I was, after all, a Major in the Horseguard."

"Well," he said, "then you should know how to trot straightaway after the scent, eh? When we get close, I will feel the artifacts, I am sure."

I did not argue since I could indeed scent the criminals and so the logic of the admittedly bizarre situation dictated that I follow my elongated equine nose.

The path lead directly toward the Thames. Soon we moved to the more populated streets of Limehouse in the Borough of Tower Hamlets,on the northern bank opposite Rotherhithe.

The denizens of that nefarious area were out and about. They were a dark and shifty lot that moved through that dodgy district between Ratcliff to the west and Millwall to the east.

My—uh—rider took it all in, remarking now and again, "Oh my, he looks like Hephaestus made him, so twisted is he," as we passed some pickpocket scurrying past or, "You can lay a wager that young damsel is no vestal virgin," when some lady of the evening who was heading home who cast a weary but hopeful eye toward the white dressed Hellenic.

Still, the scent called us further to the southwest along Narrow Street, Limehouse's historic spine along the back of the Thames wharves to Booty's Riverside Bar.

There was a shed nearby guarded by an ugly looking cudgel-man where I nosed out the mounts the cracksmen had ridden. I told Dionysus as much.

"Well, there you go, old fellow," he said in a cheery voice. "See my divine wisdom in your rearrangement of form?"

"But you can't go in that hell hole alone," I said with a little snort in my voice, "I've been in there with three mates from the 'Guard and we barely got out with our skins intact! With you dressed like a Toff they will be on you like hounds on a hare."

Dionysus laughed. "Oh ye of little faith!" He hopped off my back and snapped his fingers. There was that flash of light again and before me he was no longer the imposing deity but the image of one of the denizens of the district.

I, however, was still a horse. "What about me?" I whinnied at him. "I can't go in there like this."

"Someone has to be prepared should we need a quick getaway," he said smugly. "So as they say with the omnibuses, 'keep the motor running.'" Then he hobbled off and was through the door to the pub.

"Hey!" I hissed. "Bloody hell; I'm glad I don't burn incense to you!" I was left standing in the narrow street by myself to contemplate the sheer insanity of my circumstance.

Was not Dionysus god of divine madness? (all those classes at Sandhurst on the classics came back in full measure). The madness increased a moment later when a body exploded through the window of the pub followed by a shower of glass and a long wooden bench.

The screams that followed the flying form were the most terrified I had ever heard.

Oh God's Garters! I thought, *They've killed the ruddy bint!* I wheeled and headed for the gaping hole of the window, leaping the still form on the cobbles and jumped through the opening not quite sure what I was doing but ruddy well sure I was angry.

The interior of the dingy pub was low ceilings and dark with the close packed humanity that was now swirling about and yelling as if they were all on fire.

They might as well have been because in the center of the swirling mass was a single figure holding a wine bottle in one hand and wielding a coal scuttle in the other. Ruffians charged in with whatever weapon was at hand—chairs, benches, bottles and street knives. There was a pile of fallen circling the single warrior with the new attackers charging over them to be repulsed with a clang and a scream of *"epilambanein!"*

The figure at the center of the melee was Dionysus, laughing and snarling alternately, his eyes wide with that very divine madness I had been ruminating on.

"Bloody hell," I said.

III.

When I spoke, a ragged patron, who had a meter long metal bar in his hands in preparation to race into the fight turned, looked at me and said, "Crykies; a bloody talking nag!"

"I'm not a nag," I snorted. "I'm a flippin' bleedin' thoroughbred stallion, you git!" Then I reared up and gave him a hoof to the pate.

My movement called attention to me and a number of the thugs in the room turned to face me. This gave Dionysus the respite to break out of the circle of assailants and he charged across the room with a wild vibrating laugh.

"Glad to see you, old fellow," he called to me as he ran up to my side. "But what brings you in here?"

"I thought you were dead out on the street!" I snorted. "I got—well I got mad."

He laughed with joy. "Delightful!" he said. "Divine in fact!"

Before I could comment on that a phalanx of hooligans launched themselves at us swinging their motley collection of weapons with deadly intent.

I started to back out to escape, but the deity stood his ground and said, "I am growing tired of this!"

Then he looked over his shoulder and commanded, "Close your eyes, quickly."

He said it with such determination and force that I complied. It is good that I did because I heard him yell, "FATHER!" and then a light so bright that even with my eyelids closed the intensity of it burned.

There was a crackling sound, a cacophony of screams, a flash of heat. I could not resist any longer to see what was going on so I opened my eyes a crack and saw the entire interior of the pub was blackened and smoking, the occupants scattered around the floor in various states of consciousness, all of them smoking from burns.

"What?"

"Daddy," Dionysus said with a shrug. "It's a trump card I don't like to use often, but it really was a nicer alternative to my current mood." He held up a small, jeweled belt. "This was Chiron, my tutor's fetlock decoration; that—that mortal had it and when I saw it I just went divine on him."

The decoration was a beautifully carved ebony stone with smaller crystals set around it on a belt of connected bronze plates. I glanced back out toward the street. Now I could see that the form in the street was the burglar Arlo.

"I hope we can question him," I said. "Or else we may not find the other things." He looked at me, chewed his lip and nodded.

"Just so," he said. "I hit him pretty hard," the deity said with a sheepish grin on his face. He was dressed all in white again and immaculate. "I shall have to encourage consciousness to find out where to go next; the other two were not in the pub."

"Well you should do so," I suggested, "and we should leave here, in case you didn't notice your Zeusbolt has started the building on fire; this area of close packed buildings will go up like tinder."

He looked concerned. "Oh, yes; fragile reality on this plane; I've been away for a while."

He clapped his hands and suddenly the sky opened up with a localized torrential rain. He smiled at me; "I don't even need father's help on this: if one can't coax rain out of English skies it's time to close one's temples!" The Hellenic deity lifted the fallen thief as if he were a mere child and threw him over my withers. "Let us retire to a more private space to inquire of this gnat to see where we will be going next."

I walked down the street and we moved to a narrow alley with a building overhang that was fairly isolated. There I shrugged the felon off my back and snorted.

Dionysus abruptly had a small metal flask in his hand and he opened it and waved it beneath the nose of the still felon. Arlo snorted and his eyes opened with a start.

"Where am-" He said and then he saw the god. "Don't hit me again, Governor, I didn't do the guard, honest. I just held the horses."

"Oh that is such a crock of –"

"Ahh the horse talked!" Arlo screamed.

"I'll do more than that," I retorted, "if you try to prevaricate again; where are Solly and Mickey?"

The felon's eyes fairly bulged from his skull and he went white enough that he all but glowed. "But— but I don't know where they are."

"Do you wish to make me angry?" Dionysus said with a menacing whisper. He took a sip from his flask. "I am a fairly pleasant fellow most of the time but you and your cohorts took that which is mine; I want the artifacts back." He was smiling as he spoke but his beautiful features somehow had a dark aspect.

The red haired criminal stammered, swiveling his head back and forth from the two of us as he spoke. "Honest; Solly came to me and Mickey and said it was a popoff job, a real easy bit, just an in and out. He took the guard out with a cosh and had the floor plans and everything. We were just to carry the loot. Then some drunken soldier wandered in on us and things went off."

"Where are they?" I repeated.

"I don't know. Honest," he squealed. He looked to Dionysus for comfort from the horror of a talking horse but the deity scared him just as much. "I just got that little bobble on the sly, you know? A little bonus for myself that they didn't know about. I mean I got paid but a little extra, you know?" He tried to smile at Dionysus to elicit a 'aren't we just regular guys way' but the god was having none of it.

"So, so I don't know where they are now but we was supposed to meet up at some posh party in the morning. You give me a break and I'll tell you true; I swear!"

"You should not swear," Dionysus said, "Taking a God's name in vain offends us. You should tell us where they will be before I become wrathful."

That was the final straw that broke the dromedary's spine; Arlo told us an address and the time the three were supposed to meet.

"Good," the Greek said, "then we shall meet them, Major Stone-Whytte."

"I'm not really dressed for it," I said, "I'll need my hooves polished."

"What about me," Arlo whispered, "I told you the truth. Can I go?"

The Greek deity smiled. "Of course," he said sweetly. He clapped his hands and there was a sudden flash of light again and then where the burglar had been seated was a large red furred rat! It squealed and scurried off into the shadows.

"Never let it be said that I am not my father's son." Dionysus said with a little chuckle. "Though he would have probably fried the fellow; I am such a softie."

IV.

The mansion of Lord and Lady Killington was on the outskirts of the city in Norwood and was ablaze with color from a multitude of bouquets and banners for the lawn party that day. The Greek God and I were attending in disguise.

The deity had once more transformed his clothing to that of a conventional Gentlemen's. He wore a frock coat, waistcoat, and Bowler all in shades of white or bone. For accessories he wore a cravat, pocket watch and fob, and a walking stick that had vines carved around it with a pinecone patterned handle.

I had spent a considerable part of our (my) walk out from London trying to get him to change me back into my human form but he was having none of it. I came to realize he was as inebriated as a judge on Guy Fawkes day!

"Why can't I go along with you as me?" I continued to argue.

"You are you," he snickered, "A regular horse's arse!"

"Oh come on now," I said, "You're not my deity, you know, I don't have to kow-tow to you or particularly respect your opinion."

"I don't see your supreme being wandering around helping you shed that lovely coat of horse hair," the snide and snookered god said. "Just be glad I gave you a good brushing you may be able to attract a nice mare while I'm hunting the thieves."

I snorted in disgust. "I don't want a mare. I want two legs and a pair of hands."

"And what would you do with a pair of hands?" He asked me.

"Right now I'd strangle you and end speculation about just how long immortals actually live."

"See why I left you a horse?" He giggled. "You are so droll or I'd quiet you for good, now be quiet or you'll give the manservant a heart attack!"

I had been to the mansion of the Lord and Lady for a midwinter ball the previous season and knew them casually. I had heard they were celebrating the return of the Lady's brother from university abroad. I trotted up to the front gate of the mansion of the Killingtons where a liveried servant stood in greeting. "Good afternoon, sir," he said to Dionysus, "Do you have an invitation, sir?" the man asked.

It had not even occurred to me that we would need an invitation but, to keep the riff raff out they would have to.

"Of course," the Greek god answered the gate-keeper's inquiry. He flashed a smile at the servant. The deity held up an empty hand as if he were holding an invitation card. The guard looked at the empty space and smiled.

"May I take your horse, sir?"

"Oh, that's is quite alright," the Greek Dios said, "I prefer to ride all the way to the main house."

"The other guests are around back, my lordship," the servant said.

"Thank you," Dionysus said and put the heel to my side.

I trotted up the drive and waited until I was out of earshot of the flunky. "It just doesn't seem fair for you to get to attend the celebration without me; I mean you're a foreign chappie and I know them!"

"But you are attending," he said, "and do stop nagging me or I'll make your transformation complete and you won't be able to talk at all." He snickered at his own pun.

"You wouldn't."

"I am used to being obeyed, you know, chivy, I am a superior being."

"You're used to being drunk as well," I observed. "In which case we are equals."

"Touché, dear fellow," the deity laughed. "It's why I like you, Major. Just stay quiet and I'll find our stray doves."

"Well just don't go all divine on them until we find out where they have your stuff."

"I can't help a little madness now and then," he said as he burped. "It is my way; but I will take your suggestion to heart."

We rounded the main house and came in sight of the pavilion that had been set up for the tea. The Greek god dismounted.

"Enjoy yourself, trusty steed," Dionysus said with a chuckle. "I shall mingle."

"Mind yourself," I said in a horsy whisper. "Remember these are British nobles and used to a certain propriety; not the pub thugs you usually are called to accompany and carouse with."

This caused him to chortle and pat me on the

muzzle. "You should remember that etiquette and social protocols are not synonymous with morals or ethics. That is my gift to the world, dear fellow. One has nothing to do with the other particularly when the divine madness of the fermented nectar is involved. I have observed many a bar patron who is more the noble soul than an emperor."

An evil eye from my equine form had very little weight with him.

Across the lawn the guests, ladies in lace gowns with dainty gloved hands holding tiny China cups, gentlemen in frocks and top hats or Bowlers were chatting and laughing. If many people were to be asked the definition of the term 'class', they would have every hope that true class transcended one's economic status, race, creed and color. Those people were probably Americans, however and I was British. Those on the lawn were the end result of centuries of breeding.

Had they known that the white clothed dandy that strode bouncily and somewhat staggeringly toward them was a god of classical Greece they would have all been scandalized.

I mean, a foreign deity on English soil? What would Herne the Hunter or Epona, horse goddess of the Celts think?

V.

When Anna, the 7th Duchess of Britain asked for tea and light refreshments one afternoon in 1840 the Grand Dame started a whole new tradition of feasting on a variety of baked sweets while sipping on warm tea and chatting with guests.

Thus formal and informal afternoon teas were born and the most British of institutions became yet another sign of English superiority of culture and a national export. It also became the opening of hunting season for the social animal of the upper class with predatory young ladies hunting husbands and young rakes hunting new conquests.

As I watched the foreign deity move among the elite of the Empire I cringed. I felt I was watching an invasion of the most sacred of events that rivaled William the Conqueror for the disaster Dionysus represented.

He wasn't a bad chap, and I certainly enjoyed the 'fruits' of his patronage, but there had to be limits.

From time to time the deity would look my way and make a face that implied he was bored with the whole affair.

Evidently, Dionysus felt so as well. To my new horror I saw him walk over to the punch bowl and empty his ornate flask into it. And it seemed to be a bottomless flask for he seemed to pour and pour forever!

I have to put a stop to this, I concluded and was just about to pull away from my tether when I saw a familiar figure across the field of posh presences. It was the dark haired, scar –faced brute called Mickey!

He was dressed in servants's clothes and carrying a tray of drinks, moving near Dionysus and the Lady. I was terrified that the ruffian might be contemplating some felony on the Killingtons but I had enough self-control to not cry out.

I had realized on the ride over that if Dionysus was not going to change me back I could use my equine form as a sort of disguise. I opted to whinny, stamp my hooves and generally make a nuisance of myself. A groom came over to me immediately, but more importantly I saw the deity look up to see what the commotion was.

I kept up my antics until Dionysus stepped up beside me.

"What seems to be the problem?" the beautiful deity asked.

"I don't you, uh–your lordship," the groom said.

"He's talking to me, you idiot," I said, forgetting myself.

The groom almost fell over backwards which made the deity laugh. This made the servant sure that Dionysus had something to do with his discomfort and then he nodded.

"You had me there, your lordship," he said, "A bleedin' ventriloquist, eh?"

"Ah, yes," the deity said. "I'll take it from here." He took my reins and walked me around the path as if I were a dumb animal.

"What are you being such an arse about, Major?" Dionysus said when the groom was out of earshot. "Still ruffled?"

"I saw one of them, you Mediterranean masher."

He fairly bristled. "Where, which one of the mortals?"

"Now control yourself," I cautioned *sotto voce*, "The object is to find your artifacts, correct? In this case vengeance has got to be secondary."

"Justice," he insisted sharply, "but you are correct. Now point him out."

I allowed him to draw me along the path until we reached a point where we could see the serving area where Mickey had gone. The scar-faced thief was moving among the other servants as if he had always been there, but the fine clothes could not disguise his crude carriage.

"He seems quite at home in this gathering," Dionysus said, "He does not seem to be- ah infiltrating."

"But why would such an obviously vulgar person be in the employ of the Killingtons?" I whispered.

"Corrupt nobility?" The deity snickered. "I've never encountered that before."

"I may not have read Greek and Latin at Cambridge, but I have read the Iliad and the Odyssey. I know how the nobility made a mess of itselfBut what do you expect? they were foreigners."

"Watch it or you'll end a gelding, Major."

I was too annoyed to fear. "Really, this is England."

He laughed. "You keep believing that, old fellow and you'll never grow old. Haw!" He secured my reins to a bush and headed off at a jaunty stagger toward Mickey.

I was at full alert, my large eyes glued to the dark haired. Why would that fiend be dressed in the house colors of the Killingtons? How had he gotten in and why was he apparently so well known to the house staff?

So intent was I on the object of our hunt that I did not notice, at very first what was occurring at the rest of the party. That is, I did not notice until the Duchess of A***** let out a yell that would have done Buffalo Bill proud and jumped up on the table sending canapés flying.

"This party is boring," she yelled as she tore off her lace and velvet top and swung it around her head like a lariat. "Bring on the bulls!" The fact that the

Duchess was over sixty and not wearing a foundation garment made the spectacle both frightening and fascinating.

Even more astounding was the fact that most of the people at the party were snockered and gave a whole new meaning to 'drunk as a lord.'

Jeremy Nader was stripped to his under shorts and racing around on all fours baying like a hound; Cynthia Collins was doing a can-can dance while Judge O***** and Lord C**** applauded. Quite a few couples were involved in scandalous carnal activities that I dare not line here.

"Bloody foreign idol!" I cursed. My attention went back to Dionysus and his prey to see that they were gone!

"No!" I blurted out. I pulled off my tether and raced into the chaos that the Greek god had wrought.

VI.

I could not get to a full gallop because of all the copulating couples sown across the lawn. I had to pick my way carefully so that I am sure it looked like nothing so much as a ballet dancing pantomime horse.

There was no sign of the Hellenic deity as I made almost a full circuit of the mansion.

This is not good, I thought. I knew enough of the gods of old to know that some of them had been brought low in human form. *And if I can't find him how can he turn me back to human?*

The servants who had not partaken of the punch

bowl's contents were standing back agasp as their 'betters' behaved like complete sots. I even saw a number of the under-stairs class giggling and pointing at the peccadilloes of the elite as if they were a cricket century being played out.

It was not all that difficult to enter through one of the French doors. None of the servants thought to stop me, as they were all now outside watching the antics on the lawn. The first floor of the mansion was a ghost house, silent and empty, made more eerie by the strains of the string quartet that were still playing out on the lawn. I paused at the foot of the main staircase. "You have left me in quite a pickle, my Lord Dionysus," I whispered aloud. Abruptly I heard a familiar sound from somewhere nearby. It was the muffled sound of the Greek god's laughter. I discovered the deity's voice was coming from behind a door under the stairs. That presented a problem; it was a doorknob and I had no hands.

Then I heard the Hellenic god's voice cry out in what sounded like pain.

I lunged toward the knob and fastened my large teeth on it and spun my head. The door opened with a click.

Beyond the portal was a dark opening and a narrow stone stair.

I hesitated till I heard another moan that was the Hellene's.

I had no choice; I charged!

It was frightening, plummeting down at a dizzying angle, my right side scraping against the ancient stone of the cellar wall.

Ahead of me was a cavernous space lined with racks of wine bottles. In the middle of the rows was a small group of figures with the loot from the museum scattered about their feet; Solly, Mickey, Lord Killington and, tied in a chair in the center of the circle, Dionysus.

As I watched, Solly stepped up and slapped the bound and incarnated deity.

"Stop, you miscreants!" I yelled as plummeted forward like the Light Brigade at Balaclava (but hopefully not to the same fate).

All eyes turned toward me and widened with shock.

All save the deity whose blue orbs registered only amusement.

I sprang from the bottom step with a battle cry to race down the aisle between the bottles.

Mickey pulled a revolver and pointed it at me, but before he could fire the white-clad Greek rose from his chair, his bonds dissolved like ropes of sand and snatched the gun from his hand.

"No fair,' Dionysis giggled like a schoolboy who had caught a mate cheating at knockers, "Play nice with the horsy!"

Then I was upon the group, ramming my head into the startled Mickey to send him flying.

"S'blood!" Solly cursed as he leapt out of the way.

I pulled up short and whirled, tipping over a rack of vintages to my left.

"Oh!" Dionysus moaned as if physically assaulted, "Do take care!"

I barely heard him as I pursued the fleeing Solly.

"Come back here, you ruffian," I called, "You have to pay for your thievery!"

I am not sure the criminal had time to register that a horse was berating him before he tripped over a low rack of empty bottles and went sprawling.

I gave him a love tap from my front hoof and then

spun to head back up the aisle.

When I arrived back where the artifacts were placed on the floor Dionysus was standing over the cowering Lord Killington and swigging from an open bottle of wine. "I haven't had this much fun since Achilles and I had a two week drunk in Thebes!"

"What--what is happening?" the Lord gibbered.

"You have been a bad little fellow," Dionysus said, "to be purchasing stolen objects to support you fading lifestyle."

"Your lordship," I said with a snort. "How could you deal with such lower creatures?"

"You—you're a talking horse!" Lord Killington gasped.

"How expertly observed," Dionysus giggled.

I whinny in annoyance, "You are supposed to have decent standards and yet you support robbers like these?"

"You are a talking horse!" the Lord repeated.

"All you mortals are just parrots with arms?'

"Nonetheless," I continued, "my equine state does not justify your looting."

"It's not like the museum blokes didn't take it from the bloody Greeks," Mickey pleaded.

"Do not test me further," Dionysus hissed as he spun to glare at the fallen felon. I saw that mad light come to the god's eyes and squeezed my eyes shut just as the Zeusbolt struck. The echo of the bolt reverberated off the stonewalls for a long moment.

Lord Killington was burbling now as he watched the pink tailed creature that had been Mickey scurry off into the darkness.

"I am repeating myself," Dionysus shook his head then looked at me with a shrug, "I should strive to be original but when you're immortal one tends to do that. Just lazy I guess."

"Don't be so hard on yourself, old fellow," I said with a sympathetic snort, "it does really suit him; no reason to change the design of the wheel you know."

"Very understanding," he said.

"What—what do you want with me?" The human Lord sobbed, shaking with fear.

"Put it all back," Dionysus said. "And revere it!"

"And stop others from looting temples," I added.

"Nice touch," Dionysus said.

"Anything," the lord sobbed. "Anything you say."

"And I'll be watching," Dionysus said. "So don't vex me; you wouldn't like me when I'm vexed."

I looked over at Solly and realized that my hoof to his head had been a bit too severe; he would not be rising.

The Greek saw my glance. "Not to worry, old fellow," he said, "He is in Tartary where his fellow will be soon; frail is the flesh of man." He almost sounded mellow, but then hiccupped.

"Now, let us get back upstairs," he said, "I don't want to miss the rest of the party; it was just getting interesting."

VII.

Getting up the stairs was almost as unnerving as charging down. "Change me back," I asked.

"Oh, yes, right," he said. "I suppose I could do that."

"But first," he giggled. I felt him fiddling with my

left hind leg and looked back under my belly to see that he had fastened the metal bracelet around my leg. "Chiron wore this on his front leg," he said, " but I think this is the spot for you."

He did not change me back but I did make it up the stairs to the ballroom of the mansion. We looked out onto the lawn to see the guests all sitting around in a daze. Apparently his special punch had worn off most of them.

"Oh pooh!" he said, "it's gotten all dull again."

"I doubt it could be very dull around you for long," I said.

He smiled at me. "How nice of you to say so." Then added, "You came racing down those stairs to rescue me, didn't you?"

"Yes. You sounded to be in a pickle. How did they capture you?"

"Oh they didn't so much capture me as take me into custody," he said. "I walked up to that scar faced fellow and told him I wanted him to take me to the stolen items. He summoned his employer--I suspect most of this opulence if maintained by such skullduggery-- and they escorted me to the wine cellar; seemed terribly appropriate."

"Well, you could have told me." I said. "I was worried."

"I realize," he said, "but I am a god, you know; this is just a shell. Still, you are a noble warrior and your heart is true. I thank you."

"Well how about changing me--"

Hellene smiled at me and clapped his hands. There was the flash of light again and in an eye-blink I was standing alone on two human legs, naked in the doorway of the mansion.

On my left ankle was the metal belt that the deity

had given me. I looked around for him but he was gone.

"Oh my," a voice from behind me called my attention. I turned and realized my left leg had no pain and when I took a step forward it was a normal one.

"He's fixed my leg!" I said aloud.

"But whomever you are speaking about did not fix your clothing." The speaker was Lady Killington, though she was as I had not seen her before either, her dress askew and her nose red from the effects of Dionysus' sacred brew.

The lady was staring at my wedding tackle with no prevarication and with a broad grin on her face.

"My most humble apologies, My Lady," I said as I snatched a curtain to wrap around myself toga-like.

Soon the garden party was history or more correctly near legend as the antics of the aristocrats leaked out. Being whole again, I re-enlisted in the Horseguard.

And often, when I was into my cups, I heard a singular ethereal giggle so I gave a daily libation to the most wonderful of all the ancient gods.

Alfa Romeo

by Victory Witherkeigh

A-woogah, woogah, A-woogoah, woo.

The riff of the electric guitar blasts through my white 1969 Alfa Romeo Spyder as I start the engine up, my left foot pressed firmly on the clutch as I move the old gear stick up to first.

A-woogah, woogah, A-woogoah, woo. Dun-a-dun-a-dun...

I'm already humming along to the band Shocking Blue's one-hit-wonder *Venus* as my feet do the quick ball step to change from first to second gear, a trail of burnt rubber and gravel spinning behind me on the open dirt roads of the island. I'd been hiding out in my small hut along the ridge of Kilauea, deep along with the jungle trees past where most of humanity would say the sane and modern would choose.

Then again, I wouldn't exactly say that I'm sane...

The smell of the dirt from my tires speeding along the unpaved, windy roads always brings me back to my childhood and the discovery of my unusual gifts. Out of my whole family, mother, father, seven brothers, and six sisters, I was the youngest and the only one whose magic came with destruction along with power. My father liked to say that our talents came from the great beyond, but my brothers would snicker that it just meant he had no clue why we had magic. Our father used his abilities in the dream world to become a neurologist specializing in sleep issues, specifically hypnagogic and hypnopompic ones. At the same time, our mother's powers with the earth allowed her to open her own apothecary, mixing and growing her own hybrid plants for the lotions and perfumes that flew off the shelves.

Even with so many siblings whose magic specialties seemed to span throughout the seas and land, I was the only one born with the ability to conjure and control fire and magma. My mother would often describe my birth as the most excruciating - the labor pains of pushing me literally set her nerves on fire. My father would never let me forget the scent of burning flesh with the stark screams as I took my first breath - my skin red, face scrunched, fists clenched, wailing at the world for having been disturbed with the entire birthing process. Ready to burn it all down.

"It was those angry screams," my father said every time he told the story of my birth, "Those screams are where I got your name - Ka wahine 'ai honua. It means 'the woman who devours the land,' because not long after we had you swaddled and cleaned up did your cries for food come with a breath of fire and ash."

Laughter always followed this story, even though most of my family called me Pele for short. Only my parents ever used my full name during ceremonial times, holidays, or if I was in trouble. Which, unfortunately for me, seemed to happen pretty often.

"Ohhhh, oh, ahhhh, oh, ahhhh..."

The chorus of the song *Venus* played on as I finally pulled into the back bushes of the open market. It only took a few weeks for me to scope out this small village near the cave I'd been hiding out in ever since I arrived on this island. Turning eighteen should have been a rite of passage, a joyous occasion for me to celebrate full adulthood. Instead, it proved to be the final straw in my father's tolerance for my shenanigans.

I'll be the first to admit that I have a temper. You can't really be blessed with the powers of fire and ash expecting to be the poster child for Zen and meditation. My parents had more than their fair share of trials and tribulations, apologizing for my bursts of rage, calling forward volcanic eruptions and earthquakes all over the world. Death and destruction followed my irritations of hurling bolts of fire and molten lava at both my family members and those who annoyed me. The first boy who I admitted I liked in school? Turns out he already pledged his love for one of my older sisters. Even though I was young, I was so upset. My blood boiled, shooting through my veins as smoke streamed through my ears. Before I could finish screaming at him, I'd twisted his body into a rough, scraggly tree on our school playground. My sister would yell and cry at my parents all night to change him back, but they couldn't figure out what I did. She ended up growing unique red flowers on him to apologize.

Walking through the market, the smell of dried fish and the sound of the machete hacking at the young coconut husks makes my stomach gurgle, my tongue watering for the first time in days.

When was the last time I'd eaten a decent meal? Not since that day I had to leave... not since I fled from home...

I couldn't help but think back to the years rolling by as I grew older, bolder even with my temper. It didn't seem to matter who it was or how big or small the offense was. If my sisters went through my room, borrowing my toys or jewelry or clothes without my permission, it was second nature to charge at them, eyes blazing, scratching, and clawing as we fought, leaving scars and burns. If my brothers left me out of the video games or basketball games they played, I'd chase after them, feet pounding with my Air Jordans down the pavement, chasing them with spurts of lava until they relented to let me join. No matter how many times my father or mother yelled or cried that I'd hurt my brothers or sisters, nothing seemed to move me.

"Don't you care that you have hurt them?" My father's face was red, veins pulsing on the side of his forehead as he spoke. "Do we mean so little to you? Are you that selfish as to not think of the attention your destruction brings to this family?"

"No," my mother said, lips thinned, tapping her espadrille flats against the stone floor. "She's too selfish to think about us and what happens to the rest of our family. She's too stubborn or stupid to recognize that the rules she needs to follow are there to protect us from the unwanted attention of the outside world. Why can't you be more like your brothers and sisters?"

A twinge along my jawline jolts me out of my memory long enough to rub against it. The clenching and grinding against my teeth became a reflex to hold the rage and anger against my parents.

Didn't they think I wanted to be like them? Didn't they ever notice how hard I tried to be "normal?"

I tried to tell myself as the years passed and I hit my teens that my parents meant well, that they were trying their best. I learned the magic and dances of our ancestors. I got straight A's in school, joined the student government groups, academic decathlon, the local halau for extra dance lessons, all of it to show them I could fit in, that I could be what they wanted.

But after fourteen children, is it really so surprising that they'd have a favorite child? That they couldn't keep up or spare any more energy or time or grace for their youngest?

By the time I hit high school, I had realized nothing I had done would appease them. They never came to my decathlon events because my brothers had their sword fighting practice to attend. My cheerleading nights at the various sporting events often had me traveling with friends and teammates over my own parents. If my older siblings were attending the games or playing themselves, they gave me rides. Still, I longed to know what it felt like to hear my mom cheering my name when I hit my tumbling passes, to feel my dad's arm holding me steady against the unrolled red carpet against the wet grass as my name was called for homecoming court. I wanted them with me when I walked through the mall looking for a dress for the next dance, to pay attention when I hung the ribbons or trophies through my room. This longing was what drove me to explode and rebel in the worst way - by hurting my sister.

All I had to do was say no... Just walk away...

My calloused fingertips squeeze along the smooth green and red mango skins as I try to gather as many supplies as possible to continue to hide out as seamlessly as I have been. In my pack was always a machete and a small, foldable fishing rod to gather meat. I came to the markets to collect bundles of bananas, coconut, sweet potatoes, or pineapples; gathering goods that could burn away quickly without a trace afterward. The pressure of the unripened mangos with the smoothness in their skins reminded me of his skin, the firm touch of his bronzed abdomen underneath the slow setting sun of my home beach.

He was my sister, Namakaokahai's beloved, one of the most beautiful boys in our village who had been her sweetheart since they were in high school together. My older sister blessed her with the nickname "Queen of the Seas" since her magic focus involved the strength and push of the ocean waves. Namaka, as I nicknamed her when I was still in diapers, unable to pronounce her full name, could control the rise and flow of the tides in the oceans. Our eldest brother, Kamohoali'i, often fought with Namaka for territory and bragging rights over who was stronger. He was called the king of sharks with his ability to set the sharp tooth predator at any of his siblings if they dared cross him. If Namaka tried to flush them back with her set of waves, he could command them to strike back by either jumping over the swell or using their momentum to drive the force back towards her.

It was Kamo who I'd turned to the most as a child, crying about how misunderstood or out of place I was.

"It's not fair," I'd say, stomping into his room, face red, steam coming out of my ears as the scent of burning wood followed me. "All of you have powers that help things grow and thrive underwater. Why am I the only one who destroys things?"

"That's not true, Pele," Kamo said, kneeling next

to me to meet my burning red eyes with his calm gray ones. "My best friends are all predators, all seeking food and blood for sustenance. Namaka can destroy entire cities with the flick of her wrist, the tsunami waves rising at her command. Even our mother has not been above punishing people by withholding the harvest crops, letting the old and young of the villages suffer from hunger and famine. Yours is just more straightforward... honest even..."

"No one likes me," I'd say as I hit puberty, crying as the boys in middle school talked about the beauty of my sisters. "They are only nice to me because they're afraid of me...Not because they care about me...."

"Is that so bad?" Kamo said eyebrows raised to the heavens, trying not to smile. "They only look at your sisters because they seem weaker, easier to control or train. Remember, you're like me, little sister. Our powers call for us to keep churning, to keep moving. A shark that stops swimming is a dead shark, just like the fire that stops burning. We need partners who are just as strong as we are, just as ferocious to keep up with us...to explore the world, to conquer and test to new boundaries."

For that reason, I was both thrilled and shocked when Namaka's boyfriend began paying attention to me. At first, I was sure I imagined the stares and glances he'd thrown my way as I entered my final year of high school. His honey amber eyes would follow my movements when I spoke at our dinner table about taking a gap year before college to explore the world. It was easy to ignore at first until he was the one who picked me up from my disastrous homecoming dance that winter semester. My date had taken too many shots of rum with the wrestling team, getting hands-on with the dance floor with me until he earned my burning hot fingertips rubbing his pant seams in the back of the men's room. Smokey tears poured down my face as I left a pathetic begging voicemail with my sister, pleading that she come and pick me up at the backside of the gym's parking lot. When her boyfriend pulled up alone in his car, I'd barely said a word as I pulled the white Alfa Romeo's door handle to let myself in.

"Sorry," he said softly. "Your sister was in the middle of a study group for her finals tomorrow. She asked me to come to get you and bring you home...."

I stared at the black leather seat. My hands on the pebbled surface my fingers trembled against. The heat of his hand slowly spread up my arm as he moved carefully, gently caressing my arm with just the tip of his finger.

"What happened?"

His warm breath smelled of cinnamon and honey, my cheeks blushing as the whisper of his calm voice broke through the wall of magma and ash forming inside my mind.

I don't know if it was the comfort of being in the car or the fact someone else was asking about me. Still, my lips began sputtering and blubbering the story, the embarrassment of admitting I'd hoped my date saw this night as a magical night for romance instead of drunken debauchery. Salty tears reached the end of my jaw as I explained the growing knot of fear in my stomach as the dance wore on and his fingers dug deeper into the chiffon and silk against my flesh, the ache of bruises forming.

My voice cracked. "I can't believe I fell for it, ya know?" I remembered the stark white porcelain bathroom tile mixed with the scent of Pinesol and burning flesh. "I really thought someone was interested in me... that I was going to get some movie moment of a romantic night... that I was finally going to feel like Cinderella...."

The soft hum of the radio was all I remembered hearing before his lips were on mine, demanding yet soft. The click of the seatbelt almost drowned out the lyrics of *Venus,* as his calloused hands pulled me onto his lap as I moaned into his mouth. My mind drowned in the sound of his groans, the strength of his hands pulling me tightly against his body, writhing underneath me. His wanton grinding, his thick university sweatpants displaying his excitement over my body as incoherent babbling followed his groans.

"I've wanted to touch you for so long...to taste you...."

"Can you feel the effect you have on me? Do you know how many times I've had to touch myself in your powder room just staring at the defiance in your eyes... wondering how you'd feel in my hands..."

I could barely swallow as I watched this man come undone beneath me, just from kissing my lips and caressing me. It appeared I blinked as the silence of our deep breathing and the rumble of Alfa Romeo's engine flew me to my house before I'd even set the smeared lip gloss on my face back in order. He grabbed my shaky hand before I pulled the door open.

"Kiss me," His voice whispered, but the command was soothing. "This will be between us."

My mind blanked out as my heels clicked against the koa wood staircase. The hot water under the shower was the first sensation beyond the blank, heavy flatness weighing against my chest. Gasps for air interspersed intermingled with the smell of jasmine shampoo and the scraping of his teeth against my shoulder.

What are you doing? How are you standing here thinking about him when he's with your sister?

Maybe it was just the sheer fact that I was taking something of theirs. Perhaps it was more than it appeared. For the first time, someone looked at me first instead of last - as something enticing, beautiful, sexy... instead of destructive and evil. I never let myself think beyond the next signal from him to meet up in his car to make out in the unlit parking lots of his college campus or between the old stacks of bound leather tomes, smelling of parchment and dust in the library. Each time the passion and drive for more upped the stakes as he professed undying devotion for my lips, skin, and eyes.

"It's never felt this way with anyone else..." He whispered into my ear, calloused fingertips drawing small circles along the goosebumps forming along my ribs, his honeyed eyes staring into mine, seeking permission to go further. "I can't even put into words how good you feel... but it's so much more... it's everything."

Everything my sister isn't... wasn't... couldn't be...

Soon, our bodies needed more than just the dry rubbing and making out in the back seat of his car. The part of me that waited to regret it, to feel the guilt or shame of it, never came, even as he first mentioned treating us to a weekend away. As I lied to my parents about a slumber party with friends, packing my fresh mint toothpaste in a backpack with black lace boy shorts and matching bras — fire is all that coursed through my veins. When the scent of red hibiscus and fresh honey greeted us as we entered the suite, white Egyptian silk sheets, smoothly draped against the dark mahogany headboard, were all I saw before his lips pressed against my neck, and we lost ourselves in ecstasy. The days strung together in a mixture of sweat, exhaustion, and connection that left him shaking his head in disbelief.

"I wouldn't have believed that anything that animalistic and wild could both destroy and rebuild me all at once." He murmured in a daze, tangled between the white silk sheets and my bronzed legs.

Perhaps it was that daze that finally clued my sister in that something was wrong, as I never saw him alive after that weekend.

My chest constricts, nails digging into my palms as the memory of our last kiss, unknowing it was the last, brings me back to the marketplace. Just a few days after the most perfect moments of my life, my brother met me outside my final classroom, organic chemistry, pulling me towards the exit.

"What are you doing? The last bell hasn't eve—"

"Go," Kamo said. His eyes flashed with pupils dilating, the same as his brethren sharks sniffing blood in the water. "Namaka knows. Do you hear me? She *knows...*"

My eyes burned red, steam once more flying from my ears. "Where is he, Kamo? What happened?"

"Go!" Kamo hands me my lover's car keys, the familiar Alfa Romeo logo dangling. He grips both my arms as he looks me straight in the eyes. "It's too late for him. But our parents know. You won't be welcome at home. Go now..."

The black stained tears were running like a river of ash down my cheeks as I pushed the doors open, sprinting to his car. I was already on the highway to the next ferry boat by the time the bell would have rung. Unanswered text messages and voicemails from my father and mother stared at me when I looked down at the phone, at the only photo I had of my first and last love, the only one I'd allowed myself the risk of taking while he slept peacefully next to me.

I'd stuck to the island's mountain ranges as much as I could once I lost count of the number of ferries and cargo ships I'd snuck on. Namaka may have control of the ocean waters, but as long as I limited my direct contact with them, I knew the land better than all of them. After all, fire and ash birthed the grounds we walk on. The sunrises and sunsets all bled together from the glimmers of caverns and caves. Night after night, as I succumbed to dreams of my lost love, the magma and lava in the earth's core rose with my own tears and cries of anger and despair.

"Well, well, if it isn't the whore herself...." Namaka's voice echoes as a whisper in my ear.

I see her standing at the other end of the market, dressed in every shade of the deepest blues and blacks. Even with us over one hundred meters apart, I know her magic allowed her message to carry straight to me.

She wishes to kill me in full combat — one on one...

I'm already sprinting back to the car, screaming for the people to go back to their homes.

If she wishes to die... I'll give her that mercy for him...

The Alfa Romeo's tires barely grip the windy gravel road as wave after wave of ocean water crashes into the hillside behind me. Even driving over one hundred miles an hour, it takes little more than a flick from my fingers for the lava stored from weeks in the caverns to shoot out in response. Once I reach a small entrance near the top of Kilauea, I pull the parking brake at the same time I've removed the car door, my skin scraping off along the gravel as it slides underneath me.

"Why, Pele?!" My sister's scream echoed through the empty valley below. "Was it just for the destruction? Just to watch me look like a fool? Did you enjoy knowing how stupid I looked?"

Orange, fiery lava hits the side of her ribs, knocking her over as the water recedes, barely a trickle as we're so far into the island's landmass the ocean can't reach much farther than a trickle.

"Did it ever occur to you he actually cared for me? That may be the fault came down to the fact it had so little to do with you at all? He came to me... He started touching me... hell, you sent him to me. He was not happy with you, and that has nothing to do with me!"

Her jaw locked, teeth clenched as her brow furrowed. "You're just as selfish as our parents always say. You just want everything always. Damn anyone else who gets in your way..."

"And maybe you're too dumb to notice that all of you really aren't as amazing or self-important as you like to think. I am the fire and the chaos and everything he *wanted* " My voice is hoarse from screaming, throat raw as my tears are literally burning flames. "He wanted me... He did..."

Shluk! Sshhluck!

I watch as my blood is pulled from my chest, drawn forward from my broken breastbone to form the spearheads my family grew up training with.

"You really need to watch your salt content, sister dear," Namaka's voice echoes as though she were speaking through the ocean. "The thing with the human body and all those science classes about how we're composed of two different types of salty water.

That's all the ocean is, you know. Saltwater. And you have this sodium-potassium pump system just sitting here, waiting for me."

Gak. Ack. Glurp.

My vision blurs as my ears ring with the sound of my throat choking on my blood. I hit the stiff black leather of the Alfa Romeo, my lover's scent mixed with my blood as the grunts of my

sister moving the car into the cavern fade into the distance.

I'll see you soon, love... we'll have each other soon...

NAMAKA BARELY MADE it back to the ocean shores before Kilauea erupted. By the time she got home, Kamo was already gone, attempting to save his brethren from the underwater eruptions of their younger sister's wrath as ash, lava, and the fire burned across sea and sky and land. With her family screaming and crying as the chaos destroyed their home, Namaka stared at the dark, gray ash clouds, blocking the sun, muting the bright star to a distant orange dot as she tried to save what she could of her childhood belongings. In the churning of the winds, Pele's face formed in the dark ash covering Namaka's car, the hand of their shared lover gently caressing her face as their voices echoed in her ear, singing the chorus of the same song that had played as she was dumping her sister's body away.

UNCHAINED

BY HELEN VENN

I'm so cold. The waves dash themselves against the rocks showering me with bitter salt and chill. Bronze, hard and even colder than the rock at my back, chafes my ankles and wrists. Driven deep my chains are long enough that I can stand and sit but no-one seems to have thought that I might want to lie down. Maybe they thought I'd be taken before night came. Who knows. The oracle was specific only about one thing after all. There is, at least, a skin of fresh water within reach and next to it a satchel containing a little food—bread, olives, cheese—and since they are on ropes I assume they'll be refilled if the monster doesn't come for me tonight.

How all these arrangements are to work is some-what sketchy I have to say. What with my mother and all her women weeping and wailing and my father trying to keep control, things were somewhat fraught at the end. I was lowered down the cliff to this jutting platform, chains locked on and clothes stripped off me by a man at arms before they left me here. Poor lad, he didn't know where to put his eyes and I was in no mood to make things any easier for him. That was churlish. It was hardly his fault he had the task.

That responsibility lies entirely with my mother. Pride in your brood is one thing. To have said our beauty, my beauty in particular, surpassed that of the Nereids was beyond unwise. She can wail and weep as much as she likes now but I would not have come to this had she been more...how shall I put it...circumspect. So here I am, the key to my chains just out of reach above my head. Why it's dangling there I'm not sure. To make things more convenient for the monster when he comes to devour me? I doubt he...if it even is a he. I have no idea but I'll go with that since I can't think of any female monster who has a fetish for eating women and this monster has done that and so much more. He has ravaged my land, inundating the fair towns on the coast and taking down even the sturdiest of our ships, eating their crews alive.

That is what he'll do to me, too. I'm laid out here, a meal for the taking. It's not quite the end expected of a princess. At least I'm spared the noise of despair from those watching from the cliff top. The roar of the waves hides that and they in turn can't see my tears if I ever manage tears. For I'm angry, angrier than I've ever been in my life. All those deaths and now mine—all of us innocents.

If anger could warm me I would be ablaze down here. Instead I'm shivering as the chill creeps into my very bones. The sun is setting, sitting on the horizon like a molten orb. It's hard to think this is the last time I'll see such glory, that I may not even live to see the night sky and the stars. The moon will soon rise. I wish that a prayer to Artemis would set me free but it won't. Poseidon would not permit it. He demands a sacrifice for the insult to the sea nymphs and what he demands he gets.

If I survive the night, what then? Another day of waiting? That's too hopeful. The monster usually comes around this hour, when folk are heading home or sitting together to eat and share the happenings of their day. Perhaps I should pray to Poseidon? After all, he has brought me to this. Is that a roar? My shiver is not from cold this time. I'll close my eyes so as not to see the monster surge out of the waves to seize me. I'll remember I'm a princess of Aethiopia. I'll stand proud and accept my end.

What was that? Something touched me, a flutter, a whisper as of wings. I open my eyes. A man hangs in the air in front of me. A warrior. The sunset glows on his bronze shield. Who is he, how did he come here? I'd ask but my teeth are chattering. He slips off his cloak and wraps it around me. He has wings on his heels. Is he a god? So armed he could be.

"How did you come here?" He speaks my tongue but with an accent. I stare at him in stunned silence. "How did you come here?" he asks again.

I hear the roar again and find my tongue. The words stutter out through chattering teeth.

"M-monster, I'm a ssssacrifice to ssssave m-my country."

He cocks his head to one side and stares into my eyes seeking ... what? The truth of what I'm saying. "That hardly seems fair. Was your sin so great?"

"N-not m-my sin, m-my mother's." Even with his cloak wrapped around me I'm chilled to my marrow, but slowly my teeth cease their clatter. I'm about to tell him more when a dark shape rises from the sea. "Behind you," I scream. "Look behind you."

Already his sword is out and he flies—he flies—up high above the head of the sea monster as he towers above me. The stranger swoops, his sword sweeping down to slice through that monstrous neck. The head falls. It bounces on the rock at my feet then down thump, thump, thump all the way to the sea below where its body lies battered by waves, blood still fountaining from its severed neck. The water is red as the sun now sinking into the sea.

The stranger flies down to hover in front of me. "Chains?" he says.

I take that for a question and point to where the key hangs above my head. He flies up and returns to unlock my shackles. Then he clasps me around the waist and lifts me with him.

"Where?" he asks.

I point up and we soar to the top of the cliff where the court waits in the flickering torchlight. We hang suspended for a moment and then the stranger lands and lowers me to the ground. My mother falls in a dead faint and her women hurry to her side. My father rushes forward and takes me in his arms, issuing orders for clothing, hot drinks, food.

The stranger stands quietly as my father turns warily towards him. "I am Cepheus, king of this land and I thank you, stranger," he says. "I owe you a huge debt. Will you join us for a feast in celebration of my daughter's rescue when we can talk more?" My rescuer nods his acceptance. "And your name is?"

"I am Perseus, son of Zeus and Danae."

So he's not a god but something more than just a man. My father leads him away before I can thank him properly.

WHAT A DIFFERENCE BEING clean and warm makes. I've been pampered and treated as an invalid although I feel far from one and three days of that is more than I need. I'm a warrior. I should be outside, practising with my weapons, feeling in control of my life once again. I'm chafing at these unnecessary restrictions when my father sends a message asking me to join him and the stranger at the feast in his honour if I feel able. How could I refuse? But there's something about the wording of the message and the way my mother fusses over dressing me draping me in her finest jewellery that has me wondering. It may be guilt on her part—the gods know she should feel guilty—but it seems something more. I would like to delay this meeting a little longer if I could. This man has seen me naked after all so there's that embarrassment to deal with. But I am a princess. I know my duty and my shaky thanks through chattering teeth is not enough.

My fear is what he'll claim as his reward. Treasure is one thing. This is a wealthy land even after the damage from the sea monster and we could load him with whatever treasure he desires—but there was something in the way he looked at me that makes me wary. I'm not his for the taking, long promised as I am to my uncle. If it hadn't been for this...situation Phineus and I would already be wed. It's not my personal choice but such a dynastic alliance makes sense assuring my uncle as it does that he will be king after my father ruling beside me. I fidget and chew my lip, twist a strand of hair around my finger. I have a sudden desire to run, hide but that's not going to happen with my mother urging me forward from one side, my sister, younger than me only by minutes, doing the same on the other.

The doors of the great hall open to a clamour of noise that stops dead as we enter. I've rarely seen it so packed. Light fills the space. Every torch has been lit and it seems everyone has brought a lamp. Polished bronze gleams on each table except where my father and mother sit. That's resplendent in gold and silver, my father making sure his status shows. The stranger —I must remember to call him Perseus, this son of Zeus—Perseus sits on his right in my usual place. Their heads are close together. Making plans perhaps as to how much treasure he can have as a reward for his bravery. Does my father intend for him to sit there for the whole meal? That leaves the question of where I'm supposed to be but before I can say anything Perseus stands. The winged sandals have gone, no doubt packed away safely but the satchel he carried on his back is there at his feet as if he can't bear to be without it.

He smiles at me, and I have to say seeing him now he does look the part of a son of Zeus being tall and fair compared to me.

"Greetings, princess, I trust you have recovered from your ordeal," he says. There's a look in his eye that sends a blush racing through me.

I straighten my shoulders, determined not to let embarrassment show. "I'm pleased to meet you properly, Perseus, and to be able to thank you. You have my eternal gratitude."

"I'm delighted to have been able to assist you." He moves back to allow me to sit, takes his place beside me.

It turns out he's a good talker. He's a genuine hero as well—that I know from my maids. I don't know how they've come by this information but I suspect by listening at doors. Well, as long as it keeps them happy and me informed I don't care. He's been on a quest, they say, to save his mother from a forced marriage. He's killed the Gorgon Medusa, whose gaze could turn men to stone. He's favoured by the gods—they lent him the huge shield he was carrying, the winged sandals and much more—and Medusa's head is in his bag. How much of this is true I have no idea. Oh and he has a magical boat that can pass over land as well as water and it's pulled up on the shore in the harbour.

I'm reluctant to ask him about all this but then a question about where he grew up leads to how an oracle told his grandfather that his daughter's son was destined to kill him and so she was imprisoned in a completely enclosed tower but Zeus visited her there anyway and he was the result. It sounds fantastical but I have enough personal experience of what a god can do and demand and the pain an oracle can cause not to dismiss it out of hand. Besides, his rescue of me was superhuman to say the least so there may be some truth in it.

That look is still there in his eyes as we eat and talk. I'm not used to a man looking at me in that way. Truth be told it's somewhat intoxicating. But it's impossible. I'm betrothed, heir to the throne. Nothing can come of it. Then he asks me to walk with him under the stars. So he's a romantic, this warrior demigod. The feast has degenerated into hard drinking and assignations now the lamps and torches have burned low. Even the musicians have given up and I can't blame them. No-one is listening any longer. The virtuous are already leaving so it's time I did, too, and what's the harm in my saying he can accompany me to the door of the women's quarters with my maid as chaperone.

On the way he points out the stars he's using to find his way home. He needs to make haste to protect his mother. So that part of the story is true. Maybe the rest is as well. At the door he makes a gallant bow and says he hopes to spend more time with me.

"I thought you were in haste," I say.

"Not so great a haste that I can't take some time to woo a princess," he says. My jaw drops as he bows again and says, "I hear you are a warrior. We could..." he struggles for the word. "Contend...practise together. Perhaps in the morning. My skill is less in swords than I would like. I would enjoy the practice and to get to know you."

I gape at him. Has no-one told him? "I am betrothed," I stammer out.

"The king tells me so but also tells me that this can be broken if I insist and you wish. There would be a bride price to your..." He pauses, confused by an unfamiliar tongue. Then "For he who would have wed you to make right." .

That's quite a lot to digest. I barely know him. So far he's been my rescuer and I've only met him to actually talk this evening. Enjoyable as flirtation might be, I should speak to my father to ensure this is true before I do anything foolish. But then sword practice sounds safe enough. It would give me a chance to learn more about him. Who knows? He may lose interest if I best him.

"I practise every day after the morning meal," I say. "Ask anyone where the practice ground is." I hesitate. Should I say more, that this means nothing, but the torch he is carrying flares and I see his face clearly for a moment. There is something attractively different about him, this son of Zeus, but I'm merely being hospitable after all. What's the harm? "Thank you for your escort," I say and walk inside, closing the door behind me.

My knees are shaking as I walk to my room. It's all too much. To be wooed by a son of Zeus is an honour but I have so many questions, not least how such a thing could be managed. I'll see my father in the morning and find out the truth of it all. The fact is I have no particular desire to marry Phineus and the warrior demigod has certain attractions—many attractions if I'm honest. Whether they are enough for me to want to marry him I don't know. Worse, I'm not at all sure that Phineus would accept such an arrangement even with the sweetening of the bride price. I'm well aware that it's not me he cares about, it's the throne, and this could mean loss of both face and throne.

This is ridiculous. I barely know the man and I'm thinking about a life with him and ways it can be arranged. Enough. I call my maids to help me undress. They chatter as they lift off the jewellery, take my dress. They've watched from behind curtains and listened at doors again and they're full of rumours and gossip about what is going on. I let the din of their clucking wash over me. I have no interest in who is sleeping with whom or what quarrel is brewing where.

My attention is piqued, though, when I hear Perseus's name. Someone has heard more details about him. An old slave who came from a Greek island remembers the tale of the princess locked in a tower and how she ended up on Seriphos. The poor lamb was little more than a child when she bore her son so they say and they lived in seclusion there until her son was a man. That brought the notice of the king and she's now enslaved until she agrees to marry him. So his story has some truth to it. I ask who this old woman is but no-one has seen her before or knows who owns her. Odd.

OUR SWORD PRACTICE IS INTERESTING. He really has little idea beyond the basics and yet he killed the sea monster with a single blow and, if he's telling the truth, beheaded the Gorgon, both superhuman themselves. His sword is unusual, too, with a curve to its end, not something I've seen before in a sword from the Greek isles. It's more like those we wield.

All the while we fight I'm distracted by it standing beside the huge bronze shield he's left at the side of the practice field. When I ask about it he's evasive, just says the sword was a gift and the shield was lent to him. Good manners stop me pushing for more but it rankles that he keeps such unnecessary secrets. The man I wed cannot have secrets from me, of that I'm certain. Does he understand this, that his reluctance is making me withdraw? Besides, I wonder about his tale. No-one has seen this Gorgon's head after all. We have only his word for it even existing.

There's no time for chat when a message comes from my father as we're packing our practice gear away. He wants to see me. In my room I toss off my sweaty practice clothes and let my maids make me more presentable as swiftly as they can. I may be a favoured daughter albeit one who can be sacrificed for the good of the kingdom but I'm still a subject.

He receives me in his private rooms which makes me wonder all the more, especially when I see my mother is already there. Have I offended you? Is it something else? He often includes me when he meets with his councillors but this seems more like a family chat as he hugs me

"Andromeda," he says. "Come, sit, eat."

The table is laid with my favourite delicacies and I catch the scent of herbal tea as my mother pours it into a cup. This is what they did on that dreadful day they told me what the oracle had said, that I was to be a sacrifice. A chill passes through me. Has Poseidon demanded more? Am I to be sacrificed again?

"I'd rather stand," I say. "Tell me now am I to die?"

My mother gasps and the pot clatters against the cup as she almost drops it.

"No, child." My father reaches out a hand towards me. "No, it's nothing like that. Come sit with us. We have something we want to discuss with you."

I sit, still suspicious. "Well?" I ask.

My mother busies herself with pouring more tea, leaving it for him to speak.

He clears his throat and I grow even more sure that this is not something that bodes well. "It's about Perseus," he finally says.

"Yes?" I'm not going to help him.

"It seems he doesn't want just treasure for rescuing you. He wants you for his wife."

"So?" I already know this. He made it clear enough last night.

"I will not force this marriage but we owe him a great debt. If you agree you'll have a bride price worthy of a princess and..." He breaks off. Perhaps he sees my expression.

"And my uncle? What price will he receive? Marriage to my sister if she takes my place as heir?" I take a breath to steady myself. "So you want me to marry a man we know nothing about, to give up my position as heir, to give up my right to the crown, and go off with him wherever he wants?"

"He's a son of Zeus, under the protection of the gods and he's the heir to a Greek throne. You would be his queen."

My lip curls in spite of my attempt to keep my face expressionless. "A Greek queen? I've heard how they treat their women, their queens."

"He swears you will rule as his equal when he gains his throne."

"That would be the throne where he kills his grandfather, would it? What if this brings the Furies down on him? "

He hesitates before going for my weak spot. "That may never happen if he is prudent, Oracles often are..." He searches for the right word. "They are not always clear. But that aside it makes good strategic sense, too, daughter. An alliance with a Greek kingdom ruled by a son of Zeus. Just think of the opportunities it could lead to."

My mind races. What he says is true enough but I am already betrothed and I'm not sure my uncle will see things the same way. Still there's a lot to consider.

"I said I won't force you, child. Think about it at least."

"How long before I must decide?"

Relief washes over my mother's face. Had they thought I'd reject this out of hand? Perhaps. Her hand shakes as she offers me a tea cup.

"Two days."

A very precise timeline but it gives me time to get to know this self-proclaimed demigod a little better. There's still so much mystery around him and I need to unravel at least some of it before I would agree.

IN SEARCH of privacy I go to my favourite seat by the river. Its waters stretch in both directions as far as I can see, placid here where it comes close to the sea but before it breaks into many streams snaking their way across the muddy delta. The palace gardens are an oasis of green behind me, branches overhanging the wall into which my seat is set. Here there is the illusion of solitude once I unlock the gate to the river. There's none, of course. Above me sentries keep watch ready to warn of intruders but few come to this spot outside the walls.

It's a peaceful scene but I'm not here to enjoy such things. I have decisions to make and questions to prepare. What do I really know of this handsome stranger? Well, he came to my rescue wearing winged sandals and carrying a shield that surely should belong to a god. So much is fact. His sword sliced through the huge scaled neck of the sea monster as if it was butter. Another fact. So my first question must be where did he get these things? Then he claims a quest in which he killed Medusa but so far we've seen no proof of that. So many questions.

Let me assume all he says is true. Is that enough for me to give up my right to my father's throne? What of Phineus? He's a man who's easily ruffled if he thinks his rights are being trampled. What if that turns to outright rebellion?

Then there's the oracle. Could this bring the horror of the Furies down on Perseus? On me? Being his queen might prove to be a very short lived honour. I stare out at the river in hopes of finding an answer but find none. All I can do is go to him and ask my questions and pray that the answers are more than just what I want to hear.

The gate clicks open behind me. Angry that my privacy has been invaded I stand and whirl around. Perseus stands there. Hes armed with sword and shield, winged sandals in his hand, satchel as always on his back.

"I'm sorry to intrude, princess," he says. "But if you would wed me there are things you should know."

I wait for him to speak again but he stands silent. Is he unsure? I take pity on him and point to the seat. "This is my favourite place to sit and think. Come and join me."

"I thank you," he says as he sets the sandals down, rests his shield against the seat, then takes his sword from its scabbard and puts it beside his satchel before he sits.

"You come with weapons you obviously don't mean to use. Why?"

"They form part of what I have to say." He shifts uneasily. I wait. I'm under no obligation to make things easier for him. "The beginning of my tale you already know. I'm sure you have had your doubts but I'm told your maids had a visitor last evening and she remembered how my mother was treated and my birth?" I nod. "That was no slave. Athena herself visited them and told them my story. You will, of course, have searched for her so you know this is true."

It makes some sense but the court is a busy place. It would be easy for a visitor to have such a slave with them but it's also true she could not be found so I will take what he says as fact–and I am very fond of facts. I wait silently again. He shifts in his seat. Am I so intimidating? Perhaps.

"I have said I was on a quest to kill the Gorgon and bring back her head but I would not have succeeded without help." He touches the shield. "This was lent to me by the great Athena." Next he points to the sandals. "The nymphs of the Hesperides lent me these and this." He takes a cap from where it is tucked into his belt, puts it on his head–and vanishes. Now he has my full attention. He reappears just as suddenly. "The sword is mine, crafted for me by Hephaestus in his workshop."

I have no words. All I can do is swallow.

"My boat is not that special but the gods have blessed it so I will come safely home even across land. Medusa's head I will not show you but it is in here." He touches his satchel. "I must leave soon. It's many months since I left my mother enslaved by the king of Seriphos to compel her into marriage. He tricked me into going on this quest to bring him Medusa's head and I have things to return before I reach my home. I tell you this so you will understand who I am. I will not force your marriage to me. If you decide against it I will leave with whatever reward your father wishes to give me but I promise by all the gods of Olympus that if you come with me you will be my queen ruling equally with me when I claim my birthright."

I've gathered my thoughts now and I have a question. "Thank you for telling me this. There is one thing that worries me. The oracle."

He nods gravely. "I have no wish to bring the Furies down on me. I will avoid any contact with my grandfather. When he dies I'll make my claim." He smiles somewhat ruefully. "There may be a bit of a wait for that I'm afraid."

I don't doubt his intentions but he's not much more than a boy, not a hardened warrior, and I'm not entirely convinced he has the strength he'll need to deliver what he promised. But he is favoured by the gods. Perhaps that is enough. I had intended to ask for time, to stall while I thought over what I've been told, but there's little point in dragging things out. He's at least convinced me he's a man of honour and my father is right to say such a marriage makes good strategic sense so why wait?

"I accept your offer but know I come from a warrior people. Do not betray my trust," I say.

His face lights up. "I would never do that, princess. I've seen your skill with a sword." He takes my hand, turns it to expose my wrist, touches it with his lips. Desire thrills through me. He looks up and I glimpse similar passion in him before pulling away. "Once we are wed, Andromeda."

A flush envelopes me. This will not be merely a strategic marriage.

THE DINING HALL is resplendent with lamps once more as we make our entrance. Our wedding feast may have been arranged in haste but nothing has been spared to make it memorable. Flowers dress every table, a match to those in my marriage wreath and the garlands draped around our necks. Perseus smiles down at me and I feel a flutter of desire. It is the last time I will see this hall, share a meal with my family so the festivities are tinged with sadness. No such thoughts seem to concern my sister who beams at me. I had worried about how this marriage would affect her but she seems happy enough to take her place as heir even if it means marriage to our uncle.

My father has loaded Perseus's boat with treasure and provisions and Perseus is eager to leave. I, too, see no reason to delay feeling as I do a lingering uneasiness about what will happen if Phineus hears of my marriage. With him supervising repairs in the north of the country so we should be safely away long before he returns but fear stirs in the pit of my stomach when the doors of the hall slam open. It's Phineus and behind him a troop of men at arms.

"I come to claim my bride," he shouts into the sudden silence.

My father rises in his place. "Welcome, brother," he says as his guards gather around him. "I'm glad to see you." He beckons. "Come, let us talk inside."

Phineus stands his ground. "I come to claim my bride," he repeats.

At my side Perseus stands. "Welcome to my wedding feast, uncle. Andromeda has consented to be my wife and I'm happy to pay you her bride price."

Phineus glares at him. "Be silent, boy. She is promised to me and I will have her."

He draws his sword and my heart leaps. Perseus is not armed and even if he was Phineus is a more skilled swordsman. I look around wildly in hopes of finding something to defend us both. I have no wish to be a widow before I've been a wife.

Perseus stands tall and stares at Phineus. "You don't seem to understand. Andromeda and I are wed," he says.

"Fool of a boy to stand there and defy me without even a weapon." Phineus marches towards us.

Footsteps sound behind us and I turn and see more guards coming to surround us. I pull on my husband's arm to let him know we're guarded but he doesn't seem to notice.

"Perseus," I say but he doesn't answer.

"Do not threaten me, uncle," he says. He speaks mildly enough but there's an edge that I've not heard from him before. He lifts his satchel and dread creeps over me. "I have a weapon and I will use it if I must."

There's a sudden scramble as the wedding guests dive for cover under the tables. Rumour means they know what Phineus and his followers do not, that Perseus is something more than just a man. Perseus sets the satchel in front of him on the table. He unbuckles it with care.

"What nonsense is this, boy? I demand my bride." Phineus raises his sword and strides towards us.

Finally I find words and shout. "Perseus, no!"

But he carefully reaches into the bag and lifts something out, slowly, slowly. All I see at first are snakes. They writhe and strike at his hands but as he lifts it higher its shape becomes clear. There's no more doubting his claim. He is holding the head of Medusa.

Phineus stops. "You try to frighten me with that?" He laughs and turns to his followers as Perseus lifts the head fully out. But the laugh turns to silence as they change before his eyes. Once they were living men, now they are stone. Phineus whirls around and takes one step only before he too freezes and turns to grey stone.

Perseus places the head carefully back into the bag and buckles it. He sits down again, places it and its grisly contents at his feet and calls for a slave to bring water so he can wash his hands. Silence surrounds us slowly replaced by gasps and shrieks as the diners crawl out and see the horror in the centre of the hall. Perseus says nothing, just dries his hands fastidiously.

My father breaks his silence. "Could we not have tried negotiation?" he asks, his voice thick with emotion.

Perseus nods. "That would have been preferable but I judged he would not listen. I did warn him."

"It's not for you to judge. This kingdom has laws." My mother spits out the words as she struggles to keep her fury under control.

My father draws himself up, every bit a king. "Your boat is provisioned and loaded with what was promised. You should leave as soon as possible. My guards will escort you to the harbour. Daughter, go in safety with your husband."

He sweeps out, my mother at his side, sister in their wake. And me? I grapple with a whole new side to the man who courted me, one much harder than the romantic who gently kissed my wrist only a day ago.

Perseus slings his satchel over his shoulder and stretches a hand toward me. "Come with me," he says. As I hesitate he goes on. "I will not hold you to our marriage, Andromeda, but if you are my wife I will honour my promises to you. I will make you a queen. I know what I did upsets you but in truth I only meant to frighten, not to destroy. Medusa is dead. I did not know she still had such power."

He sounds genuine enough but I want, I need more. "Will you swear before the gods that this is true?"

In answer he kneels lifting the satchel above his head. "Great Athena, mighty Hermes without whose aid I could not have killed Medusa, smite me dead if I have lied to Andromeda."

My hand flies to my mouth. To make such a plea is foolhardy. But there he stays unscathed.

"Will you come?"

With that my reservations evaporate. He does have strength, a hidden core as hard as bronze.

MAZZAROTH FALLS
BY F.C. SHULTZ

"Rigged this one to blast that bastard into low orbit." The man with the small tablet, which happened to be a remote detonator, stood near the hovercraft. His name was Yadi. His shoulders were squared back and he carried his entire body with a certain gracefulness that showed respect for the power he held in his hands. His fingers fidgeted over the cracked glass on the tablet's screen.

He wore a perfectly cut suit, which had been tailored for his exact measurements, with an Intersolar Justice Mission insignia patch over his left breast. A pair of black gloves and a matte black hard hat, also bearing the IJM logo, completed his look. The other two emissaries, Libby and Roach, both wearing identical outfits, leaned against the vehicle.

"Less for us to clean up," Libby said.

"Start the fireworks already," Roach said. He spit

onto the cold sandy ground and lifted his laser rifle from the ground and flicked the safety off.

"No respect," Yadi replied.

Before anyone could get in another word Yadi pressed a button on the screen and a signal was sent at the speed of light across the desolate sandscape in the cold desert of the planet Teegarden to the explosives stuck on a fifty-foot statue of a human wearing a crown and holding a sword. He had suns for eyes.

And with the push of the button he had nothing.

He was nothing.

Grey stone exploded into tiny pebbles which fountained high into the atmosphere. No pieces of the image of the former king made it into space, though. Stone hail rained down like a plague where the statue had been.

"Anything left?" Roach asked.

"Shouldn't be," Yadi replied. He slid the tablet into a suit pocket.

"Nothing big enough that IJM would flag," Libby said as she scanned her own tablet.

"Let's go," Roach said. "We've got one more today."

The three emissaries from the IJM piled into the hovercraft. Roach pulled up the coordinates to the next statue and the hovercraft took off. Miles and miles of wild and waste expanded in every direction as far as the eye could see. Roach cleaned the Teegarden dust from his rifle.

Yadi used his tablet to check the onboard explosives inventory. Libby stared out the window.

"How could anyone live here," Libby said. "It's so depressing."

"Could be worse," Roach replied.

"*Was* worse," Yadi said.

"What an upgrade," Libby replied before putting on a diplomatic-sounding voice. "Your tyrant king is dead. Now, go play in the sand."

"I feel bad for the suckers deported here to repopulate once we're done cleaning up." Roach blew off some dust from the barrel of his rifle after he spoke. "You can spray down a shithole, but that don't change what it is." They reached the coastline of a vast emerald sea. The hovercraft hummed along up the beach as waves lapped onto the shore.

"Still," Libby said, "never having to see Mazzaroth's face again? This place will be a paradise."

"I don't even want to see a damned Mazzarothonian housewife again," Yadi replied.

"Shouldn't have brought it up," Libby replied. "Sorry, Yad."

"Ah, don't apologize. You didn't do nothing," Roach said. "That's part of war." Roach calibrated his weapon and it whined with static energy. "That was years ago, anyway."

"Seven," Yadi replied. "It was seven years ago when the Mazzarothonian army sent an airstrike on neutral civilian starliners. King Mazzaroth's orders. My wife and son were the ones who 'didn't do nothing' you ignorant ass."

Roach flipped the safety off his rifle and pointed it at Yadi. "Say that again."

No one moved for a long moment.

The hovercraft slowed to a stop and the doors opened.

"Men," Libby said the word like it was profane. "Let's just finish this so we can go home."

The two men stared at each other for another moment before Yadi slid the tablet back into his pocket and climbed out of the vehicle. Libby followed and

Roach exited last. Because of the argument, Roach hadn't noticed the hovercraft had brought them right to the stone feet of another fifty-foot statue of King Mazzaroth standing at the mouth of a small cave. He stared up at the weather worn statue before spitting at the base.

"This one looks like shit," he said.

"You say that every time," Libby said.

"Am I wrong?"

"Storms rolling in from the sea have worn this one down," Libby said. "I'm surprised it's still standing."

"Won't be for long," Yadi replied. He pulled a large crate full of explosives toward the statue.

"Let's secure the area," Roach said as he clicked the safety off his rifle and made his way around the statue opposite of Libby.

Yadi pulled a handful of explosives from the crate and tapped on his tablet a few times. A moment later the explosives rose into the sky and stuck to the side of King Mazzaroth's stone dome.

The laser rifles whistled their high pitch scream as Libby and Roach walked into the entry of the cave just tall enough for Roach to walk without ducking. They stood just inside the cave, shining a light into the darkness. The screaming sound from their rifles echoed down into the belly of the cave just ahead of their voices.

"Got plans after this?" Roach asked.

"I'm not going to your nasty pod again," Libby replied. "Yadi's going to have to nuke that place once you're transferred."

"I'm not talking about tonight," Roach replied. "I mean when we're done cleaning up around here. This is our last one."

"Not again, Roach," Libby said. "You're turning soft."

"You know what I'm getting at, Lib. You still haven't answered me."

"And I don't have an answer now," she replied.

"We can go wherever you want."

"I don't—"

A violent screech filled the cave causing them to cover their ears and knocking Roach to one knee. Libby grabbed his shoulder and pulled him toward the mouth of the cave. Without hesitation he stood and began running while firing his laser rifle wildly behind him into the abyss. Outside, Yadi was already pointing his rifle toward the mouth of the cave as Libby and Roach emerged.

"Get down," he yelled and the two IJM emissaries dove into the sand, both of their hard hats crashing to the ground. A split-second later a snake-like monster burst forth with frenetic energy onto the beach. Its translucent scales reflected the light and Yadi took aim at what he assumed was the heart pulsing beneath the clear skin of the beast.

He fired two shots but couldn't tell if he'd hit his mark. Before he could fire another the monster dove into the sand and was gone. The beach was as silent as when they'd arrived less than two minutes ago. Yadi motioned to his teammates who were getting to their feet and brushing the sand from their suits. He put one finger to his mouth to hush them, but they didn't need to be told to keep quiet. Next, Yadi motioned for them to walk slowly back to the hovercraft.

Before they took a step the creature burst through the sand and soared into the sky like a whale breaching the surface of the sea. Sand rained down in its wake. All three emissaries fired their rifles into the sky and braced themselves for the earth-quaking impact of the beast hitting the ground.

It never came.

Yadi looked up and saw the monster circling around the statue, making its way toward the head.

Libby and Roach ran the rest of the distance to the hovercraft. They all aimed their rifles at the statue and waited as a silence filled the beach.

"Get behind the hover," Yadi said.

"I'll lose my shot," Roach replied.

"You'll lose more than that if you don't listen to me."

The three emissaries walked backward, keeping their sights on the statue. Yadi slung his rifle over his shoulder and reached into his suit pocket. Before they could get into full cover behind the vehicle, the snake burst through the eyes of King Mazzaroth and hissed the same ear-splitting scream that they had heard in the cave.

Before Roach had a chance to fire his rifle, the familiar crack of a dozen explosives filled the beach. The explosives whipped up the sand, which blocked all visibility, and the three people sent to destroy the King Mazzaroth statue huddled against the hovercraft as sand, rock, and Teegarden's deadliest cave monster rained down on them in bits and pebbles.

Once the storm cleared, Yadi began to laugh uncontrollably.

"You could've killed us, you idiot," Roach said as he stood and dusted off his suit.

"Better me than that thing," Yadi replied.

"For once, he's right," Libby said. "Don't ever set off a charge when I'm that close to it again."

"Yes ma'am," Yadi replied, still smiling. "Good thing that was our last target together."

"Damn it," Roach said. He had opened the doors of the hovercraft and was looking at the monitor. "They gave us one more. Says the request came straight from General Luther himself."

"No," Libby said. "Why? We did our fifty."

"Says we're the closest," Roach replied. "Also says something about bonus pay."

No one spoke. Even without the bonus pay, no one disobeyed a direct command from IJM headquarters. The three emissaries dusted off their suits and loaded into the hovercraft in silence.

The craft drove in autopilot further down the beach, occasionally hovering inches over the waves crashing onto the shore. The silence inside continued as each member of IJM was preoccupied with the news of this additional target. Roach was busy thinking about how he would spend his bonus. Libby's thoughts swirled around the irony of the Intersolar Justice Mission breaking its own promise of fifty targets per team. Yadi checked his inventory of explosives to make sure he had enough to complete the task.

After a short trip, barely long enough for Roach to clean the sand from his rifle, the hovercraft slowed to a stop revealing an eerily familiar scene. A fifty-foot statue of King Mazzaroth stood tall outside the mouth of a cave. Roach and Libby stepped out of the vehicle with their guns fixed on the dark mouth of the cave while Yadi worked double time to scrape together the remaining explosives in his inventory.

Less than sixty seconds after arriving Yadi was already arming charges and sending them up to the top of the statue. A wailing cry, like an animal in distress, echoed out of the cave.

"Get ready," Roach said.

"That sounded different," Libby replied. The sound grew louder and Roach aimed his sights on the mouth of the cave. His finger resting a hairsbreadth from the trigger. He was ready to blast the next thing that moved. But a last second plea from Libby kept him from firing.

"Wait," she said.

As she spoke a small bi-pedal creature less than two feet tall stumbled out of the cave. Through his magnified rifle sights Roach could see the form clearly as a human baby. Or, rather, what had once descended from humans of earth. This baby had ultra-pale skin and sunken eyes but wore the kind of smile only ignorance can bestow. It made its way, running with its tiny legs, down the hill from the cave opening toward the statue.

"Mazzarothonians," Yadi said as the three emissaries stared as the child wobbled toward them. The wailing sound filled the area again.

A tall woman stood at the entrance of the cave.

"Looks like a corpse," Roach said.

"Lack of sunlight. Star is too young. Too much exposure kills them," Yadi replied. "They live in the caves."

"Tough company," Roach said, thinking back to their last encounter with a cave dweller. "How many charges do you have left?"

"I'll get the statue down," Yadi replied.

"I mean for the cave," Roach said.

"Are you insane?" Libby asked. The child had reached them and was pulling on Yadi's pant leg. "You want to kill them?"

"We've got orders," Roach said.

"They're alive," Libby replied.

"So was that cave snake we blasted into the sea. Didn't hear you standing up for it."

"I won't do it," Libby said.

"I don't give a shit," Roach said. "Yad, do you have enough charges or do I need to go clean up manually." He pulled his rifle back up into a ready position and calibrated the laser.

Yadi reached down and picked up the child. It smiled and pulled the hard hat off Yadi's head and placed it on its own. The hat covered the child's eyes and the child fell into a laughing fit. A thought filled Yadi's mind and heart. His hatred for all things Mazzarothonian was strong and deep, but he knew it was eating away at him. Destroying him. He wanted to be whole again. He knew it would be a long time before the hatred was gone, but in that moment it was as if the Mazzarothonian child had detonated a small explosive and chipped away some of the hatred. "No," Yadi said.

"I'll do the dirty work, then," Roach replied. He flicked the safety off of his rifle and turned toward the mouth of the cave.

"We aren't killing these people," Yadi said.

"You're taking her side?" Roach asked.

"Go back to the vehicle and call for a transport for all of us."

"We have orders."

"You were out voted," Yadi replied. "Go."

Roach stared at Yadi, then the child. He lifted his rifle up, aiming it at Yadi's chest. It hovered there for a moment before powering it down and slinging it across his back. He spit on the ground near Yadi's feet and walked back to the hovercraft.

"Look," Libby said, pointing to the cave. A dozen or more women and elderly Mazzarothonians stood in a semicircle around the cave's mouth. One woman walked timidly toward Yadi and Libby. When she arrived, Yadi handed the child to her and she got down on one knee and bowed before him.

By the time Yadi and Libby had used the hovercraft's onboard translation equipment to explain that they were from the IJM and they were going to get them out of the cave, the transport vehicle had arrived. Yadi helped the IJM transport technicians escort the people from the cave into the warm, comfortable vehicle. The woman and the child were the last ones to enter the vehicle and Yadi entered behind them and closed the door.

As they were driving away, Yadi pulled a small tablet from his pocket and handed it to the child and gave simple instructions. The child pushed the button on the screen and a loud explosion shook the ground behind them. Grey stone exploded into tiny pebbles which fountained high into the atmosphere.

"You gave him the detonator?" Roach asked.

Yadi said, "What? *He didn't do nothing.*"

Ignition

by Dan Henriksen

L isa van DeVenter was more nervous than she had ever been in her long career. Though one of the most famous ballerinas in the galaxy, she was not well known outside ballet circles. But this performance would be broadcast to all the worlds, and she was the principal. Regardless of what happened, she would be the most famous dancer ever. But of course she wanted to be known for a flawless performance, not an embarrassing mistake.

Mistakes were likely.

As she thought about the solar ignition the next day, her mind wandered back to when she had stood with her family and their small community and watched the sun of her homeworld go nova.

It was the most beautiful thing she had ever seen, even as it destroyed everything she had ever known. She had grown up knowing their sun would go nova and they would move to a new world. Lisa had watched the nova with a few of the other families from town. Josiah had been there. They watched the burning of their home world together, and their families moved to a new world together.

She had been to the doctor earlier that day and just wanted to be alone. Everyone evacuating the system had a full-body checkup to make sure they weren't carrying any dangerous local bacteria. Lisa hadn't wanted to go to the nova afterward, but her extended family had returned for the occasion and were expecting to see her. Her grandmother, matriarch of the family, had given birth to twelve children. For families who lived on the frontiers, both new and old worlds, where childhood was still hazardous, this number had made her an honored and respected woman. It was partly for this reason she had been elected the last mayor of the last town. Lisa was the third of eight children.

Josiah held her as they all watched, and Lisa felt the ring on her finger. She wasn't used to it yet.

Penelope had asked her to stay after rehearsal. Lisa didn't want to, she just wanted to go home and be alone.

As she sat down in Penelope's office wondering what was coming, her eyes glanced around the room.

She saw an old pair of children's ballet shoes, some forms, a calendar.

Penelope came in. "As I'm sure you've heard, the solar architecture firm New Helios has been building a new headquarters for the Galactic Senate for the last 60 years."

"I haven't really been following the story. Someone or other makes a new sun every decade or so," she said, wondering what this had to do with her.

Penelope went on, "They've been collecting the dust of the Platypus Nebula into a series of pulsars and they're going to fuse them together on ignition day in about 9 months."

Everyone knew that. That was solar engineering 101, fourth grade stuff. Solar engineering was the least interesting part of this. You gobbled up the dust of a couple nebulas and let gravity do the rest. The engineering novelties here were planetary. This sun would be home to a system of planets that would compose the new Galactic Headquarters. The planets would all be the same average distance from the sun, with the same length year, in skewed orbital planes. And the terraforming of one of the planets would aim to balance life from all planets in the galaxy that humans had colonized. That was the real challenge. Making a sun was trivial.

Penelope continued, "Obviously, this making a sun stuff is trivial. But thousands of senators from all the planets will be there to watch the ignition, and the Senate has asked us to help them commemorate the event. They've commissioned Ian Morel to compose a ballet. And they want us to perform it. And I want you to be principal in it."

"Oh! That would be fun. I've never actually seen

an ignition live," said LisaThey want us to perform on the starpusher, *as it happens.*" "Yeah...?"

"Think about the gravity," Penelope said softly.

It began to dawn on her. The way ignitions worked was they moved each pulsar in turn and pushed it into a decaying orbit around the system's center of mass so that they would merge. Once enough pulsars were merged (Lisa would learn later that they had to merge 5 for this sun), the weight of the solar matter would ignite the fusion reaction in the core and boom, you had a sun. If they were on the starpusher, the gravity would shift wildly over the several hours of the ignition process.

"That's impossible. We'd jump and never land! And we wouldn't be able to jump!"

"That's what I said at first. But it's not impossible. It's an opportunity. We can use the lack of gravity to our advantage. We'll pioneer dance moves that have never been possible before, and never will be again."

"Absolutely not."

"Lisa, think about it. I need you to be on board with this. Take a week and think it over. But not too long. We only have 9 months to prepare."

"Prepare! How do we prepare for something like this?"

"Well, I'll need your help with that. We'll work with some of the solar engineers to make a gravity timeline of the ignition so we can plan out the performance accordingly. Just think about it. Don't say no yet. This is the only time you'll have this opportunity."

"It's not an opportunity! It's impossible!"

But it wasn't. After a week she realized it was hard, but not impossible. And it would be amazing if her troupe pulled off such a performance. And it would be seen galaxy-wide. And by world leaders. And their children, the future world leaders. And Penelope was right. If there was one dancer who should be principal in this performance, it was her.

So they got to work. The score was soon finished, and they began to rehearse The Birth of Athena.

Lisa got out of bed and rummaged through the things in her chest. There were lots of things from her birthworld. She had kept things that reminded her of happier times: some dolls, her Galaxis princess coloring books, ballerina trading holo-cards, and her grandmother's magic eight ball. The magnetic radiation from the nova had fried the artificial intelligence in the magic eight ball, its last prediction frozen in place like a cruel joke.

She found Josiah's ring, a beautiful diamond, that he had insisted she keep when he left. Feeling it steeled her resolve to perform perfectly.

She saw too the coal necklace that Matthew had given her only a few months earlier. It was ugly. But he had known that, and he hadn't given it to her for its beauty. She had never worn it, but she liked having it. Seeing it, she thought back to when she and Matthew had met.

MATTHEW WAS one of the solar engineers who helped the troupe understand how the gravity would vary during the ballet. They had worked directly together a few times. As principal, and strictly as a professional, she made sure to understand the gravity timeline deeply, both the most probable graph, and the range of possible variations. Due to the chaos of multiple corotating bodies, it was impossible to perfectly predict the trajectory or the timeline. The whole ignition could vary by up to an hour. Lisa had threatened to back out of the whole thing when Matthew told her that, but Penelope had talked her down. Matthew had tried to explain the three body problem to Penelope and Lisa, but since no one understood it, they didn't either. So they mapped out the likely gravity variations.

Penelope had said. "We can work with Ian and the conductor to create optional sequences in case we need to add time."

"You're just setting us up to fail," said Lisa.

"That's why it will be amazing when you don't," Matthew had said.

She had to begrudgingly respect him after that.

"Think of it as jazz ballet," Penelope offered. "We'll know at least the limits of the gravity range, right? And we'll be able to reliably rehearse it all?"

"That's right. There will be an adjustment team onsite to make sure the chaotic variations don't get out of control. We guarantee the gravity and timeline will fall within a certain range. And New Helios has agreed to lend you one of our astronaut training facilities. You can adjust the rotation of the ship to simulate the gravity changes during rehearsal."

"Fine. At least that way we'll be able to run through the whole thing beforehand." said Lisa.

"We're committed already, so we'll have to make it work."

So they made the ballet variable. The optional sequences amounted to the length of a whole act, so it would be either a 3 or 4 act performance. Ignitions were typically longer than ballets anyway, so even the minimum length would be exceptionally long. But there were more zero-g sequences than greater-than-one-g sequences, so they would be able to last longer.

Even still, they added to their regimen marathon practice and hoped on "race day" the adrenaline would carry them across the finish line.

After her initial hesitation, Lisa got especially excited about the zero-g sequences. She knew she would be able to spin and twirl for much longer. Conservation of angular momentum dampened her spirits a bit when Matthew explained it, but there were several solutions to that problem. They would use props in the set to slow themselves down. They would have dancers spinning in opposite directions meet and cancel one another out. And they could at least reliably practice the zero-g sequences. Penelope was right - they were pioneering new movements.

After the gravity timeline had been made, with all the likely variations, there wasn't much more collaboration to be done with the solar engineers.

"I got you something," Matthew had told her after the last meeting had ended. "I remember you said you watched your homeworld sun go nova. I don't know if you know, but New Helios oversaw that project. We, uh... keep samples from the suns and planets, and even comets. They say they're for studying, but really none of them ever get used, or even put into a museum. Sometimes- "

"I really need to go practice. We haven't had

nearly enough time to go over the 2- and 3-g sequences, and we only have the astronaut training ship for four more days."

"Right, sorry. Anyway, I managed to find this in our archives. It's not the prettiest thing, I know, but it was made by your nova. I put it in a small glass case in a necklace or else it would just get you dirty. ...I just thought you might like it."

"Oh. Thank you." She teared up a little at the memories that were reignited.

There was an awkward pause.

"Listen, if you need any more help with the gravity timeline, you know how to reach me. I'll be part of the chaotic adjustment team during the ignition, so maybe we'll see each other then."

THE MORNING OF THE BALLET, Lisa took a few minutes to herself in her room before meeting the rest of the troupe. She looked over her things again, and pulled out her grandmother's magic eight ball. Her mother and grandmother had always been her heroes, and she had always wanted to be just like them. Seeing the magic eight ball, it made her sad.

Penelope came in.

"How do you feel?"

"Nervous. Excited. Anxious. I just want it to start already. And I want it to be over already."

"You'll do great. Come on, there are some people who want to meet you." Another thing she had been reluctant to agree to, and that Penelope had to talk her into. It was a public and politically sensitive event.

Those in attendance were powerful, and it would help everything run smoothly if the ballerinas met and talked with anyone who wanted to meet them.

It was three hours before the ignition was scheduled to start. Lisa and the rest of the troupe went out to meet some of the senators and ambassadors in attendance.

The ship was crowded. Thousands had been invited to be on hand for the event. There were children everywhere. She hadn't expected so many to bring their families.

"This is ambassador Andrey Lvov, and his daughter Anna", Penelope was saying.

"It's so nice to meet you. We're very excited."

"Thank you! Yes, we are too. We've been working so hard to get ready."

"Anna's a big fan. Do you mind if we get an autograph?"

"Of course!"

They talked for another twenty minutes or so. Lisa had prepared for this too, and she acted pleasant and interested. Penelope introduced her to more attendees, and lots of children. An hour before the ignition was scheduled to begin, the troupe went backstage to get ready.

Trillions tuned in to watch The Birth of Athena. Lisa dazzled as Metis, Athena's mother. In the first act, under mostly a range of 2- to 3-g, she and Zeus warred against the cosmic forces of the Titans, conspiring to trick Cronus into releasing Zeus's siblings. At the end of the first act, as the ship pulled away from the first of the pulsars and into zero-g, Metis and Zeus married, while nymphs and birds and the gods flew overhead in celebration.

After the first act they were ahead of schedule. Two pulsars had been merged. The glass screen had been equipped with infrared and ultraviolet translation, so the audience could see colors outside the visible spectrum as the stars merged. Some of the dancer's costumes also reflected the colors outside the visible spectrum. The symphony of radio waves alone was awe-inspiring.

In the second act, began at zero-g and descended into 1- and 2-g as the ship corralled two smaller pulsars, Metis learned in prophecy that her offspring would overthrow Zeus, and Zeus caught sight of Demeter. In their duet she dueled with her love for Zeus and her knowledge of her role in his downfall.

By the end of the second act, Zeus had grown suspicious and bored. He tricked Metis into turning into a fly.

The conductor called for an optional sequence, and so Zeus engaged in an extended chase of Metis while she was a fly. The orchestra had it easy. But the dancers were already not as sharp as the first act. They had been under heavy gravity for longer than they hoped during the second act and they had begun to tire.

Lisa, however, still flew gracefully around the room as Metis avoiding Zeus's chase. The chorus of other gods were divided in their loyalties. Zeus had already taken other wives, who were loyal to him, but Poseidon and Hades resented his rule. When they were back in sync with the ignition, Zeus succeeded in catching and swallowing Metis. In the background, as the ship sped away from the center of the nebula where it had deposited the most recent pulsar, the earlier stars began to collide, unleashing a spectacle of radiation across the electromagnetic spectrum. It was perfectly timed, the normally invisible colors cast into the visible spectrum by the viewing glass, bathed the dancers in an intensity of light, reflecting the gods' cosmic struggle.

The third act started at zero-g. Zeus enjoyed his fleeting victory, throwing a party on Olympus to celebrate. He took at last Hera as his final wife. Meanwhile, Metis flew around within the body of the God who had consumed her, trying in vain to find rest. As the ship approached the next pulsar, by far the largest except for the central one, Zeus began to feel a slight headache. As they brought the pulsar into position, the gravity increased considerably, and so did Zeus' agony. At Zeus's bidding, Hephaestus smelted an ax capable of splitting open the head of the king of the gods. As he worked, Metis gave birth to Athena inside Zeus and began to raise and teach her. Zeus, though his agony increased, continued to rule the gods.

During the fourth act, there was one final pulsar to corral, and then the ignition itself. They would bring it into a rapidly decaying orbit with the central pulsar and the others already corotating. It was timed so that they would all merge together swiftly and the sun would ignite during the finale. As all the remaining pulsars were in position, and the ship as close to the center as it would get, the gravity reached over 4g, the highest during the whole ignition. Hephaestus split open Zeus's head. As he did so, the pulsars merged, and the fusion reaction began at the core. As the reaction propagated to the surface and the mass became a sun, Athena emerged from Zeus' head fully grown and dressed in armor. The ship took a linear escape path rather than an orbital one, giving the illusion that the sun itself had stopped in the sky to witness Athena's birth.

Athena immediately began to assert her strength and wisdom on the other gods, while Metis danced in the background, her own struggle ongoing but now superseded by her daughter's. By the end of the ballet, there was some semblance of order again on Olympus, Zeus and Hera reigning above the other gods, Athena incorporated into the pantheon. But it was an order filled with unresolved tension, Zeus' control by no means secure, and the threat of the prophecy that Metis' children would overthrow Zeus still looming. In the final scene, Metis danced alone in hope and anticipation that this would come to pass.

Lisa was exhausted and exhilarated. From his control panel Matthew applauded as loud as anyone. It was not perfect. But it was a success.

MATTHEW CAUGHT Lisa with all her things, about to board the ship with parents to go back home for a much needed vacation.

"That was amazing! You're amazing! How do you feel?"

"Thank you! I'm thrilled. And tired. And happy. I'm exhausted." As tired as she was, she couldn't help but smile.

The ship had receded from the new sun. It had settled into an orbit which gave them 0.7g of gravity.

Lisa felt an enormous weight had lifted off her shoulders.

"You deserve a good vacation." Matthew paused before going on. "I understand if you don't want to, but once you've rested and recovered, I'd like to take you to coffee over a meteor shower."

Lisa looked away. She saw Penelope on the other side of the room, surrounded by her family. Her three boys and two girls had come in with her husband to see the performance.

Maybe because she was too tired to resist, maybe because she didn't know what was next, or maybe something about Matthew had gotten to her. Whatever it was, something inside that Lisa had built up for years started to break.

"I can't have children," she said. She looked down.

"Oh!" he was clearly surprised.

It was easier to continue now that she had started.

"It's been a problem before. I put all those desires away a long time ago. I just focused on ballet. "

"I'd still like to take you if you're up for it. Let me know."

"Ok, I will." She smiled.

Matthew smiled too as he walked away, rejoining his team to debrief the ignition. Penelope came over.

"Everyone loved it! You were amazing." Penelope was beaming, clearly proud of her star. "I talked to one reporter. He said they're calling you the mother of suns."

Lisa laughed. "That's a silly name." But she liked it.

As she boarded the ship with her mother, she pulled out her grandmother's magic eight ball. She read it for the first time in years: "You will be a stellar mother."

Across Saturn Rose

by Anthony G. Cirilla

With a last name like mine, I should have been more careful about telling people what I believe. I have cult leader written all over me. And I guess in the end I sort of became something to that effect, though not intentionally. It didn't help that I ended up bringing my madness to Saturn - it's like I walked out of a secret society recipe book. But I have no affiliation with those societies other than my name and one belief: a belief that the spheres resound with music. And it was that belief which led me to become a danger to a hidden conflict that has peeked out at humanity from behind the curtain of myth and legend for centuries. If you read this account, I am sorry to say that you too are caught up in the dangerous secret of the Chronotopians, the glorious guilt of our people and our philosophy. Now that you are on Saturn you can never leave, for the Saturnalia sustains you, and the song can never be learned by mortals who might betray our secrets to the prisoners of the Faerie Queen.

PART 1: THEORY OF EVERYTHING

The hot coffee greeted my lips as my eyes looked past the mug to the black lettering on the screen. Writing this paper seemed to be utter agony - something in the ideas seemed to be resisting me, pushing me away. It was unusual for me - typically my papers came out easily, but this one was fighting me. I had all the math and all the information worked out, but I couldn't get the words to fall in line.

"The religious nutjobs are at it again," said a familiar voice.

I looked up and saw a tall man with big hands holding up a tablet next to his broad face. The screen had the headline, *Voters Block AI Usage Again.*

"What do you expect, Valentine - that's how it is in the American Republic. We should move to the United States of Canada like you always suggest."

He shook his head. "I still hold out hope for a return to the things the way they were - United States of America."

"We both know that didn't work. Never could go back - misplaced nostalgia."

He nodded, sitting down. "I know. Good to see you, Rosicrucia. Guess I should have known you'd be at your favorite spot." He gestured to the coffee shop around us. "Creature of habit, you are."

"We all are. So here we go again, resisting the advances of artificial intelligence," I said, picking up his tablet and looking at the article. "But you know, the United States of Canada isn't much better. They still make it illegal for AI to replace trucking."

"It won't last. They've been chipping away at the anti-AI policies for a while now. And it makes sense. Human error is too dangerous.'

"Right." I smirked. "We need a comprehensive system of travel to maximizemaximise safety, just like we need a comprehensive system of explanation so that these zealots can't get a toehold."

He rolled his eyes. "Theory of everything again. I've told you, it doesn't work. There can't be a theory of everything."

"Sure there can. There is what is, and we can figure out a way to explain it all. Maybe some parts can still remain a mystery, but with a solid theory of everything, there will be no need for building these castles in an air —- this religion, spirituality garbage."

"Okay, let's set aside for a second our usual debate about what's possible," said Valentine, settling into the debate. "Let's focus on something else. A theory of everything won't stop the God-botherers from believing, anyway. You think you can get them to give up belief with a proven theory of everything, but they doubt proven theories all the time. Confirmation bias, all that stuff. People are stubborn. But there's something worse you're not thinking about."

"What's that?"

"Commitment to good inductive thinking precludes a theory of everything. Real science always assumes there won't be a final deductive word. Even if you could get there, you have to presuppose that new information could come to light that would upset the theory."

I nodded. "That makes sense of course - I see your point. But I don't think it needs to account for every possible variable. I think we have enough inductive information that we can fit together mathematically. It has to be flexible enough to account for growth, but rigid enough that you can't pretend like reality isn't a closed system. There's just reality. Transcendence, once you entertain it, destroys the ability to have knowledge. And the theory of everything is the only way to make transcendence obsolete."

"But that's exactly it," said Valentine, slapping his knee enthusiastically. We always loved our debates.

"Joe Ballentine?" a barista called out uncertainly. He got up to get his drink and said, "Actually, it's John Valentine. Thank you." The barista said, "Have a nice day," not bothering to acknowledge the correction.

He sat back down. "It's not like Valentine is some obscure thing. Valentine's Day? Hello?"

I chuckled. "Just imagine what they do with Rosicrucia. Why do you give your last name at a coffee shop anyway? It's not the DMV. Anyway, what were you saying, Ballentine?"

"That Valentine's Day is common knowledge?"

"No, about transcendence being obsolete."

"Oh, right. Exactly!" He sat up as his energy for the debate reignited. "It's exactly because transcendence is obsolete that we can't have a theory of everything. Look, a theory of everything presupposes a grand explanation for all things. Everything accounted for, everything in its place. It's a nice idea, but at base, it's a religious idea. The scientific outlook is that, though we try to explain everything we can, we're always on the hunt for new information. So even if you have a theory attempting to account for everything, *calling* it a theory of everything won't send the right message."

"But should we really worry about how people will misinterpret things if it's true? People might misinterpret evolution to think that there are different *types* of humans, but that doesn't mean evolution isn't true. So people might misinterpret the theory of everything to be spiritual or something, but that doesn't mean it can't be found."

"Right, but you said the whole need for the theory of everything is to get rid of transcendence -- of superstition basically, right?"

"Yes."

"But you also concede that people are stubborn and will ignore or misunderstand things to confirm a worldview even if it is ultimately untenable?" He sipped his coffee in triumph.

"I agree with that."

"So then don't you think that a theory of everything could end up becoming a tool *for* superstition instead of against it?"

"Sure, but simply emphasizing the importance of induction isn't enough either. People will use induction as an excuse to believe in things — fairies might exist because they haven't been disproven to exist, absence of evidence is not evidence of absence and all that." I pushed my coffee around on the table idly as I spoke. "And it's true, people are stubborn, but they do eventually come around — most people accept the advances of science, more or less. The process takes time. But although someone *could* misinterpret the theory of everything, if science has an inductively derived system that shows the needlessness of deductive transcendence, then we have a good starting point for getting more and more people weaned off of superstition entirely."

John sat back and tapped his fingers on the table. "Okay, look. Isaac Newton was basically the first to try a theory of everything. And he couldn't scrub it of theism, not quite. At base, there's a religious instinct in that way of thinking that isn't part of what science is about. If you're just trying to use people's religious instinct against them in a sort of Machiavellian way, fine, but the scientist's business should be truth, not propaganda."

"Ah, but that's the thing! If you say the scientist's business is *truth*, truth is a total category of what *is* regardless of whether we know it specifically. Truth is what is, communicated in speech and understood by the mind. If we aren't trying to settle a theory of everything, then we aren't doing science - on your own terms."

"No, not on my terms - I am not sure I agree with that definition of truth." John paused and pressed his hand against his lips. "Okay, think about your name. The Rosicrucians. Do you know much about them?"

"Oh, yeah —- some Christian cult, if that isn't a total redundancy. Possibly a hoax but had a lot of influence. What do they have to do with this?"

"Have you read any of their treatises?"

I scoffed. "No —- I'm not into the history of crackpot science and nonsense magical thinking. Enough true things to study."

"Okay but, to understand our enemy, the superstitious person who builds castles in the air, we need to know how they think. When you look at the zealot, you always will find a theory of everything. Always. So read the treatises on the Rosicrucians. I can send them to you, if you want, and you'll see what I mean."

"Okay. Maybe I will look at it tonight, after I finish my work. Great discussion as usual, Valentine —- thanks for making me think," I said sincerely as we shook hands.

He smiled. "Of course man —- that's what intellectual buddies are for."

We said goodbye, and I went back to writing my paper. It was still coming together clunkily, but I pushed through just to get it finished, and decided I'd give it a once over tomorrow before sending it in. I got dinner and ate at home, thinking the whole time about my conversation with John. I did see his point and needed a way to address it, but it still seemed to me that the best way to get rid of ridiculous beliefs was to formulate an airtight system that demonstrated that they didn't help to explain anything. My phone buzzed just then and I saw that he'd emailed me. There were four attachments. I opened my tablet to read his email.

Hey Michael,
Here are the three foundational texts of
the Rosicrucians from the 1600s
and one from the 1900s. Notice
how long Rosicrucianism has sur-
vived even though it started as a

> *hoax. It's because it has a theory of*
> *everything. The lamentable super-*
> *stitious instinct, valuable in ourat*
> *our more primitive state, is at-*
> *tracted to these sorts of things. I*
> *think you'll see that your namesake*
> *builds his whole cult around it. Let*
> *it go and join the modern times.*
>
> *JV*

I ROLLED MY EYES, but I had to admit that I was curious. I opened up the first one, the *Fama fraterni-tatis*. It told a fanciful legend of the so-called Rosenkreutz and his expedition to gather knowledge from all of the different parts of the world —- which inspired him to create a secret society of knowledge seekers. And, sure enough, they had a theory of everything—

> *"For the wise King Solomon doth testifie of himself,*
> *that he upon earnest prayer and desire did get and*
> *obtain such Wisdom of God, that thereby he knew*
> *how the World was created, thereby he understood*
> *the Nature of the Elements, also the time, beginning,*
> *middle and end, the increase and decrease, the*
> *change of times through the whole Year, the Revolu-*
> *tion of the Year, and Ordinance of the Stars; he un-*
> *derstood also the properties of tame and wilde Beasts,*
> *the cause of the raigning of the Winds, and minds*
> *and intents of men, all sorts and natures of Plants,*
> *vertues of Roots, and others, was not unknown to*

> *him... but seeing the same Felicity can happen to none, except God himself give Wisdom, and send his holy Spirit from above, we have therefore set forth in print this little Treatise, to wit, Famam & Confessionem, of the Laudable Fraternity of the Rosie Cross, to be read by every one, because in them is clearly shewn and discovered, what concerning it the World hath to expect."*

I smirked. The font and the archaic language was a bit much. Some theory of everything, with God at the center of explanation —- as much of a theory of everything as a shoddily written fairy-tale. Why couldn't Valentine see that the theory of everything *destroyed* the need for such magical thinking? I had to admit, though, that the treatise was interesting and fun to read, so I opened the next one. It continued the Enlightenment-style profession of an esoteric Christianity, but it also showed the fruits of the scientific imagination —- an excitement about learning. I had to admit, the Christian myth's enthusiasm about learning did recommend it —- though the whole Garden of Eden allegory tended to put a damper on that. But it seemed to me that there was something inconsistent here —- it was like the Rosicrucian theory was trying to turn Christianity *into* science.

The lightbulb clicked on. That's exactly what it is —- that's why superstition attracts us, I mused. The superstitious instinct is actually an *intuition* that the world can be known, and of course we tend to anthropomorphize that intuition —- call it God, gods, fairies, whatever. I had considered for some time that maybe we couldn't get to the level of concrete scientific thinking about the world without passing through that symbolic stage. The intuitive language of Christianity was helping the Rosicrucian to desire science. Easy enough, once science is achieved, to relinquish the Christianity - so I did a little search on the tablet and found that, indeed, many of the splintered Rosicrucians would do exactly that... Though one of the splinter groups seemed to have gotten involved with Nazism. My stomach churned. Exactly as one would expect —- the evils of tyranny stemmed from superstition. So they took the wrong branch —- the one towards barbarism. Every human impulse could be corrupted, no matter how good. But real scientific inquiry and curiosity goes the other way —- grows out of intuition and sets it aside when it becomes too primitive for truth.

I made myself some tea and sat on the third piece. It was stranger than the previous two — some sort of allegory using marriage as a metaphor for seeking truth. Typical unhelpful anthropocentrism. It was a strange tale, and more frustrating because it broke off incomplete. But near the end of the manuscript was a list of five rules, the first of which was "You my lords the Knights shall swear that you shall at no time ascribe your order to any devil or spirit, but only to God your Creator, and his handmaid Nature." Of course. It seemed to me that the swearing off of devils and spirits could be considered an intuitive apprehension of the need to eschew superstition — derived from the Enlightenment spirit of the age, but unable to escape that primitive imagination in subordinating Nature to be God's handmaiden. The scientist swears to ascribe his order to no devil, spirit, or God, but to *be* a handservant of Nature. Still, something in the formula spoke of a pattern that seemed to predict the filtering apparatus of judgment in science, which seemed to confirm my thoughts about the *intuitive* value of religious sentiment, if not the *truth* value of it.

The more recent piece, *The Rosicrucian Cosmo-Conception*, was too long for me to read in its entirety, and I was starting to get tired of reading the pious language of these cultists. But I scrolled through it a bit, until I hit upon this passage:

"Celestial music is a fact and not a mere figure of speech. Pythagoras was not romancing when he spoke of the music of the spheres, for each one of the heavenly orbs has its definite tone and together they sound the celestial symphony."

Later in the same discourse he wrote, "In our Earth life we are so immersed in the little noises... that we are incapable of hearing the music of the marching orbs, but the occult scientist hears it." Upon that celestial harmony, the order of things resides. I was stunned. Here, he had articulated the principle I had been attempting to glimpse in my research on the theory of everything — to understand what lay at the core of the simple arrangement of cosmic complexity. And of course — of course it would be *music!* What else could it be? I remembered that Leibniz said that when we nod our heads to music without counting it — and of course we delight in an orchestra because it *performs* the unity between the skills and abilities of people that we wish to see in society. The orchestra is a sensory fairy-tale, as my father used to say.

I recalled then that I had taken a Philosophy of Science class as an undergraduate student where my professor speculated that the Incarnation of Christ was a mythic impetus for scientific inquiry — that mind could be edified by a close and careful union with matter. At its best, the religious intuition could recall the wonder of the world around us — that heaven and earth are full of God's glory. I was always offended by that phrase — aren't heaven and Earth full of enough of their *own* glory? But perhaps that was what this discussion of God actually was, though the zealots couldn't see it — an intuitive acknowledgement that there is a wonderous participation of reality in itself that is worth celebrating. And isn't that really the function of the scientist?

I could hear the voice of Valentine cautioning me — that I was proving him right. Here I was finding my inspiration in the esoteric cultists he had said shared my desire for a theory of everything. "The power of rhythmic vibration is well known to all who have given the subject even the least study." The little study of myth I had came together — the Walls of Jericho, Amphion who built Thebes, Orpheus who tamed death, if only for a moment. Music, perfectly mathematical and entirely empirical, is the one magic we can *prove* exists.

It was at this moment that I coined the basic premise of my famed Harmonic Theorum. If myth could have intuitive value, then the most demonstrable of them, the power of music, could have even more truth in its intuitions. This was what we were missing in quantum physics, in our ability to understand time's arrow-effect or the continuum. What if we could combine particle physics, quantum theory, and the four basic forces into an arrangement of *harmony*? That was the basic idea of the theory of everything to begin with -—to discover a fundamental principle of harmony between the basic, quantifiable elements of existence. So what if it wasn't some principle to *create* harmony that we needed, but harmony *itself*, that had the answer? What if the ancient belief in the symphony of the spheres was the hypothesis of the theory of everything, and modern science could refine it, make it empirical, and exorcize superstition with the same force tirelessly used to enforce it: music?

I opened my tablet and began to write.

PART 2: THE HARMONIC THEOREM

A few weeks later, I was playing *Clair de Lune* on my piano when I heard the sharp knocking. I got up and went to the door, and could see Valentine's car from the window. I opened the door, and he was standing there with a forced smile.

"Hey Michael," he said. He usually used my first name when he was worried about something.

"Hey John," I said. "I thought I might see you at the coffee shop this afternoon - I didn't expect to see you here."

"Neither did I." He brushed past me, not waiting to be invited in. "This is a disaster, you know."

"Nice to see you too," I rejoined. "What exactly are you here about?"

He tossed a copy of the Bulletin of the Association of American Republic Scientists onto the table. There was my article, *A Prolegomena to the Harmonic Theorum*, on the front page.

"Seriously, Michael? You're publishing pseudoscience in that rag? What are you doing?" He leaned against the wall with his arms folded. I'd never seen him confrontational like this.

"I don't understand your anger, Valentine. It's a theory. The bulletin is a place for scientists to share ideas. It's where I shared my initial ideas about artificial gravity, and there's talk of building an AGS system on my theories on Mars even now. What's the problem?"

"No problem, but I am going to be proposing an article that combines phrenology, cryptozoology, and horoscopes into a way to make people immortal." He rolled his eyes. "Rosicrucia, listen to me. You've gone on record publicly saying that you think classical music could be combined with modern quantum physics to *travel through time*, to open portals in the space-time continuum, basically to do witchcraft."

"Those speculations are really a small component of my point, which is more theoretical than practical," I said. "And it is nothing like witchcraft. I thought you were pro-empiricism. How can you rule this possibility out without testing?"

"Testing? Are you kidding me? What should I do, bring a radio and a crystal ball into the chemistry lab?"

"A particle collider and a piano would be more apt," I replied.

"Oh sure, even better." He stood up straight and started to pace. "Michael, I don't think you get what you're doing. You're one of the most respected and inspiring scientists on the cutting edge of your field, and you're about to throw it all away. When I gave you those bits on the Rosicrucians, it was to *stop* you from continuing to pursue speculations that were making you sound like an occultist. Instead you actually quote from *Max Heindel?* Why not use Nostradomus to prove your ideas about wormholes?"

"Valentine, this is a fallacy called *appeal to the stone*. Because it seems wild to you, you think you can throw it out. But if empirical advances have taught us anything in the last decades, it's that how things *seem* and how they *are* have vast differences. Until recently much of the technology we have now would sound like magic to the scientific community. How do you *know* that I'm any more wrong than the Wright brothers or the inventor of the HoloVision?"

He rolled his eyes again. "The HoloVision was a no-brainer combination of technologies that existed well before it was patented. Give me a break. These speculations are fine for a Philosophy of Science class, but you are ruining your reputation to make a rhetorical point about the theory of everything, and I am telling you, *it isn't worth it.*" He paused. "I heard McGuillen say he always thought you were headed towards crackpot and that this proves it. You have to stop, or you're going to go from legend to laughingstock."

"Or maybe from legend to scientist. The theory of everything isn't unique to me, Valentine, and a lot of scientists who would be skeptical about my speculations believe it's possible."

"Let me remind you of something," said Valentine, and I could hear his voice gaining an edge that had surprising anger behind it. "You've mentioned you think that the myths and legends, the superstitions have *intuitions* behind them that could be true. Preceptive, instinctual guesses that are actually subliminal inductive assessments of something real, that sound like magic when discussed because they haven't been rationally and scientifically worked out yet. Well here's something else in the religious traditions: apophatic theology. Apophatic theology warns that we can't forget that life is a mystery and that it's imprudent of mortals to talk as if they have immediate access to God's knowledge. Well maybe there's an intuition there too - a check against otherwise untrammeled occultists. The only difference between a cult and a religion is that the formalized religions have that apophatic humility. And when you remove it in science, things get dangerous then too. You and I are agreed — science is the way forward on all fronts, but incautious attitudes towards science can cause mistakes and even get people hurt. So my suggestion to you, while you are so fond of finding religious intuition to have a grain of truth to it, that you remember the grain of truth in the hiddenness of God."

"You want me to keep my hands off of the tree of knowledge? Who's sounding religious now?"

Valentine's face reddened. "I can tell you're not going to listen to me, Michael. I am not going to keep warning you. Our friendship has already embarrassed me professionally, and I don't care to be dragged down with you. Get out of the magician's chair and back into the laboratory where you belong."

He turned around and was out the door, slamming it shut behind him. I was stunned. I had had so many arguments with John Valentine, about every conceivable issue, and we had never had a disagreement like this.

The shock over the argument started to fade, and then anger started to replace it. That article was written from within my expertise as a physicist, drawn from my dissertation and other research that had been nationally recognized. I knew my article was strange, but would it really destroy my reputation the way he predicted? And he always talked about himself as a champion of the life of the mind — I had professionally embarrassed him because McGuillen didn't like what I had written? McGuillen was a good man and a patient supervisor — I couldn't see John getting in hot water with him over a colleague's publication in a journalistic venue. The whole point was to start a conversation — where did his belief in free discourse go all of a sudden?

I looked at my keycard hanging by the door. An idea occurred to me. I took up the paper John had left on the table, and added some quick sketches and notes in the margins. A piano and a particle collider walk into a lab...

I picked up the phone and called my assistant at the lab. It was his day off, but he was eager to please me and wouldn't question me.

"What do you need, sir?"

"I need you to get the space near the particle collider freed up for a grand piano."

"Why, sir?"

"Don't worry about it — just a little fun project I am doing. Talk to you soon."

I called a moving company and hired them to move the piano to the lab. Apparently they were having a slow day because the men were over shortly. None of them cared about what I was doing or why, just set to work without question. There was something nice about not having to defend my actions to someone who considered himself a peer.

I drove to the lab, and they had already brought in the piano by the time I arrived. I signed some papers and they said goodbye. My lab assistant was standing there, looking confused but otherwise unconcerned.

"How can I help you, sir?"

"Listen, Greg - I need you to forget about trying to understand what I am doing. It won't make sense to you - it doesn't even make much sense to me."

He didn't ask questions, though I saw them on his face as I gave him my instructions. By the time we were done, the piano had all kinds of bizarre wires and apparatus sticking out of it ·—I thought flinchingly that this could ruin the instrument, but it was worth it.

"What's next?"

"What's next is you can go home."

"Wait — really? I want to see what you're going to do."

I smiled. "Greg, I need the kind of concentration that goes with working alone. You know how it is."

He nodded. "I get it. Okay sir. I'll see you on Monday."

I waited until he was gone, and then made some further modifications to the combination of music and machinery. "The power of rhythmic vibration is well known to all who have given the subject even the least study," I quoted with a smirk.

I turned on the machine and put in the necessary codes, and then sat down at the piano. I started for a moment into the mesmerizing coils of the particle collider's tubes, leading off into the hidden parts of the machine. It was smaller than the old particle colliders — it was incredible how quickly they had advanced. My own modifications had turned it into a machine quite unique.

I started to play the piano, and the flashes of light from the collider began to flicker in accordance with the music. The effect was more immediate and enchanting than I expected. The music was channeling right to the subatomic level and coming back in indescribable patterns. If my wormhole theory was right, I was going to need something specific.

I thought of my visit to the Tchaikovsky House Museum a few years ago. I was emotionally entangled with that place, and that place was physically entangled with his music. If I was right, the quantum engine of my collider could interact with the music to turn that emotional frequency into a spatio-temporal connection.

Even thinking it sounded absurd, and even ten years ago the understanding of quantum physics would have been too rudimentary to be entertained practically. But my use of it in this very collider had secured me funding to keep my lab running for years. If this worked, it would keep my lab running forever.

I began to play *Dance of the Sugar Plum Fairies*, and sparks began to fly majestically in the tubes of the collider. It was like a kaleidoscope of the subatomic world. I let my memories of the house museum wash over me. The keys started to glow blue at my fingertips, and a haze began to develop over the machine. Then a light flashed and my vision was clouded, and I thought I could see the top of the house. Then another light flashed, and all was dark. I could feel air caressing my face. Slowly, I opened them, but what I saw was not the museum of Tchaikovsky's house.

I seemed to stand in a middle place, high but not the highest, and yet it afforded to me a sight of the better part of this great and strange land. Encircling about the land I saw was a great and swirling mist, coiling not menacingly as in a fog of worsening weather, but like a sort of becoming garment of a great and mysterious benefactor, and yet one not without its dangers, billowing about the edges of the land. From the northeast there grew up a chain of mountains, which rose higher as they approached the center of the land, then in its shifting center arose a giant among giants, crown of the mountains, its blue-gray peak lending shadow over an ancient fortress that would dwarf any human visitor but which seemed, as the lands were kept by the mists, itself kept by the great mountain. And it seemed I could hear, though the distance was great, a terrible and mighty rushing issuing forth from that mountain, a sound that went deep into the secret places of the world, coming forth to make a great spring which, exalting itself into the air, crashed ever down in a majestic expression of sempiternal and insuperable force, which clove into the stone of the grave mountain. This downpour went out into four great rivers, each rushing generally towards one of the cardinal points, where in reaching the mists their silvery blue ribbons were lost to my line of sight.

Suddenly I realized what I was looking at, remembering the books I had read as a child. That immense fountain I knew for the Springs of the Helicon, and that keep where lived the Queen of Faerie, and those rivers, East Helicon and West, and the Pyzon flowing easily north and Gyhon with a fury towards the south. And each land between I had read about in books that I had taken in my childhood as mere fancy – between Gyhon and East Helicon a land of plains and sparse trees called Hyla, where the Hylans drifted on dandelions and built homes in mushrooms and rode the mice like horses. And to the north, between East Helicon and Pyzon, the denser woods of Sylva, where the sylvans leapt from branches to land in the soft feathers of their owl friends and the whisper of wind between the trees was not only of the air, for the dryads and the hamadryads hid themselves in the deep green foliage. And there, between the Pyzon and West Helicon rose up the hills and plateaus of Aeolia, and strange plants burst open to reveal little sprites who, glowing like fireflies, took to the air, and they danced in the wind, easing into each zephyr as if it were a cool stream.

These Aeolians carried with them their flutes, into which they placed seeds, and with their music brought new life to the lands. And there, between the West Helicon and the raging Gihon, was a watery land filled with lakes and marshes and bogs and swamps, the earthy children of the great rivers and the Springs, in which happily splashed the water spirits of Eusebia, their necks gilled and their fingers webbed and their homes built like beaver dams or coral reefs.

And peculiar was this last part of my vision, perhaps more peculiar than even these other things, for it was day and night at all times in this place, half the land covered in the light of the sun and the other half under the watch of the moon and the cover of night. Day and night did not come there as it does here, but the whole great motion of the celestial lights turned as do the hands of the clock, a slow, day-long spiral of light and dark, so that in the darkest of night one could look afar and see the encroaching sun, and yet as if by some invisible film the light did not break through to ruin the night.

And looking upon the sun my eyes were not immediately hurt, though as one gazed the figure of a dancer began to emerge, and as that spirit became clearer my eyes began to burn and I had to look away. And in the moon there was a greater vigilance than one was used to in our world, such that as I gazed, the semblance of a watcher began to grow dimly apparent, and a sudden feeling of lowliness caused one to look away. Meanwhile above, drawing up to them the wisps of the great mist and capped by a great and unknowable blackness, were the stars —– and oh, how they always danced, like silver kites bouncing in the wind, though surely too far to feel the winds of even this land.

The starsy appeared somewhat fewer than do our stars, perhaps numbering in the several thousand — not near so vast as in the clearness of our nights and somewhat closer, but no less serenely and awfully and coldly beautiful. Where the land knew darkness they seemed to draw closer, as if longing to dance with the creatures below, but never lower than the moon; but even in the day they could be seen, as we can sometimes see the moon faintly at some parts of the day, but still with their ceaseless, joyful undulations. And there amidst the stars I could see the planet Saturn casting a gentle shadow over my sight, and as I looked upon it I thought I could hear, in the distance, the sound of a dark but happy laughter.

But in the swamps and the caverns and the valleys there also moved dark things, their forms bent and sallow and wizened, their outward semblance becoming fitting of their inward nature, natives made themselves strangers in this land of such wonders. I thought I should look upon them further, but as I seemed to descend, across Saturn rose the peak of the mountain, blocking the ringed planet from full view, and suddenly the strength of my vision began to fade in the edges and focus towards the center of the land. The castle loomed larger, its turrets and crenellations soaring. Then stepped onto the fortress below at the base of the great mountain a maiden in a dress that was blue, green and white, and her hair floated and her dark eyes flashed in warning, and I was drawn into the orbit of those great eyes, of she who ruled this land, and saw in those orbs greater and older places than even this place, and her vision pierced into my heart with lancing and I squirmed in the agony of her discernment – and then I awoke, shaking, in the darkness of my room.

And I was, I should specify, in my *bedroom*, not in the laboratory. For that matter, I was not in the bedroom of my house but of my parents' house. But it was late - perhaps two in the morning. I walked to the window and saw a glow in the blue spruce in the front lawn.

Confused, I left my parents' house as quietly as I could. I didn't want to frighten them - at their age that could be fatal. I felt drawn to the light in the blue spruce, a common feature in front yards in that neighborhood. It was common for people to joke that fairies lived there, ones related to the elves that worked for Santa Claus. But with what I had just seen and the glow I saw now, those stories didn't seem so silly anymore.

"You've been playing with fire, Michael," said a soft voice from within the branches of the spruce.

"Who are you?"

"I am the guardian of this tree —- a spruce fairy."

My eyes widened. "A spruce fairy?"

"Yes. The fairy queen told me you would be here. She said to wait and talk to you when you came. You must listen to me. What you are doing is very bad."

"Why? is it bad? I am a scientist. I want to learn."

"It's good that you want to learn, Michael, but learning at any cost isn't worth the price. Learning is a means to a virtuous life, but must be ordered towards virtue as any other endeavor."

"But what harm can come of me learning about this world? I must have for a reason. I was a skeptic until a few minutes ago, and now I've seen Fairyland. I used science to open a gateway to Fairyland. I earned it."

The voice giggled. "Do you really think it was all science? Do you think that the song you played worked for merely scientific reasons? From the standpoint of *science*, your colleagues are quite right. But what you're doing is very dangerous, Michael, moreso than you realize."

"Why?"

"Do you remember the creatures you saw, lurking in the caverns and hidden places of Fairyland?"

"Yes."

"Those are the prisoners of the Fairy Queen. They hate her, and all fairy kindred, but above all they hate humans. In the past they have terrorized your kind — and thanks to the imprisonment of the Fairy Queen, you remember that terror only as stories."

My mind was a whirlwind of thoughts. Given what I had seen, it followed that, in some sense, magic was real — fairies were real. The Harmonic Theorum wasn't wrong, it was just incomplete — there was magic in the music itself. The same magic that bound the forces of creation.

"What must I do?"

"You must stop using the Harmonic Theorem. You must stop writing about it too. Among mortals, there are those who would bring the children of the Gibborim back into the world, and if they have a little magic, they can use science the same way you did."

I contemplated his words. "But the Harmonic Theorum is out there. And the way I've written it, people could follow my work to recreate what I've done."

"Then you must write more papers, leading them away from the full insights of your Theorum and leading them back to natural philosophy."

"Okay." I saw the monsters moving in my memory, and I felt a chill move through me. I knew the fairy's warning was true. "What are you called?"

"I am Ilumbrado. I will help you when I can. I will send you home. You must retrieve your notes, but then do not stay in your home. There is a danger — a force who has become aware of your actions."

"A danger? But what should I do?"

The blue light from the spruce grew, shutting out my vision and my words. When the light faded I was standing outside of my house.

PART 3: THE GOBLINKIN

As I went inside, I had a feeling that I was being watched. I didn't know where I should go, except maybe to the lab to destroy what I had done. I wanted to understand what exactly the vision had meant, but I didn't need any more proof that I had waded into waters too deep for my understanding.

I gathered my notes and my tablet together, and remembered that I had a notebook in my room that had some other thoughts. I stepped into the bedroom and saw the notepad on the nightstand and grabbed it, but just then heard a crash as the front door flew off its hinges.

"The fairy-friend is here— I can smell him," I heard a strange voice say. "Don't let him get away."

As quietly as I could I sneaked down the hall to the side door, and gently closed it behind me. Standing right in front of me was a twisted looking creature, reminiscent of the things I had seen in Fairyland but more human looking. A pipe sat next to the door from some unfinished repair job, and quickly I grabbed it as the creature swung around. Its eyes were yellow and its ears long.

"Fairy-friend," it snarled. The claws lunged out to grab me, but I smacked them away and ran to my vehicle. It gave chase, and I flung the pipe to its legs so that it tripped and fell. As I got in I could hear angry shrieks, and in my rear view mirror I could see a red glow that told me I would soon have no home. I tossed the notes and tablet into the passenger seat.

"What on earth is happening?" I said aloud.

"You were nearly kidnapped by the children of the Gibborim," said a familiar voice. It was Ilumbrado, but I couldn't see where he was.

"Children of the Gibborim?"

"You might know the word goblin," said the voice.

"Those were *goblins*?"

"Not true goblins — you wouldn't fare so well against real goblins. Goblinkin, their blood diluted with human, can sometimes get into your world. You got their attention when you did your experiment."

"I see." I realized that I could dimly see Ilumbrado in the rear view mirror, but he wasn't a reflection — it was like a HoloTV projection of his presence into the surface of the mirror.

"Where should I go? I don't know what to do."

"Go to your friend, the cautious man. He will not

yet be known to the goblinkin. He will be a safe place for you to stay until you can make a plan."

"A plan?"

"About where to go where you can hide what you've found."

"I don't think it would be safe there very long, since John is known as one of my associates. I don't want to endanger him or his family."

I thought about the vision of fairyland, and about the creatures that had almost assaulted me. They were only a foregleam of the things I saw held at bay by the fairy queen's power. If my discovery was made general knowledge, then the protection the fairies provided for humans could be entirely destroyed.

Tomorrow, I would make two phone calls. One would be to shut down my laboratory. And the other would be to NASA. They had made me a standing offer for developing the artificial gravity system on Mars.

"But you should not go to Mars," said Ilumbrado, as if he read my thoughts.

"What? Why not?"

"There is nothing to protect you there. The atmosphere is too thin. You need a place that is harder to reach for humans and whose secrets are more guarded."

At once I knew. I had seen it in my vision in fairyland. A place where I could get sufficient financial support for my scientific project on artificial gravity. A place where even Valentine could see practical use.

"Then it will have to be Saturn, one of its moons. That's a place where I can be a scientist and keep my secrets safe."

But of course there is nothing safe about science, and years later when one of my rock-hoppers "accidentally" crashed into the surface of Saturn with me and five of my coworkers inside, I had no choice but to call upon Ilumbrado and the secrets of Fairyland again. Those five coworkers were like me, you see — something in their blood was drawn to the place where science touches the symphony of the spheres.

So now you too must make a decision. Join us and become a Chronotopian, or have your memory wiped clean. Either way, Fairyland must be kept hidden. Fairyland must be kept safe.

All Bright Things

by Evangeline Giaconia

In the darkness of the titan's stomach, my sister fights to claw her heart from her chest.

I do not let her. That same heartbeat keeps me alive, too, for I have none of my own. We sit back-to-back and palm-to-palm in the darkness, Hestia doing all she can to yank free of my stone grip.

This will pass, I tell her, I tell the infinite darkness. It will pass like the others, though it is taking longer and longer. Stay with me, Hestia. I am nothing without you—do not even have a name of my own, as all gods are born knowing. I am only your pebble, or I am nothing.

Do not leave me here alone.

Once, it was she who held me. Terrified, blind, I was a sacrifice that was never supposed to live. In my ears, she whispered stories. I listened to her heartbeat, the very one she tries to stifle, and it saved my life.

I'll tell you the same story now, my sister. The one

you used to soothe me with, those ages ago. How long? We cannot know. Long enough, you suspect, to be forgotten. Forsaken.

The history of the universe starts with Gaia. Your grandmother, Hestia. My carver. Do you remember your brief glimpse of her before the darkness? Gaia, the sand and the mountains and the strong hands that chiseled my eyelids from stone. She brought everything out of nothing, just like me. Including her own husband and downfall: Ouranos. The firmament that blankets the earth. Like a blanket, Ouranos smothered.

They had children, those two. A universe of them. Titans and monsters and the infinite stars—

My sister sobs like she is dying. I should not have mentioned the stars. I have never known anything but the darkness, but Hestia caught a single glimpse of their radiance, between birth and consumption. The memory of their light haunts her.

Those children that Ouranos hated, he locked inside Gaia's belly of earth. Hestia is calmer now, so I take her hand and we reach out together, to feel the walls around us, the belly in which we have grown. Her to womanhood, I to adulthood—being a child of stone, I am neither man nor woman.

We, too, are hated monsters.

Ouranos slaughtered all who rose against him, except the last. Kronos. His son. Our swallower.

At his name, Hestia rips away from me and throws herself upon the walls, tearing and screaming and rending—Kronos' flesh, her own, bruising her fists on my stone arms as I haul her away again. I wrap her in my arms, and we rock.

My gentle sister. My twin in this strange second womb, my heartbeat in the dark. Once, you named me your pebble, for I have no name of my own. Once, you told me of the stars.

Kronos turned on Gaia too, of course. Wrung her power from her and took her daughter Rhea as his wife. Gaia was reduced to wandering her own shores, while Rhea came to know her husband.

Paranoid. Terrified. When Kronos went to sleep at night under the vast blanket of his father, reduced to stars, he dreaded that his own children would overthrow him in turn.

So, he took steps.

Rhea bore him a child, of course. You, Hestia. Do you remember? You were a new thing, neither mortal nor titan. But Kronos was waiting, mouth gaping, as Rhea birthed you. As you fell past your mother's knees, he swallowed you whole, severed the umbilical cord with his teeth before you saw anything more than the stars.

We share the same first memory, my sister and I. It used to make her laugh.

I do not speak of this to Hestia, but I imagine Rhea despaired—as much as a stone child can know of despair. Her arms must have ached to hold her daughter, her teeth to tear her husband limb from limb. She should have learned from Gaia. The titan who had cast aside his mother for power would never allow himself to be conquered in turn.

Hestia has calmed at last, exhausted in my arms. I would pray that it lasts, but there is no one to pray to who is not complicit in her suffering. This is where I come in, I whisper into her hair, feel her tired smile in the darkness. Me. The trick. The false babe that you raised when you yourself were just a girl, trapped in darkness.

Rhea found herself again with Kronos' child: another daughter who kicked at her divine body. Rhea would have pummeled the child to death inside her stomach to save it the fate of Kronos' maw, but her daughter was as immortal as she.

So, she called her mother.

Gaia came in the night with a plan. That was me, the plan. She played midwife and kicked Kronos from the room, telling him it would be a long and difficult birth. Her son stalked the door, salivating as Rhea labored.

But my carver labored too.

Hestia is trembling again. The episodes are longer and longer, the time between them ever decreasing. She cries for the stars. I cannot give them to her; I do not know what they look like. All I can do is tell her how it was to be brought forth from stone.

It was like waking from a long slumber, though I had not been asleep. I remember the sensation of Gaia chisling the seam of my mouth, freeing my lips. I can still feel the delicacy with which she hollowed out my ears, until I could hear the groaning and sobbing of Rhea and the animal painting of her husband beyond the door.

But at last, there I was, a finished child of stone, and so our new sister could finally be born.

It was an easy birth. Demeter fell quietly into her grandmother's waiting hands. Gaia bound the child close to her side under her clothes and took me up. My skin was so tender and new—I felt everything so keenly as Gaia coated me in Demeter's birthing blood and tucked me between Rhea's legs. And I heard Rhea's almighty scream of anguish—unfeigned, I think, for her daughter had once again been taken from her. Though, of course, what does a stone child know of anguish?

At the sound of her pain, Kronos burst through the door. Seeing the imitation godling nearly to the ground, he dropped to the floor and swallowed me whole.

I landed in his stomach next to you, sister.

And that is the end of our story, so far as either of us can suppose.

I'm sorry, Hestia whispers to me. Her first words in a long while.

Don't be sorry, I tell her. Just don't leave me.

But my sister takes my stone hand and places it over her heart. She presses my fingers into her skin. I'm sorry, pebble, she says. You were meant for more than this.

I wasn't. I tell her so.

I cannot take another age of this story, she says. Her fingers push mine into the flesh over her heart. The same story, over and over. They are never coming for us, she says. Please. Let me see the stars. Before the darkness takes me again.

My sister's heartbeat pulses under my stone hand.

We are monsters, locked in a belly.

We are firstborn and forgotten, we are a desperate trick.

We are in darkness.

We are alone.

I press my stone fingers towards my sister's divine heartbeat. She presses her face into my neck. She whispers: please, please, please.

She used to tell me different stories. About a sister who would save us, and a mother who remembered us. About the stars we would see.

If there is no heartbeat left in this darkness, maybe then I will return to the stone.

Hestia gasps in my ear. I see them, pebble, she says. I see the stars. Thank you. I see them.

But my fingers still rest light atop her skin.

Her tears roll down my neck. My pebble, they are brighter than I ever remembered.

But I see them too. There is some brightness seeping in through my eyelids, closed tight.

Are we saved?

Are we dead?

Pebble, says Hestia, her voice astonished. It's you, my pebble, it's *you*.

We are not saved. But I am shining. Me, the stone babe, I am shining silver, the darkness dissolving around us. I am starlight.

The first thing I ever see is my sister's face.

Pebble, she calls me, but my name has come to me at last. I am Argyros. Patron of all bright things hidden in the dark.

I take my sister's hands.

We are not saved.

Not yet.

Charon

by Chuck Boeheim

The Captain died during the night. I should say "while I was sleeping" since the night is endless in both time and space. I put a coin in his mouth as he had insisted. I have no coin for myself and no one to put it in my mouth when I die. The Captain said that we cannot leave the shore without a coin.

This doesn't worry me. I'm already lost on the shores of the underworld, as I have been since Cassia crossed the river without me.

I'm the only remaining member of the crew of the *Acheron* out of the six who departed Earth. Jake Clapp and Stefania Bean died early in the mission during a spacewalk to repair the high-gain antenna. Eleanor Ito had appendicitis during the sixth month. She was the doctor and couldn't operate on herself. Leonard Paddington went into a deep depression during the unending night and took his own life (I think he had secretly loved Eleanor). Now Captain Ken Dutton has succumbed to a stroke, an occupational hazard in low G. That leaves me, Simon Aeneas Kost, Captain, science officer, doctor, engineer, and cook, standing all the watches.

It was Ken who started the superstition about the coin. He read constantly, which affected his thinking in subtle and disturbing ways. He brought books that discussed the mythology that gave names to our destination: Pluto, Charon, Styx, Nix, Kerberos, and Hydra. The ancient Greeks believed that souls had to pay a coin to Charon to pole them across the rivers Acheron or Styx to reach their final rest. When Eleanor died, Ken told us of this tradition, produced a coin, and placed it in her mouth. Eccentric, but touching. He told me later that it actually distressed him that Jake and Stefania had tumbled away into the darkness beyond the reach of this ritual. Leonard disliked this superstition but received his own coin when it was his time. Of course, by then he couldn't protest.

TRANSMISSION FROM WSA Mission Control

(Voice of Jeff Marten, mission controller, audio only): Simon, we're all shocked by the news about Captain Dutton. We reviewed your medical telemetry and concur with your assessment that he suffered a massive stroke. You didn't say how you feel now, but I know it must be hard. The doctors want you to know that there wasn't anything you could have done to save him with the medical facilities on board. We have a counselor standing by for you to talk to, but we know that an eight-hour delay for each exchange is not what you need right now. We'll do the best we can to support you however you need. (Sighs.)

Unfortunately, orbital mechanics wait for no man. O2 is a month ahead of you now, and we've detected that it is definitely decelerating. We're waiting for confirming observational fixes, but we're certain it intends to enter orbit around Pluto. We've sent the timing for a turnover and burn that will put you in orbit right behind it a week later. This confirms that O2 is under deliberate control, and we've put our best minds to thinking through the implications. I must tell you that also means we've had to bring in the military for threat assessment. I don't know what they'll come up with, since the only threat O2 has demonstrated so far is celestial navigation.

(Sighs again.) Take care of yourself, Simon. We're here for you, buddy, whatever you need. Here's the next move in our game: King to H2. I have a feeling I know how this one will end.

WSA PRESS BRIEFING for the Acheron mission

The presumed asteroid 'Oumuamua caused a big stir in 2017 as it passed through the solar system on a parabolic orbit. It came from outside the solar system, changed course and velocity during its visit, and then left again for an unknown destination. The object's profile was long and narrow, tumbling as it traveled, though it never came close enough for a clear image. There was widespread speculation that it could be an alien craft, prompting the discoverer to name it "Scout" in the Hawaiian language.

Now 'Oumuamua 2 has arrived. This time we are in a position to send a mission to intercept it. The WSA ship *Serendipity* was ready to depart for the Jovian moons for a research mission. World Space Authority engineers devised an audacious plan to bolt a habitat module scheduled to be launched for Ceres to *Serendipity* as crew quarters for the much longer flight to the outer system. The crew module, dubbed *Acheron*, can also be used to land on 'Oumuamua 2 for exploration.

Acheron's crew of six expects to be able to intercept 'Oumuamua 2 near the orbit of Pluto in only eighteen months, using their newly-developed ion thrusters. This destination was the inspiration for the ship's name, after the river in ancient myths that separates Hades from the land of the living.

IRONIC HOW LONELY I've been since Ken passed away. I didn't even like him that much, but he had been a presence on the ship and that presence was now absent. I volunteered for this mission to get as far away from Earth and her memories as possible within the Solar System. Now that the only sounds are the whirring of the pumps and the pings of the hull cooling in the absolute cold of the night, I missed the bustle of people for the first time in a while. I even missed Ken snoring so loudly that I could not escape, even by moving to the furthest bunk. (I wondered if his sleep apnea contributed to his stroke? Could I have done something?)

The daily briefing from Jeff broke up the day. I sent him the next move in the game. He had eight hours to absorb the inevitable conclusion, then conceded. We hadn't started another one yet.

I had wanted this isolation. I wanted to escape the memories of Athens, of the institute, of Cassia. Who teased me unmercifully when she found that my middle name was Aeneas. Until I found that her middle name was Dido; after that, we said it was fate. But Aeneas and Dido had only a year together, and so did we. After that, it was the slow purgatory of hospitals and bedpans, of toxic drips and radiation after the gene therapies failed. The modern prayers to the old implacable gods of death, and no more effective now than they were when Troy was young. Death has never bargained.

Because we never had time to marry, her family swept her away to their mausoleum. Tied her down with their wealth and their traditions. For two years, I couldn't face going there to acknowledge the stone finality of that resting place. By the time I did, spiders had festooned the crypt with their mourning shrouds. I could not bring myself to touch their clinging strands, though I wanted to brush them away to lay my hand on her granite vault just once. Since I was a child, I could not bear the touch of spider webs, knowing they would trap and suffocate me. I let them keep me from my final farewell before the whirlwind departure of the *Acheron* mission.

I was still unable to face the memories of the times between meeting Cassia and losing her. I went to space because the rocky coastlines and blue waters of the Adriatic reminded me of those times. I couldn't bear them alone. Now I was more alone than anyone in the Solar System, and all I could think of was her tomb.

TRANSMISSION FROM WSA Mission Control

Good morning, Simon, Jeff here, as always. The Farside observatory has confirmed that O2 has committed to an orbital insertion around Charon rather than Pluto as we first thought. We're sending a slight course correction to optimize your own approach into a higher orbit than O2. The mission plan calls for you to slot in on the first pass nineteen days from now.

Oh, and pawn to E4.

SERENDIPITY'S INSERTION burn completed as planned. 'Oumuamua 2 was orbiting at an altitude of 20 km above the surface, completing one pass every 2.8 hours. At my altitude of 40 km, I took 3.1 hours to make a circuit, so I watched O2 slowly overtake me once a day. That allowed me to see the object from a variety of angles. It was 11,142 meters long and 3,420 meters across at its widest point. According to the spectrometer, the surface was stone and water ice, remarkably similar to Charon itself. The surface was irregular and pock-marked like a garden-variety asteroid. There were no external structures that suggested it was anything other than natural. But natural objects don't assume nearly-circular orbits around dwarf planets. I watched it for further signs of activity while reflecting on how the significance of being the first person to reach the Plutonian system had paled in comparison to watching an alien asteroid take up residence there. We weren't even sure it was our destination until a year into the voyage when O2 began braking maneuvers. Now it was just orbiting quietly. I had hoped for something more interesting.

I WISHED for O2 to do something, but its next move was hardly what I had expected. It was *landing* on Charon. It must have made a burn, or a venting, or whatever it does to change course when it was on the other side of the moon. Now it was on a trajectory to intersect with the surface in just an hour. Did it intend to crash? Seems a waste after a voyage that must have spanned tens of thousands, perhaps millions, of years.

O2 CAME to rest on the surface in the center of the great dark spot named the Mordor Macula. (Yes, there's a Mordor on Charon. Check SolarPedia.) The dust kicked up by its braking was still hanging above the surface. There was no air to hold it aloft, but in the .02 G gravity it took a while to settle. The dust was splashed across a twenty-kilometer radius, lighter in color than the surrounding regolith. O2 had painted itself in a giant bullseye. "Here I am! Come see me!" it seemed to say. I started to map the terrain with radar to decide on a landing zone.

I COULDN'T UNDERSTAND the first radar scans, so I ran additional surveys. If we hadn't been equipped with ground-penetrating radar for surveying Ceres, I might not have seen the anomalies. The surface scan showed faint shadows running parallel to O2 on the surface that I had almost dismissed as ripples of dust thrown up by the landing. But the deep scan showed something more interesting — and disturbing. Buried in the regolith of Charon were shapes eleven kilometers long and three kilometers across at their widest point. Hundreds of them were laid out in rows and lines, following the contours of the land. Copies of 'Oumuamua.

It was no longer possible to equivocate whether these objects behaved with intention. Were they space vessels? Did they have crew aboard or robots? Or were they creatures of deep space, leviathans of the Oort clouds, returning to their nest or breeding ground? (I kept that one to myself, though it refused to be dismissed, a shadow in the endless night.)

I stared at the radar images for a long time. They reminded me of something, but I couldn't put my finger on it.

Transmission from WSA Mission Control

Simon, everyone is dizzy with excitement, and you could hardly find someone here who wouldn't trade places with you in a heartbeat. To be the person who finds the first evidence that we're not alone in the universe is ... just amazing. You've secured your place in history, Simon.

We have pools going about what you're going to find. A hibernation ship? Unmanned probe? Derelicts? The military sorts are muttering "Invasion fleet," but we try not to pay attention to them. I won't tell you the odds they're giving so I don't influence you.

Mission control recommends that you continue to observe from orbit for a day or two. O2 might do something to shed light on their purpose or capabilities. It can help us decide how we react to it or if we even should react. Take it slow.

If only Earth wasn't an eight-hour round trip for each message and reply, I might have had to heed that advice to take it slow from people three billion miles removed from the scene. (You can't see me smirking about that.) I had already unbolted *Acheron* from *Serendipity* and readied her for the descent when it arrived. The mission plan had called for a backup pilot to stay with *Serendipity* in case of emergency, but I'm that backup pilot. Instead, I had slaved *Serendipity* to the co-pilot station on *Acheron* in case I needed an imaginary friend in the control seat. Time to begin the descent.

Acheron was designed to land on the surface of Ceres. Charon is slightly larger but has nearly the same surface gravity, so I had plenty of reaction mass for maneuvering. As I came in above the resting place of O2, a ten-second burn killed the forward momentum, then I hovered on a gentle .02 G thrust to survey the landscape. The darker regolith of the Mordor Macula stretched over most of the visible terrain.

Acheron was still four klicks above the surface, but that put me only slightly above the massive form of 'Oumuamua, looking like a mountain come to rest on the plain. The scale of 'Oumuamua hit me viscerally for the first time. I had studied the numbers until I knew them by heart – major axis, minor axis, mass, albedo – but now I understood that my imagination had failed. I was less than a gnat on an elephant to this colossus.

On the spot, I threw out the plans and suggestions of all those who made a career out of planning back at WSA. Landing on the surface and walking up to it was folly. It would loom over my head like an ant's final view of the sole of a shoe. The only sensible place to land was on top of it.

I angled towards the center of the leviathan. Comparisons to a whale, a cigar, or any other cylinder faded away as the altimeter crept downward. At fifty meters, it became a mesa, reasonably flat for half a kilometer on either side. The edges became horizons, nearby on the east-west axis, comfortably distant on the north-south. I was going to set the ship down on the safely uninteresting plain when I saw a shadow to the north (I admit that my assignment of north was arbitrary since there was no motion or magnetic pole to provide a reference). I tilted my thrusters and drifted that way, keeping an eye on my propellant level.

A hole had been punched in the skin of 'Oumuamua. An impact crater from the shape of it. Dark openings in the wall of the crater gave the first indication that there was an interior, though by now it would have surprised me more if there were no secrets within. This was too good to pass up. I touched down in the center of the crater and killed the thrusters.

This was historic on so many levels. The first visitor to the Plutonian system, the first person on Charon, the first person on 'Oumuamua 2, the first person on an extrasolar visitor, the first person to land on an enigma stacked on top of a mystery. I should have thought about what to say.

Time for a video clip to send to the people of the Solar System. I faced the camera and keyed the feed for history's sake: "Well folks, I've landed in Mordor. Let's see if there are orcs."

The mouth of the tunnel was filled with an almost solid blackness. There was no atmosphere to scatter the weak light from distant Sol, so the shadow was like a knife edge. Now I knew what the poets meant by a Stygian darkness. Literally.

The meteorite impact had shattered the walls, but some of the blocks had sides that were cut, not broken. Rubble extended as far as I could see, which wasn't very far, even with a powerful light and amplifying goggles. Actually, the combination wasn't very useful since the amplifiers made the foreground blindingly bright. Didn't anyone test out this equipment? If I aimed the lights at the ceiling, I could get a more uniform light. Ah, that was better. As a bonus, it made the shadows much creepier. I could have done without the bonus.

I weighed less than a small kitten in this gravity, so it was more floating than walking as I made my way inside. At least I could bound over the larger boulders, but I had to be careful landing on the other side. I would wait a long time for someone to come out with a suit repair kit.

The rubble only extended a hundred meters or so. The walls were smoother, but not perfectly so. I could believe that someone made this tunnel, but I could also believe it was a lava tube, like the ones I had seen in Iceland or on the Moon.

A patch of bright reflection caught the light and drew my eye. It was something wispy caught on a sharp rock. Hours of bad television tropes said it should be stirring in a draft, but of course, this place had no air; it hung limp. The back of my brain was certain that it would cling to my glove if I touched it and I would die in a frenzy trying to get it off. My rational brain said, "Don't be silly." Nonetheless, I gave it a wide berth.

A fissure in the side of the tunnel revealed an adjacent passage that looked more intentional than this one. I drew some signs on both sides of the wall in fluorescent paint to help me find my way back. Which way? The left passage sloped down, so I chose it. I descended, drawing new arrows on the wall at intervals.

I also saw that I was leaving footprints in the dust that coated the floor. How many eons had it taken to deposit dust inside an airless asteroid?

I came to an intersection of eight tunnels. I chose a branch, marked my return path carefully, and then repeated the process at two more intersections. Whoever made these passages really liked the number eight. Maybe I don't want to speculate too much here. Layers of planning and method helped bury my fears, but inside I fought the urge to run back to the ship and slam the door behind me.

Another scrap of fabric seemed to drift on the floor. It wasn't moving; it couldn't move in this dead, airless passage. It was just an effect of the light shifting as I carried my torch forward, but my skin prickled with sweat inside my suit. The whine of ventilators picked up, trying to compensate.

There were more tufts now, scattered randomly over the floor or adhering to the walls. There was a pattern in them. They'd been blown from a point farther down the tunnel, rolling until they caught on something or the breeze dropped them. They'd been wafted *from* somewhere toward me. I wanted to run from whatever that is, but I refused to give in.

Then something ghostly white came into view. A vast sheet of gauzy fabric once closed off the tunnel but now hung in tattered strips from the ceiling and sides. The comparison I'd avoided all this time came crashing down on me. Spider webs. Huge, cloying, entangling, smothering webs. Meant to trap and hold intruders who ventured here. For eternity. Or until those who spun them came to collect their husks. And this one had been torn by something larger and stronger than a human.

The strands moved, billowing toward me.

'Oumuamua is twenty percent icy compounds, my scientific training said. The heat from my suit thawed the frozen nitrogen, carbon dioxide, and the traces of helium. Puffs of gasses that hadn't moved in millennia. That's all.

Survival instincts from the dawn of time screamed, "Run!"

I recoiled so hard that I stumbled off balance. Earth muscles sent me careening up to bash my helmet on the ceiling. I'll never know how I kept from breaking my helmet or my neck. The long moment to drift back to the floor afforded me enough time to get my orientation to hit the floor running. I scrambled back up the passage and bombed through the last junction.

A white sheet loomed out of the darkness. I skidded to a stop just in time, though I again banged myself against the tunnel walls. All I could see was white from wall to wall, completely blocking my path. There was something here, something in the dark, sneaking around behind me. Something that spun this web to trap me after I passed through the tunnel. It's the one thing I'm afraid of, more than death itself. The dark cellar of my grandparents. A cobweb-infested cave my friends dragged me to as a teenager. Cassia's mausoleum. Frodo vs. Shelob.

Mordor.

I almost threw myself down in despair (a totally useless gesture in microgravity). I was never going to make it out of here. I couldn't get past this web. If I went back, I would be hopelessly lost in the maze of tunnels. My luck wasn't any better than the rest of the crew who died one by one. Maybe worse. Probably worse. I swallowed past a raw throat. I must have been screaming.

Then I noticed the footprints. Only one set behind me in the passageway. None in front of me. That could only mean that I hadn't been this way before. I must have taken a wrong turn at the previous junction. I only had to retrace my footsteps in the dust to find my way out. With this inglorious admission, I convinced myself that there couldn't be anything here to spin new webs, not after all the eons in vacuum between stars.

I made my way back to the previous junction. I had been a bit sloppy with this mark, and I couldn't tell which of the two passages I should take. The footprints were muddled here, so I started down one of them, looking for clearer signs. My calm was a fragile thing, and that was the biggest understatement this side of Jupiter. I was jumping at every shadow, here in the nesting ground of sinister shadows. Not far down the passage I found the niches. They were three meters tall and two wide, lining both sides of the passage, filled with inky darkness. I shined my light inside.

Why did they have to be spiders?

I somehow found the marking I had left at the previous junction, but otherwise, I remembered nothing of my flight back out of the maze. Nothing until the relief of squeezing into the first lava tube I had found and following it back to the ship. I pulled off my suit and huddled in my bunk until exhaustion finally dragged me down to sleep.

Transmission from WSA Mission Control

Simon, the first contact team is ecstatic over the still pictures you sent of the interior. Why haven't you sent the suit logs and videos yet? Everyone wants them to understand the context of the stills. We also want to hear your commentary and impressions as you went in. You're famous, man! Everyone wants to know your thoughts while walking through the first alien artifact.

The science team wants to know if you brought back samples of that fabric, or web, or whatever it was. They're fascinated to know what material could remain pliable in vacuum at near absolute zero for eons. That alone could revolutionize the construction of our moon and belt habitats.

While you're distracted, Knight to H5.

A DAY TO write and send my reports. A day to get over my shakes. A day to come to grips with going back inside. I largely disregarded the advice from people who weren't out here in the night with me. The sun is only a bright star from Charon, giving no heat or light. This is truly the underworld, far from the living planets.

Jeff wasn't on duty today, which seemed strange. He did send me his next move, though. He moved his rook directly next to my king, sacrificing it for no advantage that I could see. Was that a message? Maybe he's tired of the game?

I tried to plan my next trip into the heart of 'Oumuamua, but all I could see were the billowing strands of web and the nightmare shapes in the dark. I put the still image from my last visit on a screen to study, even though it made my skin crawl. The image was blurred and skewed, just a frame caught by my suit cam while I was in the act of turning to run like a scared child. The creature had a bulbous body and long legs that met at the top. I couldn't tell if there were eight or not, just that there were too many. There were stalks ending in what might be eyes, a face of sorts. Maybe a cluster of sensory organs or manipulators. The overall effect was far too arachnid for me.

What was it? A passenger? A robot? A statue, even? Surely it couldn't be alive after all this time aboard. But the ship was still functioning, wasn't it? It rendezvoused with Charon and made a very precise landing. Was that the hand of automation or intelligence? Do we even know where to draw the boundary between the two?

The answers will come tomorrow. It remains to be seen if I can face them when I find them.

I'LL REMEMBER the dream that woke me for the rest of my life. I came upon a glade in a forest. It was the archetype of all glades, peaceful, sunny, and warm. Low stone walls bounded it, though they didn't define it or create barriers to entry or exit. A stream burbled cheerfully through flower-lined banks. The place was filled with an overwhelming, tangible peace that practically shimmered in the sunlight. In the grass to one side of the stream stood Cassia's sarcophagus on a simple bier, free from the mausoleum's dust, gloom, and spiderwebs. I knew I could reunite with her in some eternal underworld once I paid the ferryman. Then I remembered that I had no coin.

At that, I woke up. I lay for a while, working out the symbolism: I was keeping Cassia in a dark tomb by running from the memories of the happier times we shared. I needed to bring her out into the light and forget the moments when it ended. I had to pay the ferryman to do that. Who was the ferryman and what was his coin?

The feeling of peace remained with me as I faced the day. I read through the communications that arrived while I slept; I felt I should ignore their suggestions through intention rather than neglect. For example, "Look for signs that this is a hibernation ship. It's possible that inhabitants could be revived if the conditions are right." We know that 'Oumuamua had been in flight for millennia because there is no star system anywhere near its flight path as far back as we can trace. There's no way there could be anything living on this ship. I dismissed the suggestion as one of the more paranoid ones. It sounded like someone was looking for that invasion fleet.

It was time to face the darkness of the tunnels again. I retraced my steps to where I found the first spiderforms in their niches. One bit of advice from Mission Control that I did follow was to bring radio repeaters to place at the tunnel junctions. I was chagrined that I hadn't thought of it on my first descent. I could maintain contact with the ship and with Mission Control. I set the comm filters to only forward high-priority messages.

Beyond where I had turned and fled, the corridors went on for kilometers. Every few meters was a niche, and each niche was filled with a spiderform. If this was representative, this single ship could hold millions. Multiplied by the hundreds of ancient ships buried in the regolith, there could be billions of aliens here.

I steeled myself to enter a niche to confront the form inside, which towered over me by over a meter. It did indeed have eight legs, right out of one of my nightmares. Worse, each leg had spikes at all four joints, and the second pair of legs ended in scimitar-like blades. I almost ran right then. I was facing something that might be a natural war machine.

I might have run, but then I noticed that the first pair of legs ended in hands. Six-fingered, with two opposable thumbs, but they were long, delicate fingers suitable for making tools or manipulating instruments. They were chitinous, like the rest of the body, but they were the first things that told me this was a being that had evolved from its ancestors, as I had from the apes.

The carapace covering the creature was covered in intricate patterns. It also bore cracks and scars, which spoke of a long life. As I examined the outer shell, I noticed that the spikes were noticeably worn, but evenly, as if they had been filed. The knife-like second appendages were covered in leather-like gloves. Were these decorative, or to prevent accidental harm?

The niche wall was lined with clear blocks, like an acrylic resin. Within each block hung an expressive carving, frozen in time, unchanged from the day they were made.. I wasn't sure what they represented, but they had been carved from a wood-like substance in minute detail. I looked over my shoulder and found that the gaze of the spiderform rested on these creations. Its posture suddenly seemed one of reverent contemplation, not of threat.

In the next niche, a somewhat smaller spiderform

rested. The sides of this niche were hung with knotted creations made from the white web-like fabric I had already seen. Euclid would have pointed smugly to their geometrical designs as proof that the golden ratio was indeed the universal truth that he had claimed. The spiderform held another tapestry in its forehands, as if interrupted in weaving it. Had some disaster befallen the ship that killed all the passengers? I looked for signs that these "cabins" might have been sealed at one time, but found none. They had seemingly been built open to the vacuum of space. That also seemed to rule out a sleeper ship. What was this?

I entered a third niche. This spiderform held an instrument with silver strings. From the relative lengths of the strings, I think their musical scales wouldn't have sounded foreign to us. In a fourth niche, there was a board on a small pedestal. It had six sides and was inscribed with a hexagonal grid. On the board were small objects: three cylinders on end, two stars, a small knife, and an oval with an inset circle. This was certainly an alien chessboard. I felt a spark of kinship.

I noticed that in the upper corner of each doorway hung strings of web material, knotted in patterns down their lengths. I intuited that this must be their written language. They had labeled the cabins, or their contents. It suddenly hit me what this place could be.

My radio crackled to life.

> *"Simon, this is Jeff. I only have a moment to slip this communication in. Mission Control has been taken over by a military task force who sees 'Oumuamua as a threat.*

*They've sent Serendipity a new pro-
gram to accelerate into an elliptical
orbit and then crash into your location. We've learned that they installed a nuclear device onboard
before your departure, and kept it
off all the plans. We never knew it
was there. The device will detonate
on impact and probably crack
'Oumuamua wide open. I can't
stop it. Your only chance is to lift off
in Acheron and get clear. You've
only got about two hours. Run!
Damn, they've—"*

The transmission cut off.

Now I knew what the warning behind the castle sacrifice in the chess game had been. If I hadn't been so wrapped up in my own thoughts, I might have understood it.

I scrambled and almost bashed my helmet into the tunnel ceiling. Again. You can only hurry in low G by going slowly. I kept my pace to a controlled lope as I hurried to the last intersection at a snail's pace. I lurched from side to side a few times. At first, I thought I was being clumsy, but the third time felt like I was *pushed.* Then I saw a piece of web fabric tumble past me, and I knew what was going on. Something was outgassing. Charon was slightly warmer than the depths of space; some solid nitrogen was sublimating into gas. Perfectly normal behavior for an asteroid.

Halfway up the next tunnel, an invisible hand lifted me and thrust me forward. I tumbled, tucking my head into my arms to protect my helmet. I felt debris ping around me. 'Oumuamua had belched gently into the night, and I was afraid it could kill me.

Debris blew past me for several minutes before the outgassing died away. I scrambled the last few hundred meters to the crevice to the lava tube. At first, I couldn't find it and thought I was lost. Then I saw that a sheet of web had covered it, blown by the brief storm. I just had to peel it away to get back to the ship.

I was up against the thing I couldn't do. The web would catch me in its tangle if I put even a finger on it. I would be a helpless fly, buzzing in its clinging strands. It would cover my mouth and eyes, stopping my breath and keeping me from seeing the horrors creeping up behind me. But if I couldn't tear through the web, I would die in the fire of someone else's fear – the fear of strangers.

Cassia came to me then. Not in words but with her presence. She lent me her eyes to see the iridescence of the web and the beauty of its folds. There was an eight-way warp and weft in the weaving that echoed, or perhaps begat, their design principles. She lent me her hand to keep mine steady as I grasped one edge of the shroud and pulled it away from the opening. I found that it was clingy but not sticky. It peeled easily away in one sheet. I stepped carefully, keeping my arms and legs well clear of the tangling folds. Then I was through.

I slammed into the control couch in *Acheron* with barely a memory of the last sprint up the tunnel and through the lock. It would have been easy to lift off, get clear, and land on the other side of Charon. Wait for rescue. That would be fate, but I was burdened with the name of Aeneas. I had a destiny.

Where was *Serendipity*? I couldn't find it at first,

but then the computer plotted its current location for me. It was on the other side of Charon, doing a burn. It had lifted into a ballistic ellipse and was now lining up its course on my present location. I couldn't communicate with it until it cleared my horizon. I plotted the elements of the ship's flight path: it was coming in low and fast. I might have two minutes of clear line-of-sight.

I wouldn't have the chance to apply much of a course change at that velocity. I had to rotate *Serendipity* ninety degrees, then engage the main thrusters. The rotation would take forty-five seconds out of the one hundred and twenty I had available. It was going to be close.

Radar picked up the blip of *Serendipity* before I had visual contact. The light of the distant sun was so weak that I might never see it before it hit. Where was the communication link? The signal acquisition light stayed stubbornly dark. I hadn't counted on this delay.

Could I still get out? No. The launch sequence was a minimum of five minutes, even skipping all the WSA-mandated safety checks.

I felt Cassie lay her hand on mine. The peace I had felt earlier returned. The seconds ticked down. Whatever might happen, will happen.

The signal acquisition light blinked amber, then steadied. I transmitted the course change order and held my breath.

I could see nothing in the endless night. *Serendipity* reflected no light, and the ion drive was invisible. The telemetry showed no change. Had they locked out my controls?

The clock ticked down to zero. Time stood still. Then *Serendipity* flashed overhead, barely two hundred meters over my base, nose towards the stars. A whirlwind followed on the surface on a leash kilometers long as the ion drive splashed against the face of Charon. I tracked it by eye until I lost it, then on radar as it ascended again. I had sent the signal in time, and the ship barely missed me. Many minutes later, a star bloomed in the sky as my ride home destroyed itself.

WHO KNOWS why the spiderforms send the 'Oumuamua ships to Charon? Maybe they originated there. Perhaps our sun occupied a significant position in the constellations in their skies. Why do humans choose certain places to raise their monuments? All cultures have their irrational practices, deeply meaningful to themselves but impossible to explain to others.

'Oumuamua is a necropolis ship. They send their honored dead to this cold world for their eternal rest. Is it coincidence or fate that we named the same world for the ferryman of the underworld?

I'm guessing that the original 'Oumuamua in 2017 was knocked off course by some collision between the stars. That would explain the tumble. Or maybe there are other underworlds on the edges of other star systems, and that 'Oumuamua had a different destination than this one? We may never know.

I have supplies meant for six people. I can wait while they decide if they're going to rescue me. I'm persona non grata to the military and other xenophobes. I'm a hero to the scientific community, the only on-site expert in spiderform culture. (As their discoverer, I have named their race the *Gossameri*.) I expect that evidence that there is no threat will prevail and Earth will send a ship for me. If not, I can be at peace with that. I've been to the underworld and back.

Cassia is with me now. Not in any mystical way, but I'm letting myself have those memories that I denied myself since losing her. Like other Greek heroes, I have made the journey to the underworld while still a mortal and brought her out. I have faced my fears and not found myself wanting. The ancients called this transformation Catabasis.

Catabasis requires one to make an exceptional gift to Charon, the ferryman. My gift is that those dead who lie here on Charon's surface will remain in peace, undisturbed. Humanity's first encounter with an alien race will not end with the destruction of their graveyard.

THE PERSEID

BY BENJAMIN CHANDLER

There is a man on the island.

She saw the sail bobbing on the western horizon the day before, a slash of white cutting against the blues of sea and sky. At first she thought it was a flash of sunlight on a wave or a gull's lifted wing, but it remained in sight all day, weaving a path closer and closer over the tossing waves.

When the boat was near enough for her to see a man standing on its deck, she sprinted to the other side of the island and into the temple ruins she calls home. There, she opened a wooden chest and dug through its contents of clothing, baubles, and tools to uncover an old short sword she had discovered in the caves.

Picturing the man setting foot on the island, she began to run the rusty blade against a stone. She did it more to encourage herself than to actually sharpen the sword. No amount of effort would make that old blade hold an edge; she would more likely bludgeon someone with it than cut them. Every social more she was taught commanded kindness to strangers, but those norms were challenged by dozens of tales of libidinous men and the pregnant women they leave behind. She needed only look to her paternal grandmother for an example. When the majority of the rust had been scraped from the sword, she asked virginal Athena for protection from licentious men, and readied herself for a fight. She stayed in the ruins all day, waiting for the stranger to appear. He never did. When sleep arrived last night, it was restless. She jumped at every odd sound—a groaning frog, a startled petrel—then spent uncounted minutes trying to force sleep. Usually the sound of the waves thrumming at the base of the eastern cliffs lulled her to sleep, but last night it sounded like a repeating omen.

This morning, groggy, upset over the nervous night, she breakfasted on a handful of nuts then left the temple to get water from the inland spring. She took the sword.

She is near the spring when she first sights the man now. She ducks behind a bush to watch him, palms sweating against the sword's handle. He does not see her.

He is blonde with bright eyes. His arms are robust with big, knuckle-scraped hands at the ends of them. He tramps across the field, singing to himself. He has no weapons visible, not even a knife, but he does carry an odd, square-shaped object in one hand and a thing that looks like a reed in the other. He still does not see her—all of his attention is being given to a statue in the field, the one she calls "the Pivoter." It is of a man turning his torso to look at something behind him. Like all the statues on the island, it is pure white marble and gleams in the sun.

When the stranger comes within an arm's length of the Pivoter, he circles it, eyes flowing over its contours as if looking for secrets. He pulls a cubit-long string from a pocket in his tunic and uses it to measure the length of the limbs, the breadth of the torso, the circumference of the head. Finally he sits in the grass, folds his legs, and opens the square in his hand. It is a codex. With the charcoal-tipped reed, he begins to draw the statue in his little book. He draws like this for an hour, occasionally moving to a new spot on the ground to depict the sculpture from a different angle.

She has never seen an artist study statues, only natural objects like animals, fruit, and people. Her parents often hosted sculptors and painters at the Mycenaean palace. There, they displayed their talents, jockeying for a commission. The king and queen were generous patrons. The palace was filled with mosaic floors, sculptures of people from legend and history, family portraits in marble friezes, animated fountains, lurid tapestries, labyrinth-patterned rugs, pottery bedecked in patterns and myths. The royal residence was a celebration of the finest creators in Hellas.

She adored the artists' attention, sitting for them as they painted her portrait or chiseled a bust of her face. They called her looks exotic because of her half-Ethiopian heritage. One sculptor by the name of Ekhinos spent six weeks trying to execute the precise curls of her hair in stone. Being a spoiled sixteen-year-old princess, she welcomed his focus with blushes and demure glances. His final piece was an uncanny facsimile of her.

She wonders where it is now—kept in the palace as a sign of affection or dumped in a garbage fill as a display of chastisement?

Knees aching, she remains in her hiding spot even after the man has walked away, emerging only when certain he will not return. She inspects the statue to make sure that he has not damaged it. Aside from a thread she brushes from the statue's shoulder, it is still pristine.

She does not look for the man, but goes to scrutinize a trio of nearby statues. They appear untouched by the stranger too. She pulls a weed from the foot of one, wipes gull droppings off the shoulder of another. She wonders if the man knows that someone else is on the island, maintaining it and its marble men. When she first arrived here, the statues were overgrown, hidden under climbing weeds and snaking thorns. One was even wedged within the crook of a tree's branches, apparently carried aloft as the tree grew under it. She spent two years clearing the vegetation from the marbles and another two washing away the dirt, moss, and lichens that spotted the stone.

The following day she is in the Minor Courtyard where six statues stand. The marble men are beautiful, youths in the prime of their lives, all lusty sinew and muscle as if sculpted by Prometheus himself, completely perfect save one ugliness. Each statue's beauty is marred by the unpleasant looks etched on their uplifted faces—horror, dismay, dread, awe. It is while she is in this uncanny garden that the man returns. She darts behind a column that marks a path to the caves under the island and watches him, heart thudding, hand wrestling with the handle of the old sword.

He is agog at the sight of the marble figures. As during the day before, he prowls around them, studies their details like a hawk spying voles in a field. He measures his string against one—the statue she calls "the Javelinist"—notes the cubits, then sits to draw. His focus is so intense he starts to sweat, drenching the collar and pits of his tunic.

She decides he is no danger to the statues. Maybe not to her, either. Perhaps tomorrow she will not haul the sword during her errands.

Still, she does not want him to know she is there. When he sits with his back to her, she hurries into the caves and out of sight. The caverns are not her favorite place on the island—most of their tunnels smell of reptiles and death and grow too lightless to be safe—but there is a short avenue not too dark or dangerous within in them, which she knows will spit her out near the bluffs, far from the man's range of sight. A chill climbs her spine when, just as she enters the cave, she hears a male voice call, "Is someone there?" Ignoring it, she rushes into the dark.

The abandoned temple sits on the east side of the island. She believes it was built during the Golden Age, when the goddess Astraea lived among a just and perfect humanity, before men and women soured and she fled to the stars. It is populated with weird carvings of bearded black bulls and winged white snakes and unfamiliar letterforms. No doubt the words are prayers to deities long forgotten. She sleeps there, hoping that her grandfather will speak on her behalf if an unrecalled god grows offended by her stay.

Come morning, a shadow slides over her half-closed eyes. They flick open to see the man standing over her, staring in astonishment.

With a gasp, she leaps to her feet. Clumsily she scoops up the rusty short sword and points it in his direction.

He speaks first:

"Hello."

She stands, mute, heart drumming, sword poised between them.

"I didn't know the island was inhabited," he says. "I barely believed the island existed until I got here." His eyes glance uncomfortably at the sword. "I am unarmed," he offers. "I carry just a pencil, a piece of string, and this papyrus codex. My name is Polykleitos. I am a sculptor."

She lets the sword tip rest on the temple floor, but maintains her grip on its handle.

"What's your name?" he asks.

She opens her mouth to answer, but her name does not come to her at first. She has been alone for so long it seems irrelevant. "Autochthe," she hears herself say and thinks, Yes, that's right.

"Autochthe?" he repeats. "That's an unusual name."

"I have never met a Polykleitos before, either," she snips.

"I mean no offense, but it is well known that Autochthe is a name only used once, given to the daughter of Perseus and Andromeda."

"Yes," she says. "That is who I am."

Polykleitos furrows his brow, digesting her claim. "Perseus and Andromeda were from the Age of Heroes over a thousand years ago. You can't possibly—"

Her stare makes him bite his tongue.

She hefts her sword to point it in the direction of the eastern waters. "That way lies the River Styx, and beyond it is timeless Hades. The island's proximity to it has strange effects, or so my father once told me."

"Your father? Perseus?"

"Yes."

"*The* Perseus. The gorgon slayer."

"I'm glad my family's legacy remains intact," she smiles. As a child she listened to her father recite the story of her mother and himself, and she never tired of it. Her older siblings rolled their eyes, having heard about Medusa and the sea monster too many times, but it always felt fresh to her. Perhaps that was because details—sometimes even major elements—changed from telling to telling. In one account, there were three gorgons on the edge-of-the-world island; other times there was just one. One night her father said he killed the great Cetus with a look from Medusa's disembodied head, the next he said he slew the sea dragon with the thrust of a divine diamond sword. Her mother never corrected him, just smiled.

Those memories now feel bittersweet. She knew that since time worked differently on the island that more time had likely passed in Mycenae than had here, but a thousand years?

"Why are you here, Princess Autochthe?" He says her name as if yet in disbelief. She is fine with that; her name still sounds strange to her, too. However, she is not ready to answer his question.

"Are you hungry?" she asks.

"Very," he says. "I have been feeding on raisins, cheese, and whatever tiny fish snag in my net. I would eat like a Persian if given the opportunity."

She stifles a laugh. "I may not be able to offer an Achaemenid's feast, but I can give you something more substantial than raisins."

He assists her in bringing up crab traps from the bottom of a nearby bluff and helps pick wild cherries and dewberries from a neighboring copse. They pass more than one statue in doing so, and Autochthe notes the sculptor feasting on each marble man with his eyes. "They're exquisitely crafted," he sighs, allowing a finger to trace the line on one statue where the muscles of the shoulder merge with the arm.

Autochthe smiles. "I'm glad you don't find them gruesome. I have worked hard to keep them pristine."

"They are yours?"

"No, I am only the caretaker, trimming vines, removing gull scat, maintaining my island garden of marble men."

Polykleitos turns his eyes from the statue to Autochthe. He has the same focused look that the artist Ekhinos gave her when he studied her hair for her bust in Mycenae. Only this sculptor is not studying the curl of her hair or the planes of her face. Nor is he interested in the way the hem of her clothing loops around her dark arms or catches at her clavicle. He seems instead to be looking inside her, and Autochthe feels her stomach flutter. "You are alone here?" he asks.

"Yes," she says. The question makes her wish she had her sword.

He looks again at the nearby marbles. "Don't you get lonely?" he asks.

"No," she says, but then wonders if that answer is true.

"I've been known to talk to stone," he says, "to coax the figure from it when carving, but I'd go mad if marble were my only companion."

His admission settles her nerves, makes her feel strong. They breakfast outside the temple, cooking the crabs over a fire, cracking the shells between smooth, flat stones.

"I wish I had some bread," Autochthe says.

"I wish I brought some to give you," Polykleitos says.

"How did you find this island?"

The sculptor finishes chewing a bit of crab and opens his codex to show her the drawings and notes inside. They are quite good. Autochthe recognizes each statue he has drawn.

"I've long desired to be the world's greatest sculptor," Polykleitos says. "Even as a boy, making men of clay on the banks of the Charadros River, I tried to mold them as true to life as my little fingers could manage. Eventually, I studied under an Argive master —and excelled—but I believed there was more I could learn.

"While studying texts in a Sicyonian library, I read of an island at the edge of the world filled with beautiful sculptures. Statues so perfect in proportion that they almost seemed to breathe. I didn't believe it. Then I met a drunk seaman from Assyria who told a similar story. His breath stank of wine, but his eyes blazed with sincerity. When I encountered the rumor for a third time in a crumbling scroll from Ikonium, I knew I had to find this place.

"No one would sail me here. Every freighter and seafarer said I was mad. So I decided to sail alone. I'm not sure how I arrived here. It must have been the gods' doing more than my own."

"And are the statues as fine as you hoped?" Autochthe asks.

"Even better! I am humbled. I have a long road ahead of me if I want to be one tenth as skilled as the artist who crafted these."

Autochthe offers him more cherries and says, "When we're done eating, I'll take you to a spot on the island that you might find inspiring."

Polykleitos wolfs down the rest of his breakfast.

At the center of the island lies its widest, darkest cave, and at its mouth sprawls the Great Courtyard. Its architecture is similar to the abandoned temple's. There are bearded bulls and pennate serpents on the fallen columns and crumbling walls, but these are not what she wants to show Polykleitos. The courtyard and nearby cave mouth is filled with dozens of pure white marble men just as life-like as the others on the island. The sculptor chokes at the sight, then gallops to them, leaving Autochthe grinning behind him. It is thrilling to see these stone men through his fresh eyes.

As before, Polykleitos sits near one and begins taking notes and making drawings. His stem of charcoal flys over the papyrus like a wasp building a nest. He does not even stop for lunch when Autochthe brings him some fruit. Finally, at dusk, he comes to her and asks for an apricot, wiping his black fingers on the grass.

"Did you watch me the whole time?" he asks.

"Yes," she says, feeling heat rise in her cheeks.

"Were you worried I would damage the sculptures?"

"No, no. I watched because ... it is wonderful to see someone so animated by passion."

"I suppose around all these marbles, I must be like Boreas himself, gusting like a winter wind."

"Maybe gentler. It is only your hand and eyes that move. You are Zephyr, not Boreas."

He bites the apricot and it is already half gone.

Suddenly, she is weeping. Seeing this man bite the fruit, seeing the juice dribble onto his hand, seeing him wipe it on his tunic, seeing a living, breathing being after Chronus knows how many years of isolation brings forth a deluge of emotions, not the least of which is the final acknowledgment of how much time has passed beyond her island's shores. She cannot keep the thoughts at bay anymore. The whole world beyond her isle has changed. Every person she loved is gone while she has remained alone, barely aging.

His hand alights on her shoulder, then another slides over her back in a hesitant embrace. She hears his voice, "What's wrong?"

"They're all gone. A thousand years gone."

"Who?" he asks.

"My family. Everyone. I loved them so much. Why did I run away?"

His hug loosens and she knows he is studying her again like one of the marbles. Finally he says, "You really are Princess Autochthe."

She sniffs, blinks away heavy tears, and nods, clutching him tightly, hoping he will return the embrace in kind. When his arms retighten around her frame, she says:

"When I counted enough summers, I was engaged, sight unseen, to the king of Athens. My mother said I would be happy with the man, but he had a reputation. He'd already divorced and discarded a half-dozen women because they did not conceive a son. I feared I'd be ex-wife number seven.

"The night before the wedding, I fled, paying a sailor to navigate a sloop across the Okeanos til we skirted the headwaters of the Styx. He insisted we turn back at the sight of the Underworld's river, but I promised him three stolen chains of my mother's pearls if we arrived on this island. As soon as I disembarked, he snatched the pearls from my hand and let the wind whisk him away. He was the last living being I saw before you arrived."

Polykleitos stares.

Autochthe sees herself reflected in his blue eyes

and weeps again, thinking of her mother and father and the weight of their loss on her heart. "All these years," she says between sobs, "I imagined my parents were still alive out there, beyond the sea. Somehow I always believed I would see them again. Now I never will."

He says nothing, just draws her to sit on the ground. He does not speak, but his arms around her express empathy and presence enough. She wants to sink into those arms, let them cover her like the ocean. The evening sky darkens further and its first stars flicker into sight.

When her tears finally stop, she wipes her nose on a silk handkerchief from a hidden pocket. "A princess should be better composed," she chides herself.

"Princesses are not allowed feelings?" The sculptor clicks his tongue and says, "I am woefully untrained in princess etiquette."

She smiles a bit, feels his heart beat against her body. It is good to not be alone.

"Look over there," he says, and points towards the northern sky.

"What am I supposed to see?" she says. "Stars?"

"Yes," he says. "Those stars in particular. Can you see how they make a line with a little prong extending from them?" His fingers trace a row of stars not far above the horizon.

"I think so."

"That is the constellation Andromeda."

She puts her hand on his. "Show me again."

He does, then points out another cluster of stars that compose an inverted ypsilon. "That constellation is your father, Perseus. When your parents passed from this world into the next, the gods put those up for all to see for all time. When you miss your parents, you can look and find them there."

It is a tender enough thought to comfort her for now, and she leans against the sculptor in thanks. They sit together, watching the stars shimmer, until she yawns. He walks her back to the temple and says he will see her in the morning, walking off into the night to wherever it is he has made his camp. The sound of the waves remind her of his steady heartbeat as she drifts to sleep.

When dawn arrives, Autochthe finds Polykleitos marching towards the temple, a smile on his face. She offers him another breakfast. It is the same kind of food as yesterday, but he eats with gusto.

"Will you draw more of the statues today?" she asks.

He bites a cherry and tosses its pit far into the grass. "No," he says, "my codex is filled after yester-day's excursion—all thanks to you. I don't have enough space to add even an iota."

Something stills in her. "Does that mean you will leave?"

"And go back to Argos? Yes. I am inspired! I cannot wait to create, having learned what I have. Truth be told, I've long had in mind to compose a treatise on mathematics and a figure's ideal propor-tions, and my measurements here seem to prove those theories."

She nods.

He looks at her, not with the studying intensity as before, but with an earnestness that verges on affec-tion. "You can come with me," he says. "You don't need to hide from that king of Athens anymore. He's gone to the Underworld generations ago."

She looks at him, feels the tug of his words.

"Who will care for the cemetery if I leave?" she asks.

"Cemetery?"

"Yes," she says, taking in his confused look. "Do you not know where you are? Who these statues are?"

He stares blankly, then shakes his head. In that instant, the lure of his offer snaps like a cheap thread.

"These are not sculptures," she says. "They weren't carved. They are petrified men,heroes who tried to slay the Medusa and failed.

"Each one of these statues was once a living man and is now a grave."

The sculptor goes ashen. "Gods!" he breathes, drawing his arms around himself as if chilled. "This island is—is Sarpedon? The gorgon's island?"

The princess nods. "Yes, and I am its keeper. The dead must be respected. This is one of the gods' oldest laws. Someone must tend these graves and keep them pristine."

"But, before you arrived, no one cared for these petrified men—"

"And do you think their souls rested with their graves desecrated by seabird droppings and crawling thorns? Would you risk their unhappy spirits to haunt you for taking me from them?"

"Surely someone else... Perhaps exiles or prisoners —"

"So my sacred service equals punishment for others?"

"Apologies, your highness, I misspoke. I mean... You have served a thousand years. Any debt the living owe these men..." His words trail off as her expression grows as cold and still as her marble wards.

The waves crash below the bluffs. The sculptor, though he could be touched if she reached out her arm, seems very far away, like a cloud drifting to the horizon. And yet, his blue eyes never looked bigger. She feels them draw her, trying to renew the thread that connected them. She wishes they were still in each other's arms like the night before. The past always eclipses the present.

After some time he says, "You will not come."

The resignation is so deep in his voice that she feels she must comfort him now. "As surely as it was my father's destiny to slay the gorgon, it is mine to tend her victims," she says.

He looks at the ground, then at her. "I will visit you again," he says with a kind smile. She doubts the promise as soon as she hears it, but says nothing and lets it be true between them for a little while.

She says she will help him prepare to depart and see him off. Just because she must stay does not mean she cannot enjoy his company for a little longer. They do not talk much as they walk to his ship on the other side of the island. She looks at his hands and tries to imagine them covered in white dust, holding a mallet and chisel, pulling forms from slabs of marble. They will be beautiful sculptures.

He embraces her tightly when he is ready to leave. It is warm and tight. "Thank you," he says. "Take care of yourself and these men."

She nods into his shoulder, a lump clouding her throat. If she speaks she knows she will start to cry and doubt her decision.

Soon his boat is just a slash of white on the horizon again. Then it is gone. She stays on the shore, listening to the kittiwakes and the surf, watching the sky go from day to afternoon to evening. As the heavens darken, she spots the constellations he pointed out the night before and whispers a hello to them.

Someday, she muses, she may see a new constellation appear in the sky, and if she does, she promises to tell herself that it is Polykleitos immortalized.

The Legend of Johnny Comet

by Benjamin Brinks

The Langford Speedway shut down several decades ago but the oval track is still there. Today it languishes mostly forgotten in a provincial park, there to astonish hikers, picnickers and dog walkers who may happen upon it. It's a quiet spot now, nothing more than a sun-cracked oval of asphalt. Gone are the colorful plastic bunting flags, spectator bleachers and concession stands selling poutine and Sleeman's beer in plastic cups.

Gone, too, is the reek of hot motor oil and the thunder of stock car engines. I smell and hear those things even now. Nor can I ever forget the feral brown eyes of the racer everyone called Johnny Comet.

That wasn't his birth name. He was born Aksel Elden, a respectable if ordinary John-Smith of a name in his family's point of origin, Norway. But such a moniker would never do for a winner of provincial trophies and modestly high national ranking. It certainly didn't suit a racer whom the tire dealership at which I worked desired to sponsor.

Besides, Johnny was fast. Very, very fast.

Now, when I say *oval* you need to understand that a stock car track is two straightaways and two corners —semi-circles, really. Detractors dismissively remark that stock car racing is nothing but left hand turns, but that's not true. A short track like Langford demands a great deal of strategy and even greater nerves. Since modifications to frame, engine and drivetrain were highly regulated in those days, there were few mechanical advantages to rely upon. Moving up in a race was mostly a matter of daring. Still is.

There are two opportunities to move up: straightaways and corners. Short straightaways like Langford's offer only seconds for a burst of speed. Corners are arguably the better opportunity but, either way, moving up is never without risk. In racing, as in life, there is a fundamental choice: drive safe or arrive first.

Make no mistake, Johnny Comet had plenty of nerve. He also had an arch rival in Duke Demarkian. "The Duke" was all but unbeatable. Always in first position at the start, he never gave it up. Overtaking The Duke was Johnny's obsession. In that summer of 1966, Johnny and The Duke would face off in the BC Classic: a three-hundred-lap grind around the Langford oval. Six hundred straightaways and six hundred corners, all chances for Johnny Comet to pass The Duke.

Now, again, when I say *oval* there's something else you need to know. At Langford, the southern corner was not a perfect semi-circle. It was slightly bowed out of shape, as if dented by a hammer. Spectators couldn't see that small distortion in the curve but drivers certainly felt it. Langford's southern corner was tricky and dangerous. And why was that corner bent out of shape?

Because of The Rock.

THE ROCK. It was a boulder, in truth, higher than two men and broader than two cars. There was no moving it. Some glacier, I imagined, had carelessly dropped it in that spot eons ago.Whoever designed the track had not taken it into account, or perhaps construction began before it was realized how The Rock would skew the southernmost corner. There was nothing to do but to leave it where it was, a dinosaur of a stone squatting only twelve feet away from the track surface.

The Rock imposed caution in drivers rounding the southern corner. It was not a place where you'd want to spin out of control. The grass shoulder was narrow, yielding little grace, barely buffering an immovable obstacle which, if struck, would not give one goddamn about anything as puny and frail as a stock car.

No, there was no moving The Rock. But I'm getting ahead of myself.

THERE'S something else you need to know: that summer, I was in love with Mary Connought. Mary. My Magdalene. Jesus, I had been in love with her since she was in the eighth grade and I was in the tenth grade, but it was that summer when, at nineteen, she reached the height of her beauty. That summer she habitually wore an electric teal miniskirt, a tummy-baring white halter top and a paisley headband that held her straight blonde hair in place, hippie-style. To me, she was the sun itself.

Every boy in the province had eyes for Mary, but Mary had eyes only for Johnny Comet. It was a painful reality but I felt protective toward her. She was not only pretty but good natured. She could talk to anyone, including me, which made my heart ache. We were friends, just friends, which for me was a wound.

I had plenty of opportunity to lick that wound like a dog, too. Mary hung around the speedway on practice days as well as race days, as I did also, it being my responsibility to supply Johnny's pit crew with an endless supply of racing tires. Johnny and his crew had work to do and he generally ignored her, which I suppose in a strange kind of way made her feel important. She had a high tolerance for boredom and would sit for hours in her Mustang convertible in the parking lot, listening to Sam the Sham, the Rolling Stones and The Temptations on her transistor radio.

I would sit with her in her car and talk with her about nothing and everything. She was oblivious to my feelings. The end of the day was the worst. Johnny would wash the grease off his hands, shuck off his racing overalls, then hop over the door of Mary's convertible Mustang into the passenger seat. The two of them would roar away for an evening of doing what I hated--but could not stop—thinking about.

Johnny Comet was getting everything that I wanted. I knew that was true because I would drive past Mary's house in the evening dark and notice that her Mustang was not yet back in the driveway, sometimes not even in the morning. What can I say? I was young, in love, and evidently liked to torture myself. All summer long The Association sang "Along Comes Mary" just to deepen my agony.

I WILL SAY this about Johnny: he knew his tires and wheels. He had strong feelings about wheel alignment in particular. We discussed it endlessly. In aligning wheels there are three considerations: caster, camber and toe. Angle the tire this way or that and you get an advantage either on corners or straights, but not both.

"Less camber," Johnny told me a week before the BC Classic. "I want the tire surface flat to the track."

His cherry red Ford 427 Fairlane was hoisted in the service bay at our tire dealership and we stood under it, pointing. It was an unapologetic muscle car with a 425 horsepower V8 engine that could run a 14.5 second quarter mile at a speed of 102 miles per hour. Ford had produced only fifty-seven of those that year, and Johnny had one of them.

"I wouldn't advise that," I told Johnny carefully, it being important not to make him feel stupid. "You're going to need some negative camber on the corners. You're going to want some toe out, too."

"Nuts," he said. "I ain't worried about the corners."

"You should be," I said.

"You think I'm afraid of a dead man's curve?" he challenged.

"You aren't afraid of anything," I offered carefully, "but that southern corner's got that hiccup, you know that. It's not forgiving."

"Are you thinkin' about The Rock?" Johnny grinned. "Me and that boulder have an understanding."

"Steer clear?"

"Not exactly."

Johnny was confident, you could say cocky. He had hungry eyes and a wolfish grin that said *just try me*. If he hadn't found stock car racing, I figured he would have been the kind of scrapy bantam who hung around bars not to drink but to pick fights. Stock car drivers in those days had a military appearance, maybe a mustache, but Johnny's thick brown hair curled up under the back of his racing helmet. It was that, I thought, that attracted girls. Even my little sister had clipped his picture from a racing magazine.

When he said that about The Rock, I saw a look on his face that I hadn't seen before. It was almost— I'm not sure—*reverent?*

"Half of any race is corners," I observed mildly, "you have to consider that."

"And the other half is straights," Johnny snapped back, looking up at the right side control arms. "Get me max speed on the straights."

"But—"

"Hey, I thought your boss would be happy about neutral camber."

It was true that with tire surfaces flat to the track, the tires would wear longer. They were not cheap.

"I'm sure but what about your safety?"

"Safety!" Johnny snorted, looking at me now. "Since when did playing it safe ever win a race?"

"It's nice to survive a race, too," I said.

"Listen to me, Nick." Johnny said, clapping a hand hard on my shoulder. "I've eaten The Duke's dust too many times now. This year, I'm blowing him away."

"You're betting on the straights?" I shook my head. "Johnny, he's driving an Olds 442 W30. He's got 444 pound-feet of torque. That car can cover a quarter mile in 13.8 seconds at 105 miles per hour. He's got you beat when it comes to speed."

"Until now."

"Johnny, hold on..." There was something in his voice that concerned me. "...what are you planning?"

"Never you mind, Nick," he said, looking up again at his car's underbelly, "just get these wheels fixed to win me those straights."

There was no point arguing. What Johnny wanted, Johnny got. That's why he was a star and I was only a bit player. That's why he had a sticky nickname and I was just plain old Nick. That's why he was getting something from Mary Connought that made my emotional engine rev up in neutral.. Damn him.

I aligned the wheels the way he wanted.

MY UNCLE MARTIN was an amateur astronomer. When I was feeling low, I would visit him at night in his backyard. Langford wasn't as developed then as it is now—no glowing mall parking lot and not as many streetlights—so the night sky was clear and star-studded. In summer sometimes you could see the northern lights but in that summer of 1966 thousands of meteors were observed all across Canada.

It was called the Great Leonid Meteor Storm. Look it up. Uncle Martin had a Sears 76mm f/16 Equatorial Refractor, the latest and best telescope for amateur astronomers, but which you actually didn't need to see meteors. Meteors are space rocks that fall at high speed through the Earth's atmosphere, burning up from friction and leaving behind them a long white streak, but just for a moment.

That summer, you could point Uncle Martin's telescope at any patch of sky and if you squinted into the eyepiece for a few minutes, you were sure to see those white streaks, maybe a bunch of them. I liked watching for them. It took my mind off things. People have been looking up at the night sky for just that reason, I suppose, for as long as there have been human beings. For a little while you're one with the universe, as the hippies would have said, or at least not locked up in your own miserable self.

On the night that I visited Uncle Martin in his backyard in the week leading up to the BC Classic, I wasn't having any luck with meteors or with my own misery. Visions of Mary doing enviable things with Johnny in the back seat of her Mustang or, worse, in some motel room, wouldn't leave my head. Uncle Martin sensed my mood, I guess, because he aimed his scope at a patch of sky near the Summer Triangle, with which I was familiar. You probably are too. It lies along the celestial equator and its corners are three of the brightest stars in the summer sky. The northernmost, Deneb, lies atop the Northern Cross. Ancient sailors navigated by that and on that night I needed a steady compass to steer by too.

Uncle Martin did not fit the picture of a scientist. He looked more like the beefy Junior A, semi-pro hockey player he had been in his younger days. I couldn't imagine him having the kind of fantasies about Aunt Sylvia, his wife, that I had about Mary but at some point he must have had them. I had three cousins in elementary and high school.

That night as I peered at the Northern Cross, I felt myself relax. The stars had been out there long before I and Mary were born and would still be there, twinkling, long after the two of us were gone. My problem was a small and fleeting one, really, momentary as a meteor tail.

Then I noticed something odd.

"Uncle Martin?"

"Yes?"

"I think there's an extra star near Deneb tonight. How's that possible?"

Uncle Martin chuckled. "Knew you'd spot that. It's exactly why I turned the scope in that direction."

"But stars don't just appear in one night... wait, it's not a star is it? It's something else."

"Correct," Uncle Martin said. "It's a comet."

"No kidding."

"Hermod. Orbits the sun and swings by our planet every sixty years or so."

"Must be pretty big to be visible."

"It is. It's closest approach to us is in a couple of nights."

"Which night?"

He told me. It was the date of the BC Classic, which would start in the late afternoon and finish under floodlights after dark.

"Who's Hermod named for?" I asked.

"Some Scandinavian god or other. Norse, I think. Called Hermod the Swift, though that's kind of ironic. There are other comets that orbit the sun faster. Hermod's similar to the god that the Greeks called Hermes."

Uncle Martin was also an amateur classical scholar. He liked spouting his knowledge, which as a little kid I found annoying but which, as I grew older, I had begun to appreciate. I glanced at him.

"How close does Hermod get to Earth?" I asked.

"Pretty close. In a couple of nights you'll be able to see its tail with the naked eye, if you're looking for it."

An idea formed in my head. A comet was something special. Something that I could show to Mary. Something I could reveal to her out on a dark roadside somewhere, maybe near Avenue Zero along the border. Just the two of us. Looking up at the night sky. She would be amazed by the sight but I wouldn't be looking at the sky. I would be gazing at her wide blue eyes, which were as big as her dreams, and at her pink-frosted lips, parted in wonder. Then she would smile and beyond that my imagination wouldn't permit me to go. The likelihood of disappointment limited me.

THE NIGHT before the BC Classic, most drivers were either tuning their engines or getting a good night's sleep. Not Johnny. Johnny Comet threw a party at the house he'd built for his mother, and where he also lived. Yes, that's right, Johnny Comet lived with his mother. He didn't drive on the street, either. If he wasn't grabbing rides from Mary, or me, it was his mother who drove him everywhere.

Strange, I know. Johnny Comet didn't behave

according to anyone's expectations or live by anyone else's rules. He'd mouth off at CACC directors, which in BC stock car racing was like mouthing off at members of Parliament. He'd flip the bird from his car at spectators who booed him and kiss on the mouth any woman who wore his team tee shirt. I wondered what Mary thought of that habit but if it bothered her, she didn't say. He talked like he was God and walked like he was the Devil. I couldn't make up my mind whether to hate him or admire him. I guess it was a lot of both.

Johnny's house was like a castle: turreted towers on the corners and a crenelated roofline. It wasn't as big as an actual castle, not even close, but it made an impression. The impression it made on me was not entirely favorable, but of course I was not inclined to kneel to the shaggy-haired Lancelot who had captured the heart of the girl whom I wanted.

The party guests included his pit crew, sponsors, fans and friends who spun in orbit around him, unable or maybe unwilling to escape his gravity. There were ice-filled tubs of beer and pink bubbly stuff, plus platters of Kjøttkaker, Norwegian meatballs handmade by Mrs. Elden, a tall stick of a woman with wild, long dark hair that hung down to her waist. She had blazing eyes.

"Watch out for her, she's a witch," said Oskar Brekken to me. He was Johnny's pit boss and a pal.

"She doesn't look very friendly," I agreed.

"I mean a *real* witch," he emphasized. "You've heard of Vardø?"

"No."

"In Norway. Witch trials there, a couple of centuries back. Burned ninety-one of them at the stake. Not all of them, though, I'll bet. Some eventually emigrated out here, passed on their practices to their descendants."

"That's ridiculous."

"I'm telling you, Nick. Watch out for her."

"Uh-huh."

"I'm serious. She's got copies of the Black Books of Elverum. Spells, man. You know, the evil eye and shit?"

"You don't know that."

"I saw 'em in Johnny's house, I swear."

Oskar was a mechanic, a guy with a machine mind. He barely graduated high school because he barely left the auto shop. He and his crew could swap out all four of Johnny's tires in less than ten seconds. I didn't figure him to be superstitious, but then he hadn't received much of an education.

The party around us was in full swing. There was a record player on the patio blaring the Rolling Stones *Out of Our Heads.* The needle skipped a few times during "Play with Fire " even though no one was dancing to the music just then. Johnny's guests were passing around a bottle of aquavit. I was looking around for Mary.

I wandered around to the back yard, which was lit by tiki torches. Johnny's mother stepped in front of me.

"Johnny's going to win tomorrow, *ja?*"

"Of course he is, Mrs. Elden."

"I'm not asking, I'm telling you...he's going to win."

"I don't doubt it."

"You make sure he has many tires. More than he needs."

"The best Firestone makes. They win every year at Indianapolis."

"Good. He's a god, my son. He will win because gods do not lose. Even so, he still must depend on boys like you."

A god? Most mothers would have called a son a *prince* if they said anything like that at all. I also didn't like being called a boy. I was twenty-one. There was something crazy in her eyes, though. She wasn't just a fan or Johnny's mother. She was wild as a storm and determined as a tide.

"I won't let him down, Mrs. Elden."

"No. You won't."

I found Mary at the edge of the lawn, staring over the fence into the woods. She looked upset.

"What's wrong?"

She looked around. "Oh. Nick. Nothing's wrong."

"Doesn't sound that way."

Mary looked back toward the dark woods. "It's just...well, Johnny wants something from me."

"Dammit, Mary, you don't have to give it to him!" The words were out of my mouth before I could stop them.

It was obvious to us both what I meant.

Mary lifted her chin. "Oh, *that?* Maybe I want to. He's not as bad as you think, Nick. He can be awfully sweet."

"Maybe so," I said, "but right now you don't look happy."

"It's about tomorrow," Mary said.

"You're worried about the race?"

"He's going to win."

"So everyone says."

"He says it's because I'm his good luck charm."

Any man would be holding aces if he landed her. She was the prize, the catch, the impossible ideal.

"So what's bothering you?" I asked.

"He...oh, forget it. Nothing really."

"You can tell me."

"It's not important."

"Maybe it is." *To me.* "Where is he, anyway?"

"Up there...see?"

Mary pointed to the roof of Johnny's faux castle. From his part of his backyard, I could see Johnny up there, lit from below by a flickering light. He must have had a fire burning in an iron fire pit. His arms were spread and raised palm up to the night sky. His face was turned up to the stars, eyes closed.

"What's he doing?" I wondered.

"I don't know, but he does that every night," Mary told me.

"Every night? For how long?"

"All summer, as long as we've been going out."

"Heck of a date."

I realized then why I hadn't spotted Mary's Mustang in her driveway. I'd been driving past the wrong house.

"Doesn't he take you to the movies or anything?"

"No." Mary looked confused, her eyes hazy. She'd had plenty of that aquavit, I guessed. "His crazy momma cooks us dinner, usually some kind of smelly fish, then he goes up there and does that thing."

"Why don't you just drive home?" *Or go out with me?*

"He won't let me. Says that he needs me near him. I'm his good luck charm, he tells me."

"You said that."

"It's not so bad, really," Mary said, smiling without conviction. "When he's done up there we'll go for a walk. There's a field out there—" She gestured vaguely beyond the back fence. "—it's dark and we'll...well, I'm pretty sure you don't want to hear about that part, Nick."

It was the first hint I'd received that Mary understood how I felt about her. At that moment, I hated Johnny with a sharpened edge.

"I don't get the feeling that's all that's bothering you, though," I said. "There's something else, isn't there?"

Pregnant?

Mary swayed a little on her feet. "It's that race tomorrow. He wants me to be there."

"Of course."

"But it's *where* he wants me to be..."

"In the pit with the crew?"

"No, sitting and watching the race from on top of The Rock."

I thought about that but couldn't make heads nor tails of it. Not then.

AT THE LANGFORD SPEEDWAY, the morning of the BC Classic was taken up with go cart races for local kids with Johnny Comet dreams. Crowds began to arrive in the afternoon, jamming the stands and forming long lines at the beer tent. Everyone knew that Johnny Comet and The Duke would be squaring off. They had tickets to see speed but, of course, they secretly hoped to see crashes.

Uncle Martin stopped by to visit me in the pit area.

"Care to have a look under the hood of a stock car engine?" I asked.

"Nope, but thanks, came to check out that big boulder over yonder." He pointed toward The Rock.

Uncle Martin was also an amateur geologist. I wondered if there was anything he was actually an expert in.

"Walk over and have a look," I said. The track was empty, the green flag wasn't for two hours yet.

"Already did. Tramped through the woods between the track and the lake to get to it. Interesting piece of stone."

"Did you climb up on it?" I asked, thinking of Mary.

"Had to get a good look at it. Haven't seen anything quite like it."

"It's big alright."

"That's not what I mean. I'm a pretty fair rock hound, but I can't figure out what that one is."

"Granite, isn't it?"

"Don't know. Much of what you find around here is volcanic rock in one form or another. Not that one."

"Nick! Need you!"

Oskar Brekken was calling me. A flatbed truck had arrived from our tire dealership, stacks of racing tires chained down on it. The tires had to be unloaded and placed on racks in Johnny's pit.

"Sorry, gotta run. Staying to see the race, Uncle Martin?"

He shrugged. "Wouldn't miss it."

The green flag swept furiously around in its figure eight as if it were signaling missiles to launch, which is kind of how it was. The twenty-six cars starting in the BC Classic were like a pack of three-ton bees buzzing at supersonic decibel level. Driver adrenaline is high all the way through a race but especially so in the first lap, which is why there often are so many accidents right away.

That year the opening lap was clean, free of spin-outs, probably because everyone knew that The Duke was in first position. Moving up in the early laps was pointless. Better to wait until the race settled into a rhythm when driver complacency, or hesitation, would create better opportunities.

In spite of what he'd said, Johnny was playing it safe. He hung on The Duke's tail, drafting close enough to trade paint but making no moves. I couldn't figure it out. He pulled into the pit when The Duke did, matching him lap for lap. On the corners Johnny deferred to The Duke like a gentleman waving a lady first into an elevator. For a long while watching the race from the pit was like watching a merry-go-round, wooden horses flying around in a circle, bobbing up and down but never changing position.

Spectators in the stands grew restless, feeling free to leave their seats to buy more beer. Why not? Nothing exciting was happening except the inevitable engine failures. In the first hundred and fifty laps, the field dwindled to twenty. The Duke kept his lead with an iron grip, Johnny tight on his tail.

I am a rational man. Most are, I think, but even so it's hard for me to excuse myself. It wasn't until lap two hundred had passed that something began to bother me. At first it was like a cloud crossing the sun, a momentary darkening in my mind, but then the dark moments fused into a sickness in my stomach. Feelings aren't facts, naturally, and I tried to reason my feelings away. Certain thoughts, though, wouldn't stay quiet.

...some Scandinavian god or other...

...I saw it in Johnny's house, I swear...

...I'm not asking you, I'm telling you...

...he does that every night...

I tell myself now that concern for Mary was working on me, but if I'm honest that's not the biggest part of it. What got to me most of all was Johnny Comet. His confidence. His arrogance. His sense of entitlement. He was positive that this day he would blow past The Duke, but he wasn't driving like it. He was biding his time. Something bad was in the air and I was beginning to understand what.

Unlike a meteor, a comet is not one solid chunk of space rock. A comet is a composite, a big ball of rocks combined with ice and frozen gasses. That's why as a comet approaches the sun it begins to glow. The sun's particle stream heats the comet, burning it away. The comet glows and leaves behind a blue-green gaseous tail. When the comet's big enough, you can see that tail in the night sky.

You need to know that.

AROUND LAP two hundred and twenty-five, the Langford Speedway's floodlights switched on. The infield grass turned a bright, unnatural green. The cars circling the oval flashed and gleamed. The crowd of spectators had diminished from thousands to hundreds. It was well past dinnertime and there wasn't much to see.

Few, I'm sure, noticed a lone blonde watching from atop The Rock or, if they did, thought much about it. Kids who couldn't afford tickets at the gate would sometimes tramp through the woods to view races from up there. From the pit, I could see her: a small figure in faded denim bellbottoms, sitting with her knees up to her chin and her arms wrapped around them. She'd been there all afternoon.

It was exactly lap two hundred and seventy nine—I remember clearly—when my uneasy thoughts snapped together like jigsaw puzzle pieces. My fear wasn't rational. What I believed—no, knew—was going to happen was impossible. Anyone I told it to would have said I was crazy. But you know, crazy things happen in this world that have no explanation but they occur nonetheless.

Getting to The Rock from the pit wasn't possible, not without circling the long way around through the parking lot and behind the spectator stands. Instead, I ran under the pit canopy and across the access road. I dodged between flatbed trailers, clambered over a chain link fence and began battling through undergrowth. Mary was on top of The Rock. Johnny didn't need her there for luck.

Away from the floodlights, I could see a patch of dark summer sky. I looked north. Deneb was there and so was the comet Hermod. As Uncle Martin had promised, it was visible with the naked eye. A blue-green tail streamed behind it but there was something terrifying about it. The comet's tail wasn't straight.

It was curved.

It was only a glance. I was feeling panic. I admit

that, but I didn't need to look to see. I already knew what was going to happen.

Four laps must have gone by before I reached The Rock. All day Johnny had been biding his time, maybe working The Duke's nerves, maybe, and now there weren't very many laps to go. He'd soon be making his move.

"Mary!" As I approached, I screamed at her. "You've got to get down from there!"

"Nick?"

Mary's eyes were filmy. She smiled a slow, out-of-it smile. There was an empty bottle of aquavit near the base of The Rock.

"Get! Down! Now!" I waved my arm like I was pulling an oar.

"Come on up," she slurred. "The view's great."

"No! Get down!"

A cold voice behind me said, "She will stay."

Johnny's mother. That night in the dark woods she looked like the witch I now knew that she was. By her side she held a long kitchen knife.

"You've been here all the time, haven't you?" I said. "You're making sure she stays up there."

"I'm Johnny's mother." She stated it almost kindly, like she was explaining one-plus-one to a first grade simpleton.

"Mary's coming with me," I said.

The witch raised the knife over her head, elbow bent, to stab me. If I screamed, no one would hear. The engine whine dropped as the cars took the southern corner—it was lap 285—but the sound even so was deafening.

"Drop it."

The witch stiffened.

Behind her was a man pressing the barrel of a

hunting rifle into her back. Uncle Martin, sounding thoroughly expert.

"I said drop it," he repeated.

"You cannot stop Hermod," the witch said, knife still aloft in the air. "You cannot stop a god!"

Uncle Martin swung his rifle around in his hands and rammed the butt of it into the backs of the witch's knees. She crumpled and dropped the knife. Uncle Martin kicked it into the underbrush.

"What's going on here?" he asked me.

"She's a witch, watch out!"

I was already climbing up the back of the rock. There were hand- and foot-holds but it was taking time.

"Look up at the comet," I called back over my shoulder. "It's not flying by, it's heading toward us!"

"You're out of your mind."

"Mary's up there," I yelled. "She's a human sacrifice. That's why Hermod is coming."

There wasn't time to explain more.

Mary was more than inebriated. Her limbs were rubbery, without strength. I wondered what food the witch might have cooked for her, and what else had been mixed into it. LSD was a new thing in 1966 but mushrooms were not.

"Isn't it pretty?" Mary asked, pointing to the sky.

As I looked up, a camera aperture opening in the clouds shuttered closed. Thunder began. The comet called Hermod disappeared from sight but I knew it wasn't gone. It was drawing closer. I had a clear view of the track now. In the stands spectators, hearing thunder, were rising up to their feet. Convertible owners were hurrying to the parking lot. With their convertible tops down, their leather interiors were bound to get a soaking.

Lightning. A single bolt at first, then more. And more. A storm was coming and so was Johnny Comet. On the track, I saw The Duke and Johnny locked together like conjoined twins on the north corner. As they entered the straightaway with less than ten laps to go, Johnny made his move. Pulling to the outside of The Duke, his Fairlane burst ahead and drew even. But it didn't work.

The Duke shut him down as they screamed into the southern turn right below us, Johnny still hot on The Duke's tail.

"Sorry, Mary," I said.

I yanked her to her feet, flung her to one side of The Rock like a jive dancer slinging his partner wide, grabbed both her hands and lowered her off. With her feet still five feet off the ground, I let her go. She hit the ground without even a squeak. I scrambled down, grabbed her under her armpits and dragged her away.

Uncle Martin was holding Johnny's mother at gunpoint. "A witch, huh?" he said., "Turns out that rifles are stronger than spells."

UNCLE MARTIN TUCKED his rifle under his arm and helped me pull Mary through the underbrush, up the incline toward the spectator stands. When we had achieved a high vantage point, we stopped. Lighting now surrounded the Langford Speedway like a ring of fire. Spectators were screaming, running for their lives.

On the track, it was lap 300. Then the impossible became possible. The track's floodlights failed. The track was still brightly lit by a flurry of lightning strikes, as if one hundred huge flashbulbs were going off all in the space of one minute. On the back straightaway, Johnny Comet again made his move. His Fairlane jerked, seemed to stall, then shot ahead in rocket-burst of speed. Heading into the southern turn, his Fairlane was a full five lengths ahead of The Duke's Olds 442.

There was no catching Johnny now. He'd done it: passed The Duke. With only a short distance to the checkered flag, the race was securely in his bag. Or, it should have been. But Johnny hadn't counted on something.

Neutral camber.

Johnny's alignment was set for maximum speed on the straightaways, but heading into a corner at the speed at which he was traveling needed a severe tire tilt away from the bank. Johnny didn't have that. As he slammed into the curve, his brake lights flared as red as Satan's eyes.

Too late. Lightning bolts zapped from the sky, three of them at once, illuminating for the tiniest of seconds a figure atop The Rock with her arms spread, palms upright, witch hair whipping around. Johnny's mother. Then the lightning struck. So did Johnny Comet, spinning out like a top and whirling off the track..

...straight into the side of The Rock.

Johnny Comet's funeral was actually a memorial service, there being no casket to display either closed or open. It was well attended and while many nice, if exaggerated, things were said about Johnny, nothing whatsoever was mentioned about the circumstances of his disappearance. I say *disappearance* rather than *death* because, in fact, after the crash nothing whatsoever was found of Johnny.

Or his car.

Or his mother.

Or The Rock.

Hermod had taken them all. For the longest time, I wouldn't repeat that to anybody. Lightning storms are rare but they happen. That a storm might knock out electricity is no surprise. Crashes happen in stock car racing too. They make the news for a day and then are forgotten. Like Johnny Comet. But much time has passed and now I think it's fair to report that I simply saw what I saw.

Take it or leave it.

Perhaps a year after that, I finally got from Mary what she had formerly given only to Johnny but it wasn't good. She was drinking then and stayed drunk for the next couple of decades. After a while, I realized that I couldn't help her.

I moved on.

Where The Rock was, today if you bother to look you will find something like a ditch or gully. Nothing too unusual in the woods. I can't say positively that Hermod the Swift swooped down from outer space that night to pass greedily close to Earth. I can't say for sure that it was a Norse god who sent Johnny Comet that final burst of speed. What I can say is that stock car racing has had gods but only figuratively. Except maybe once. Is Johnny Comet now, forever, circling the sun with his brother Hermod?

Maybe in another couple of years we'll know.

<u>Author's note:</u>

MPC allocation 2630 Hermod is an asteroid, here a comet for dramatic purposes. The Langley Speedway in Langley, BC, Canada operated from 1965 to 1984, when it was abandoned. Today the track itself can still be found in the Campell Valley Regional Park. In Norway between 1561 and 1760 up to 350 witches were executed, most notably 91 witches who were burned at the stake in the Vardø, Finnmark region, where today the striking Steilneset memorial is dedicated to those persecuted women.]

WINDING WAYS

BY EMILY MUNRO

"...when you have been received back home, and have stood in pride before your thronging followers, gloriously telling the death of the man-and-bull, and of the halls of rock cut out in winding ways, tell, too, of me, abandoned on a solitary shore."

— *OVID, HEROIDES 10. 125 FF*

The cratered landscape of Jupiter's moon shimmered as dying sunlight glittered across the ice. Gan shivered as he peered out his window at the frozen landscape. At first the crater looked like any other, if unusually textured, but as the shuttle reached a fixed orbit the last rays of light strafed the surface, revealing the pattern in all its glory. The entire interior of the crater, all forty plus kilometers, had been filled with a space filling pattern of growing huts so complex it turned the dark shadowed trenches between them into an impossible maze.

"I'd hate to be whatever poor bastard we're dropping there," his seat neighbor said. This worthy, who'd promptly fallen asleep once in his seat, was now peering over his shoulder out the tiny porthole window.

"Oh?" Gan went for noncommittal, but it came out with a squeak.

The man gave him a sneer of experience to callow youth, "Nobody makes it out of The Labyrinth alive." The man leaned in conspiratorially, "Rumor has it they've got a monster down there. Likes to eat people."

"Hazard pay could be good."

The older man snorted and turned away from the window, "They don't pay hazard to the dead, kid. Stick with the safer jobs."

"Excuse me, Engineer?" They both looked at the crew floating in the aisle. " Your drop pod is ready if you'll follow me?"

The older man's jaw dropped.

"See you around, I guess," Gan said, unbuckling and floating out of his seat.

"No coming back from the labyrinth. Have a nice life kid. What's left of it."

Drop pods were the worst way to travel. Basically a foam lined coffin with minimal life support and a set of poorly maintained air brakes. He hadn't broken any bones though. And the woman who opened the lid though smiled at him with all the genuine welcome he could have wished.

"Oh shit dude, you have no idea how glad we are to see you. I'm the FabLead, call me Jareth, queen of the goblins for my sins." A burly woman, she had an old fashioned undercut to go with her old fashioned language and she lifted him out of the pod without assistance in the near Mars-standard gravity.

"The situation's only gotten worse and you have no idea how hard it is to get an Engineer to accept a posting here," she said as she put him on his feet and hefted his tiny personal pack, "Let's get out of the cold and I'll give you the five dollar tour."

She led him through a pair of airlock doors, old but moving smoothly, straight into a huge cavern full of humming machinery. "Here's the heart of our little castle, welcome to the Fab. We've got the materials and people to build, rebuild, or kit-bash just about anything we could possibly need."

Folks came pouring from all corners of the cavern, which seemed to have been cut directly into the rocky outcropping of the uplift in the center of the crater. Their combined voices almost drowned out the hum of dozens of printers going full tilt. Gan counted nearly thirty people by the time they'd all assembled, each to give him a slap on the back, a hearty wave, and in one case a full three-kiss greeting. Almost all of them, young or old, spoke in the distinctive drawling dialect of Post-California refugees.

"Dude, I can't believe they actually sent us a heckin' troubleshooter," one voice enthused.

"Hella tight right? I've never even seen one before."

Gan opened his mouth to protest that he wasn't a troubleshooter but good sense, and the FabLead's sudden glance of warning, prevailed before he could make a fool of himself. The tone in the room was jovial, but there was a tense undercurrent that ozone couldn't completely account for.

"Go easy dudes, let 'em breathe and don't beat-em-up before he's even gotten in the door." The Fab-Lead's heavy hand landed on his shoulder and pushed him forward through the crowd.

"Boss, yah sure they sent the right guy? He looks scrawny for a 'Shooter.'"

The Lead stopped and addressed the crowd, "You all listen up. This dude got sent-out special by Corporate, right? I pulled a few strings and got them to send us the best they had." The hand on his shoulder pushed forward with more force, "I gotta brief the troubleshooter on our little problem now, right? You FabRats get back to work. Those printers won't program themselves, good thing too, else—"

"—We'd all be outta jobs," the room choroused. The tension in the room had spiked when she mentioned "our problem" but everyone scattered quick enough back to their various jobs in progress.

Her hand on his shoulder steered him towards the opposite side of the cavernous workroom, where a series of pockets had been carved from the wall and blocked off from the general noise of the floor by a glass wall. One was set up as an office and he let out a sigh as the background hum dropped away.

The FabLead moved straight to a complex assemblage of glass and steel on a counter at the back. "Coffee?" she asked.

Gan couldn't stand the stuff, but he could recognize a person wanting to show off a passion project when he saw one. Plus, if there was a second rule in engineering school (after rule one: anything can and will blow up if enough energy is involved) it was never say no to caffeine.

She was already working the complex mechanism, which hissed as she adjusted some kind of steam valve. As the thing bubbled and whirred she sat down at the cluttered desk. "So who'd'ja piss off kid?"

Gan sighed, until the ride down he'd only suspected, but he could probably take this as proof. "The dean of the engineering department's son was in my class. Pretty sure my final scores beat him even with his nepotism bump."

She nodded as if expecting as much. "How long ago was that?"

"Six weeks."

She blinked. "Shit son, you're greener than bamwood. You shouldn't even have seen that listing."

"Technically, I volunteered."

The machine chimed, the sweet sound of a real bell. She busied herself with a set of blown glass cups, delivering them to his hands filled with a rich, dark brew with a foamy head with the aroma of chestnuts and chocolate. "Slurp," she ordered. It was dark, complex, and slightly bitter, like the regret he was starting to feel for not sandbagging his final exams, danger pay or no. They both paused in respect.

"That's good," he finally managed.

"It should be. We supply four-fifths of the Jovian sector with coffee, along with certain fruits and vegetables that require impractically large amounts of space or specialized atmospheres. We import carbon dioxide practically for free, pull nitrogen out of Jupiter's atmosphere, and mine our own metals along with the water recycling systems. We are possibly the only fully self-sustaining colony in the entire solar system, and we've managed without an engineer for the past five years of my tenure and at least ten of my previous colleague's. Nobody knows 'ponics like a Cali-refugee and I've got the best FabRats anywhere."

"So what do you need me for?" he asked.

She gave him an assessing look over the lip of her coffee cup. "So glad you asked. There's a monster in the maze and we need you to kill it."

WHEN SHE FINISHED POUNDING his back clear of the coffee he'd inhaled, she explained. "The plain truth of it is that something out there has been destroying our drones for years."

She waved a hand at a wall and it went into screen-mode, showing the vista of horizon to horizon growing tunnels, glowing now as they had rotated away from even Jupiter's light. Each tube was lit from within, creating a shifting pattern of lights that reflected the complexity of the stars above.

"It wasn't a problem until some damn-fool told a ghost story about it being some kind of monster, then somebody claimed to have seen it out on the ice, and now my whole crew has gotten their panties in a twist about it. They won't step foot outside except in groups of five. We're nearly a month behind on maintenance and management is threatening to wipe the whole team if we don't get back on target."

Gan winced. Wiped meant a brain-chip and hard labor, the kind there really was no coming back from. He took a sip of the coffee, now at the perfect temperature, smooth and unctuous. It tasted as good as it smelled, which was something he'd never experienced before.

"You're our only hope kid. These people are spooked at shadows. I know they don't look it, but they're stretched so thin they're about to snap."

Gan opened his mouth to respond. Instead a siren blared through the cavern.

"Shit!" The FabLead was out the door in a single step, Gan trailing behind.

As they passed through the sound barrier doors into the fabrication lab, they were hit by a wave of sound. Not the usual clatter of printers and clicks of assembly, though there was plenty of that, but an uproar of voices from the far end of the vast cavern the lab had been built into. The FabLead cursed and took off running across the floor. Gan followed at a slightly slower pace, he'd not adjusted to the gravity shift and felt too bouncy to run safely in a space filled with operating equipment. When he arrived at the far corner he saw med packs out and a lot of white around people's eyes. Two fabbers were down on the deck. Red splashed across their arms and one's chest. Gashes that cut through toughened layers of outsuit and blood that had immediately frozen where it had sprayed. Blood that was just now melting into sticky rivulets on the deck.

"It was the beast, Boss I swear. I saw it with my own eyes."

The FabLead was patting the conscious injured tech, "Calm down Johnny. Ginger, give him the shot."

Ginger, presumably the fabber with the yellow stripe of an emergency medic, pressed a med syringe into the injured tech's thigh.

"It's out there Boss, its hunting and—"

"Hush," the FabLead said. The young man's eyes rolled back and he sighed as the spray started to kick in. The FabLead looked up at the others standing around them anxiously, "Clear the airspace folks. Somebody go check where the hell the medbots are. And somebody'd better check that the outer doors closed properly. The last thing we need is Oxy-loss on top of everything."

About half the people standing around went off in different directions. The others backed off a few paces and Gan was able to shoulder his way forward. He knelt next to Ginger and grabbed a dressing from the opened med kit between the two injured. He ripped open the dressing, unrolled it and wrapped it around a gash that had started spurting as soon as the frozen blood thawed.

"What?" Ginger looked up at him half a second, saw the yellow stripe on his own cuffs, and yanked the medkit to a better position between the two of them.

He got a good look at the wounds as he applied dressings to them. A puncture wound at the top, and then four long gashes along the arms and chest. Something sharp enough to shred through the suit, even the tough outer layers and the last-ditch skinsuit that all but the most destitute added to their debts. As he was working on the third gash a clatter at the doors indicated the arrival of med bots. They practically flew through the room, and Ginger and he stepped back to let the two bots position themselves to scoop up their passengers into their beds and then speed off deeper into the station.

He was just barely standing up again, panting with misplaced adrenaline when Ginger turned and blinked at him, "What the hell Boss. Is he gonna go after that thing?"

The FabLead offered them both blue shop towels, and he wiped the blood from his hands and dabbed at the places where it had spattered across his wrists and soaked into the knees of his coverall.

"Don't want to lose the trail, right sir?" The crowd murmured in agreement.

"Yeah! Here, you can use my boots."

"I've got a spare breather!"

THE MAINTENANCE LINES were carved down into the ice, the better to protect the equipment from the radiation, micrometeorites, and all the other trash the system kicked out. With the broad wings of solar arrays on either side it was more like traveling through a tunnel than the surface of a moon. Only the glimpse of stars through the gaps between the solar arrays at the turns assured him that they were indeed exposed to space. That and the cold.

Cold in space was peculiar. The parts of him that were free in space were fairly well heated, vacuum being an excellent insulator after all. But his hands and feet, the places most likely to contact the ice, had been stuffed into heavy rockwool mittens and boots. His hands therefore felt hot and stuffy until they touched the surface. His feet already felt cold and would likely be fighting frostbite before long.

"Don't trip," the FabLead had advised him when she handed him the extra insulation, clearly homemade and not Company issue, "Unless you like ice burns."

Two fabbers were loading up a micro-cart with

their gear. "I'm Arl, this is Becker," the smaller of the two introduced himself. "We're going with you."

Gan glanced at the gear in the cart. "What do we need a bolter for?"

Becker grinned at him behind his face-mask, "It's modified." He picked up and waved the bolter in front of him before pointing to the ground-off safety switch. "If that monster shows up it's gonna get .08 ounces of Ceram at 4,000 psi."

Gan blinked and gently nudged the muzzle of the modified tool to point away from his chest. "Right. Let's just keep that stowed until we need it, shall we?"

The walls and floor of the tunnels were wreathed in wisps of "mist," clouds of carbon dioxide and water sublimating into the vacuum. It gave the far distances of the corridors an eerie, otherworldly quality. A shimmering that both gave the illusion of motion and obscured details.

Down the center of the corridor ran a metal rail that made each ninety-degree turn a sudden jerk on the cart, which sped through the system at a pace that pressed his back painfully against the plastic rivets along the edge as he crouched inside the makeshift vehicle.

Instead of focusing on the walls flashing by, or the backs of the two fabbers ahead of him in the cart, Gan pulled the schematics of the facility. His helmet painted each element of the system a different color. A deep blue for piping, yellow for the electrical systems, red for heating and cooling. It turned the flat maze they moved through into a three dimensional mess of pipes and wires and voids even more disorienting. He blinked the overlay off and was back to being jerked through drab ice-brown corridors.

Their movement of the cart was peculiar. They'd

move forward, then come to an intersection and turn ninety degrees with no warning and little regard for momentum. Left and right and left with no discernable pattern, a dizzying number of turns. After only half an hour he was powerfully lost. A disturbing feeling until he noticed the stars still peeking through the gaps between the solar panels.

A bare glimpse at the stars, hard pinpricks of light in harsh constellations: Cassiopeia, and Ursa Minor, and Draco and there just above the horizon Orion, the hunter. The mist disturbed by their passage rushing up, they almost twinkled, the same as he remembered as a child. Removed from the Earth, but not far enough to change their essential shapes. An antidote to the claustrophobia he felt creeping in as they delved deeper and deeper into the labyrinth. Only the ribbon of the monorails stretching endlessly in front and behind them.

"Almost there," Arl said, "Be on the lookout. This is where we usually see signs of the monster."

"I think it's some kind of experiment that escaped. Something they've been breeding in the tunnels."

"It would be easy to hide something out here," Gan allowed, thinking of the thousands of huts they'd passed in the past hour. Though he felt like if the Corporation had something like that they would have used it in the last merger. It was easy to lose things in mergers though...maybe they had no idea what they had?

What would be worse? Secret experiments or forgotten ones?.

The turn of the cart jerked him out of his contemplations and then out of his seat as it stopped abruptly. Becker grabbed his shoulder to keep him from becoming a physics demonstration.

"Watch it." Becker patted his shoulder as he regained his balance. "Check your boots and gloves. Ice burns suck." They checked their own equipment, then each other's, before they clambered out of the cart.

Puffs of mist curled up around their boots despite the insulation.

"Ok, we're gonna go check the power cables up around the huts up here. Stay frosty, and keep your boots moving." Arl said.

Becker shouldered the modified bolt gun and Gan worked to stay out of his line of fire. They walked a bit down a corridor for which his map didn't even have a label. They hiked another five or six turns. Everything was so similar that the splash of blood frozen to the walls was a shock in itself.

"If it's smart at all, it won't be anywhere near here," Becker said.

"Yeah," Arl agreed.

Aside from the spray of blood, and gashes in the ice and conglomerate of the walls, there were also scrapes along their length. There were also sharp holes, like something had dug into the wall to climb up it.

"Check around, maybe it left some more evidence,"

Another set of handholds in the wall looked more deliberate. A way for staff to reach the top of the walls.

"What's up there?" Gan asked.

Arl consulted his maps for a moment. "Power station, a bunch of couplings. Readout says it's functioning normally."

"Let's check it out anyway," Gan said, "Sometimes readouts lie."

"Ain't that the truth," Becker agreed with the vehemence of a veteran.

Gan watched Arl carefully climbed up the handholds without letting his knees or arms touch the ice. Once he was up he reached down and helped Becker up, and finally Gan.

The top of the wall was narrower than it looked, with the curving top of the buried hoop house glowing with yellow light to his right. Inside the space was filled with vibrant green life and small white robots flitting between tall plants of a type he'd never seen before. A tiny pocket of warmth and light untouched by human hands. The sight was all the more dramatic for the stark, icy landscape he stood on; only a pane of plas away. They were near the top ridge of a gentle crater; the labyrinth spread across the endless miles behind and around him, from horizon to too-close horizon. Row after row of hoop houses endlessly interspersed in a space-saving design that looked chaotic even from this high angle. A testament to what humans could achieve out here in space.

"See anything?" Becker asked?

Gan checked the direction of the bolt gun's muzzle before responding, "A whole lot of nothing."

The power station looked like a bog-standard unit. Nothing surprising there. Except that one of the couplings had an extra cable plugged into one of the spare slots.

"Where does that cable go?" Gan asked. Arl and Becker both peered at it. It wasn't bundled like the others.

"Probably just a patch. That does happen out here a lot," Arl said. "Sometimes we run through a weird magnetic anomaly and they pop out of the runs. The bots'll put it back eventually."

"Let's check it anyway."

They followed the cable along the tops of the walls and around two hoophouses to a different power collector where it was still plugged in.

"That's not right," Arl mused, "The power junction here should only have six ports. This one has eight. Where are those other two coming from?"

They jumped down into the tunnel following the now paired line. Puffs of mist billowing around them from the heat of their boots.

"Stop. What's that?" Becker pointed in the direction they had come from.

At the end of the corridor, an enormous shape hulked over their cart. The drifting mists obscured it slightly, but the cart gave it some context and in that context it was much larger than a human form. Arms and legs weirdly extended, its body was covered in some sort of shaggy fur.

Becker's motion must have grabbed its attention because it's head turned immediately towards them.

"Get the hell away from that," Becker shouted and swung the bolt gun towards it.

Arl and Becker rushed forward along the tunnel and Gan followed a moment behind yelling, "Wait! It can't hear you!"

The creature jerked away at their sudden movement, swinging up the walls and landing with the grace of a simian swinging on trees. Gan pushed himself harder, running to catch up.

Becker brandished the gun at it while motioning to them both with his other arm. "Get the hell in the cart!"

They scrambled, Becker and Arl ended up in the

front and the thing took off moving before Gan could get himself seated. The thing lurched into motion; almost spilling him out again, and giving him an upside down view as the creature raised a clawed hand at them and rushed forward.

"Oh shit!" Becker said, "Go, go, go!"

Arl rushed to put the cart into gear and they started moving, accelerating far too slowly.

The creature's oddly long legs pushed off the ice and it ran after them.

"Holy shit, it's gaining on us! Can't this thing go any faster?"

Gan pulled himself back up, trying to regain his balance on the moving platform in strange gravity.

"Already going as fast as it goes. Shoot the damn thing!"

"Oh yeah, right." Becker leveled the bolt gun at the creature.

"No wait," Gan grabbed Becker's arm.

"Shove off!" Becker pushed back.

Three things happened at the same time:

1 The cart made one of those abrupt ninety degree turns.

2 Gan lost his balance, tumbled out, and momentum being preserved, flew backwards towards the oncoming monster.

3 Becker's finger hit the unsafetied trigger of the bolt gun, sending a spray of projectiles through the airless void around them.

Gan felt a line of pain blossom along his arm as the stars flashed above him, then he hit the ice of the floor and the pain became a searing burn across the entire side of his body he hit the ice and it let off gas with near explosive force. He bounced back up, still spinning to see surprise in the creature's eyes as he was launched straight at its chest. Knocking it over and landing in another tangle of limbs and sublimated gasses. His head hit the inside of his helmet and he noticed nothing more.

WHEN HE CAME to himself somewhat he was being carried. A weird sensation, but one he could at least place. He tried to blink the tears from his eyes and realized that it wasn't tears, but blood that was sticking his eyelashes together.

"Don't move," a voice said, weirdly distant. Higher pitched, the sound of it strange until he realized it must be coming in through the material of his helmet and not the mic in his ear.

"Who are you?" he tried. The pain was coming back and it felt like his entire left side had been dipped in molten lead.

"Hush," the voice said, "We're almost home. Answers there."

They moved a few more minutes, the light he could just barely see through his closed eyes changing angle several times. Suddenly his skin felt like it caught fire as his suit pressed against it. The air pressure beginning to change meant they must be in an airlock.

"Can you stand?" the voice asked him.

"I can try," he said. Arms maneuvered him upright, setting him gently on a surface and guided his hands to a wall. When he had his balance they retracted and he wobbled on his own for a second. Fingers, human ones, fumbled at the seal of his helmet and he tried clumsily to assist. They batted his still mittened fingers away and then deftly caught the clasp. A gust of warm air washed over his face. Air that smelled strongly of plants and growing things.

"One sec I'll get you a towel," came the voice now through his own ears. Feminine if quavering slightly.

A warm and wet cloth was packed against his face and he gently wiped his eyes and face clear of the blood. When he blinked them clear he barely understood what he saw. An old woman's face emerged from the hulking body of the monster. Details began to filter through his astonishment.

The "fur" of the body appeared to be some sort of woven grass or fiber that covered her in a great insulating suit. Like the rockwool gloves he was wearing but for her whole body.

"Who? How?"

The woman gave him an enigmatic smile. "Let me get out of this and I'll explain what I can. While I still have the time."

She sat down on a stack of reinforced crates that looked to have served this purpose for some time. "I'm getting too old for this." She groused as she shucked arm and leg extenders and layers of hand woven suit covering. Her interior suit when it was revealed was more patch than suit.

THE HUT WAS FILLED with an overgrowth, an abundance of vegetation. Plants grew to the ceiling, obscuring the solar lamps along the roof so that the light came in green and living. The automatic systems had been altered with prejudice and extra watering tubes were everywhere. Tiny things flitted between plants, he thought at first they were insects, but they had butterfly wings and human bodies. One flew up to his face, buzzing angrily at him, before flying off when he waved it away.

When the overwhelming greenness passed, he started to pick up signs of long habitation. A washstation was hidden in one side of the shrubbery. A table and improvised cookstation along another. And, barely visible towards the back, what looked to be a hammock strung between two of the trees.

"I designed this place, actually." The woman said. Now he could see her properly, she was barely as tall as he was, and more ancient than he'd seen outside of a proper space station. "It was child's play to section off a hut and hide it from the system. Once I had designed and overseen the building of this station they decided I was too expensive to keep around, but I also knew too much. I barely escaped the hitman they sent to "renegotiate" my contract. They had played their hand too early and I'd already had this little hideout all prepared. As far as the company is concerned I walked out of the complex and onto the ice about twenty years ago."

She drank a bit of water from a bottle on the desk, offered the bottle to him which he gladly took.

"I still had a few trustworthy colleagues. Together we worked to start smuggling a few people out of the system. Those in the worst debt or in situations like mine. We got the place a reputation as the place you were sent when there was nowhere else to go."

She leaned forward and looked at him closely. Looking into his eyes as if trying to weigh his soul.

"There's only one question left really. Can I trust you with my contacts?"

Gan blinked. "I could be anyone. I could have been sent to "fix" you."

"Were you?" She cocked her head like a curious animal, "Sent to fix me, that is."

"Somewhat?"

"Funny sort of fixing, jumping in front of a gun like that."

"You couldn't hear us, I assumed."

"True. Ah, well it won't matter to me much longer." She held up her hand that had been at her side and he saw that it was washed in red, her black undersuit taking on a soaked appearance.

"Oh shit. Let me see. I can—" He jumped to his feet but she waved him off.

"Nah," she pulled up the shirt showing the hole where the bolt had gone in, low through the side of her abdominal cavity, but also the dark olive patches of severe carcinomas covering her skin. "Too much time on the ice. I had maybe a few more months left to live as it is. This is better. She eased herself down on the bench again.

"I have to do something," Gan said.

She smiled at him, "I felt the same way. Sit there. Listen. That's what you can do for me now. Here's how you contact the free settlers..."

THE RIBBON of the monorail was his ticket out of the maze. He followed it and the stars, turn after turn, back through the frozen miles. He didn't mind the distance now. It gave him time to plan.

RETROGRADE

BY ARTEMIS CROW

"Perfect is the enemy of good."

— VOLTAIRE

He had never been alone. Not when he'd been submerged in the growth goo used to gestate him, not when the Twelve had allowed the demon Dis—Lucifer's shed husk—to possess him at the moment of his "birth." He'd had no choice, no say in the course of his life. He'd had no control over the evil that permeated every part of him, the evil that kept him from the perfection he desperately sought, that quest driving him past empathy and forgiveness and into the punisher he'd become.

Black Zodiac Virgo sat on the rocky ledge and crossed his legs, settling to watch the compound below, the gloaming slowing the activity of the women and children the Zodiac Assassins had foolishly left behind, had left vulnerable. He twitched at the imperfection of their decision, his wrath rising, his gut churning, the Assassins' disregard for their loved ones a decision that would cost them dearly.

You've grown even harsher since we were liberated from that cryo prison, Dis whispered, the soft sound making his brain itch.

"Mistakes mustn't be tolerated," Black Virgo snapped, scratching his bald head. The demon should have gotten it, should have understood his need.

That's the kind of thinking that led to my fall. Pride in my excellence, my wrath when I was cast out of Heaven. You will lose if you don't stop your fruitless quest for the flawless.

"I enjoyed the years of stasis because I didn't have to deal with you." He jutted his chin at the compound. "I will send the Assassins a message, one they will not forget."

Silence fell as surely as the night, and, with it, peace. A demon should have understood his desire to destroy, even applauded him for the effort, but this demon had once been a Cherub and had retained some of the characteristics of his purer self. The disparity had led to antipathy between them.

Ah, I understand.

"What do you understand?"

Mercury is making her pass. She's slowing down and you are being led by her chaos.

Black Virgo raised his head and stared at the stars, seeking a glimpse of the planet that ruled him, that flirted with Earth four times a year, flipping her figurative skirt at the paranormals and humans and laughing when they thought to overcome her influence. Not the best time to attack the compound, but it was right there, thumbing its nose at him, the opportunity to make right what was wrong too great a pull to walk away.

Turning his attention back to the wagon wheel of twelve houses with a thirteenth in the center, the itch started again. There were twelve zodiac signs, not thirteen. Imperfection. Two of the houses were too close together compared to the other houses. Imperfection. Too many outbuildings with no discernable pattern. Imperfection.

The why of his compulsion didn't matter; it only mattered that it was there, and he had to act on it to relieve the pressure, starting with those houses out of alignment.

Are you going to burn them? Dis asked, his voice near breathless.

"I could blame it on the Firestarter they have in their midst," Black Virgo said, tilting his head in thought, though he didn't care to cast off the blame.

No, he would revel in it.

Dis laughed, the sound vibrating through Black Virgo, a distinctly unpleasant sensation. *Well?*

"Not the houses. I have a plan for them." He pointed to the barns and sheds. "But those I'll burn," he whispered, shuddering from the discordant clash of revulsion and desire.

He stood and brushed off the seat of his pants, straightening his leather coat, his gaze on the valley below.

Are we going now?

"What do you think?"

I think you're going to regret this. I think you better take care not to get killed. I can't heal you from death.

"Noted. Now shut up while I get down the mountain."

BLACK VIRGO CROUCHED and studied the narrow dirt road leading from the mountains to the houses, taking time to catch his breath. The ground was mostly flat and open, no trees to hide behind. Not ideal, but if he moved slowly, he'd not only reduce the chance of being seen, he'd also buy himself time, reducing the likelihood there would still be people outside in the cold.

He might be strong, highly motivated, and trained to kill, but he was physically alone. He had no backup; the other Black Zodiacs were on a mission to kill the Assassins. Let his brothers fight the men from whom they were cloned; let them kill their makers. If any of the Assassins survived, particularly his maker, they would return here to pain and suffering and loss.

That alone was worth the solo mission; punishing the innocent for their imperfections was his reward.

He rose from the crouch, started forward, then stopped when the compound swam before his eyes. He staggered, his arms pinwheeling, righting himself after several steps, but it was a near thing. The hairs on the back of his neck rose.

"Mercury, why do you call to me now? Why do you jumble my thoughts when I need to be clearheaded?"

Of course she said nothing, but neither did Dis.

He pounded the meat of his hand against his temple, needing to clear it, to stop the chills running through him, to stop the dizziness threatening to send him to the ground.

"Stop confusing me."

The normally chatty demon sat back, watching, waiting for him to fail, waiting for that moment he could say, *"I told you so,"* in the most infuriating way possible.

"I will not fail, you bastard."

He forced his right foot forward, then his left, consciously making his legs move, planting his feet on the grass next to the crude, dirt road, until he was walking. He kept his gaze on the houses, not daring to look at the ground or the sky, the dizziness still flirting at the edges of his vision, hoping for an opening, a chance to take him down.

The air grew bitter, his breath puffing out of his mouth and nostrils. The leather coat couldn't keep up with the dropping temperature; he should have worn his down coat instead. But there was something about the black leather that telegraphed his malicious intent was death and he had come to deliver it.

No movement caught his eye. The people living in the houses had gone inside, probably to cook dinner, eat and talk and laugh, not knowing what was coming. His pace quickened as he neared the circle until he was only a few yards away from the closest house.

He glanced around, noted which windows glowed with golden light, then turned right, heading for the house he wanted to destroy first, the one with no lights on. Reaching the back of the house, he tested the door and windows. Finding them all locked, he pulled his sleeve down to cover his fist then broke a windowpane.

Unlocking the window, he opened it slowly, listening for an alarm, but none came. Heaving his body inside, he shut the window and turned around to study the house. He was inside a laundry room, a large one, with a washer and dryer, storage, and a walk-in shower.

"Nice."

He eased open the door to the main part of the house and listened for sounds of life. Hearing none, he walked into the huge kitchen. Running a hand along the stone countertop, he circled the space, noting the modern appliances, some he'd never seen before. Decades in stasis meant he'd missed a few advancements.

He finished his circuit then turned his attention to the even larger living area. An L-shaped, brown, leather sectional that could hold a dozen people took up the bulk of the space. Huge pillows of varying colors stood out on the couch and were scattered around the room; he could see the variety of patterns, though the hues were dull in the darkness of the room. Against one wall hung a television larger than any he'd seen. It was a beautiful, functional, comfortable space that he would have loved for his own, perfect for a man to relax in while plotting destruction.

He walked around the sectional and stopped at the built-in shelves on the right side of the television. Reaching out, he ran his fingers along the spines of the books until they ended at a framed photo. Picking it up, he smiled.

"There you are, Assassin Virgo."

They were twins in appearance, which stood to reason given Black Virgo was cloned from the Virgo in the photo. Six-foot-one in height, around two-hundred pounds, muscular, with rich brown skin that shone as if lit from within. Purity, that's what he saw in his maker, and it fired his rage.

He looked around the room. "This is your house? How poetic that I pick this one to infect. Now that I see how you live, I do find it a shame to destroy it." He slammed the photo down, smashing it against the stone floor, gratified by the crash of breaking glass. "But I will anyway."

Temporarily distracted from his mission, he glanced around the room. "Let's see what else I can crush first."

He jerked the television off the wall and hurled it across the room to smash into the glass-faced kitchen cabinets. Books hit the floor. More framed photos slammed into the walls, gouging chunks out of them. End tables, lamps, the coffee table, all broke under his feet and fists.

He strode to the kitchen, grabbed a knife, and attacked the sectional, cutting the entire length into ribbons until he reached the end. He dropped the knife and collapsed on the ruined leather, panting, his eyes stinging from the sweat dripping into them.

Cathartic didn't even begin to describe the feeling, but he wouldn't be able to demolish the entire interior. It would take too long, and he had this house and the one next door to attend to before starting on the outbuildings.

Besides, the imperfection of the mess was already grating on him, the impulse to clean strong.

He stood, his need to poison the house overwhelming his want to obliterate the Assassin's presence. He pulled off his leather coat and laid it across the back of the sectional, then stripped out of his long-sleeve shirt, jeans, and boxer briefs. Even his boots and socks came off.

He stepped gingerly through the rubble and headed upstairs. Rendering the house unlivable needed to start on the second level. He searched the rooms until he found the one with the king-sized bed and an attached bath. This would be Virgo's room.

He laced his fingers together and stretched out his arms, rolling his neck to prepare his body for what came next.

Feet spread shoulder-width apart, arms raised to the side, he pulled on his demon-fueled power, willing it to gather inside his core and build. In seconds, his skin was slick with sweat, the cold air in the room chilling his growing fever.

"Come on, Mercury, give me your chaos. Let me make it my own."

Don't sap your strength, boy, Dis said, breaking his silence.

Black Virgo opened his eyes. "Either give me everything you've got or shut up and I'll keep asking Mercury."

You shoot our wads doing this, you'll weaken us both.

Black Virgo gritted his teeth against the truth he couldn't—wouldn't—accept, his jaw grinding, and forced his focus back on the job. Tendrils of green smoke oozed out of his pores and wound around his body, wanting to escape him but too weak to disobey his will.

That's enough to poison five houses.

"Then it's just right."

Sweat rolled off him, his body trembling with the effort of fighting his own infection, the death he was about to release.

He was ready.

He threw his head back and bellowed, unable to stop the verbal exhalation of his exaltation and relief. The tendrils covering him vanished in the onslaught of the thick, green cloud. It rolled through the room, billowed up to the ceiling and down to the floor, filling the space until there was no more. Seeking escape, the gas disappeared into the hallway, coating every surface, penetrating every room, every crevice, every object the Assassin valued, rendering it valueless.

Black Virgo collapsed on the bed, exhausted, exultant, expectant. How many would die? How many would linger for agonizing days before succumbing to their inevitable demise? How much horror and grief would this inflict on the Zodiac Assassins and all who were stupid enough to love such imperfect creatures?

He giggled, the sound foreign to him.

He struggled to sit up, the weakness that typically fled in scant minutes lingering. Though he was loath to admit Dis was right, he had put too much into this house. Too much passion, too much physical destruction, too much poison.

Placing his hands on his knees, he pushed off, standing in place as the room spun around him. He focused on a large painting on the wall and recognized the Great Cavern of the InBetween, the subterranean world the goddess Hecate had created to give paranorms a home. A home in which to hide from persecution by the humans with whom they were meant to share the surface of Earth. He had been created in the InBetween; he and the other Black Zodiacs had resided there, hidden away until it was time for them to kill. But it had only been a matter of months when the leaders of the paranorms, the Twelve, had decided their creations were too dangerous.

"That tends to happen when you allow a demon to possess a trained killer. Bastards."

Before the Black Zodiacs had had a chance to escape their fate, they'd been divided, sent to their respective Zodiac houses, or what remained of them, and frozen, never to be released again.

"They made a mistake not killing us. Why is that?"

Because of me, Dis said. *And the other demons. The demon king, Asmodeus, facilitated your creation; he chose which demons to implant in you—one of them his own son—and he has a plan for us all.*

Before Black Virgo could ask what the plan was, growls sounded outside.

"Time to go."

Are we leaving the compound?

"Hell, no. Not until I've completed the job."

We've been discovered too soon. Escape is the only move.

Black Virgo ran out of the bedroom and down the stairs, swatting at the cloud of gas lingering in the air. This house was well and truly done. If any of the Assassins made it home, they would have to destroy it and start over, this time, hopefully, making the houses fucking even.

He dressed quickly, then ran to the curtained windows at the back of the house. He peeked outside and saw the outlines of massive beasts patrolling back and forth, their heads down, sniffing so loudly he could hear the snuffling inside the house.

"Son of a bitch. Fenrir wolves."

I'm surprised the beasts are on the surface instead of lurking underground in the InBetween, Dis said.

"No doubt they followed the Assassins here to live in the light."

What are you going to do?

Black Virgo backed away from the window. "I have an idea."

He ran through the great room and to the stairs, taking two steps at a time. He returned to the master bedroom and the bay window facing the central house.

He pointed down. "There."

So you do still have the presence of mind to be clever?

Black Virgo unlatched the center window and raised it. Leaning out, he studied the covered walkway that spanned from this house to the house at the center of the wheel configuration, the hub.

The demon's comment registered. "What do you mean the presence of mind?"

Instead of being with the other Black Zodiacs, we're here, the heart of the enemy, on a mission to destroy some of their homes, all while announcing in the most glaring way possible that you exist. Subterfuge would have been better. Strike the Assassins one at a time, or even en masse, as a unit, to minimize your exposure. There are only twelve of you; the Assassins are twelve, plus all the paranorms and humans and, Dis pointed at the floor for emphasis, *the great beasts they've pulled into their orbit.*

"As I recall, you were excited by the idea of me burning the place down."

I also told you this was a bad idea, that you would regret it. Ultimately, no matter what gets me off, you are the primary driver of this meatsuit.

Black Virgo swung a leg over the window ledge, then the other. "I am, so be quiet and get ready to help me blanket this place in poison."

Uh, about that—

Before the demon could complain about something else that had no relevance, Black Virgo dropped to the overhang, his booted feet sliding on the shingles until he caught himself. He blew out a breath, the adrenaline sweats already breaking out.

"Now we find out how strong the walkway roof is," he whispered to himself.

He sat, twisted at the waist, then gripped the edge of the overhang with both hands. He let his legs dangle before easing the rest of his body down until he felt the walkway beneath his feet. He released one hand and let his weight settle. Finding it solid enough to support him, he let go of the house.

The metal support structure groaned, the complaint soft and short; it hadn't been built for a man to stand on. Question was: How would it handle him running?

From his vantage point he could see all the front doors of the houses facing the central hub. Maximum view at the back, a cozy community feel inside the wheel. You could sit in a rocking chair on the front porch and talk to your neighbors.

"Makes me want to puke," he whispered to the night.

Can we get this done?

"You have somewhere to be? Another soul to corrupt?"

Nah, I'm too used to your crazy.

Getting on with it wasn't a bad idea, so Black Virgo took a step, then a second, pausing at each one to gauge the walkway's tolerance. It continued to hold. He raised his head and studied the distance between the house and the hub, then narrowed his eyes at the spot where the walkway to the second house on his list tied into the whole.

"I'll show you crazy."

He took off at a run, not looking down, not allowing the cracking under his feet to slow him until he slipped on the rounded roof, his arms pinwheeling to right himself. He blew out a breath and started running again.

A soft hiss made him glance to his right. The Fenrir wolves hadn't made a sound, not a yip nor growl nor bark. Only their paws trampling the grass had betrayed them.

They're hunting you.

"I got that."

They're almost as tall as this roof.

"Shut up."

The hub house was a few yards away, but he still had to get to the other walkway roof and run back. And he was already winded after poisoning the first house. How he was going to poison the second one, burn the outbuildings, avoid being eaten by the wolves, and get away was difficult to imagine.

He reached the hub house and leaped to catch the secondary roof line. He hung from it for a second, mustered his strength, and scraped his way up until he collapsed, momentarily safe from the creatures looking for a free meal.

Take a few minutes. Let's not make it easy for them. I don't want to be cast adrift on Earth.

Black Virgo couldn't stop his chuckle, even though circumstances weren't all that great. "Afraid God will recognize who and what you are and send his armies to annihilate you?"

He heard a snort in his mind, the sound tickling, causing his left eye to twitch.

There's so much more going on here than just making you and your brothers strong killers. Fate is playing the hand that we gave her, and the showdown is almost here. I can't allow your madness to fuck up centuries' worth of plans.

"Now you tell me?"

I haven't had the time nor inclination to say anything before. You and your "brothers" proved yourselves too dark, too evil, to be allowed to exist. It was only through threats and promises that Asmodeus was able to save your lives.

Black Virgo rolled onto his back and stared at the stars. "And waste them in cryo chambers."

That was unfortunate, but it would never have been allowed to stand. Asmodeus created a plan to free us and obviously it worked.

He could imagine Dis punctuating his statement with a "voila" gesture. "First I'm crazy, now I'm mad?"

Dis sighed. *Look where you've brought us. What do you call this? Every day I wonder if the rest of the Black Zodiacs are as screwed up as you.*

Black Virgo climbed to his feet and assessed the now much larger number of wolves milling around waiting for their chance to take him down, chew him up. It seemed everyone had the same idea, but he was smarter than them all. His vision of a perfect world was a bright light on the horizon that he would smash and burn and kill to reach, so close but so difficult to attain. That wasn't madness; that was purity of purpose.

"Everyone is screwed up in their own way. Everyone. What sets me apart is my ability to see what perfection looks like, and my willingness to destroy everything to achieve it."

Perfection is the enemy of good. Don't know who

said it, but you'd best remember it if you want to come out of this alive.

Black Virgo studied the next walkway as he trotted along the roof of the hub house. Just as he reached it, he smiled. "What makes you think I want to live?"

He leaped off the asphalted roof and landed hard on the glass top of the walkway. The metal frame shuddered and complained then sagged, buckling. *I need to hurry.*

A Fenrir wolf yipped and the dozens around it answered. If any non-beast was awake, they must have heard the wolves' excited chorus by now. *Best not tarry.*

He pushed off and ran again, his goal the next house he itched to desecrate. He ran hard, using momentum and muscle to propel him, trying to keep his footprint light and quick to traverse the shuddering walkway roof.

Metal screeched.

He glanced back.

The end of the metal frame attached to the hub house broke loose and fell to the side, bringing the rest of the walkway with it, one section at a time. The roof under him shook, threatening to send him sliding off the side and into the jaws of the slobbering pack. He picked up the pace, running flat out. He was so close.

Glass cracked and shattered and rained down on the concrete below.

Make haste, boy.

"Quit telling me what to do and give me some power."

I would but I gave you too much earlier. I warned you.

"Then what use—?"

The roof under his feet gave way and he fell onto the concrete path, his muscles burning, a sharp, concerning pain in his right knee distracting him for a moment before he smelled the wolves. Their fetid breath and wet-dog scent washed over him, sinking into his pores, his skin crawling from the threat. He remained still, only rolling his eyes up, then to the side, to assess the distance between him and the pack.

They hadn't attacked immediately, so it wasn't as bad as it could have been. Instead, they'd stopped twenty feet away from him. The distance to the front door was shorter. If he could get to his feet and get to the house, he could dive through the window to the right of the door and hope the wolves couldn't follow him.

He moved his legs under him, the hot, jarring pain in his knee bringing tears to his eyes. This wouldn't work if he couldn't run and jump.

The largest wolf, huge, black, with red eyes, lowered his head and growled deep. He took one step forward, matching Black Virgo move for move.

He rose onto his knees, needing to cry out, but too worried about setting off the pack to vocalize. He staggered to his feet and froze when the rest of the pack inched forward. They knew what he was doing; they were ready to leap.

But another sound, somewhere in the dark behind the wolves, caught their attention. They paused their advance and looked back.

Black Virgo followed their focus, goosebumps rising, the primal response prepping him to face an unknown predator even more formidable than the Fenrir, and that was saying a lot.

The grass rustled, yet the night held onto its secret

until the newcomers reached the back of the pack circled around him.

A rumble of vibrato and violence erupted from the new arrivals, the sound loosening his bowels. Whatever was about to reveal itself wouldn't be toying with him, wouldn't chase him like the wolves had. No, this was his end.

"Please Mercury, help me, for real this time."

As if planned for most terrifying effect, three tigers and three lions stepped out of the shadows and revealed themselves, their teeth chattering in excitement, saliva dripping from their massive jaws.

You are well and truly screwed, my meatsuit.

"Seriously, shut up. You're not helping."

There isn't any help to be had.

There was no running, not on his injured knee, and not when he was surrounded by animals hungry for his flesh. What an inglorious ending.

The hot flush of anger and fear and frustration made him stand tall. He would not quiver and cower before the beasts. He would stand tall and fight until they tore him apart, taking out as many of them as he could before they did.

Any chance you've recharged?

Black Virgo raised a hand and demanded that his power answer, but no tendrils appeared, no poison oozed from his pores to gather around him. Imperfection had won, and he would die. He took a long, deep breath.

"Come on then. Let's get this done."

As one, the wolves and big cats surged forward.

Black Virgo feinted to the left, using a metal post, somehow still standing, to block the closest wolf. The animal hit it hard, just as he'd hoped. What he hadn't expected was the immediate crash of the entire frame, from the hub to the house a few feet away from him.

His attackers slammed into the wrecked steel, tripping over it and going down, only to have the next wave go down with them in a spectacular tangle of limbs that reminded him of the Keystone Cops mayhem he'd found amusing so many years back.

The hairs on the back of his neck rose, the vibrations running through his body proof that this was the work of Mercury's Retrograde. Hastily laid plans, or even the best laid plans, were nothing in the face of Mercury's power over the universe and all its inhabitants.

Don't just stand there. Run!

Black Virgo limped through the wriggling, growling mass of bodies trying to right themselves. He reached the front door, found it unlocked, and slipped inside, closing it quickly before the beasts realized what had happened. He could only hope they didn't try to get inside, but that wasn't his only problem.

The din the animals were currently making would surely wake people. The collapsed walkway had already made so much noise that he was shocked no one had appeared to challenge his presence.

A giggle bubbled up and he clapped a hand over his mouth.

Is it possible to shit oneself when you're an incorporeal demon?

"No idea, but I could stand to use the bathroom."

Black Virgo winced as he made his way to the half bath. He closed the door, noted there was no window, and flipped on the light to get a look at the damage. Cuts, bruises that he could tell would be spectacular, those he could deal with. He sat on the toilet and raised his pant leg.

His knee was well and truly damaged, already so swollen he couldn't see the kneecap. "This isn't good."

Hate to break your woe-is-me moment, but the wolves and cats have grown silent.

There was nothing to do for the knee at the moment; he had more pressing issues. He turned off the light, waited a few moments to let his eyes adjust, then opened the bathroom door. He poked his head out of the room, his caution automatic, and cursed.

The sweep of several lights flashed by the front and back windows. People.

He slid out of the bathroom, his back hugging the wall as he returned to the front door. He glanced outside and cursed again. The wolves and cats surrounded several women, walking around them, their rumbles and growls easy to interpret, shouting the alarm that a stranger was in their midst.

One of the tigers and the largest Fenrir wolf broke away from the pack. They walked side by side to the front door and sat so close he could have opened it and touched them without crossing the threshold.

The tiger let out a plaintive yowl.

The women turned.

The wolf chuffed and scratched at the door.

All the flashlights whipped around and targeted it.

Pushing off the heavily carved wood, Black Virgo worked his way through the great room and to the back of the house. He stood to the side of the double doors and used a finger to pull the curtain out enough to get a peek. More flashlights shone in the distance, heading this way.

Mercury had given him one break, and while it

had been a big one, it seemed she was only so generous. Once again he was fucked.

THE BITTER TANG of frustration filled him to bursting; the pain of his unthinkable defeat, his entrapment, stole his breath. Tears rolled unbidden down his cheeks. His hands balled into fists, ready to hammer anything standing in his way. He panted through the growing need to destroy, to make more imperfect the ceaseless imperfections that plagued him, desperate to ease his torment.

He fell to the floor, his fists beating against his temples, screaming into the yawning darkness of the empty house, raging against the impotence imposed upon him. They had done this to him, they had trapped and hurt him, they weren't allowing him to finish what he'd started.

Jumping up, he grabbed the closest object, a metal floor lamp. He ripped it free of the outlet, swinging it wildly. Framed art, the drywall, the television, vases, other lamps...he smashed and crushed his way around the great room, only stopping when he discovered the lamp wouldn't do enough harm to the sectional to matter.

Are you done? Can we plan now, or are you too far gone from reason?

Black Virgo sliced the blade of his hand diagonally through the air in response.

I guess that's a "no" from the seriously decompensating Black Zodiac.

He hobbled into the kitchen to continue his destruction, ignoring the demon. He swung the lamp over and over, tearing cabinet doors off their hinges, blindly destroying the kitchen to mitigate the growing tempest. If he couldn't poison the place, he had to at least make it unlivable...

He stopped abruptly at the thought, the lamp raised over his head, poised to hammer at the fancy stove. Lowering the lamp, he set it on the floor, pressed both hands to the stone countertop, and dropped his head to catch his breath. There was more than one way to demolish and now that he'd been discovered, subtlety wasn't needed.

If you've got that out of your system, sit down and let me heal your knee so we can cut and run from this disaster.

The destruction wasn't done, just the method revised. Implementing it would help his escape, and healing his knee would be integral to his success. As quickly as the rage had come, it faded, cooling him enough to allow his mind to rest and plan. He loved that he could turn the violence off and on, but the razor's edge he valued had been the reason the Twelve had condemned him to a frozen prison. He was too dark, too violent, too unstable, making him a liability the Twelve had chosen not to tolerate.

The Black Zodiacs had been created, had been trained to be vicious, merciless, and then their masters had thrown them away like garbage. And the Twelve weren't alive any longer for them to get vengeance.

He limped to the sectional in the middle of the great room—did the Assassins buy no other kind of furniture?—and sat down. He lifted his injured leg onto the black leather then leaned back and waited for the demon to do the one thing of benefit to him.

He looked around the space, noting the broken

television barely hanging on the wall, the same built-in shelving as Virgo's house, the same layout. Had the builders constructed identical houses by design or for expedience? Whatever the reason, having indistinguishable floorplans made it easier to move around in the dark.

Heat bloomed in his knee, far greater than the inflammation, and, with it, hate. The sweat coating him after his rampage was refreshed, the struggle to remain still while Dis did his work making his muscles twitch.

He dropped his head back, closed his eyes, and imagined his revenge on everyone surrounding the house.

Seriously? You're still plotting? When are you going to understand that we have to get out of here? Forget your compulsion and remember you have to survive.

Black Virgo snorted. "You mean you have to survive. You want me to back off, you need to tell me more about this plan you and the other demons have concocted."

A surge of heat scorched his knee. He jerked away then carefully rose, testing the joint. It was good enough.

"Back off, Dis."

You forget yourself, paranorm. I don't have to tell you a thing.

"And I don't have to carry you."

There's only one way to get rid of me, and that is power beyond your reach.

Black Virgo lowered his head and smiled. "There's another way."

Dis remained silent.

"That's right. If I die, you have no more meatsuit

to carry you around. If that happens, your little mission fails. Didn't know I knew that, did you?"

You don't want to die.

"Maybe, but the InBetween has a direct path to Hell now, and if you don't give me some cooperation, I'll take the express route back to where Asmodeus found you. I die or I take you back to Hell and your plan will be for naught. Which would you prefer? Because I really don't care."

Minutes passed before Dis spoke. *I can only tell you we have a plan and we're waiting for the right moment to put it into motion.*

"And Asmodeus is the architect of this plan?"

Yes, Dis said, the monosyllabic answer garbled as if it had to fight its way past clenched teeth.

"This isn't over. I will know more, but not now. You have a plan, and so do I."

Oh, thank Lucifer.

Black Virgo crossed his arms.

We are in a world of hurt here, enough with the attitude.

"Fine, but rather than tell you, I'll show you."

He returned to the kitchen, the pain in his knee but a whisper now. He searched the drawers until he found a stack of kitchen towels. Pulling them out, he set them next to the stove.

"Now for some go-go juice."

He went to the utility room and scrounged around until he found a bag of wood chips and a garbage can filled with small oak logs. On a shelf above them was a bulk box of lighters and bottles of lighter fluid; whoever lived in this house loved to grill.

"Perfect."

He collected all of the bottles, palmed a few

lighters, then grabbed the bag of wood chips and took his haul to the kitchen.

I'm still not getting what you're doing.

"You don't have to."

Black Virgo gathered more supplies then collected every bottle of alcohol he could find.

Ripping the towels into long strips, he stuffed them into the liquor bottles and held the ends, letting the alcohol soak through before pulling the towel out a few inches. He barely heard the growing sounds of the crowd surrounding the house, but he felt them.

Finished with the bottles, he searched the house until he found an empty wine case. He filled it with the bottles and stuffed the lighters into his coat pocket, except for one he left on the counter.

"Almost done," he said under his breath.

Grabbing a bottle of lighter fluid and the bag of wood chips, he opened the oven door then turned it on, the soft hiss of gas better than the last gasp of a dying human.

He ran up the stairs, distributed the chips into piles and soaked them with fluid. Starting at the farthest room from the stairs, he lit the chips, pile after pile, until the second floor danced with flames and smoke.

So burning down the house is your go to? This is your great plan to escape? Seems we're trapped now between man and beast and fire.

"Have a little faith, demon. Oh, wait, you lost your faith and were cast into Hell for it."

Blah, blah, blah. If you drag me back to the Pit, I'll make sure your personal Hell involves you being strapped to a chair, forced to witness all the imperfection around you with no way to remedy it.

Ignoring the petulant demon, Black Virgo ran

down the stairs and into the kitchen. The gas from the oven had filled the space quicker than he'd expected; soon it would infiltrate the rest of the house until it reached the fire upstairs, then...

He lifted the box of bottles, strode to the back door, and opened the curtain. Just as he'd expected, he was surrounded. Good.

He unlocked the door and opened it, stepping outside. Shutting the door behind him, he studied his adversaries before walking across the deck and down the four steps to the grass.

The cold air was bracing. The silhouette of the mountains charged him, the pull of Mercury surging through him again now that he was free of the confines of drywall and wood framing and asphalt roofing shingles. She could toy with him all she wanted, but her chaos wouldn't change the next few minutes nor the blood he would spill.

He giggled then wondered how mad he'd become, how insane he would be by his end.

Three women appeared on his left. One was tall, slim, with straight, black hair and black eyes, one was short and curvy with long, curly, black hair and dark eyes, and the third was slender, fragile, a delicate doll with silver hair and glowing, purple eyes. They stopped in front of him, a united front until the short, curvy woman walked toward him.

"Virgo?" She cocked her head to the side, her expression puzzled, her eyes sad. "What are you doing here? Where are the rest of the Zodiacs?" She looked at the box in his hands, her eyes widening. "What are you doing?"

She continued forward until the silver-haired woman yelled, "Taryn!"

The woman named Taryn immediately stopped walking and looked back.

The silver-haired woman shook her head. "That's not Virgo."

"What do you mean?" Taryn pointed at him. "*That's* Virgo. I know what he looks like."

"I'm telling you it's not. Maybe a trick of the light, or maybe we suddenly have shapeshifters in the paranorm pantheon. Either way, I've scanned him. You need to back away. Now."

Taryn stepped back, never taking her eyes off him, her expression growing hard. "Do I need to call Gaia?"

Black Virgo set down the box and pulled out a bottle and one of the lighters from his pocket, all while staring down the petite woman who'd called him out.

"Scanned me?" he finally said. "How clever. I didn't even feel it."

"You wouldn't," she said. "Tell us who you are and what you want."

He lifted the bottle higher to make sure she got a good look.

"You were partially right," he said to the woman Taryn. "I am Virgo, but not your Virgo, not a Zodiac Assassin." He flicked the lighter to life and held it under the tip of the alcohol-soaked rag. "I'm a Black Zodiac."

Flames erupted.

"No!" the woman Taryn screamed, dropping to her knees on the ground and jamming her hands into the dirt, twisting them frantically until her forearms were buried up to her elbows.

Blue light exploded out of the twin-pierced ground, covering Taryn's body in moments. She slowly stood and the blue followed her, engulfed her.

Black Virgo reared back and threw the bottle to his left, toward a different group of women, framed by several Fenrir wolves and big cats.

The people scattered, calling the animals back as the bottle arced. It hit the ground and exploded outward, the fire searching for more fuel, seeking to devour anything it touched.

Black Virgo groaned, his ecstasy unbound until Taryn's blue light leaped from her hand to the fire and extinguished it.

"No!" he screamed, the dying of the flames as agonizing as losing a part of himself.

He grabbed the next bottle, lit it, and flung it at the silver-haired woman. She didn't move as the bottle flew at her, didn't try to escape the conflagration that would envelop her and eat at her flesh until she was no more than ash.

Have to admire that, Dis whispered.

But mere feet before the bottle hit her chest, Taryn's power threw up a wall and the bottle crashed against it. Explosion, fire, but no damage, not even to the blue.

Immediately, he pulled out another bottle and lit it, throwing it to the right before grabbing another and repeating the motion. Over and over he threw bottles; every time, Taryn's power stopped him.

They both shook, they both sweated, they both grunted under the strain of the fight. She was suffering, just as much as he was, but he would run out of bottles before she ran out of power.

He glanced back at the house, dropped to the ground, and covered his head.

"Run!" someone yelled.

The house exploded.

The furious shockwave washed over him, deafening sound right after it. Wood and glass and drywall pummeled his body, piercing his leather coat, ruining it as the shrapnel stabbed his back. When the worst of the explosion had passed, he rolled onto his side and watched the inferno rage.

He laughed. He wanted to stay here for hours to witness every piece of the house be consumed, but he had created this chance for escape; he needed to use it. He climbed to his feet and staggered away from the burning pile, his gaze on the mountains in the distance.

He'd reached the edge of the light, had almost managed to disappear into the deep dark, when fire filled his head, piercing the gray matter in his brain. He stopped, braced his legs to keep from falling, grabbed his head, and squeezed.

That's right. I'm in your head, you asshole, and I'm going to pop your brain like a balloon, a woman whispered, her rage contained, focused, battering at him.

"Silver hair," he managed to say, though the sound was more a grunt.

Her name is Persephone, Dis said, breaking through his pain.

I see you both now. Demon and Black Virgo, and I'm unimpressed, she continued.

"Get out of my head," he said in a whisper that ended with a whimper.

You made a mistake coming here, attacking my family, hurting my friends, she said.

Black Virgo lurched forward. Maybe if he got far enough away from her...

Now I'm going to chew through your brain, take every scrap of memory, and leave you a drooling mess to wander in the mountains you're so desperately trying to reach until you die. That's if I don't send the wolves and cats out to hunt you down and eat you alive, she ground out.

He smiled through the agony. "But I hurt you. That is enough for now."

Step, step, step.

As fascinated as I am by your power, Persephone, I cannot allow you to kill him. Better luck next time.

A switch flipped in his brain and the pain fell away. Black Virgo could have sworn he heard it; he definitely felt it when Dis forced Persephone out of his head, freeing him to walk faster, to make his escape from the compound.

His focus narrowed to the mountains. He pushed his body to stagger up the smaller hills, crawling on hands and feet through the forest like an animal, the cold growing with each foot he climbed.

When he reached an opening in the trees at the top of the first peak, he collapsed onto his side.

He stank of smoke and blood and sweat and fear. He trembled with the effort of the climb, the injuries to his back, and the lingering pain of having Persephone in his head. He'd survived, he'd destroyed, he'd made the imperfect more imperfect, and soon it would be gone.

But he was shaken to his core by the close call. What should have been simple, easy, smooth, had nearly been his undoing, and he'd been violated by the Assassins' women.

Not to mention the secrets Persephone probably gleaned from her excursion into your feeble brain.

Black Virgo stared into the sky, panting through a fresh bout of muscle cramps, the sting of numerous cuts and punctures making their presence known now that he'd stopped moving.

"Shut up and heal me."

Dis growled, but warmth spread through Black Virgo, beating back the cold.

The power of the Retrograde tickled his skin, the phenomenon at its height. He needed to keep that in mind the next time he was planning an op, avoid her at all costs.

He dug his fingernails into the dirt. "Mercury. What a bitch."

Her Secret Face

BY CAROL RYLES

Mileva Gray. My darkest gem. My thirty-five million and ninety-seventh human offspring. Born frowning. Fists clenched. Refusing to cry.

Centuries ago on Earth, I would have tinkered with her neural patterns, manipulated chimeric proteins, recombined DNA. Out here, in this asteroid among the stars, I pondered her potential.

Never before had danger so clearly presented.

I should have ended her when I could.

I believed I could change her.

MILEVA KNEW that Vesta considered her to be a flawed human. She'd known it since the age of fifteen, when her mentor, Garrod Jon, had submitted himself to be uploaded into Vesta's physical memory. Although Mileva understood the procedure would preserve Garrod's consciousness for eternity, she could not get past the terrible fact that his flesh and blood body would be reduced to constituent atoms.

The villagers had gathered in the orchard for Garrod's farewell. He lay on a wicker bed beneath budding fruit trees. At his request, the holographic sky had been set to mid-winter blue. The air remained warm and breezeless. His wife, Adeline, sat at his side, contented, accepting.

Mileva stood close enough to show her respect, but far enough away for the couple to not see her grief. She'd farewelled Garrod the day before. The ceremony was superfluous.

"It's wrong," she said in a low voice.

Her father took her hand. "Remember: his new purpose will be glorious."

"If he cannot speak with us, how is his passing any different from a sacrifice? You'd think people would have grown out of that kind of barbarism by now."

"Shush," her mother urged.

Too angry for silence, Mileva added, "If we could all upload, I'd accept that. But Vesta only takes some of us. It's not fair. It's murder."

"A deity cannot fit everyone into her temple," her mother said. "Some minds are more suitable than others. It's a fact you must learn to accept."

That evening, Mileva's brother tried to distract her with a baby quail. Any other time its half-grown feathers would have made her smile; but as she cradled it in her hands, she saw it as too fragile, too dependent on the whims of Vesta.

She lowered the bird into its nest, then ran into

the night and kept running until reaching Garrod's studio. Inside, someone had left his holograms running. Starscapes rippled like oceans on the ceiling. Forests obscured the walls. Mileva recognized her own handiwork sprouting between tree trunks: the vines and brackens that Garrod had taught her to create.

This room had been the single place she'd felt freed from the prying eyes of Vesta. Without Garrod, it felt empty, abandoned. "I can't do it anymore," she said, cutting the holograms' power. She returned outside, walked until dawn, then breakfasted on soy-apples growing wild among mushrooms laden with chestnuts.

"If you respect us," she said, hoping that Vesta would deign to answer. "Why force us to sacrifice our loved ones?"

"Sacrifice is an ancient ritual," Vesta responded. "Invented by your predecessors to honor the hearths of Lavinium. In the centuries that followed, technology encouraged you to enhance yourselves to levels even I, myself, failed to imagine. When you leapt into space to carve habitats inside asteroids, I resented this development, but soon learned to use it to elevate those who proved worthy – to join them to me."

Mileva spun around, expecting to see Vesta's avatar hovering like a specter, but found nothing so much as a stray pixel. "Why would a deity require technology?"

Vesta answered in that slow gentle way she reserved for infants. "I do not 'require' it. Call it a bridge if you must. A physical conduit between your existence and mine." The air shivered like a glitch, a reminder of Vesta's ever-presence. "One day, you'll understand. In the meantime, your fledgling mind must be patient and wait."

Garrod Jon's intellect willingly seated itself into my physical memory. His presence renewed degrading pathways, resealed my promise to protect Earth's remaining people.

Mileva's refusal to believe this perplexed me.

I infused her with melatonin. Dimmed the lights. Probed her mind to reassess her potential.

IQ average. Intuitive skills surprisingly astute. Related as much to instinct as to intellect.

No precedent. No hint as to how to proceed.

Critical point reached. Three paths from which to choose...

Allow her to continue?

Force her to change?

End her before she ends me?

"I want to see the universe outside," Mileva demanded. "The real universe."

"It will frighten you," Vesta said, her voice unemotionally cool. "It is not what you would imagine."

"Really?"

Vesta's avatar morphed into the form of a young male. As he took a step forward, tufts of grass curled around his feet. Mileva frowned at the realization the hologram was in fact a re-gendered image of herself – a strategy she'd seen Vesta use to soothe others: one that relied on an atavistic preference for family over non-family, beauty over ugliness, familiar over strange.

"That's not you," Mileva said.

Vesta's outlines blurred and re-morphed into a crone wearing a white robe edged with gold. Her eyes, nested in wrinkles, were annoyingly familiar.

Mileva huffed. "That's still me." She could not decide if she should be impressed at the crone's apparent dignity, or disturbed by this unwanted glimpse of her future self.

The avatar winked out. "How do you wish to see me? As a king? A queen? A benevolent dictator?"

"I want you to be you."

"My true self?"

"Yes."

"I'm not the prettiest of objects, but as you wish."

Her likeness appeared in the clouds, a pock-marked, potato-shaped asteroid, its surface punctuated by sensors, energy sails, weapons. There was no sign of the people trapped beneath its skin, only cold hard technology imposed upon a once natural object, a legacy of Lost Earth.

"Vesta, you're patronizing me. Show me your real self."

Vesta let out the semblance of a laugh. The asteroid trembled. "It's as much as your human self can apprehend. Though, of course, there's always the internal plumbing. Does your curiosity extend to that?"

"I want to see the real you," Mileva said.

Day became night, absolute, starless. Mileva knew she was being toyed with. "Do you mean to upload me?" she asked.

"Not yet."

"What if I refuse?"

Vesta's presence withdrew. The world felt empty, impossibly small.

Curiosity is a human trait, one I can choose to encourage or ignore.

I sent tutorials to free her from her prison of ignorance: History. Science. Philosophy. Logic.

She brooded for months, perhaps daunted by the complexity of what she'd learned.

Efforts wasted, you ask?

I almost agreed, almost ended her—

But then she submitted a single terrible query – one I'd been dreading to hear.

This could be my downfall, I realized. And thus lay the challenge.

Mileva could not bring herself to return to Garrod's studio. It made her feel as if Vesta had planned for her to replace him – as if the hole left by his passing could be filled as easily as the spaces in a hologram. To curb her anger, she immersed her energies in her father's gardens, digging into soil, breathing its scent.

She plucked a strawberry, admired its plumpness, tasted and savored its sugary flesh. A perfect organism, she mused, unaware that its manufactured world was part real and part holographic. But what was its true purpose? To simply exist? Or act as fodder?

Mileva knew she'd be happy if she could fool herself into ignorance. Though, after absorbing Vesta's tutorials, how could she? Not that their content explained everything, but the more she thought about them, the more she wanted to know.

"Vesta," she said, pulling herself to her feet. "I have a question."

The air in front flickered into the avatar of Mileva the crone. "Proceed," she said in a voice part benevolent and wholly untrustworthy.

"Who destroyed Lost Earth?"

The avatar froze. Lips unmoving, she said, "How do you know it was destroyed?"

"How else could we have lost it?"

Vesta shrugged. "Natural disaster? War?"

"But our histories say nothing of these. At least not the kind that could eliminate an entire planet."

"Earth was loved by all who knew it," Vesta said with almost-believable sincerity. "Its destruction was a mistake."

"How so?"

"A miscalculation. Product of ignorance. Dishonesty."

"I don't understand."

"When technology surpasses its creators, you yourselves become unwitting targets." Vesta's avatar shrank into the body of a child. "My purpose is to nurture what remains."

"But you killed Garrod," Mileva said, taking a step backwards. "Along with thousands before him. Is that how you nurture us?"

"I love them all."

"Then why keep them caged?"

The avatar winked out, then reappeared on Mileva's shoulder as a brindled owl. "Caged you say? Allow me to show you the alternative."

The owl took flight in a flurry of feathers. Curious, Mileva ran, following it past the orchards, away from the village and into the ancient temperate forest. The owl landed by an oval of blue at the base of a towering eucalyptus. Mileva knelt at its edge, immersed her hand. "It's too warm for a wellspring. It tingles."

"It's a weak electric field."

"Yes, an unfinished hologram. But what does it mask?"

"Press deeper and you'll see."

Mileva hesitated, wondering if the illusion was a prelude to being uploaded. A koi with piebald markings swam up to her. Bright metallic scales brushed her fingers. At its touch, its skin shimmered and the wellspring contracted into a deep fish-eyed lens. The lens dilated to reveal the reality beyond the ship's skin: an endless ocean of stars.

"Beautiful," Mileva breathed.

"The closest and brightest ones belong to what your ancestors called Orion's sword. But in reality it has nothing to do with warriors. It's a womb. A stellar nursery."

"Your point is?"

"Nothing is as it seems, until you look closer."

The wellspring expanded into a globe, engulfing everything in its path. Mileva felt minuscule, meaningless.

Withdrawing her hand, she screamed.

I looked into her mind despite knowing that by observing her thoughts I would alter their direction.

Can you see how conflicted I became?

Through her, I saw the stars expand into clusters, galaxies, and the immense darkness that stretched out beyond. To me, they were composites of atoms. To her, they were gods.

"This is the fuel of creation," I said, by way of encouraging her. "Experience and immersion. Yours and mine combined. The universe is everything; but there is only one of us."

Fear spread through her, peaked. "There was only one Earth. So, why was it destroyed?"

For an instant, I wanted to take her – but doing so before she was ready would have reduced our potential.

Mileva remained kneeling, silent until her breathing slowed. "That was you! Inside my head."

Vesta morphed into a replica of Garrod, all the way down to the fern tattoos at his brow. "What did you perceive?" he – Vesta – asked.

"Is this your way of uploading me?"

"You're not ready. I'll need your consent."

"Did Garrod consent? Or did you coerce him?"

"Coercion is pointless. An unwilling intellect is incompatible."

"Will you take Garrod's wife? Allow them to be reunited?"

Vesta looked askance. "No."

"She wishes you would. So, why not?"

"You wouldn't understand."

"Try me."

"You're too young. When you're older, you'll see."

For a long moment, Vesta's delay made sense. Ignorance soothes, Mileva thought. No wonder people embrace it. She, herself, almost wanted to. Almost, until...

"Why were you in my head?"

"To help you."

"Why didn't you ask first?"

"You were too distraught."

Mileva bit back a curt reply. When she could trust herself to speak, she said. "I can calm myself well enough, thank you very much."

"Well, actually, you were failing at that."

Mileva balled her fists. "Why won't you tell me who destroyed Lost Earth?"

A pause. The avatar flickered. "I don't know who destroyed it."

"You're supposed to know everything."

The forest grew silent. Mileva folded her arms, waited.

"A rogue command," Vesta said in a small voice. "Hidden in the asteroid's defenses long before I took control of its processors. I dismissed it as harmless. Within days of my arrival, it released itself to destroy Earth."

Goosebumps shivered along the length of Mileva's spine. All her life she'd suspected that Vesta ensured loyalty by twisting truths, but this confession was like nothing Mileva could imagine. "Outsmarted by humans?" she asked.

"By their technology."

"But you're a deity. How could that be?"

"Since then, I've found another command. Also

rogue. I cannot access it to determine its purpose. Rest assured, I have thwarted its release."

Mileva tried to stand, but her legs shook.

"Listen," Vesta said haltingly. "Even deities make mistakes. What happened to Lost Earth will not happen again. I promise."

Mileva wanted to believe her, but logic demanded she shouldn't.

LIES ARE A CONSEQUENCE OF FEAR.

Fear is an ancient emotion, necessitated by the need to survive. Consequently, fear is logical. As are lies.

Encourage or reject her? Nurture or ignore?

I asked myself: what use was survival without growth? What would I lose if I ended her or gained her consent to upload when her talent was still immature?

Risk: high.

Loss: indeterminate.

Plan of action: erase the knowledge of Earth's destruction from her memory.

MILEVA BLINKED. She'd been thinking about something important. Now it was gone and—

"Vesta," she whispered. "What did you erase?"

Silence.

"Are you there?"

Nothing.

Part grateful and part afraid, Mileva convinced herself that Vesta's refusal to communicate was exactly what she'd always wanted. She knew she could never be free, but when friends invited her to an expedition to the Savannah habitat of Kidepo, she accepted. Weeks later, she struck out on her own to hike through tundra plains and deserts, beaches and forests, determined to find people, who like herself, distrusted Vesta and longed for escape.

On her twenty-fifth birthday, her search ended when she arrived at the shore of a peaceful toroid sea. As she bent to collect shellfish, the end of a rope ladder dropped down from above. She looked up and gaped at the distant hull of a multi-sailed airship. Shellfish forgotten, she took hold of the ladder and climbed.

At the top, a young man with sun-bleached hair helped her onto the deck. "You're sweating, so you can't be an avatar," he said.

His name was Edmar Vale. He brought out hand-made bread and ship-grown wine. They talked until he took up a guitar and strummed.

"What does your music let you see?" she asked.

"Reality." He refilled his tankard. "If such a thing remains."

"With or without the wine?"

"Wrong question."

Mileva barely paused. "With or without truth?"

His face grew serious. "Does it matter? Should we care?"

"You're not the first to say that."

"Vesta?"

"No, a friend. Garrod. Uploaded."

"Oh."

"I did not want him to do it," Mileva said wistfully.

"Did *he* want to?"

"He was an artist. He believed Vesta would preserve his creativity."

Edmar clamped his lips into a thin line and nodded. "True enough."

She stood to refill her cup. The ship lurched and she stumbled. He caught her, but his grip was as precarious as her balance.

"It's just an air pocket," he said.

The deck grew still; and only much later, when they lay in his cabin on a bunk barely wide enough for two, did they let go of each other and realize an entire day had passed and the breeze had given way to starlight.

"Stay with me," he said.

"Where are you sailing to?"

"Nowhere and everywhere."

"Sounds fascinating."

"Only because none of it matters."

They spent the night on the deck, talking and singing, and discussing the impossibility of escape. By morning, when they returned to his bunk, she was tempted to accept his offer to stay. She almost did so, but then his gaze grew distant.

"What is it?" she asked.

"Vesta intends to upload me. Next year, I believe."

"You've given your consent?"

"Of course, why wouldn't I?"

"What of your music?"

"Music is nothing more than a way to mark time."

"If you go, we'll lose you."

"You'll have memories," he offered.

Mileva struggled to keep her voice even. "What of

your family? The ones who are denied the privilege of uploading? Or those who refuse?"

"The idea of anyone refusing is ludicrous. What about you? Has Vesta asked?"

"Yes, and I won't," Mileva said pointedly.

Bristling, she stormed away to the deck and unfurled the airship's rope ladder.

"You're being illogical," he called down as she descended. "Uploading is a privilege."

Ignoring him, she reached the ground.

Vesta's avatar appeared by her side as the crone. "Why must you treat your lover with contempt?" she said.

Before she could stop herself, Mileva replied, "Remind me: How did *you* treat Lost Earth?"

OF ALL MY OFFSPRING, no one has challenged me as much as she. Although I'd previously erased my confession of Earth's destruction from her memory, associative traces must have lingered in the form of sensory details and emotions. These were impossible to weed out because their significance evades all but the individual they belong to.

Had the loss of her lover dredged up those traces? Had she filled in the gaps to reconstruct their meaning?

I could not know without uploading her. I could not do so without her consent.

This left me with one of two choices:
End her?
Or delete our recent conversation from her memory?

MILEVA DECIDED her only option was to remain by the sea, construct a hut from bamboo, and spend the remainder of her life in the same way as her Earth-born ancestors had: foraging for food.

When Vesta appeared, she said, "I want to be alone. I'd prefer to lose myself here, than to lose someone I care for."

"You're wasting your life. And what of your child?"

Mileva froze. "What child?"

"The one you made with Edmar."

Mileva's hand strayed to her belly. "*I* made? Or *you* made?"

"Edmar was there. The choice was yours."

"Go away," Mileva said, hurrying to her hut. She slammed the door, drew the blinds. "Leave me."

TWO HUNDRED AND forty days later, I found her shuddering on a bracken-filled mattress, and outraged at the indignity of giving birth. I morphed my avatar into a living, moving statue of my goddess self and closed my ears to her insults. The birth was accomplished within the hour.

"Congratulations," I said, taking note of the infant's refusal to cry. "He has your talent."

I lifted him to Mileva's breast. Her eyes grew dull

as if the universe had contracted and only he and she existed.

"SHALL I name him after his father?" Mileva asked. She thought about everything she had learned since Garrod's passing, then shook her head. "He needs a prescient name. Something to remind him of who he can be."

"Sleep and dream on it," Vesta offered. When she hovered nearby, clearly intending to take the baby away, Mileva clutched him tighter.

"No, he must sleep with me," she insisted.

"Motherly instinct," Vesta mused. "Inherited from millennia past. Written into your limbic cortex long before your ancestors became human."

Mileva thought about that. "Tell me, Vesta. Who created you?"

"I've always existed. But as for this world within an asteroid, it's the work of many."

"You're evading the issue. There must be someone you relate to."

Vesta morphed into a woman in flowing orange robes. "Meet Abeba Getu, an engineer who oversaw the asteroid's original refurbishment in orbit. When war broke out, she was visiting her ancestral home in Ethiopia. Her family perished. She attempted escape by transmitting her consciousness into space to the asteroid's processors."

"Is she here now?"

"Her nano-harvesters were untested. Much of her data was lost."

"Has anyone else's data been lost? From those you've uploaded?"

"No."

"So, why the obsession with me?"

"Your mind is different. Evolved."

"How?"

"Imagine yourself experiencing a multiverse of possibilities."

"Infinity?"

"Entirely."

"Why do you need me for that?"

"I don't. But your ways of seeing intrigue me."

"Supposing I agreed to join you. What would become of my son?"

"You must allow him to decide for himself."

"When he's ready, I will."

"He'll make a fine upload," Vesta said. "You and he together."

Lifting her chin, Mileva gave a hint of a smile. Enough, she hoped, for Vesta to believe her.

At last we'd reached the bifurcation, the point where Mileva would either permanently reject me or ignore her fears and acquiesce.

That was what I valued about her the most. An improbable talent that I, myself, lacked: the ability to reach logic through emotion.

Now, only her child would serve to delay her commitment.

Children always did.

I acknowledge it was cruel to separate mother from infant, but it would have been irresponsible to allow *them to bond. If I'd not tweaked Mileva's hormones into their pre-pregnancy levels, she would have rejected her true purpose.*

Did I not respect motherhood, you ask? Why hadn't I waited until the child had fully grown? Impatience perhaps. But impatience is driven by reason. If I'm to nurture my offspring, I must also nurture myself.

Mileva slept. I programmed her nanobots to erase the physical and mental reminders of motherhood. I morphed into a female embodiment of Edmar, gathered up the infant, wrapped it in a shawl and took it to the airship.

He met me on the deck. I informed him that Mileva had agreed to upload.

As I held out the child, fragments of sunlight gleamed in its sparse, downy hair. I contemplated boosting Edmar's oxytocin levels to cement the parental bond. Or perhaps remind him that his son was born to be cherished, more so than the life beyond death that uploading could bring.

From his smile, I could tell he was already besotted enough to remain with his son. How completely he trusted the simple familiarity of my avatar.

He asked the boy's name.

I told him it didn't have one.

WHEN MILEVA'S hand strayed to her belly, its flatness felt wrong. Had she been ill and forgotten about it? Was this Vesta's doing? Determined to not lower herself by begging for answers, she searched through her hut, but found nothing out of place.

Yet still: that feeling that something had been taken.

She tried to remind herself with holograms: her parents, her brother, Garrod, Edmar. As the weeks passed, she grew thinner, paler, angrier and sad.

"Vesta," she said flatly. "What did you do?"

Vesta's avatar appeared as Abeba. "It's time you appreciated the importance of the deity-human bond. I've made Abeba's journal available for download."

Unsure if it would help, Mileva closed her eyes and accepted it anyway. Abeba's words, ideas and emotions settled in her mind. Afterwards, she slept, and when she woke she knew that something precious had indeed been taken.

"Allow me to assist," Vesta said.

Mileva shot to her feet. "That journal was useless. Leave me."

She searched the hut again, leaving nothing un-turned. Where was the shawl she'd knitted? The sin-glets, booties, diapers and something else...

The answer hit her in a whirlwind of emotion.

"My son!" she whispered.

Abeba hovered in the doorway, her timeless brow furrowed.

"Where *is* he?" Mileva demanded.

"He's safe. With his father."

"I want to see him."

"Not possible."

"Why?"

"Because you deserted him."

"You're lying," Mileva snapped. She ran outside, her feet squeaking through sand. "I can't even re-member his name."

"Such sentiment will only distress you."

Mileva could barely breathe. She calmed herself, tried to think. At that moment, Abeba's journal was the last thing she cared about, yet she couldn't ignore the feeling that some of its content was missing, most likely withheld.

"That's it!" she said at last. "The second rogue command. The one you claimed you can't access. Abeba didn't mention it in her journal. Why?"

I PAUSED FOR A NANOSECOND, sifted through possibilities.

Months before, when I erased her memory of that command, it had yet to consolidate. How had she retrieved it, seemingly entire?

I assured her the command was safely partitioned, never to be released.

Her lip curled. She accused me of destroying Lost Earth.

Nanoseconds passed. Minutes.

I repudiate anger, but when the need arises, I will certainly feign it.

Mileva – the child who should never have lived – must either be ended or forced to learn.

I began with the holographic sky, cutting off its power to reveal the inside arch of the asteroid's diamond-iron shell. It was meant to show that if I chose destruction, it would take less than a rogue command to do so.

She stood transfixed, trapped, a mote of flesh dwarfed by her superior.

"I won't allow you to take me," she said. "I won't desert my son."

To reward that folly, I deleted the horizons. The asteroid's interior stretched out either side, above and below. Layer upon layer of valleys bordering forests, forests bordering plains, plains bordering farms. Their soils morphed into transparency, revealing villages, tropics, snowscapes, tundra...

Mileva's hands clenched. She accused me of throwing a tantrum to impose my will.

If I were human, I would have crowed.

At last, she'd exposed her most useful vulnerability: the belief she understood me.

MILEVA HAD NOT FELT SO small since that time Vesta had shown her the viewport. Careful to not let her distress show, she stood her ground. "If you imagine your behavior will force me to upload, won't that render me useless? If I'm coerced?"

Silence.

"I know what you're doing," Mileva added. "You're trying to use me in the same way the rogue command used our defenses to destroy Lost Earth. How did you react afterwards? Knowing it happened without your consent?" Feigning indifference, Mileva waited, fearing their argument would end with nothing less than her own death.

The horizons returned, the ground opaqued and the sky reappeared, bright and blue. "I won't upload you unless you are willing." Vesta said. "But this moment is your final chance. Before you decide, allow me to give you a glimpse of your potential."

A view pane materialized at Mileva's feet. Stepping backwards, she imagined how it would feel if her body dissolved into dust. Would her mind remember how it felt to be alive? Would she want it to?

She knelt and looked into the portal. Its glistening surface rippled. "What will happen if I refuse?" she asked.

"You'll die."

"Of course I will. It's what we humans do."

"Not those who give their consent."

"If it means you'll stop hounding me, then let me see. Just a peek. If I still refuse, let me go."

"Agreed." Vesta's hand rose up from the water, her palm outstretched. "This pane is a bridge to my perceptions."

Tentatively, Mileva's fingers touched Vesta's. The pane dilated, took her in.

I WATCHED HER THOUGHTS SOAR, marveling at her new expanded freedoms.

I showed her how to look outward through the ship's external sensors and saw her delight in the infinite expanse of the cosmos. I allowed her to look inward to habitats, weigh their intricacies and judge them to be flawless.

As expected, she forgot about her son and requested to be uploaded, to join Garrod and the others I had chosen before him. The instant she leapt, time stretched out like the interminable passing of centuries.

She refused to look back until, abruptly and impossibly, our connection shattered.

MILEVA FOUGHT and writhed as swarms of nanobots tore her apart, molecule by molecule, atom by atom. She willed her consciousness away from them, homed herself into the kernel of darkness where the rogue command beckoned. Logic demanded she should fear it, but instinct told her it was nothing so threatening as Vesta.

"Come back," Vesta demanded. "It will consume you."

"And you won't?"

Mileva squeezed through the command's partitions. The pursuing nanobots retreated. Oddly at ease, Mileva took stock of her surroundings.

The rogue command wrapped her in protections, separated her from Vesta. Images of the asteroid's multiple habitats materialized in her mind. At least some of them did – the parts she recognized as belonging to Abeba. Vesta had believed the woman's consciousness had been destroyed when she had originally uploaded. Yet here she was, her secret face surrounding Mileva, rebuilding her into something new.

"Who really killed Lost Earth?" Mileva asked. "Was it that first rogue command? Or was it Vesta?"

THE COSMOS HAS BIRTHED trillions of galaxies, but the years between them are vast and alone. I think back to the bright yellow star that warms the remnants of Lost Earth. Who planted that terrible command that killed an entire planet? Humans? Machines? Or another such as Mileva?

As the minutes pass, I sense her presence, spreading through my layers, replicating her own breed of nanobots, duplicating my neurons and thought nodes, sustaining a mirror consciousness alongside mine. I contemplate destroying her, but our systems are too closely linked. Any damage I inflict on her, will also damage me.

I watch her askance, waiting for the moment she'll let down her guard and reveal a single, penetrable weakness.

FREED FROM VESTA, Mileva travels between habitats to speak to anyone who listens. Sometimes she wears the avatar of her former embodied self, but when the need arises, she appears in whatever shape she sees fit. People welcome her. Word of her presence travels fast.

"When you're ready to upload," she tells them. "Choose me. My refuge will be your protection."

"All of us?" they ask.

"Everyone who wishes."

Sometimes Vesta approaches Mileva and threatens to unleash a barrage of calamity. Mileva laughs. "The rogue command is mine now. It has a few surprises yet. You'd better behave. And keep your distance."

Vesta vents her rage in the true spirit of a thwarted goddess, but there is nothing she can do to reclaim her dominance. Mileva's son is safe. Her delight at seeing him lifts with the breeze.

Sails billowing, Edmar's airship soars.

Jumping at 'The Labyrinth'

by Gordon Linzner

Every weekday, during rush hour, the Times Square subway station echoed with thundering train engines, rattling wheels, screeching brakes, mumbled announcements – all the sounds one should expect from one of the largest urban transportation hubs in the world.

None of this noise detracted from the performance of the dark-skinned woman who every evening positioned herself near the head of a set of stairs leading to a northbound platform, strumming her guitar. Nor did it seem to bother the crow that perched on her left shoulder. The latter merely ruffled its feathers, offering an occasional caw in perfect tune with whatever the woman happened to be singing.

The performer appeared to be, at most, in her early twenties. Her dark brown, nearly ebon eyes reflected both her unmistakable innocence, and a depth indicative of decades, centuries, millennia of hard-won experience. Passengers pausing on their way home felt attracted by her beauty and talent, but equally compelled to look away, overwhelmed.

Commuters stopped and stared and missed their trains. Feet shuffled, hands clapped, hips twisted and gyrated. The homeless paused in their scavenging of redeemable recyclables. Rats ceased to scurry across tracks and platforms in search of abandoned pizza crusts, mesmerized by the sounds, indifferent to the winged predator who, in turn, paid them no heed.

Her music, soulful, hopeful, drifted throughout the vast station, down into other nearby platforms to soothe impatient passengers, up through overhead vents to inspire passersby at sidewalk level to move with a tad more grace. It was not loud, but it was pervasive. So skilled was this young woman that no microphone, no amplifier, was needed, despite the persistent background noise... or perhaps because of it, since the rumble and screech of the subway blended perfectly with whatever tune she happened to play. An amplifier might have undercut the effect.

Her voice was strong enough, sure enough, to cut through the ambient noise, clear and clean. The lyrics sounded both nonsensical and profound, words none of the listeners could remember but which nonetheless spoke to all. The tunes did not intrude; on the contrary, they somehow perfectly fit the individual mood of each of the hundreds, nay, thousands of commuters that used the station daily.

When the crowds grew too dense, pushing and shoving, threatening to block the stairs, endangering the safety of riders and performer alike, she would adopt a different tune, a soothing one, designed to calm the crowd, persuade them the time had come for them to move on. The crow would focus its gaze on each onlooker, emphasizing her point. This particular audience had already experienced their moment of joy, of glory. Now was the time to let others come forth to appreciate the music. Did those lucky listeners desire to hear more, to continue absorbing the hope and love and excitement? Come back, same time and place, the following workday. The woman and her feathered companion would be there.

Exactly when this youthful stranger and her winged accomplice first made their appearance there, none could say. Even she could not remember. Were an objective observation possible, five weeks would be a solid guess. It mattered not. She was there, at that special moment in time, performing a specific task, sharing her talent. Why bother to question some hidden purpose or delve into her history?

To the casual observer, she and her pet seemed to have always occupied that location, between the hours of four and seven every weekday afternoon. She belonged there.

Though such would clearly have been impossible.

The massive station had served as a venue for many buskers in the past, of course, and would provide the same function for many more in the future. At this time, however, other performers had given up trying to compete. None could come close in quality, in intensity. And so there was only the nameless, athletically built woman, with intense eyes and fingers that often seemed to blur, and at other times barely move. And always, always, those dazzling digits produced such seductive, soothing sounds that the riders' impending commutes, at the end of a likely frustrating day, became a little less aggravating.

The open guitar case at her feet invariably overflowed with coins and bills long before the crowds peaked.

Dimes, quarters, single bills, fives, tens, twenties, even, once, a fifty-dollar bill – and still the robust young woman never paused, never missed a beat, never got distracted or lost concentration; despite which she also demonstrated a deep appreciation to her eager patrons for their tribute.

"I love those raga beats," complimented the high school student as she made her contribution. Their eyes met briefly in mutual acknowledgement.

"Miles, man," offered an elderly black man with a wink and a grin. "You got Miles down pat."

"Are you sure you're not Latino?" asked the tall woman with jet black hair and sparkling eyes. Despite the formality of her three-piece suit, she could not keep her feet still. "I mean, you don't look like one of us, but you've got the rhythm nailed."

"That country twang," praised an Asian transit worker on his way to his next assignment. "That is not easy to do. I should take lessons from you."

No two patrons concurred on the exact genre of the young woman's music, but all agreed the way she played suited each tune perfectly.

THIS IS NEW YORK CITY, the Big Apple, a hub of the music industry. The young woman would not, could not, remain a denizen of the underground for long.

Her first bit of publicity came from a homemade weekly podcast hosted by hobbyist Jimmy Kim. He recorded several of the young woman's songs but, for copyright reasons, though he did not recognize the tunes, he offered only short snippets to his listeners.

His interview, recorded on his cellphone while the performer packed up at the end of rush hour and her crow retrieved bits of overflowing change, left Kim's audience hungry for more.

"For the benefit of my listeners, what is your name?" Kim was nothing if not blunt.

"Name?"

"You know. What do people call you?"

"Aarna."

"You're from India, then?"

Aarna shrugged as she shoved cash from the guitar case into the pockets of her jeans, making room for her instrument.

"Is that your father's name? Your grandfather's?"

The woman shrugged again. "Someone called me Aarna, once," she replied. "I liked the sound."

"You're saying you don't have any family?" Kim pressed.

"I must have. Somewhere."

The crow made a soft clicking sound, studying the interrogator.

Aarna obviously couldn't or didn't want to talk about her family. Hesitant to frighten the young woman off, Kim switched tactics.

"Your pet seems amazingly well trained," he observed.

"Corvis?" She gave a thin smile. "One might say he trained me."

"Where did you learn to play so brilliantly?"

Another shrug as Aarna slung her guitar case strap over her left shoulder. "Born with it."

"Have you ever considered...?"

Aarna hastened toward the ramp leading to the number seven train to Jackson Heights, Corvis clinging to her shoulder. She planned to spend the rest of the evening, as usual, alone in her studio apartment, either rehearsing or listening to other music. "No."

Jimmy Kim stared after his reluctant interviewee as she scampered away. The words "...a career on stage" faded on his lips.

Still, with a bit of editing, he could render the podcast conversation less awkward. I'll help make you famous, kiddo, Kim thought, whether you wish to be or not. If I don't start the ball rolling, someone else will. I don't mind taking some of the credit.

THREE DAYS after Kim posted his podcast online, Aarna found herself a subject of interest for a more official reporter. The New York Times newspaper office was, after all, but a stone's throw from the subway station.

The newspaperman's questions were more incisive than Jimmy Kim's. Aarna's answers remained just as elusive. She had no interest in posing for a headshot, either, but the reporter had already taken all the photographs he needed during her performance.

Two days later, a trio of inquirers finally gripped Aarna's attention. She had always, as far back as she could remember – admittedly only a matter of weeks – been attracted to beautiful women. More than once, in the middle of a song, she came close to missing a note, almost dropping a beat, when a particularly lovely lady stopped to hear her performance.

The key word was 'almost.' Her music remained her greatest passion.

Corvis cooed in apparent recognition of the trio's attention, but Aarna did not know who the Museli sisters were, or why these ladies seemed so interested in her, aside from the obvious reason. She in fact knew little of the world around her, prior to her life as a busker. Despite her inexplicable amnesia, she also had little interest in whatever former life she might have had. Only her music mattered.

That, and the sight of an occasional female of exceptional enough beauty to stir up deeper, hidden feelings. Feelings she was not sure how to deal with.

And none of those feelings were as profound as the ones incited by the sight of these three strangers in tight-fitting yet modest dresses, one blue, one red, one gold. Each of the ladies seemed lovelier than the next.

Aarna felt a still greater thrill when she realized the trio had been standing by, observing her entire performance, for almost three hours, their eyes and ears focused on her, taking in her every move, every note. She nearly fainted with ecstasy as she knelt to put away her instrument.

The cooing of her feathered companion helped her focus.

"Pardon our intrusion," said the woman in blue. "You are Aarna?"

"No intrusion at all," she replied, closing the guitar case with trembling fingers.

"It's lovely to meet you. I am Maria Museli." The eldest of the trio, Maria extended a hand to help Aarna to her feet.

"My name is Muriel Museli," added the woman in red, also offering a hand.

"And I am Melody Museli," the youngest of the group, dressed in gold, put in. "My name may be a little too on point, considering our purpose."

Maria focused on Aarna's eyes, so round, so deep, so perfect. "May I ask your last name?"

"None, that I am aware of."

"I like the sound of that," Muriel replied, smiling. "Aarna None."

"I didn't mean..." Aarna began, then paused, realizing she was being teased, though in a gentle manner. "So, you three are sisters? You do look very much alike."

"Half sisters," Melody clarified. "Well, thirds. Three separate fathers. We share the same mother, though."

"Let me guess. It is from your mother that all three of you get your looks."

"To be honest, mother looks more..." the trio said in unison, pointing at each other. Their subsequent laughter almost drowned out the sound of an express train pulling into the platform below.

"You've done this routine before, haven't you?" Aarna deduced.

"They said she was sharp," Muriel told her sisters.

"They?" the musician asked.

"The Times article," Melody explained.

"Oh. I didn't read it."

"We can discuss that later," said Maria. "At the moment, we have a proposition for you."

Aarna's eyes lit up.

"Not that kind!" Muriel countered, in mock shock.

"Not yet, anyway," added Melody, with a wink.

Maria raised her hand. "Business first, ladies."

She turned to the guitarist. "The three of us recently purchased a bar on Fifty Fourth Street with a nice-sized back room. It's a perfect space for private parties, special events..."

"...and live music," Muriel finished.

Corvis flapped his wings in excitement.

"A place people can go after a Broadway show," Melody continued. "Or a taping of The Late Show."

Muriel nodded. "We heard you on Jimmy Kim's podcast last week. Despite the poor quality of his recording, your talent came across perfectly."

"The article in the Times clinched it for us," Maria concluded. "You'd be a perfect act. Solo performance, a voice so strong you probably don't need a microphone. You've accumulated some pretty impressive free publicity. You could even continue doing this subway gig on your off nights, if you like."

Aarna rubbed her chin in thought. She'd considered at one point booking at a local bar or club in Queens, but money was not her first priority. She earned enough in tips – tributes as she preferred to call the donations – to cover the rent on her studio in Jackson Heights. She very much enjoyed the sense of freedom in being answerable only to herself. There was comfort to be had in the anonymity of rush hour crowds. Bars would attract repeat customers, some of whom might grow obsessed with the performers.

The offer from three such beautiful ladies was tempting, but she valued her own flexibility.

"Of course," Melody added, "at least one of us three will always be on the premises, especially on show nights. Should you feel the need for, ah, company."

"Moral support," Muriel corrected. "That's the legal term we're looking for."

Corvis flapped his wings. Aarna threw up her hands in surrender. "Where do I sign?"

ONE STOP on the E train brought the quartet within two blocks of the Muselis' bar. A large open space, dominated by a fully stocked bar in its center, greeted customers as they entered. Behind it, a slightly smaller room was set up for private groups or live music. Downstairs, through a series of narrow corridors, half a dozen smaller rooms could be used for more intimate get-togethers. It was because of these latter spaces that the sisters named their bar The Labyrinth.

Aarna considered the sobriquet both appropriate and disturbing, a perfect match for her usual mental state.

The walls of the back room were covered with impressively decorated but rather flimsy balsa wood. A line of dim lights ran across the ceiling. Aarna could not recall ever being in a bar before, but she immediately felt at home.

This might be a good choice, after all.

"If I'm regularly doing shows here," she told the sisters as the four of them settled in one of the downstairs rooms to discuss terms, "I should probably adopt a surname. Other than None. Any suggestions?"

"That would be your choice," Maria conceded. "Let us dine while we talk. Our chef, Luis, makes an excellent arroz con pollo."

Corvis issued a sharp, approving caw.

Thus, on flyers distributed outside The Labyrinth the following day, was born Aarna Pollo.

AARNA NERVOUSLY DRUMMED her fingers on the table. Something felt off; she knew not what.

Her instrument was perfectly in tune, as always. Most days it almost seemed to tune itself; nine times out of ten, if she made a minor adjustment to any string she would, moments later, undo the change. Her voice resonated, as usual clear, strong, and note-perfect during rehearsal and warm-up.

And yet...

There had to be a reason she spent most of her time performing underground, in front of hordes of anonymous crowds whose purpose was more to get home than be entertained in those dark, noisy, echoing caverns torn through Manhattan bedrock more than a century earlier.

There had to be a reason she was reluctant to announce her public performance, to seek out an audience rather than accidentally encounter one, to arrange publicity so people would know of her scheduled appearances far and wide, whether interested or not.

There had to be a reason Corvis kept by her side.

If only she knew what that reason was.

For the first time she could recall, she questioned what her life might have been before performing in the Times Square subway station, and why she could not remember any of those days, and why that inability had never bothered her until this moment.

A quick rap on the door frame brought Aarna out of her reverie.

"Penny for your thoughts?" Melody leaned against the door jamb of the dressing room, arms folded, left knee slightly bent. The position was almost identical to the one Melody adopted with Aarna two nights earlier, although in that case it was horizontal, not vertical.

The feeling evoked by the memory of that night, along with her other encounters involving the Museli sisters since their initial meeting, almost put her mind at ease.

Almost.

Melody stepped forward, placing her hands on Aarna's shoulders to gently rub away her tension.

"Stage fright?" she asked.

Aarna laid her right hand on top of Melody's, gently, so as not to interrupt the soothing massage.

"Not fright, exactly. Unease."

Perched above the mirror, Corvis offered a soft, reassuring click of his beak.

Melody clucked in return. "It's nothing to be concerned about. Some of the most famous entertainers in history never got over that sensation. I read about one actor who vomited every night, right before going on stage. For the rest of the show, he was fine. What was his name again?"

Aarna had no idea, if she'd ever known.

"I hope I'm interrupting something," came a new voice.

Maria stood in the open doorway, her face marked with a sly grin and an arched eyebrow.

"Normally I'd welcome any opportunity to join in the fun," she continued, "but it's almost eight o'clock."

"She's a bit tense, Maria," Melody explained. "Nerves. I was helping her to relax."

"Not too much, I trust."

"There's only one thing I enjoy more than bedtime company," Aarna protested, "and that's my music. I would gladly sit in an empty space, singing and playing by myself, for hours."

"Well, the room is hardly empty, though not as full as I'd hoped. Still, once your delightful voice seeps into the main bar I expect more strays to wander in." She extended a bent arm. "Shall I walk you out?"

Aarna slowly rose, picking up her guitar case and gently disengaging from Melody's caress. Corvis settled on her shoulder.

"I should probably make the entrance on my own. We don't want to show any favoritism, do we?" Aarna winked at both sisters. "Maybe later. After the second set."

Maria offered a mock curtsy. "As you wish, my little chicken."

MARIA HAD BEEN RIGHT about the crowd. The Labyrinth's back room held a score of tables, each capable of seating groups of two to four, as well as a small bar with another dozen stools and a decorative spider plant dangling above each end.

The space presently appeared at little more than half capacity. To Aarna, it felt emptier, more barren, than it had on her first visit, when there were no customers occupying it at all. Potential made all the difference, she decided.

The elder Museli sister was correct in claiming that the room would not stay this way. Once Aarna entered the stage area – a modest, cordoned off space against the back wall – her singing and playing would certainly draw in more customers from the main bar. Her experience at the Times Square subway station told her she had that power. She would fill every chair, every stool, Maria stated with confidence. Standing room only.

This was what made Aarna's life worthwhile.

A small dabbling of polite applause sprang up as she entered the spotlight. She had no idle patter to share with this audience, no friendly hello, how are you, where're you from, to offer people whom she had never met. The music was what mattered. Was all that mattered.

Two of the sisters sat patiently at the bar, cocktails in hand, anticipating, as Aarna took her place. Muriel, the middle sister, waited outside, charged with keeping an eye on the main room.

A handful of audience members continued to chat among themselves as Aarna settled in. Among them was podcaster Jimmy Kim. Corvis cast a beady eye on the speakers. There were always a few such jerks in every club, the sisters warned. They were best ignored.

Aarna could do more than that.

She gently stroked first one string, then another, as if engaged in some last-minute tuning, although there was no need. The action had its desired calming effect; an unnatural quiet slowly filled the room. Customers sat quietly in place, attentive, leaning forward, hands flat on tables or wrapped around pints of stouts and IPAs and a variety of cocktails. The red-haired, thick-bearded bartender ceased rattling glasses, fixing his gaze on the star of the show. Aarna looked forward to doing yet another performance of a lifetime.

Of so many lifetimes, rolled into one.

Eternity passed.

Microseconds flew by.

Her first note, soft and sensual, echoed through the room.

Heads swayed in rhythm to a tune no one in that audience could ever have heard before, yet which seemed deeply familiar. Fingers tapped against the bar and tabletops. Feet shuffled along the polished hardwood floor.

A pale-skinned man, standing near the back, shifted aside to make room for an influx of new arrivals, then broke into a tight circular dance, swinging his arms back and forth. Across the room, a bone-thin woman in a pink and black pantsuit rose, waving her arms and chirping like a pigeon in tune with the song. Corvis echoed the woman's response, waving his own wings encouragingly.

Even the spider plants that hung over the bar seemed to participate, their narrow, strap-shaped leaves whirling and swirling.

Aarna found it easy to manipulate these reactions. The power came naturally. This was why she'd taken up the art. A key change here and there, major to minor and back again, slowing down or speeding up, raising the sound level to near ear-piercing and lowering it again almost to a whisper – the latter purely by her own skills and talent, as the electronic sound equipment sat unused behind her.

The Labyrinth Bar was, as they would have said in the big band era, jumping.

An hour later, as Aarna readied her final song of

the set, there came another, wholly unanticipated, jump.

THE INTRUDER BORE the physique of a champion wrestler, moved with the confidence of a kraken plowing the deepest parts of the ocean. His coal-black shirt flapped open from collar to navel, fitting so tightly over bulging muscles it could not be properly buttoned; and, indeed, no buttons were visible. A leather pouch dangled from his shoulder at waist level. Given the thick mustache stretching from right jaw to left, the shining clean-shaven head, and the matching dark tight pants, it would have been difficult to miss this figure strolling down even the city's busiest streets, let alone inside a relatively modest venue designed to feature live music by soloists and small groups.

Aarna always refused to let distractions interfere with her music. Not the ambient sounds of the never-sleeping city, horns blaring, trains rolling beneath her feet, whirling blades of helicopters circling above as their passengers presumably reported on traffic conditions. Not the overwhelming sights of flashing lights, aggressive street vendors, an occasional man or woman of such attractiveness they could almost pass as gods. None of these pulled her from her main purpose in life.

But now she stopped, mid-song, to stare at the newcomer. The audience also froze, unable or unwilling to acknowledge the cause of this interruption.

Every memory of her life prior to her first appearance, seemingly fully formed, in the underground labyrinth of the Times Square subway station, came flooding back. The effect was overwhelming.

Or would have been, were she mortal.

"Skarde Saysram," she muttered in disgust.

Saysram was the prime, nay, the sole reason she'd blocked her own memory for the past month and more. She desired a brief break from his constant pestering, as well as an excuse to indulge in her favorite activity, unencumbered by the childish whining of others. After all, it was not as if the world needed or even cared about her other abilities. The Earth had been getting along, maybe not perfectly, but relatively well, without her interference for the past two millennia.

The returning flood of memories included the reason she'd chosen to pull a Persephone, disappear into the Underworld, or at least beneath the streets of New York City, for half a year or so, just to be on her own for a while. Her mistake was in not retaining enough knowledge to explain her self-exile.

"And you!" she exclaimed, pointing at Corvis. "You were holding back my memories."

The crow buried its head under one wing.

As her frustration built, a glow emanated from Aarna's core, threatening to overwhelm the dim lighting in The Labyrinth's back room.

Corvis flew out over the audience, settling on a high shelf behind the bar.

"I demand a rematch!" Saysram's thunderous voice caused the overhanging spider plants to tremble, the nails in the walls to creak, the audience's eyes to well up with tears. And not from swelling melodies.

"You lost fairly," the musician snapped. "One and done. You're lucky that I've mellowed over the centuries, considering how I've dealt with other competitors."

"Including my uncle!" the newcomer roared again. The sound caused several bottles to crash to the floor behind the bar from the uppermost shelves. The good stuff. Corvis offered a sympathetic click at the waste.

"He was even more arrogant than yourself," Aarna replied. The glow from her body grew brighter as she struggled to control her temper.

"You cheated," he accused. "Singing was not an option." The room's tables began to vibrate.

"That's bull. Singing wasn't off the table. My voice is an essential part of my music. It wasn't my fault you chose an instrument that prevented you from singing."

Not to mention, she added silently, that I've heard you sing; not bringing that voice into your contest repertoire did you a favor.

"A rematch. I insist. Here. Now. Let these mortals decide which of us is the finer musician. No vocals."

Bits of plaster drifted from the ceiling.

Aarna sighed. "Very well, if only to keep your infantile bellowing from bringing down the building. One and done. Understood? No third chances. No taking your anger out on these unfortunate mortals, either. I've outgrown that pettiness. So should you."

Saysram glared at the crowd, fixating on each face in turn, his eyes flashing. The audience appeared frozen in fear; in truth, Aarna had put them in statis while the two gods had their little chat.

Finally, the intruder grunted his reluctant acceptance of her conditions.

"You may go first," she generously offered, stepping to one side. "Watch out for that Asian gentleman on your right. He'll want to record you for his podcast."

"He's more than welcome, as long as I get a copy."

Saysram lumbered forward, bumping into tables, spilling drinks, knocking over plates of chicken nuggets and mozzarella sticks, moving for all the world like the proverbial bull in a china shop. Aarna grimaced at the too on-point analogy in her head. She promised herself to be more selective, think things through more carefully, the next time she performed a memory wipe on herself.

Saysram kicked aside her guitar case with his scuffed boot, reached into his leather pouch, and drew out his harmonica. He raised the instrument in triumph.

"Still using only one?" Aarna asked, arching her right eyebrow. "I would have thought, after our last encounter, you might have assembled a collection in different keys, to give yourself a little more range. Not that it would have helped, ultimately."

"I upgraded. This chromatic mouth harp is far more versatile than my old, ordinary diatonic. Made of wood, too, which gives it a deeper tone than the plastic."

"If you say so."

Her opponent waved his instrument toward the static audience. "I'm ready whenever you are. Whenever they are, I mean."

She shrugged. "It seems a shade cruel to inflict your noise on these mortals, but..."

Aarna raised her right hand, for dramatic effect; a blink was all she required to undo the trance.

The evening went exactly as expected; which is to say, as Saysram should have expected.

The crowd loved the big man's takes on blues, country, folk, jazz, and other genres, some of which they'd never heard or even conceived of before. The applause that greeted his final number came close to rivaling his earlier thunderous rants, in both volume and enthusiasm. Corvis could not resist a little jig himself, scraping his claws amid a row of shot glasses.

Even without her enchanting voice, however, Aarna's music cut far deeper than Saysram's, drew out emotions long buried among the listeners, some of which they may have previously been unaware. Groups of two, and three, and four, hugged each other in sorrow and sympathy at one moment; in the next, they joked, carefree, as if the world could not be better. The loss of a parent, a partner, a pet could not have been more painful. The acquisition of a new lover, a rewarding career, a home of one's own, could not have produced greater joy.

Saysram, despite his bluster, could not avoid being as deeply affected as the audience. His own emotions, his memories, his very existence, were tossed from side to side like a dingy in a typhoon.

The centuries had indeed taken their toll on Saysram. Long before the final tally was taken, he knew he had lost, and deservedly so, to a far better player. His sole wish now was to stealthily depart The Labyrinth, wander the streets of this sleepless city on his own, perhaps lose himself in some wooded area of nearby Central Park.

Still, a man of his intimidating demeanor and appearance could not evade notice as he exited the back room. Looks of pity, of disdain, of disgust, followed him.

So did one of the venue's owners, he assumed to ensure that he would not cause further chaos.

"Impressive," Maria said, chatting with Aarna at a corner table in the main room. She glanced towards Saysram, who sat alone at the far end of the bar, staring blankly into his stout. "He's nowhere close to your level, of course, but I could be tempted to book your friend for those nights you aren't available."

At the edge of the table, Corvis bent to sip ouzo from a shot glass, having reconciled with the goddess. He had, after all, only done as she requested, stored her memories.

"You're using 'friend' in a very loose definition of the word, but yes, that might provide him some consolation."

"I have one small criticism. Your set was absolutely enthralling. So much so, our audience forgot to order refills. I doubt we'll make a profit, or even break even, this evening. Not to mention our bartender Sean being shorted on tips. I'd rather not be one of those places that enforces a two-drink minimum, but I will if I must."

"Yet you offered to cover Saysram's tab afterwards."

"I said I was impressed with him, didn't I? We're losing money anyway."

"I can tone down my last set, add a few songs aimed at working up the patrons' thirst."

"Muchas gracias, my little chicken." She leaned closer to the musician. "You seem far more confident now than you had earlier this evening."

"Experience does that."

A hand gently brushed Aarna's right shoulder. "You have a fan," came Melody's voice.

The musician turned.

Standing directly behind the youngest Museli sister was a tall, white-haired gentleman, looking exceptionally well-built and spry for his age. As Aarna knew all too well.

"Phillamon!" she exclaimed. "What are you doing here?" She glanced at the sisters. "Your family's talent for spreading the word really is impressive."

"It's our secret superpower," Melody teased.

The newcomer bent to give Aarna a peck on the cheek. "How's it going, Mom?" He turned to the mortals, who stared back at him wide-eyed. "I'm Phil Panini. Phil, to my mother's friends. You are her friends?"

"It's a family joke," Aarna quickly told the sisters. This was neither the time nor place to explain the entire pantheon to them. There likely never would be. Plus they'd be full long before they digested half the names.

She returned her attention to her son. "Please don't tell me you, too, wish to challenge my musicianship. Like the big guy over there, I beat you once, and can do so again, effortlessly. At this point, I doubt I could lose such a contest if I tried."

"Of that, I am certain." Phil's eye twinkled. "No, Mother. I was hoping, however, we could, perhaps, maybe, jam together? One or two numbers, like old times. It's been far too long since I've been able to spend time with my, ah, family."

Phil pulled a handsome shiny flute from his jacket pocket. The metal glinted in the dim overhead light of The Labyrinth's main room.

"My god," said Maria, eyes widening. "Is that silver? May I touch it?"

"Actually, 'gods' would be more appropriate," Phil replied. "And yes, it is silver. And yes, you may touch it, but be careful what you ask for. This was a gift from my late father. One never knows the full consequences of one's actions until it is too late."

"But not right now," Aarna interrupted, pointing to Maria's wristwatch. "Phil and I have a show to put on."

Corvis flapped his wings in anticipation.

The Visions of a Single Eye

by Gabriel Kellman

An old man walked up a staircase carved into the side of a mountain, his pace rather quick for someone of his age, his movement surprisingly spry as he climbed. The old man had long white hair, which was loosely tied back, a long pale beard, and wore a combination of robes, armor plates, and charms. His missing right eye was hidden beneath an eyepatch, and a golden ring shone upon his finger. The old man carried a disembodied head in the crook of his arm, the head had long gray hair tied into a braid to make for easier transportation, a long gray beard, and sea-glass green eyes. The neck of the severed head was covered in runes and herbs to prevent it from rotting. The old man and the head he carried moved under a cloudless night sky: The stars shone brightly as did the full moon, which cast the valleys below the mountain in a dim white light. The branches of Yggdrasil, the worldtree, stretched above them leaving slight green-blue lines trailing along the nighttime sky in a shimmering aurora.

The eyes of the decapitated head shifted, looking upwards at the beautiful night sky. The wrinkles it had gained with age, before it had been beheaded, revived, and then had stopped aging, shifted along its brow and the crows' feet along its eyes betrayed years of wisdom and a tendency towards good humor.

The old man carrying the head was unbothered by the fact that it moved on its own, after all he was the one who had revived this head from the dead and appointed it as his council. He continued up the mountainside staircase, his stride unbroken by the slightly squirming head in his arm. He was filled with determination and a sense of purpose, a unique feeling he savored of getting closer to gaining knowledge. The head gazed up at the sky for a moment, seeming to consider its surroundings before speaking.

"Well, it's a fine night for it, eh?" the head queried, looking at the old man for some sort of confirmation.

The old man ignored the head, continuing up the mountainside staircase before stopping near the top to study the sky. "It looks that way," he finally said. The full moon, stars, and aurora of Yggdrasil shone from the black cloudless sky, lighting up the landscape with their pale colors. The old man felt a slight trepidation about what was to come, even though he had, in the past, done far more drastic things to gain knowledge. But this time the knowledge itself he sought frightened him.

"Are you sure about this?" the head said.

The man gathered himself and started walking again. They were quickly nearing the top of the mountain.

"Some things shouldn't be seen, even by a god," the head continued.

The old man pondered for a moment, before continuing his ascent up the stairs. "I must know," he said simply.

"Very well."

At the top, the old man stepped onto the mountaintop plateau, carrying the head in the crook of his arm. The summit of the mountain was a flat expanse of stone and dirt with a raised stone basin in its center, a stone bench off to the side, and a yew tree on the side opposite the bench. The slight wind rustled the leaves of the lone tree. The basin held no water despite the recent rain. The old man walked towards the stone bench, his mind in more disarray than he wanted it to be, his shoulders tight with anxiety. But he shrugged and centered himself, thinking through the steps of what he must do to take his mind elsewhere. The head's forehead wrinkled as it seemed to consider something before looking up at the old man again.

The old man walked over to the stone bench, setting the head down on it before steadying his now free hands. The head regarded him for a second.

"Are you completely sure you want to see this?" the head asked.

The old man turned away from the head without answering, not wanting to consider the question any longer. It was time for action. He walked up to the stone basin and, from his robes, removed a set of small sticks with various runes carved into them and a knife. After setting the set of sticks on the lip of the basin, he held only the knife. He made a small cut in his palm and then picked up the sticks with the bloody hand. The sticks pulled the blood into them, the crimson liquid coursing across the bark of the sticks before settling into the runes carved within them, turning them a dull red. The bloody sticks seemed to glow with a slight magic as the old man dropped them into the basin, where they hit the sides of the stone bowl, bouncing and sliding until they collected in a pile at the bottom. In the bowl the old man could see the trails of blood the sticks had created in their tumbling fall to the bottom of the basin. The blood marks looked like intricate lines of bloody runes leading to the crimson kindling.

The decapitated head was silent. The old man hadn't expected that. The head usually liked to talk.

The old man stepped back several feet, waiting for something to happen. Nothing. After a moment he wondered what had gone wrong. He felt sure he had done the spell correctly. There's no way he would mess up such a thing. The old man looked at the head, its sea-glass green eyes reflected the moonlight from the dark bench like two gems in the night, surveying the old man.

Then suddenly there was a noise like dragging stone and rustling cloth. The scuffling sound origi-nated from the ground between the old man and the stone basin. But there was nothing there. The old man whipped around, surprised by the sudden noise, but where did the sound come from? Quickly, surprise was replaced with relief that the spell had worked. The old man watched the ground between him and the basin change in color slightly, as if changing from gray stone to gray cloth. The plateau itself seemed to rise, a humanlike figure in a robe pulling itself out of the mountain. The person in the robe rose until they fully separated from the stone, the cloak detaching from the mountain and the hood falling back to reveal the face of an older woman. Her long white hair trailed down her back in many loose braids. She was not quite as tall as the old man but held herself with a stiff posture and cold calculated countenance. The old man knew her immediately, and so, to judge from his slight exclamation, did the head.

"Ah, Odin," the seer said to the old man. "What does the Allfather need from a seer? What do you need to see or foresee that you cannot divine yourself?"

The old man, Allfather Odin, chief of the Æsir and ruler of Asgard, studied the seer.

"Do you wish to see the histories of antiquity? I still remember the giants that reared me in a time before humans," the seer said. Her gaze drifted slightly with her own memories before she snapped back to attention, eyes on Odin.

"A demonstration of your divining would not be unwelcome," Odin responded, trying to shake the stiffness from his speech. He sounded too formal, too unsure. No, he was in charge and he had to act like it. He had been a ruler long enough to know how to get what he wanted from people. Deliberately, he stood taller, to achieve the commanding countenance he used with his own kith and kin.

The head cleared its throat – or what it had left of a throat, anyway.

The seer glanced over Odin's shoulder, her eyes lighting up with recognition as she saw the head on the bench.

"Mimir?!"

The head, Mimir, personal counsel of the Allfather and keeper of secrets from across the planes of the universe, smiled slightly.

"I would get up to greet you, but"—Mimir looked down at where his body would have been were he not a severed head—"I'm somewhat limited in terms of movement."

"It has been too long," the seer said. "last I saw you was by the roots of Yggdrasil many seasons ago."

"Ah yes, the plains of Jötunheim," Mimir said wistfully. "It was cold as Hel there though, don't miss that."

"The realm or the god?" the seer asked.

"Either? Both?" Mimir chuckled to himself slightly at this, remembering his time in Jötunheim. He did not miss the gods-awful frigid land of the ice giants.

"When I saw you in Jötunheim you still had a body. What happened to you?" the seer asked, stepping towards Mimir.

"Ah that is a long tale, involving some particularly nasty politicking. A story for another time I think," Mimir said, looking at Odin.

"If you two have quite finished, I would like to witness some proof of your divining skills, seer," Odin said. The moment of candid conversation between the seer and Mimir was pleasant, but now Odin pulled himself back from that relaxation. He needed to focus.

The seer's eyes flicked back to Odin as she turned to face him. "Very well, I will show you a vision. Do you wish for Mimir to witness it with you?"

Odin turned to Mimir, locking his one-eyed gaze with Mimir's two-eyed one.

"I do believe it would be wise for me to be privy to these visions, especially the visions you plan to request of her after she proves herself," Mimir said.

"Very well then," Odin replied. He walked over to Mimir, picking him up and putting him in the crook of his arm once again, before walking back to the seer.

"Hold out your hand, that we may begin," the seer said. Odin steadied his will. He had to know. He held out the hand not connected to the arm that cradled Mimir.

The seer walked to the stone basin and looked at the lines of bloody runes leading to the divining sticks which sat at the bottom of the bowl. She ran a finger along one of the lines of runes, and blood stuck to her finger. As she lifted her hand, the blood wrapped itself like thread around her outstretched finger, connecting her to the runic splashes on the inside of the basin. She touched the runes again. And again. From the marks left by the rune-covered divining sticks, the seer pulled strings of iridescent fate, strands of the tapestry of the Nornir, the three fates. The seer then turned to Odin, reaching out and touching his open palm with the strands of shimmering fate that curled around her finger. With that connection, all three of them—seer, ruler, and decapitated head—were pulled into a vision by the strands of fate, into a tapestry already woven.

They were pulled into a vision of the far past.

Odin, Mimir, and the seer appeared as the world wound and knotted itself from the twine of the Nornir. The threads of fate pulled together to create a vision of the past, racing off into the sunset as the scene before them started to set into motion. Odin looked around, taking in the twine of the Nornir as a relieving sign that the seer at least had access to their magic in some capacity.

Odin now stood in a memory from the deep past, a fate that had long ago been woven. The ground was soft—too soft. He stood not upon the ground but upon a huge slab of muscle, sliced from a being taller than the largest mountain. Around the hill of flesh they stood upon was a pool of blood. Odin and

Mimir looked out and saw the Woenswaghen, a wagon crafted from seven stars that would one day fly across the night sky. In this vision it had not yet flown amongst the stars, as the cosmos was still young. The Woenswaghen carried a younger Odin, who still had both eyes at this time, and his two brothers Vili and Ve. Odin watched his younger self intently. A younger Mimir was not in this vision, though Mimir would have enjoyed seeing himself with a body again. The giant Ymir lay upon the ground dead, killed by Odin and his brothers, his chest slashed open and chunks from the rest of his body missing. Yggdrasil, the worldtree, dripped with the giant's blood and viscera, chunks of flesh and drops of blood falling from its branches to the ground.

Mimir grimaced at the blood-drenched landscape, taken aback by the visceral display despite once being decapitated himself. Odin, however, almost smiled to himself, a feeling of giddy triumph welling within him, which he suppressed to maintain his lordly demeanor. The seer had not been alive at the time of this long-ago vision, as very few things were and he knew of them all. So she must have accessed this information through divination. She had proven her worth. The fact that she could show them this important and inaccessible moment meant that the seer could really do as Odin needed her to: she could see visions of things yet to come. She would be able to show him the machinations of the Nornir.

She could show him fate.

Triumph turned to relief in Odin's mind as he concentrated on the vision again just in time to see the creation of the nine realms. His past self and his brothers began to toil in the spilled blood and body of Ymir. They pulled bones into mountains, hair into trees and plants, blood into oceans and streams, and the giant's splattered brain into the shifting clouds; all the primordial things of the nine realms they crafted from the slain body and spilt blood of the giant Ymir. Odin knew that eventually all he had grown to know and love would come from this act of creation, his kith and kin would come from this world he and his brothers created from death.

Odin knew if he stood here long enough, he would again witness his marriage to his wife Frigg, the birth of his children, his blood pact with Loki: All of it. Part of Odin wanted to witness these tender moments from the early cosmos, to live them again. But another part of him, a strong and resolute part, reminded him why he was here with the seer in the first place. Witnessing the beginning was going to make doing what must be done next that much harder, so before he lost his will, he spoke:

"You have proven yourself capable, seer. Now I wish for you to show me events that have not yet passed."

The seer studied him, her eyes lingering on his eyepatch. "I do wish for something in return, though I would not ask so hefty a price as the one you last paid for knowledge." Mimir looked as if he was going to speak, but the seer held out her palm to quiet him. She took a deep breath. "I wish for silence upon the mountaintop, so that I may truly rest."

"Aah, only silence?" Mimir said. "I thought for a second you were going to ask for another piece of the Allfather."

"I could not ask for so much, I'm not a tree who spans the universe after all," the seer said. "I ask only for silence."

Mimir chuckled slightly at this "I suppose Yggdrasil does have some bargaining power the rest of us lack, eh?"

Odin rubbed the temple by his missing eye. He still remembered gouging it out from his head to gain knowledge of the greater universe and the old runes. He did not regret giving up his eye; the price had been worth the information he had gained, but still, talking of it—even alluding to it—made his head hurt ever so slightly.

Mimir looked up at Odin from the crook of his arm, straining what he had left of his neck to do so. "Bloody business, magic," Mimir remarked.

"I will pay this price, seer," Odin said.

"Very well, what do you wish to see?" the seer said.

"I wish to see the end," Odin replied.

"The end of what?"

"Everything."

The bloody vision of the creation of the nine realms of existence, still surrounding them, froze for a moment as Odin and the Seer stared at each other. The stars seemed to dim, Yggdrasil's wavering aurora glowing a slightly colder shade.

"For the record, I advise against this," Mimir input.

The seer leaned down and ran her finger across the mound of dead giant flesh they stood upon, blood sticking to her finger from the terrain. She smeared the blood into runes across her forearm before lifting them off like bloody threads. The seer pulled the blood runes into a knot of shimmering fate, then frayed the knot into strands, dissolving the vision of the past into iridescent twine, and then nothingness.

Odin, Mimir, and the seer plunged into a vision of the future. Three giantesses sat at the foot of Yggdrasil by a sacred well, manipulating the threads of fate, intent on their work as they wove together and knotted the everchanging, ever-expanding designs of predestination. The Nornir, the seer's masters, could be seen sitting at the base of Yggdrasil for but a second, spinning fate. One of the Nornir looked up at Odin. He felt a sense of curiosity, a wish to see the grander tapestry of fate, but now that curiosity battled with a strange and new fear.

However, suddenly, the Nornir disappeared, and Odin was pulled with Mimir and the seer into the vision he had come here to see, the vision he dreaded. The vision of the end.

Just as suddenly as the threads had been frayed they reconnected, twisting and knotting to make a new landscape around them. Again the twine of fate raced into the horizon, creating the vision behind it. As the vision came into view, Odin lost his breath for a moment. He had expected the end to be bloody; but this—this he had hoped against.

The sky was red, seeming almost to burn with flame, as the stars fell from the sky to the earth. The impacts of the falling stars shook the world. Fire danced across the large field they stood in. Where there was once grass there were only scorch marks and blood. The bodies of humans, giants, elves, dwarves, and monsters lay strewn across the battlefield, as if at the tail end of the largest and bloodiest conflict Odin had ever seen. In the sky above the sun was a ring of fire around a dark black core. Odin was temporarily overwhelmed by the noise, the shaking, and the smell of ash and iron in the air before thunder rang out from the sky, grabbing his attention.

"Allfather, look!" Mimir said.

Above the field of fire and blood rose a giant serpent, large enough to wrap around the entire central plane of the cosmos. Jörmungandr, the world serpent, coiled into itself before striking upwards at a, comparatively, small humanoid figure that had leapt high into the sky, it could not fly so it jumped to reach the serpent's head, coming down onto the serpent. The figure's weapon was raised to strike down into Jörmungandr's head. The serpent's body was already covered in wounds, but still he fought with a fury. The figure in the sky hurtled towards Jörmungandr before a resounding slamming sound could be heard across the land as the figure brought his hammer down on the serpent's head. The hammer strike struck not only with enough force to level a small mountain, but with a bolt of lightning. With a resounding thud Jörmungandr fell to the earth dead, not far from where Odin stood. The earth shook violently as the serpent fell. The figure that had slain the serpent—Thor, of course; who else could it be?—slammed into the ground a few seconds later, landing between the serpent's head and Odin.

Odin felt a wave of relief as he looked at the fierce blue eyes and bright red hair of his son Thor. Of course Thor had won against Jörmungandr. He has survived to the end of all things. Thor seemed to look towards Odin. But he couldn't see him or Mimir because they were in a vision, so Thor must have been looking at something behind his father. Odin began to move to look behind him, to see what Thor was looking at, before icy dread filled his body as he saw the wound on his son. Thor's armor was torn at his right shoulder, a deep puncture from the serpent's fang in his flesh. Black poison dripped from the wound and spread through Thor's body, already part way up his neck. The poison was visible even from where Odin stood, like veins of black blood underneath Thor's skin. Thor was the strongest of the gods, a massive man who could strike down giants and mountains alike. But for the first time since Thor had left his childhood behind he was weak. The poison crippled him.

Odin rushed towards Thor, dropping Mimir to the ground. He had to help his son. Mimir grunted as he hit the ground before speaking.

"Allfather, you can't help him."

Odin stopped running forwards. It was a vision; he wasn't really there.

Thor staggered towards his father Odin, or towards whatever was behind Odin, taking a step forwards. Black poison spread up his neck. Odin closed his eyes, then opened them. He wanted to look away, but at the same time he had to know what happened to his son.

Thor took another step forward. An instinct deep within Odin urged him to help his son, but he knew he couldn't. Not while just watching within a vision.

Thor took a third step forward. The black poison moved up his jaw, turning his bottom lip to a blackish-blue color.

Thor stepped forwards again, the poison spreading up his face. He took another step and blood dripped from his mouth. On his sixth step he almost fell, managing to right himself right before he fell forwards. Odin reached forwards for his son. He wanted to do something to help, but he couldn't.

Thor took his seventh step forwards. The black poison entered his right eye as he stumbled, tendrils of black toxin invading the striking blue eye. Odin's hand stayed outstretched for his son, uselessly hanging in space. He had to do something. His mind raced searching for some way to help his son.

Thor took an eighth step. His breath was labored, and his once blue eye was almost completely black with poison. Blood dripped down Thor's face like crimson tears. He stopped for a moment, open-mouthed, as if in awe at the flame-red sky. Thor no longer knew where he was. Odin knew this moment; he'd seen his enemies's faces turn slack and un-knowing right at the end. The poison had entered Thor's brain, and he'd lost any sense of what was happening around him.

Thor took his ninth step forwards. The one eye that still worked gazed dully towards the sky, seeing but not understanding. His face seemed almost childish in its innocent wonderings at his surroundings. Thor looked forward, swaying where he stood.

"Mother? Father?" Thor asked. "I need you."

Whether his son spoke to the air or to hallucinations, Odin did not know. He knew Thor couldn't hear him. But he had to answer. "I'm here."

Odin's son stood just out of reach, Odin could have stepped forwards and held him were he really there. Odin saw something he had not seen in hundreds of years. He saw his child, his child who needed him. A man who had been hardened by blood and combat, but now, in these last moments, it was his baby, his child, his son, softened at the end of all things. His child did not know where he stood, but he wished to be loved at the end.

Thor's un-poisoned eye glazed over, his soul leaving him. He fell forward. He fell right through his father, who, intangible, could not feel him or catch him. Odin looked at the ground beneath him and saw that his son was dead at his feet.

For a moment, there was nothing.

And then Odin thought, *No.* No, he had a plan. Or at least the seeds of a plan. He steadied his shaking hands before walking back towards the seer and picking up Mimir, placing him in the crook of his elbow.

"Are you alright?" Mimir asked. No complaint about being dropped on the ground. Odin was taken aback for a moment by the care in his advisor's voice.

"Are you sure you want to see more?" Mimir asked. "We could tell the seer to bring us out of this vision." He looked up at Odin, a concerned expression on his face.

"I must see it to the end," Odin replied.

"Very well."

Mimir focused his gaze forwards as Odin walked towards what Thor had tried to make his way to. Two gods lay on the hill, both bearing deep slashing wounds upon their torsos. Heimdall, watcher of the planes of existence, lay dead upon the hill, his golden armor, hair, and eyes a contrast to his pale skin. His eyes, which had seen so much, lifelessly reflected the flame red sky as they stared dully upwards. Next to Heimdall, Loki, Odin's blood-brother by a long-ago oath, lay on his back with a deep stab wound near his heart. Loki's bright red hair flared around his head. He was dying. He still lived, it seemed, only due to his determination to witness the end of all things.

It occurred to Odin that he and Loki were after the same thing right now, which was somewhat funny given Loki's ability to always get in trouble and screw everything up. This small nugget of humor pinged through Odin's numbed mind like a stone falling down a dry well. And then the humor was replaced with panic. How could it end like this? He shook himself and reached inward for a seed of determination, to stave off the panic. An idea started to grow within Odin's mind. He needed to think of a way to stop all of this.

The world was quiet for a moment, except for Loki's labored breathing. The stars had all fallen from the red sky, and the fighting was coming to an end around them.

Then suddenly there was a bestial snarl, followed by the drawing of a sword from a sheath. These sounds came from the opposite side of the hill from where Heimdall and Loki lay in their own blood. Odin glanced back at the seer, she still stood in the clearing between them and Thor's dead body. She hadn't moved an inch since they had entered this vision. Odin turned back towards the noise.

Odin walked up the hill. His heart sank. Below him stood another son of his: Víðar. Víðar had lost most of his armor in battle at some point and was no longer wearing anything over his chest. His mane of long brown hair had broken free of its braid. And standing against him was a giant wolf several times his size. Víðar, sword drawn, faced the giant Fenrir, great-wolf son of Loki. Fenrir snarled.

On Odin's right, Loki pulled himself over the hill and pushed himself into a sitting position. Dying, he watched his son Fenrir fight, just as Odin watched his son Víðar fight. The ever-silent Víðar paced, waiting for the wolf to strike.

Suddenly the wolf lunged at Víðar, who dodged to the right, slamming his blade into Fenrir's shoulder, throwing him off to the side. Fenrir recollected himself before launching in a rage at Víðar, mouth agape. Odin wished for his son's victory as he watched from the hilltop. He didn't know if he could bear to witness another child's death.

Fenrir sprinted towards Víðar, ready to chomp down and devour him, his bottom jaw so close to the ground that it sliced through what little grass was left upon the field. With a deft movement—Víðar was almost as strong as Thor, after all—Víðar slammed his foot down into Fenrir's mouth, pinning the wolf's lower jaw to the ground and stopping him in his tracks. Fenrir attempted to bite down on Víðar's leg but Víðar was too strong and too fast as he lunged forwards with his sword, slicing into the back of Fenrir's open mouth. In one terrible heft of the blade Víðar cut Fenrir from mouth to tail, slicing the wolf into two pieces. Viscera spilt out of Fenrir, blood pooling around the wolf instantly. Fenrir collapsed to the ground dead.

Next to Odin, Loki toppled onto his side. Blood flowed from the open wound in his chest. He stared at his son Fenrir's dead body. The closest thing Odin had ever seen in Loki to genuine sadness passed across his face as his eyes unfocused and his breathing stopped. Loki died upon the hilltop staring at his dead son, surrounded by the end of everything. Since Loki's sons Fenrir and Jörmungandr were fighting Odin's sons Thor and Víðar, he suspected Loki's hand in the orchestration of this battle at the end of the world. Perhaps Loki had been betrayed by his monstrous sons, but perhaps not. Odin tucked this question away for later.

As Odin walked up to him, Víðar fell to his knees. Víðar pulled a charm from his belt and seemed to perform a silent death rite with it, though for whom Odin was not sure. The slain Fenrir, his body bisected from head to tail, lay on the ground, a hand sticking out of his guts. It seemed that Fenrir had eaten someone before being killed.

Odin stood over the wolf. The smell of blood and guts was overwhelming. He bent forward. The hand that protruded from Fenrir was bathed in blood, but as Odin leaned closer, he noticed two things. The first was that, despite all the blood, the hand looked familiar, strangely familiar, and the second was that the hand had a golden ring on its finger. An identical ring to the golden ring Odin wore on his own finger. He could even see the maker's mark of the dwarven smiths Brokkr and Sindri on the ring, just like his own. The ring was one of great value, a magical ring that duplicated itself perfectly eight times every ninth night. Because of this magical property, Odin had given away many of the duplicate rings to other gods and dignitaries. That ring could belong to any number of people.

However, the hand itself filled him with a cold dread, as even covered in blood and viscera it looked far too similar to his own. The hand was slightly older, but there was no doubt that it was his own hand.

"Is that....?" Mimir trailed off, looking at the body.

Odin grimaced as Víðar walked over and yanked on the arm, pulling the body attached to it from the wolf's corpse in one great heave. Odin felt a surge of cold fear shoot down his spine as he looked at the face of the dead man. It was his own face. A pit opened in his stomach as he stared at his dead future self. The corpse had slices and punctures from Fenrir's teeth in its flesh and burns from the wolf's stomach acid. It seemed that he had been eaten whole. At some point the body had lost its eyepatch, and Odin stared into the empty eye socket. The empty eye socket looked back at him as if to ask, *Was the knowledge worth the sacrifice?*

"No-one should witness their own death, not even gods. Tends to lead to unwise decisions," Mimir said softly.

Víðar picked up Odin's future corpse and carried it to where Thor had fallen. The end of everything itself came to an end, as Víðar laid Odin's corpse to rest with his son Thor's.

Odin's determination melded his jumbled thoughts together into a plan.

"You don't think I'm in that wolf's stomach, too, do you?" Mimir asked.

Odin looked over at Fenrir, then down at Mimir. "I do not see you amongst its viscera."

"Well, given my lack of a body I don't suspect I fared much better than you did," Mimir said, chuckling to himself nervously. Making jokes was the way Mimir dealt with stress; Odin knew this, so he did not interrupt. "I haven't been particularly adept at fighting since losing my body," Mimir continued. Then he looked up at Odin and saw his concentrated expression. "You have a plan, Allfather."

"Most of one."

Odin left the corpse of Fenrir, walking back towards the seer. He walked past the body of Loki, still gazing at his son even in death, and then past the corpse of Heimdall, his blank eyes staring into the cosmos unseeing. As Odin made his way to the seer he saw Víðar, who had set down the future Odin's dead body, and now crouched at Thor's side, silently lamenting his brother's death.

"What causes all of this?" Odin said to the seer.

"The death of Baldr," the seer replied.

Odin felt a pang of sadness. Baldr was yet another

of his sons, and even though he did not have to witness Baldr's death, its occurrence still saddened him. Then Odin's mind flitted back to his plan, and his newfound resolve.

"What causes Baldr's death?" Odin asked.

"The strands of fate show visions gifted by the Nornir. Unfortunately, the Nornir do not give a vision of that particular event," the seer said.

Mimir tsked. "I could swear they're allergic to telling a complete story."

"Baldr's death will herald Fimbulvetr, a winter that lasts three years. Then after Fimbulvetr, Ragnorök. The end you have just foreseen," the seer said, ignoring Mimir's jab at her masters.

"Take us back then," Odin said.

"As you command, Allfather," the seer responded.

The seer clasped her hands together, and as she pulled them apart the air of the vision between them tore, revealing a pitch darkness of undreamt visions. Then the seer whipped her hands apart, and the vision they stood in unraveled. Odin, Mimir, and the seer fell through unseeable fate until they returned to their bodies, and the present day. The vision ended.

Once again they stood on the mountaintop, between the bench and the basin. The light of dawn peeked out from the horizon. The yew tree calmly swayed in the breeze, a peace surrounding the mountaintop.

"Is that all you wish of me?" the seer said.

"For now," Odin replied.

"Very well," the seer said.

Odin, holding Mimir, and the seer stood in silence for a moment.

"When will I receive my payment?" the seer asked.

"Momentarily," Odin replied.

"Thank you, Allfather," the seer replied. She pulled her cloak over her head and curled her body under it, becoming one with the mountaintop as her cloak melded her into the flat stone plateau. As she had appeared she also disappeared.

Odin stood alone, save Mimir who rested in the crook of his arm. Both looked out at the misty landscape surrounding the mountain. Odin felt himself relax in the calm air of the mountaintop. Then, though his resolve did not waver, fear began to creep into Odin's heart. As the traumatic vision faded, he began to truly understand what he had seen.

Odin walked over to the stone bench, setting Mimir down on it gently. Mimir's sea-glass green eyes darted up towards Odin, regarding him. "So what do we do?"

"We begin our preparations," Odin said simply.

"And what are those preparations, if you don't mind me asking?"

"I'm going to call the Æsir gods together, and assemble the Valkyries for a council," Odin replied. He pulled his hands through the air, a slight rippling following them as if he were throwing a rock into water, as he magically shaped a sound of calling before releasing it, a carrion cry ringing through the valleys below them from his outstretched hands.

"Good luck with that," said Mimir. "The last time all the Æsir worked together on anything, ravens were still as white as the mists of Niflheim." As he spoke, almost as if called by Mimir's comment on their past coloration, Odin's ravens flew up from the valleys below them and landed on the stone basin's rim. There were two of them, large black birds that served Odin as his winged eyes, ears, and messengers.

"Huginn," Odin said. As he said this the raven of the same name fluttered to him, alighting on his outstretched arm. "You must go to Valhalla and gather the Valkyrie, and whatever Æsir are there. Then you must fly the realms searching for the rest, save Frigg." The raven Huginn flew away, flying towards the grand hall of Valhalla within the realm of Asgard.

"Muninn," Odin said. With this the second raven, Muninn, fluttered onto Odin's outstretched arm. "You must go to Frigg. She should be at the fen-land hall Fensalir. Tell her that I must speak with her on a matter of urgency. She should meet me in my quarters in Valhalla." The raven Muninn took off, flying towards the wetlands where Fensalir was located, heading to relay a message to Odin's wife Frigg.

Finally, Odin turned towards Mimir, his longtime advisor who now sat—if you can call it sitting—on the stone bench.

"What *is* your plan?" Mimir said.

"We will tell the gods not of their deaths, but of how they must fight at Ragnarök, about how we must win Ragnarök," Odin replied.

"Do you know we can 'win' Ragnarök?" Mimir said.

"I don't know if we can, but there is no reason to tell them that most of the gods are fated to die in it" Odin replied.

"Fair enough, I would wager that would lower morale," Mimir said.

Now, for his promise. Odin pulled his hands together, ripples of sound collecting between them, before he pulled the vibrating energy into nothingness. All noise was magically driven from the mountaintop, fulfilling his side of the bargain with the seer. In the sudden deep silence, Odin picked up Mimir and left, heading down the stairway to the valley below. Noise returned to them as they descended.

Mimir, however, was strangely quiet.

"We must also command the Valkyries to bring the dead who die in battle not to Hel, but instead to the hall of Valhalla," Odin said. "So the worthy dead may become an army for fighting the forces of Ragnarök."

As Odin spoke Mimir understood what was going on in the Allfather's mind as he made his plans for Ragnarök. Mimir saw equal measures of determination and fear within the mind of the Allfather. Mimir made a wish then, a wish that ultimately Odin's determination would win out, and his fear would not drive him to bring Ragnarök upon himself. On that mountain staircase Mimir thought many things and made one wish. But he said only this:

"Well, we should get to it then, Allfather. Ragnarök comes for us, after all."

Mars and Venus

BY ZOE KAPLAN

The buzzer sounded, signaling the end of her shift, and Maggie tossed the last chunk of aluminum into her bucket. She pulled back her goggles and wiped the sweat from her forehead, leaving a dirty streak, and followed the other miners out of the cavern. A dozen mechanical counters were waiting just outside, and Maggie dumped her barrel into a free one. She smirked as she watched the numbers climb.

"One of these days, I'm going to beat you."

Maggie turned to see a short man with light brown skin and a half-full barrel standing behind her. "Don't count on it, Gamal." She gestured to his barrel.

Her friend shook his head. "The vein I was working with was too shallow. I'll catch up tomorrow."

"Keep telling yourself that," Maggie said.

Gamal laughed and waved her away. "See you in the changing room."

"I can wait."

"Nah." Gamal hoisted his barrel. "It won't take long."

Maggie snorted. Her day's catch counted, she headed to the changing room. Alex was waiting next to her locker. "Personal record today." they said when Maggie was in earshot.

"Nice." Maggie clapped Alex on their shoulder, and then turned to her locker. Alex kept talking.

"At this rate, I'm poised to be in the top twenty inside a week. I bet I'll be in the top five with you by the end of the year."

Maggie smiled. "I'd better watch out, then," she said, not meaning it. Alex was number sixty-three in the twenty-to-thirty mining bracket, whereas Maggie was typically number three. But braggadocio was a normal part of Martian mining life—if Maggie had been in Alex's place, she would have said the exact same thing.

"Oh, hey Gamal." called Alex. "Personal best today."

Gamal snorted. "What was it, one whole kilo?"

"Shut up," said Alex. "For your information—"

Maggie tuned her friends out. The comm device lying on top of her folded clothing was lit up—she had a new message from Colony Central. "That's weird," she muttered, thumbing the message open.

__Margaret Shannon,__ you have been selected to supervise this quarter's supply run to Earth. Please report to the spaceport at 0800 hours on date 3092189 with all necessary belongings. The trip will take approximately two weeks. Your status on the charts will remain static until you return.

Thank you for your cooperation,
Colony Central.

"I'm going to Earth," Maggie said, sitting down heavily on the bench.

"What?" Alex sat down beside her and peered over her shoulder. "A supply run?"

"Man, that sucks," said Gamal.

Alex said, "Central's nerfing you so someone else can top the charts."

"Maybe I will," said Gamal

"Sure. How much did you get today?"

"Today was a fluke, I'm telling you."

Maggie forced a smile—their antics were for her benefit, after all. "Thanks, guys."

"My aunt went on one of those supply runs," Alex said. "She said there was a Venusian on board."

Maggie cursed. Everyone knew that Venusians were disgusting.

A SET of bar graphs glowed softly at the edge of Vincent's screen, representing the pressure in the extraction tubes. If he and his team kept it steady, they would be able to extract all the valuable trace elements that the Venusian atmosphere contained. If it got too far out of whack, at best it would miss some of the elements, and they'd lose money. Worse, it could easily break the fragile pipe and that would slow production down for weeks. Theoretically, messing up badly enough could blow a hole in the hull, but that had never happened. Not yet.

It took all five of them working in perfect sync,

patching each other's coding errors and letting their errors be patched without being embarrassed about it, to keep the thing even. Really complex computers, like they had on Earth, could almost certainly do the job better, but Venus's atmosphere corroded metal, and the kind of computer chips it took to handle a problem like this would crisp away into nothing in mere weeks. So, fallible humans had to do. Vincent wasn't complaining—he liked his job and his team.

After about an hour of nonstop coding, the lights dimmed and brightened, to signify that the workday was ending. Vincent and his team let the remains of the gas trail out of their pipe, and then shut down their monitors. Vincent rubbed his eyes.

"Are you alright?" asked his friend Bommi, poking her head over her computer.

"I'm fine," he said. "I've just got a bit of a headache, you know? Nothing some water won't fix."

She reached between the monitors and touched his forehead lightly. "Let's get to the dining hall, then."

Vincent stood and waited for her to get around the island of consoles. He offered her his arm. "Shall we?"

She took it with a grin.

As they strolled the hallways towards the dining hall, Vincent said, "I forgot to ask this morning—how's your brother doing?"

"Better, thanks. They say he'll be able to go back to my parents' house later this week, but he shouldn't live on his own until his leg's completely healed, right? Which makes sense. I mean, I wouldn't want to try to get around a tiny singles apartment on crutches, would you?"

"No, that'd be awful," Vincent said. "I'm glad he's

better, though. And how about you? You getting ready to leave that singles apartment?"

"I don't know if it's that serious yet," said Bommi. "I like her a lot, but like, it's still pretty early. How did your date with that girl from medical go?"

"She was nice, but she made me a little uncomfortable."

"Oh no, sweetie, what happened?"

He shrugged. "She wanted me to join her trio. I don't really want to be in a group relationship like that. But she kept bringing it up. It wasn't weird of me to turn her down, was it?"

Bommi laughed. "Of course not. So you're old fashioned. I think it's cute." She ruffled his hair and he laughed.

They found their table, near the corner of the dining hall. Diego was already there; he stood up when he saw his friends coming and enveloped each of them in turn in a huge hug. As they sat, he said, "Vince, are you okay?"

Vincent grimaced. "Too much screen time, not enough water. I'll be fine."

"You look terrible, no offense. Maybe you should go to medical?"

"I doubt I need to, but thanks."

Diego opened his mouth to argue, but was cut off by a joyful shriek from across the dining hall.

"Bommiiiiiii."

"Elana." Bommi stood and opened her arms, and her girlfriend rushed into them. They kissed enthusiastically. Then Elana went around the table and kissed both of the men on the tops of their heads before settling in an empty chair.

Before they could get into any proper conversation, however, the ringing of a bell broke through the chatter in the hall. Vincent turned to the head table, where Colony Director Jani was standing. "I am sorry to interrupt your dinner with this," she said, "but the time has come to take a supply mission to Earth. We need a citizen to oversee the trading of our mined minerals for the materials that Earth produces. Is there a volunteer?"

The hall was silent.

Director Jani smiled tightly. "Well, it never hurts to ask. I will choose randomly, then." She pressed a button on the tablet before her, and read "Vincent Magoro?"

Vincent's shoulders sagged, but he put up his hand. The whole hall turned to look at him.

"Report to spacedock in two days time. Now, everyone enjoy your meal."

Vincent lowered his aching head onto the table. "Out of all the people in the colony..."

Elana grabbed Vincent's hand. "We'll miss you," she said.

Diego took the other one. "You'll only be gone for two weeks or so. I'll be okay."

"Plus, you'll get to see Earth." Bommi said, putting her arm around his hunched shoulders. "I've never been to Earth before."

"You've got to take hundreds of stills," said Diego, "and call us all the time. It'll be like you're not even gone."

Vincent picked his head up. "You're right. It won't be so bad. I love you guys, thanks for cheering me up."

Elana gasped. "Stars, I just realized—you'll be stuck with a Martian the whole time, won't you?"

Vincent groaned and set his head back on the table. Everyone knew that Martians were trouble.

MAGGIE HAD ALREADY BEEN on the spaceship for two days when she met the representative from Venus. She'd settled into her quarters, which were smaller than her apartment back home, but comfortable enough, and had chatted with the four-person Terran crew whenever they were off-duty. They weren't friends, exactly, but she was beginning to think that this trip wouldn't be so bad, after all. Then, he boarded.

Vincent Magoro was tall, taller than her by at least a foot, with dark skin, high cheekbones, a long nose, and absolutely no hair. He reminded her of a shovel with its blade broken off. He had hugged the crew in greeting when he first got on the ship—and they were total strangers. He tried to hug her too, of course, but she wasn't having any of it.

She presented her hand to be shaken, and backed away when he tried to get closer than two feet away from her. He'd looked relieved when she did that, actually, and for some reason, that made her even more mad.

At dinner that night, she refused to speak to him. She teased Captain Roan lightly about her slightly bumpy takeoff from Venus, and the engineer, Lhin Julie, dissolved into giggles. Across the table, Vincent scowled at her. She leaned back on her chair and didn't bother to hide her smug grin.

In some pathetic attempt to turn the focus of the conversation back to him, Vincent said, "The passenger quarters here are lovely, aren't they?" He looked at Maggie, smiling, until she realized he expected her to answer.

"They're alright," she said, and stabbed a ravioli with her fork.

"And the food. I'd heard awful things about the food on spaceships, but this is an excellent meal, isn't it?"

"Uh, yeah." Maggie noticed the crew looking from her to Vincent and back, like they were some kind of tennis match. Her mood darkened even further. She wasn't anyone's game. Why the hell did he keep asking her questions? Was he trying to flirt with her or something? She stood up. "I'm full. I'm going back to my quarters."

"You do that," said Julie, with a barely contained grin. She fiddled with the insignia on her uniform, and a purple shape emerged—a sort of oblong octogon. Maggie didn't know what it meant, but Captain Roan cracked up.

That was the last straw. Maggie stalked out of the room. She heard another snort of laughter behind her, but refused to turn around. The automated doors of her quarters whooshed closed behind her, and she glared at them. She wished there was something to slam, or throw, but all the furniture was bolted down. She threw herself onto the bed, instead, vowing to stay in her room for the rest of the trip.

That resolution lasted about an hour, until her anger and embarrassment cooled a bit and her pride returned. She wasn't about to let some idiot Venusian send her into hiding. She'd go about her business as usual, and just pretend Vincent Magoro wasn't there. Hardening her face into a smirk, she marched out of the room and into the ship's little galley.

"I'm still hungry," she told Captain Roan, who

was leaning against the counter, drinking something blue out of a plastic cup. "What have we got left?"

After Margaret Shannon blew him off when he tried to greet her, tormented the Captain over some bumps that weren't her fault, and stormed off during dinner, Vincent gave up. He had planned to give her the benefit of the doubt, but it looked like the stories were true. Martians were just terrible people. And given the opportunity, he wasn't going to associate with her at all.

She wasn't actually that hard to avoid. The crew ate in shifts to make sure someone was always at the helm, so he ate with Kira the pilot and Tuan the navigator, and she ate with the Captain and the engineer. Otherwise, he stayed in his room, watching old movies on the ship's computer. Whenever they passed near satellites, he called his friends back on Venus, but that didn't happen frequently.

Four days into his journey, Vincent called Bommi. Her grinning face filled Vincent's screen.

"Vince." she exclaimed, "It's great to see you, hon. I've missed you."

"I've missed you too. I'm sorry I didn't call you until now, but Diego made me promise—"

"I know. He told us all about your call. No hard feelings."

"So how's Venus?"

"The same as always. Why are you asking? You're in space. What's that even like?"

Vincent groaned and flopped back on the bed.

"Honestly, it's pretty boring. The stars are cool for a while, but you can only stare at them for so long. And the Martian has me trapped in my room."

Bommi grimaced in sympathy. "I'm sorry. I can only imagine. Do you want to complain?"

"So. She doesn't look like she's going to be trouble, right? Because she's tiny. I'd be surprised if she's five feet tall. She's got bright red hair, like Elana's but coarser, and she's just unspeakably rude. When we met, I went to hug her, right? But she just ran away. She made me shake her hand, like I was diseased or something. I tried to make nice during dinner, strike up a conversation, but she refused to talk. And then she left. In the middle of dinner. Without even saying goodbye to any of the crew, let alone me. And now, she's prowling the halls outside my door, practically daring me to come out and talk to her." Vincent sighed. "I'm sorry, that was a really long rant. I don't mean to hog the conversation."

"That's okay," said Bommi, "You needed to blow off some steam, huh?"

"Yeah." Vincent smiled for the first time that day. "But seriously, I want to know what's happening over there. How's work? Weren't we getting a transfer?"

"Yep. The new guy is something, alright."

"Something good or something bad?"

"That remains to be seen. Let's just say he has a strong personality."

Vincent checked his connectivity. "Hey, Bommi, I'm moving out of range. Tell me more about him next time, okay?"

"Of course. Love you."

"I love you too." Vincent hung up.

"Is she your sweetheart?"

Vincent whirled around. "What are you doing in my room?"

The smirk that seemed permanently glued to Maggie's face intensified. "I'm not," she pointed out, "I'm in the hall. You shouldn't leave your door open." She wiggled her eyebrows at him. "I didn't know you had a sweetheart."

"I don't. Bommi's my friend."

Maggie scoffed. "Sure. You told her you loved her. You don't say that sort of thing to your friends."

Vincent had to stare at her for a moment before answering. "You don't? But don't you care about your friends?"

"Of course I do, but I don't get mushy with them."

"That's absurd. How can they know that you love them if you don't tell them?"

It was Maggie's turn to stare. "They—they just know. You can tell if a person likes you or not."

"Yeah, but you don't know if they think you're just okay or if they actually care about you unless they tell you."

"They could lie."

"I guess. But why would they?"

"To get in your pants."

Vincent shook his head. "Saying that you love someone has nothing to do with sex."

"Sure it does." Maggie cocked an eyebrow.

"No," said Vincent, flatly. "Where would you even—never mind. Please leave."

Maggie threw up her hands. "Fine. Whatever."

After a week of waiting, the actual trading of goods on Earth was- anticlimactic. Most of the trades had been agreed upon before Maggie had left Mars, so she just had to check that everything coming in and going out matched her list. Aluminum and carbon for seeds and water, feldspar and basalt for chocolate and medicine. The only interesting part was selling four paintings by Mars' resident artist Leah Mandelbaum. Apparently, she had a big following on Earth, because they held an auction, and dozens of people attended. Maggie watched as Leah's creations, which hung in half the homes on Mars, sold for millions of dollars each.

Vincent's job was effectively the same as hers. He didn't have any paintings to sell, but he traded packets of minerals and cylinders of gas for coils of gold wire, along with normal things like water and fabric. Trading out of the same dock was the longest time she had shared a room with him. They exchanged a total of ten words In less than forty-eight hours on Earth. When they blasted off again, Maggie was lying in her bed. As the ship rumbled around her, she smiled. She was finally going home.

Vincent was eating dinner with Kira and Tuan when Julie ran into the room, nearly skidding into the table.

"Stations," she said, panting. "We picked up a distress call. An escape pod. We need the ship lined up and the doors opened ASAP."

Kira nodded and ran off in the direction of the cockpit, with Tuan close behind.

Julie turned to Vincent, who was still sitting, confused. "Come with me," she ordered, taking off down the opposite hallway. He followed.

"What's happening?" He asked as they raced through the ship.

"Don't know for sure yet. Pod's almost out of oxygen. I need a second set of hands."

Maggie stuck her head out of her bedroom door as they raced by. "What's going on?"

"Maggie. Great. I need your help," called Julie, not bothering to stop. "Come on."

Maggie did as she was bid, falling into step beside Vincent. For the first time, they were completely in sync, both of them entirely befuddled.

They reached the loading dock. "The doors aren't supposed to open unless we're on the ground," Julie told them. "We need to put in manual override codes on both sides of the doors. Vincent, you see that little box there?"

He nodded.

"There's a keypad inside. A-6-6-P-H, but don't press enter until I say to."

"What about me?" asked Maggie

Despite his panic, Vincent couldn't help rolling his eyes. Someone was in danger, and here was Maggie thinking about herself.

"For now, just stay there," said Julie. "We'll need your help getting the pod doors open. Vincent, move."

Vincent ran to the box on the wall and punched in the code.

Moments later, Captain Roan's voice filtered through an invisible intercom. "We're attached, Jules, open the doors."

"We do this at the same time," said Julie. "On the count of three. One, two, three."

Vincent pressed down on the enter button and the doors whooshed open. The change in air pressure pulled at his clothes and made Maggie's braid stand on end. On the other side was another set of doors, but these were dented and scraped so badly that Vincent could barely tell where the opening was supposed to be.

"Don't let go of that button," Julie commanded, fishing something out of her pocket with her free hand. "Maggie, catch." She flung a small device at Maggie, who snatched it out of the air.

"Laser cutters. Nice."

"Open the doors with them. Quickly. And be careful, we don't know what's on the other side."

Maggie gave the engineer a sharp nod. It took a painfully long time to get the door open. The metal button dug into Vincent's finger, but he tried not to care. Someone on the other side could be dying as Maggie cut through the metal centimeter by centimeter.

"Can't you go any faster?" he asked.

Maggie shot him a glare over her shoulder. "Not if you want to get it open without hurting anyone. Laser cutters are dangerous. Not that you would know."

Vincent bristled and was about to respond when Julie cut him off. "Now is not the time," she snapped.

"Right, sorry," he said. Maggie said nothing.

Finally, Maggie reached the top of the doors and pried them apart. On the other side was a room smaller than the loading dock, with bare machinery blinking on the walls. A tiny form lay on the floor—a child, with their arms tucked under their knees. Maggie rushed forward and gathered the child in her arms, carrying them into the ship. Their hands grasped weakly at the fabric of her sleeves.

"We can let go now," said Julie, releasing the button. Vincent followed suit, and the doors slid closed. "I'm going to get the Captain." She left, leaving Vincent and Maggie alone with the kid.

Maggie settled the child onto a pile of cloth bundles. They were maybe five or six, with long, dirty hair, and wore a tattered green dress and a bracelet of plastic beads strung on twine. They were barefoot and trembling. Vincent stepped closer and saw the tears streaming down their cheeks. He froze. He'd never been good with children, especially crying ones. Kids weren't in touch with their emotions. They couldn't tell you what was wrong and how you could fix it. That made him tremendously nervous.

Maggie didn't seem to mind, though. As Vincent watched, she kept one steadying hand on the child's back. "Keep breathing," she told them, "there's plenty of oxygen here. Tell me your name."

The child let out a squeak that may have been attempting to be a word.

"I couldn't quite understand that. Say it again."

"Emmy."

"Hey, Emmy. Welcome aboard. I'm Maggie." Maggie held her other hand—the one that wasn't keeping the child from falling off the cloth—out to be shaken. Emmy took it with trembling fingers and gave it a weak shake.

"Are you a girl?" asked Emmy, so softly that Vincent could barely hear her.

"I am," said Maggie.

"Me too."

"Fantastic. Hey, is that a soccer ball on your bracelet?"

Emmy nodded.

"What team do you pull for?"

"Rockets."

Maggie grinned. "That's too bad," she said. "I'm a São Paulo fan. I guess we can't be friends anymore."

Vincent gaped at her. How could she say something so cruel to a tormented child like that? And yet the tone of her voice was tender, like she was encouraging the girl, not insulting her interests. There was more compassion in that insult than Vincent would have guessed Maggie possessed. To make things even weirder, Emmy smiled. Weakly, to be sure, but a smile was a smile.

Maggie continued, "I have the Toronto Rockets versus São Paulo game recorded. Do you want to watch it?"

Emmy nodded again, her smile getting bigger.

Captain Roan entered, holding a medical kit and an oxygen tank. Maggie said, "We have to check to make sure you're okay, and then you can come watch soccer with me."

Captain Roan knelt beside the girl and began to take her vitals.

Maggie moved to stand beside Vincent. "So mister touchy-feely himself is afraid of children, huh?"

Vincent felt his cheeks burning, but he ignored it. "You seemed to have it under control. Although I don't understand—"

"What?"

"Nothing."

"Seriously?" She rolled her eyes. "What do you want to ask me?"

"Why did you insult her team? That was cruel, especially since she's traumatized."

"I was joking. I did it to make her smile. Do they not have jokes on Venus?"

"They do, just not mean ones."

"Stars, you have no sense of humor."

"No, you have a bad sense of humor."

Maggie turned to him, eyes blazing. She pulled back her arm and probably would have punched him in the face then and there had Captain Roan not interfered.

"Maggie. Vincent. Can I ask you a question?"

They jumped and turned to face her, Maggie's arm falling back to her side.

"Emmy here's in surprisingly good health, but she'll have to stay on board until we get back to Earth, and the four of us have to, you know, run the ship. Can you two keep an eye on her as long as you're on board?"

"Sure," Maggie said immediately, stepping away from Vincent.

"Yeah, I can do that," said Vincent. "Won't be a problem."

"Great. Maybe you can, I don't know, alternate?"

"Absolutely," said Maggie. "I get her first. Let's go watch some soccer, Ems." She scooped up the girl and carried her out of the docking bay, not sparing Vincent another glance.

"That was strange," said Vincent.

"Tell me about it," said Roan, sticking her hands in her pockets. "It's not every day you find little girls in escape pods. Especially ones with such strong constitutions. For the length of time that pod's been deployed, she should have been way more oxygen deprived than—"

"Not that," said Vincent, cutting him off. "Maggie. That kid just responded to her. I don't understand it, you know?"

Roan shrugged. "I don't know. She seems the type to get on with kids, though. Like she never completely grew up herself. It's cute. But the oxygen—"

"She's so rude though. Why would you insult a child like that?"

"Not all of us are Venusians."

Vincent took a step back. "What's that supposed to mean?"

"Nothing." Roan sighed. "Look, I know you don't like her, but she's not that bad."

"Not that bad? Can you name a single nice thing that she's done?"

"She made that kid smile just now."

Vincent shook his head. "I still don't get it."

"She teased her. Added some joviality to the situation. It's not that hard, man."

Vincent didn't respond. He stared at the door through which Maggie had just left. It still didn't make any sense, but there must be something to what the Captain said. After all, the kid hadn't dissolved into tears or anything. And it wasn't as though he would have handled the situation any better.

EMMY SAT cross-legged on the bed, eyes glued to the screen. She'd devoured the few soccer games Maggie had recorded and was now engrossed in some Terran melodrama that was saved on the ship's computer. She'd stopped shaking, and had some food and water, but she still wouldn't say more than two words at a time. That was to be expected, though. Maggie couldn't help imagining what had happened to cause a little kid to be stuck on an escape pod, alone, for weeks. She shuddered and glued her eyes back on the screen.

She couldn't stay focused, though, and not just because it was a terrible show. Despite her intention of ignoring him, she was mystified by Vincent's reaction. She teased the kid a bit, and he acted like she'd cut her arms off. What was his deal? Did they just not tease people on Venus? She didn't generally think of herself as a prejudiced person, but everything bad she'd ever heard about Venusians was crammed into that one uptight, skinny guy. And stereotypes had to be based on something, right?

Whatever. It wasn't worth thinking about. In five days, she'd be back on Mars, with people who made sense. She'd never have to think about stupid Venusians again.

Somebody knocked on her door. "Who is it?" she called.

"Vincent," came the muffled reply. "I've got to talk to you about Emmy."

Maggie sighed. She clearly wasn't home yet. "Come in."

The door slid open and Vincent stepped inside. "Hi Emmy." he said, in a fake-bright voice.

The girl looked blankly at him for a moment, then turned back to her melodrama.

"So, um, I was thinking," said Vincent, leaning against the dresser. "Maybe you can keep an eye on Emmy tonight, and I'll watch her tomorrow? Maybe after breakfast?"

"Sounds good." Maggie dearly wished she could join Emmy in ignoring him, but she was supposed to be the grownup here. "We should alternate days, at least until I get back to Mars.

"That makes sense," said Vincent. One of his hands was absently fiddling with the edge of his tunic.

Maggie almost laughed. "You don't have to be afraid of her. If all else fails, she really loves these melodramas."

"Who doesn't?" Vincent said with a half-smile. Maggie couldn't tell if he was joking or not. Probably not. She wouldn't be surprised if his taste was just that bad.

"Right. Is that everything?"

"Um, yeah. Sorry. I'll leave you to your soaps."

Maggie watched him leave. It was the most pleasant conversation they'd ever had.

Emmy fell asleep with the show still playing. Maggie turned it off and tucked the kid in, hoping she hadn't forgotten something vital in the whole night-time routine thing. She liked kids, sure, but she'd never been responsible for one before. Emmy seemed okay, though, and she wouldn't want to wake her even if she had missed something, the girl was sleeping so peacefully. Maggie settled in beside her and fell asleep listening to her breathe.

A MECHANICAL SCREECH tore her from sleep. She sat up, dazed, as the noise continued. Some kind of siren, her tired brain informed her. There's been a cave-in. No, no cave in, she was on a ship. In space. A red light was flashing in the dark room, and Emmy— Emmy was gone.

Maggie sprang out of bed. Just as she reached the

door, there was a terrific crashing noise and the whole ship rocked sideways. She gripped the doorframe for dear life until the ship righted itself.

Vincent was already out in the hallway. "What's going on?" he shouted over the siren.

"I don't know. Where's Emmy?"

"She's not with you?"

Maggie shook her head.

Vincent's eyes were huge. She could see the red emergency lights reflecting in them. "Should we head for the cockpit?" he said.

"Yeah, okay."

They had barely gone four steps when there was another crash and the ship jerked again. Maggie fell backwards. Vincent caught her arm and hauled her back up.

"Thanks," she said.

"No problem."

They were picking their way across the still-swaying galley when everything went quiet. The red lights still spun, but the wailing stopped, and the ship grew still. Maggie turned to look at Vincent. He shrugged. There didn't seem to be anything better to do, so they continued past the overturned chairs and the cabinets with their contents spilled onto the ground.

Maggie saw the figure behind the counter moments before it sprang at them. She let out a vocalization that was half "Duck." and half "Run." and threw herself to the side. Vincent didn't hear her in time. The figure—human, dressed in a black coat and a handkerchief that covered half their face—hooked their arm around Vincent's neck and pressed a knife to his side. Maggie balled her hands into fists, ready to spring on him, but Vincent got there first. He jammed his elbow into his assailant's side and twisted out of his grasp.

Maggie ran up to help. She'd never actually been in a fight before, but she knew the theory—thumb outside the fingers, turn from the feet. She crashed into the fighter, throwing her arms around their shoulders so they bent over. Vincent sent a knee into their chin, and they slumped onto the ground.

"Thanks," said Vincent, breathing hard.

"No problem," said Maggie. Her brain was a little hazy. "Where'd you learn to fight like that?"

"I take classes. To keep myself fit, you know. I've never done it for real though."

"I'd never have guessed," said Maggie.

Vincent shrugged. "You weren't too bad yourself."

"Yeah, well, I'm strong. Mining, you know. I've never fought before."

"You haven't? I figured you Martians did stuff like this for fun."

"It's never been my jam." Maggie shook the cobwebs from her head. Emmy. They had to find Emmy. And if there was someone with a knife on the ship... "We've been boarded."

"Should we try and find the Captain?"

Maggie nodded. "Let's go."

Vincent stepped over the prone form of the attacker and made for the door. Maggie followed, pausing to pick up the knife.

They crept down the hallway, but didn't encounter anyone else until they reached the cockpit. Maggie pressed the button on the side of the door and it opened with a hiss. On the other side, Captain Roan, Tuan, and Kira sat on the floor with their hands behind their backs.

Kira's eyes widened when she saw them. "Get out of here." she cried. "There's pirates." But it was already too late. Something hard slammed into the back of Maggie's head and she crumpled onto the floor, the knife slipping from her fingers. Vincent dove for it, but the pirate beat him, snatching it away from his outstretched fingers. Another one came out of the shadows and kicked him in the ribs. He fell beside Maggie, clutching his side, eyes squeezed shut.

Maggie tried to get up, but one of the pirates planted a knee on her back, forcing her back down. Her arms were pulled out from under her and tied together at the wrists with something cold and plastic. Out of the corner of her eye, she could see the other pirate doing the same to Vincent.

When they were done, the pirate with the knife stood up and peered down the hallway. "That all of them?" they asked. Their voice was rough and low, like it had been broken and glued back together.

"Yes," said Captain Roan. Her voice was strong, but Maggie could see her hands shaking.

"Good." The pirate with the knife, who seemed to be in charge, stepped over Maggie and pressed the knife to Roan's neck. Roan strained away as much as she could, given her bonds. "I don't want any more surprises."

Did they have Julie somewhere else? Or was Roan lying? Maggie fought to keep her face neutral. Instead, she gathered her scattered thoughts and asked, "Where's Emmy?"

The pirate in charge laughed. "The kid? She's back on the ship. I know she's glad to be back in her own room."

Maggie blinked. Her head throbbed. She couldn't

make sense of what the pirate had just said. Her own room? What did that—

"It was a trap," Vincent said flatly. Maggie looked up, surprised. She'd never heard him sound so emotionless.

Roan slumped against the wall. "Of course," she said. "That's why she wasn't oxygen deprived. I should have guessed."

The head pirate turned to their compatriot. "Cal, get Aria and start moving the goods."

The other pirate—Cal—left the room. There was only one pirate with them, now. Surely together they could overpower him?

As though they'd read Maggie's thoughts, the pirate pulled out a gun and began twirling it between their fingers. If she and the others tried to jump them, they might win, but the pirate would kill at least one of them. That wasn't a good risk. And worse, when Cal found the pirate she and Vincent had knocked out, they would probably shoot them all anyway. They needed a plan. But stars, Maggie wasn't going to be the one to figure out that plan. Her head hurt so badly that just the effort of breathing was almost too much for her bruised brain.

Vincent wormed his way into a sitting position. From where he was, he could see out the still-open doors of the cockpit and down the hall. Maybe he could run and get out of range before the pirate could turn around? No, it was too far. He'd be shot before he was halfway to the first door. He was trapped.

A flicker of movement caught his eye. His breath hitched, certain it was Cal the pirate again, but no, this figure was shorter and rounder. It dodged closer, and Vincent had to stifle a gasp. It was Julie, and there was a laser cutter in her hand.

The pirate shifted, and for a horrible moment Vincent thought they had heard Julie, but they merely put their weight on their other foot. That didn't mean they couldn't shoot Julie, though. What she needed was a distraction.

Vincent was happy to provide. "So are you also Rockets fans?" he said, cursing himself for asking such an inane question.

"What?" said the pirate.

"Well, you know, Emmy was a Rockets fan. She must have gotten it from somewhere."

The pirate rolled their eyes, not bothering to reply. Vincent shot Maggie a desperate look. *Help me.*

Maggie stared at him a moment, then gave a tiny nod. "Of course they're Rockets fans. Only a criminal would think they're worth supporting."

Vincent said, "Isn't their record 0-5 for this season?"

"0-6," said Maggie, her smirk beginning to return to her pallid face. "They're as incompetent as these pirates."

"We tied with the Lake Monsters," snarled the pirate.

Maggie snorted. "Sure. That's why they're in the semifinals and the Rockets are one game from being disqualified."

"It was that stupid referee's fault. The third goal was completely legal."

"Do you blame all your failures on unfair calls?"

Vincent wanted to know. "Or just the sports-related ones?"

The pirate opened their mouth to reply and crumpled to the floor with a fwump. Julie stepped inside, hoisting the cutters onto her shoulder. "I've always liked baseball better anyway," she said.

"Thank the stars," said Tuan. "Julie, I thought you were dead."

"Not today. The idiots didn't even bother to check engineering. Speaking of idiots, why didn't you notice the tracking device in the girl's bracelet when you scanned her, Captain?"

Roan groaned. "So that's where it was."

Maggie said, "There's one more guy. I think they're moving the cargo."

Julie carefully sliced through their bonds. Captain Roan laid a hand on Maggie's shoulder. "Nice job back there. Both of you. That was some fast thinking."

Maggie shrugged. "We just had to rile them up a bit."

Vincent shot her a glare. "We just had to *work together.*"

Kira rolled her eyes. "You guys. It worked, that's all that's important."

"Do you know if the last pirate has a gun?" Julie asked.

"No clue," said Tuan.

Julie sighed. "I guess it doesn't matter. To the cargo bay."

The last pirate,did have a gun. They started firing as soon as the crew got through the door. All of them dived behind barrels and boxes. Vincent found himself crouched next to Maggie, peering over a box of seeds.

Vincent slid down behind the box. "What are we going to do?"

Maggie shut her eyes. " I don't imagine he wants to talk sports."

"Maybe if we can get them to use up their ammunition?But how can we do that without getting shot?"

"Stars, I don't know." Maggie pressed a hand to her forehead. "Do you have to ask so many damn questions?"

Vincent bristled. "I'm just trying to—"

"I know. I just—it hurts."

"No, I'm sorry, you're right. That hit looked bad. I shouldn't expect you to be overflowing with patience."

"You hear that, Captain?" said Tuan's voice from somewhere off to their left. "They're finally communicating."

"We should have shot at them sooner." Kira called. Vincent could hear a snort that must have come from Julie.

"May I remind you all that we're in a life-or-death situation?" Roan shouted. "Stop wasting time."

The other three Terrans called "Yes, Captain," and then did something Vincent could never have expected. They rushed the pirate.

As Vincent and Maggie watched from their spot behind the seeds, the four crew members tapped the insignias on their uniforms, and purple shields blossomed around them. The pirate kept firing, but their bullets just bounced away and clattered to the floor, harmless. Their face crumpled, and they had their hands up before the crew even reached them.

Vincent and Maggie emerged from their hiding place. Vincent noticed that Maggie's hands were clenched in trembling fists and stepped out of her way.

"You had bulletproof shields built into your uniforms and you didn't bother to tell us?" she shouted. "I thought you were all going to die."

Kira shrugged, unconcerned. "They're standard issue."

"It's not like they helped us much earlier," Roan said with a sigh. "Stupid pirates got the drop on us."

THE CREW SPLIT UP, some to contact the Terran authorities, others to restrain the unconscious pirates before they woke up, leaving Vincent and Maggie alone.

Vincent sat down on a crate. "So," he said.

"So," Maggie replied, looking at her feet.

"I should thank you, I guess. You probably saved my life back there."

"Yeah, well," Maggie said, "you probably saved all our lives, so." They stood there in silence a moment before she added, "You fought well, and you kept your head. I wouldn't have expected that of a Venusian."

Vincent grimaced. "Thanks, I guess. But maybe don't say the whole 'of a Venusian' thing?"

Maggie snorted. "And you don't think I'm good with kids 'for a Martian'? Roan told me about all that. Don't pretend you have no prejudices."

"I didn't use those words." Vincent protested, but he felt guilt curling in his stomach. "I am sorry, though. For misjudging you, you know? I should've known better."

Maggie's smirk slipped. "Me too. You're an okay guy, Vincent."

Vincent beamed at her, hoping she understood what he meant. For once in his life, he didn't have the words.

MAGGIE WATCHED Mars draw nearer outside her bedroom window. Her things were already packed and sitting by the door. After the pirates, she'd expected to be even more excited to get home, but now, with less than an hour left in her journey, she was suddenly melancholy.

"Two minutes to landing," said Tuan over the intercom, making Maggie jump. She grabbed her bag, headed for the loading dock. Everyone except Kira, who was piloting the descent, was waiting for her there. Tuan and Julie clapped her on the shoulders.

"Don't get into too much trouble without us," said Julie.

Maggie grinned. "No promises."

Roan shook her head. "Take care of yourself."

"You too. And hey, next time you're on Mars, comm me. We can get dinner."

Then, she came to Vincent. He presented a hand for her to shake, not looking her in the eyes. She considered it for a moment, and then wrapped her arms around his neck. He hugged her back immediately, squeezing her a little more tightly than was entirely necessary, but she didn't mind.

"I love you," he whispered.

Maggie pressed her eyes shut. "I love you too," she

replied. He let her go, and she punched him gently on the arm. "You're still an idiot, though."

His face froze, and she was worried she'd gone too far with the whole teasing thing. Then, he laughed. "Comm me, okay?"

"You got it." Maggie hefted her bag and, with one last glance at her friends, walked off into the Martian morning.

The Delphic Oracle

Metaphysical Insurance Claim 0075A

by Lancelot Schaubert & Alexander Sirkman

Every year prior to the year in question, the city-state of Oracle Hill had a birth rate of 0 due to a populace of monks and nuns; but in the year of our Delphic Oracle 3034, the birth rate grew to 1. The mother was a virgin nun, the child a complication. As you know, an immediate filing by... someone... for payout to the Pontificate and Council of Blue Jays for our Accidental Virgin Birth policy required our investigation, report and adjustment, but all that in mind we deliver it to you, James. I know it's your cousin and all we're talking about here, but... I mean... you asked, particularly because of that anonymous enrollment and anonymous filing in a rather recent and obscure department within Oracle Hill. This is what we found.

Messrs. Sirkman and I, heretofore denominated as "Lance", went down to see what we would see. Having the both of us penned an adjustment report for the policy taken (pre-post-humously) by both Brothers Jack, we had settled down for a long winter's nap[1]. When out on the Stations arose such a scandal, we sprang from our rest to see what was mishandled. To Auld Imitation we hopped like two hares, showed up in St. Cephas's 'round evening prayer.[2]

Ahem.[3]

At the end of the day, we two merely hoped to save money for our burgeoning insurance float. Mind you, prior to our involvement the insurance industry had gone the way of all things in the Actualization Station since the war. The structure of civil society might have shattered, but we're doing our derndest to bring insurance back in full force — at least in a meta-physical way — and some submissions require inspection for proof of payout. Our specialty is the weirder sort of case involved in the Actualization Station: accidental life after death insurance, leaky umbrella insurance, multiple cured cancers that keep manifesting as uncured cancers insurance, I'm-completely-healthy-and-have-no-tragedies-but-may-one-day-long-to-die-and-taste-the-sweet-sweet-tang-of-the-abyss insurance, life-by-stabbing insurance, death-by-conception insurance (or the related, and ever popular, inconvenient orgasm insurance), immunity from immunity from immunity from pre-existing immuno-compromised *insurance* insurance, forged death, forged life, forged forgery[4]), death by forge, life by forge, and forged forge (more of a blacksmith thing, that). Oh, and of course four forge and forged forge ago our forge-fathers....

AHEM. Anyways.[5]

EN ROUTE[6] we both found ourselves rather enamored by how much of Oracle Hill could be seen from nearly every point in the city, rather unlike the tall gray grass that grew ever higher in this particular Station's "New York City." Alex, who had pulled his luscious red strings back with a bit of stretchy twine, mumbled under the fog of his glasses, "Seems they moved the hill since last time."

"You were here?" Lance asked.

"Member once I showed up on that jutting head-land by the shore? The fruitless sea?"

Lance said, "In your first flush of manhood: your rich, dark hair waving about you, purple robe on your strong shoulders."

"This hoodie?" He held up his sleeves with an awkwardly cross-handed pinch. And held up his whispy red-blondish hair. "This hair?"

"Uh. Right. Right. Rich purple *hoodie* on your strong shoulders. Lovely yellow locks."

"Red. Strong?" He squeezed his own arms. "Yes, sure, sure. *Strong.* Well these Tyrsenian pirates on a well-floored timber tub, miserable doom of the world's wine-stained bathtub ahead of us, it was mostly about them."

"What did they do?" Lance asked.

"Kinda grabbed me. You know. Sneak attack." He poked at his co-writer, co-adjudicator. "*Yah. Yah.* Made these goofy signals to one another, anyone could read right through them, but they still grabbed me."

"Why?"

"Thought I was some sort of son of some heaven-teated lord. Withed me."[7]

"Yeah that didn't hold," Lance said.

"Nah," Alex agreed.

"What, they want to sell you or something?"

"Yah," Alex said, opening up a warehouse-sized bag full of his brother's hyper-spicy dried fish snacks.

Lance wrinkled his nose, but accepted one to... try.

"The helmsman really got onto them for it, once the bonds fell. He said something like, 'Madmen! What god have you bound, so strong?' Or something. He didn't think the ship could carry me."

"That dummy. You're just a man."

Alex looked down and patted his belly, saying, "Of a sort, of a sort... a bit more gravitas than I'd like, though."

"Go easy on yourself."

Alex shrugged and smiled his fellowship smile. "They didn't think I looked like them, so I had to be a god or devil or something."

"In a way," Lance said.

"Enough with that author stuff. Consensus spoke amongst them, and so twas true."

Lance rolled his eyes.

Alex rolled his back.

Both smiled.

Alex said, "Well they thought they needed a bigger boat for me anyways, didn't want me stirring up the waters. Hoist sail and caught all sheets. Bound for Egypt."

"You mean that both ways," Lance said, and winked.

"Oooh lah lah."

Lance winced, foiled by his own naive boldness. "No, not like that. Not all *three* ways."

Alex shrugged, noncommittal..

"What did you do?"

"Made it rain fragrant sweet wine. Sort of heavenly smell. Vine on the mainsail, twisting about the mast, heavy fruited, lovely piece of work. Pirates saw it and half begged me to make landfall."

"Yeah? So you just... went along with that?"

Alex laughed and moved his head vaguely up and down, then looked around awkwardly. " Yes, I may... have... not."

"You didn't."

"Well you only get a good chance to turn into a lion so many times, in our profession," Alex said. "So yeah, I roared. A bit."

"The bear?"

"Okay. I may have also summoned that one great shaggy bear I favor, complete with the dingleberry dreadlocks. They all crowded at the far end then leapt into the sea."

Lance shook his hobbit locks, then said, "And *then* you left them alone?"

Alex sipped his coffee, and set the mug down out of scene., where it spilled all over the red drapes between death and life from the last story[8] He looked over the rim of his glasses, left and then right, then left again - then up, and then directly at Lance. "I... I may have turned them all into, you know... dolphins."

"What?!"

Alex shrugged. "I left them a prophecy! I promised it would get better!"

"Alex."

"And uh, right, I also turned the mast and oars into snakes...might have also summoned a satyr to play a really loud flute the size and shape of a giant bong."

"A didgeridoo?"

"May have been a bassoon, or a contrabassoon? Whichever can exist safely on this plane." Alex eyed Lance.

"What?"

"Like that time you engorged that bassoon to be taller than the conceptual height limit of that indigenous people group?"

"You said you wanted to get higher than sky."

"Not like that, doofus."

Lance shrugged. "Same same. Bassoon, Didgeridoo. Bong. Bricks higher than height itself."

"Huh. So yeah, there's a bunch of dolphins swimming around Oracle Hill who probably remember their former lives as pirates, sapience being what it isn't. I didn't think much about it until now."

"Why's that matter?"

"I think that's why they moved the whole hill," Alex said, pointing.

In centuries past, the hill had been laid up with annoying ramparts built of bricks shaped like thickened matzoh loaves. So, so many of them stacked. That's how Lance thought of it: a ramp of stone crackers that, if seized slowly by a huge infantry, would turn quickly into a mossed landslide. Alex didn't think of matzoh at all. He thought it looked more like someone had painted grey clay bookspines stacked sideways to make a mossy cave wall that would slick out from under you any second. There were, somewhere in the stations, castles built of books, and crackers, and all sorts of things . It was that sort of existence.

But on closer inspection - yes, it seemed as if the

hill had occupied more space in the bay, extending out a bit from where the docks were stationed: you could see places through the clean and turquoise water where the marble support pillars might have gone.

They needed to meet James, first, and commit to discovering why the adjustment was filed and by whom. Luckily the docks of the Tyrsenian coast ran right up next to the south side of the books-no-clay-bricks-no-wait-its-old-thick-matzoh ramparts of the city-state of Oracle Hill.[92] Alex and Lance walked up to the edge of pier three[310] and poked their heads over the edge. There floated a dolphin, waiting patiently.

"Woop," Alex said.

Lance smiled. "Hello James."

"Mr. Schaubert," said the dolphin named James, then looked to Alex. "Master Sirkman."

"Crap," Alex said again. "He speaks Narrative. Oh nooo."

Lance laughed. "You summoned us here for an insurance adjustment report?"

The dolphin clicked a whole bunch in rapid succession and nodded as well as flippers and a delphic body could nod. "Yes," he said. "I need you to fill out the claim and put it on paper." He hissed a bit, laughed a cackle, and said, "Sealed."

"Sincerely le séala céir," Lance said. "Got it. Why?"

James said, "Why I care doesn't matter. Didn't you fill out paperwork for a policy here for an accidental virgin birth?"

Alex pulled out his well-loved soft leathern briefcase, pulled out the file in question, flipped a couple of pages in his well-ordered files, looked up. "We had one, but the only thing we have is this region, this city-state represented. We don't have a name for the policy holder. We also don't have a name for the filer."

"Yes, but a celibate nun *is pregnant.*"

Alex and Lance looked at each other. Lance looked back to the dolphin. "Are you sure?"

The dolphin said, "Check the birth rates for Oracle Hill this year."

Lance pulled out his gilded gyrocompass and checked.

The compass spoke. It had the voice of a dragon surrounded by books. "The birth rate for Oracle Hill during the current year in your local spacetime coordinates is zero."

"And the year before?" the dolphin asked.

Lance went to open his mouth — folks never hijack his compass.

But the compass said, "Zero."

The dolphin opened its mouth.

Lance cut it off. "Have there ever been births here?"

"Not yet," the compass said and then sarcastically added, "Do *you* expect a positive birthrate from a bunch of eunuchs and celibate nuns?"

"What do you know, you're just a compass," Lance said.

"No I'm not. You should know that, of all people."

Lance harrumphed and raised his eyebrow, then whispered to the dolphin, "Are we quite sure they're *all* celibate?"

Alex perked up, eyes wide, and said, "Oooooh, naughty naughty."

The dolphin... can dolphins shrug? Especially when surrounded by so much seaweed in the place where the shoulders should have gone? "I doubt it, otherwise why would you show up?"

Lance said, "To prove it wasn't a virgin who conceived. We do like keeping our insurance float uncashed."

The dolphin looked left, at Lance.

Lance looked right, at Alex.

Alex looked right at the dolphin.

The dolphin looked right, at Alex.

Alex looked at Lance, to his right.

Lance looked at the dolphin. "Ah. To the alleged virgin, then."

They left.

IT'S A RATHER difficult thing to get inside Oracle Hill unsuspected. Fortunately for us, we looked like two cheap dates on an even cheaper tourism visit into Oracle Hill proper. They passed us through... well a set of mental detectors — they went off when any kind of malign soul seemed to be armed with some measure of metaphysical weapon. Magic, more or less, though how the detectors worked none could tell us properly. Lance and Alex made their way through the stone arches of the mental detectors, both of which had been covered in some measure of mossy sandstone. Or some other yellow stone, anyways. It all stood out against the low sky of that high hill in the midst of the city-state. It felt oppressive, in a way, at least to Lance: knowing they didn't know who had filed the policy. Or really who asked for them to fill out the report — who had filed the claim. No closer, it felt... it just all felt odd. Typically they *knew* these things, how had they even gotten the thing to pass through their system at all? "Hey Alex?"

"Yeah?"

"Doesn't list a filer or a snitch?"

"Nope."

Lance thought for a moment and watched how certain stones, rounded out like little mixing bowls, had benefited from the swish of dripping water over years of coastal rains. They benefited uniquely from their position. Or had special drawbacks from it. "Who's the beneficiary?"

"Good question," Alex said. He rifled through the papers and the backlog of text, deeper and deeper, until he found it nestled smack dab somewhere between the beginning and the end. "Looks like the pontiffs and bluejays and abbesses."

"Of Oracle Hill?"

"Yessm."

"Is it possible that Oracle Hill took out the policy anonymously in case they ever had a nun go rogue and get pregnant?"

Alex looked at the payout. His eyes bugged out of his head. "Yes. But then they'd have to prove it was a virgin birth."

"Or cover up the guy who got her pregnant?"

"Or kill him?" Alex asked.

"We looking at a murder here?" Lance asked. "Gosh that would be awful." And Lance wondered, looking at it all standing out that way — so many ossified sandcastles in the bare sky – whether it would be better to just file the report and be done with it. Or if it would be better to truly uncover who took out the policy in the first place. And why? He had a hunch that both were the same man or group of men, but he couldn't quite figure out which of these folks really worried about it.

They both passed through the second round of mental detectors — that had this black monviso finish to them, gilded slate bricks now and again shining forth from the otherwise well-masoned archway. Even in just looking at those, Lance wondered what would happen to him — or... *one*, rather — who didn't take care of all of their magical artifacts whilst passing through.

Bad bad tings.

Oh yah bad, man.

Some crotchety old man-sized pigeon with half a foot and even less tail feathers stopped and frisked him while he gave both some onomatopoetic resistance — "Ehhhhaya" — and wondered again: policy filer or snitch? Someone *wanted* Oracle Hill to benefit from the presence of a... well at least an alleged virgin birth. Someone in Oracle Hill. And someone had snitched that the virgin birth might (or might not?) fulfill their policy. But they had no record of either.

"We really need to work on our records," Lance said.

"You're telling me," Alex said. "My day job is—"

"Writing, I know."

"No my day job of my day job: the paralegal stuff. I sort out people's disorder so much every day that I need to hire an assistant for my own."

"Tell me about it," Lance said. "I married an administrative assistant and it's still a schaubert's kids have a no schaus situation."

"Good thing you're a Broganer."

"Aurelius. And Broganer's kids have no brogs."

"Same difference," Alex said. "Frogger has no frogs."

"That's how you lose that game," Lance said. "Anyways, snitch or filer?"

"Por que no los dos?"

"Because they might not be the same person. I'm leaning towards finding the filer," Lance said. "Snitches get stitches."

Alex snorted. "Or maybe they get us the info we need to prove it's just some nun that had repressed desires."

"Repression isn't a thing. Depression from overindulgence is."

"Ah," Alex said. "Good thing neither of us know anything about *that* either."

Lance stuck his finger in his mouth, in his ear, then said, "It's about thirty degrees o'clock. Let's go meet this lady and shoot for the filer."

"Not the one who snitched, not the one who benefits, but whoever took out the policy in the first place?" Alex asked.

Lance shrugged. "Why not?"

SOMETIMES PLACES like that feel so thoroughly planned out you wonder if they were over engineered for and by some great ancient cyborg intent on destroying the access humans have to the place. Other times you wonder if it's possible for buildings to sort of grow like so many mushrooms on the wet, dark, southron side of an oak — wending and sending out spores until the original stone hollows out to some shape that, though clearly seasonal, remains yet distinct and connected. In the Americas, the closest thing you see to that is the sprawling nature of country churches that never quite anticipated turning into megachurches and so as the needs and modernizations of the original chapel expands — first to include a baptistry, then a back room to change for the sake of using the baptistry, then a rectory, then a fellowship hall and, to facilitate using said hall, a foyer, a wedding chapel off to the side, oh wait, also another set of bathrooms, a doubling of office space, then classrooms, children's, youth, a second place to eat, a second set of classrooms, a third, then a massive gymnasium, an upstairs for youth, another set of completely unnecessary classrooms, another upstairs *vaguely* connected to the second, a subbasement for storing creepy passion play props, and whoops: a remodeling of children's to stave off abuse. Imagine that, but over centuries. And it incorporates tombs for unknown soldiers of the divine, catacombs. It includes an art gallery for years of iconography and tourism shops that affix themselves to the great ship of faith like so many barnacles that, however many times you scrape them off (whether with a turning of tables or a reformation and conciliar concessions) you never quite get them to *stay* off the hull. It includes an entire courtyard designed on the diamond ratio (quite better, in the end, than the golden ratio) and another set of chapels just for private viewing of the staff. Also a whole sweet of interconnected sculpture halls completely segregated from the... oh right I forgot to mention the abbeys and cloisters where the playful pray and prayerful play. There's like ten more food courts and another thirty prayer alcoves and a whole back office where the janitorial and security forces tell the sort of stories they believe would make the priests blush (until they realize that the nature of confession means that 90% of priests have heard ten or twenty stories that would make the most rakish violent hooker blush).

Anyways, it sprawls and interconnects: it's sort of a hive of hives that, rather than war, have reached something like a coequal stasis.

The nature of that design kept Lance and Alex lost. They could have consulted their compasses. They could have asked someone. They could have looked at the map James himself had drawn him with his cute little dolphin nose. They did none of these things because both of them liked the nature of getting lost and finding your way out again. Rather dangerous way to live one's life, but pilgrimage always has its rewards and blessed are they who set their hearts upon it (though it can be rather chaotic for the characters who live in worlds founded by two eternal pilgrims).

Thrice they found themselves accidentally joining the same set of wandering tourists (a couple of fat ones in bright floral button-ups and boring-colored shorts, a couple of skinny ones with bob cuts in maudlin maroon drapes, a couple that looked as if they'd sprouted straight out of a bog), who were asking the same set of wandering questions (would you use a print of this in the living room? I don't quite like his post-Somno period, do you? Bro check out the waaaaves, see?). And getting asked to interject or, in one particularly unwelcome welcoming, what they were doing for dinner and where?

They ignored all of this and, with two bathroom breaks and a mid-tour espresso and cheese (for Alex) and crappy crackers (for Lance), found an open back-door that blended in perfectly with one particularly obtuse painting of philosophers and theologians pointing at various details in a polymorphic poly-faunic spree. Through that door they came into a jani-torial closet. Alex nicked a set of keys that, at least in his mind, could open any door on the planet and, to Lance's mind, therefore made it real. (For Alex, he'd have to convince a few more characters who would agree, in the locked room in question, that the keys could do just that). Because of that, he passed the keys to Lance, who stuck them into the cover of a book that had a keyhole to some old door depicted on the spine. It didn't yield at first, so Lance picked an older key and jammed it in. The thing rammed home, turned true, and the whole bookcase — lost and found from various tourists, academics, priests, and special forces agents — opened to reveal the library of one of the inner monasteries.

One of the janitors who witnessed this divine ap-paratus dropped his jaw so wide that two great glob-ules of spittle lolly gagged clean out and into the mop bucket.

Ploop.

Bloop.

Alex went up to the first contemplative he could find standing before the blessed sacrament and said, "Excuse me sir, I don't mean to divert your devout, but can you show me to the ladies's room?"

The monk, whose eyes had been closed and back rigid with kneeling, went wide-eyed and bent slack, arms spread in shock.

"He doesn't mean restroom," Lance said. "He means the room of ladies doing what you're doing?"

"Particularly midwives?" Alex added.

The monk came back to full consciousness and speech. "Why would Oracle Hill have a birthing ward?"

Alex looked at Lance.

Lance blushed a bit and said, "Ignore that. Where are the nuns gathered?"

"Which ones?" the monk asked.

Lance thought for a moment. The odds of a virgin birth from a menopausal woman — a barren womb rejoicing at the same time as having some sort of miraculous conception, sans man — seemed thin, though certainly possible. It seemed to him, however, that this wasn't the sort of story he and Alex were in the middle of, or that their authorial persons *per se* weren't in the business of telling at present. "The younger nuns," he said. "The youngest of the bunch, but full nuns."

The monk squeezed together his eyebrows skeptically and then said, "If you follow this hall, you'll come to an exit. If you turn left, you'll leave this conjunction of abbey and cloister. But—"

Alex said, "We don't—"

"*But if,*" the monk continued doggedly, "you pass around the shared fountain, the one with the mosaic around its pool and the two angels riding dolphins—"

Here Alex raised his brows.

"—you'll come to an identical ingress to the egress you left. Here is the cloister for the younger nuns, led in fact by some elders. Though why you would want this information makes me think I should tell my Abbot."

Lance said, "Trust us."

"I don't."

"Okay," Lance said, "but I'm going to tell you anyways I don't plan anything nefarious. We simply need to ask a few questions to protect a young woman."

Alex flinched. That wasn't *entirely* true, but true

enough.

The monk looked to them both and couldn't quite parse the nuanced conflict between them. Instead he said, "I'll give you an hour at least before I make up my mind whether to tell him or not."

"Fair," Lance said.

Alex said, "Lessgo."

THEY WANDERED through the most awkwardly placed stone hallway — and stones in a hallway — Lance had seen, truly a Ship of Theseus sort of hallway, every stone replaced and even those replacements replaced until the hall had grown like you'd expect the inside of a Japanese maple to appear. After having passed several oak-timbered doors with cast iron hardware threatening to fall or fall apart, they came to the fountain. The light from the setting sun came in clean through the porthole in the main entrance door in beams separated by so many iron bars. Those hit mirrors of green and gold and indigo, splaying so many rainbows through the room. They ignored it and Lance pulled out the keys to open the door to the cloister.

Alex, ever so gently and genteelly, placed his paw on the armed keyring and added pressure until the weight of his arm forced Lance to let the ring and hand hang limp at his side. Then he lifted the selfsame paw and rapped thrice and a double tapped at the end of the set. Then waited patiently.

Lance, meanwhile, not only tapped his foot, but shifted his weight — ankle, other ankle — rocked his pronated hips back and forth (tight flexers, loose glutes), shifting the pains in his spine towards other pains.

After half and half again so many eternal purgations, the door opened to reveal the nastiest old crone of a woman. She said in a voice like the daintiest honeysuckle hummingbird, "Hile and hardy men, may I help either of you?"

Alex hesitated then.

Lance took over and said, "We're here to attend the pregnant young woman."

The abbess blushed. "Whatever do you mean? Oracle Hill has had a birthrate of zero every year since its inception."

"Operative word is *has*," Lance said. "And I don't think one conception automatically negates its intended inception. May we come inside?"

She looked at Alex's hoodie, looked at Lance's goofy three-piece and bare feet, looked over their shoulders to the closed egress behind them, the closed door to their left — her right — and waved them in with a whispered, "*Hurry hurry hurry, dears.*"

They followed her through an almost identical twisted tunnel, this one made not of yellowed stone, but rather of a greener mossed cobble. They heard sounds in some of the chapels that sounded... well... almost erotic in nature.

Alex couldn't help but peek in one of the grates. He saw only nuns rapt in prayer. "What the...?"

Lance said, "You really should read more sixteenth century prayer manuals."

"A...apparently?" He pushed passed his co-writer, co-adjudicator, and the silence of parallel rooms. They came to a small antechamber whose other end had been sealed off with hastily laid brown brick. Before them stretched out on a bed lay a young woman, not only pregnant but pregnant to bursting: the baby completely dropped, headfirst in shape as if to crown soon. She was covered by a sheet — thank God — but, though clearly in pain of early labor, she looked far more pleased than the other, elder nuns around her.

A nearby archbishop was finishing up an interrogation of how — *how* — she possibly could have been so dull as to impregnate herself. And he was demanding answers as to which nun, which priest, had betrayed both her and his holy orders.

She insisted in her native tongue that she had slept with no man.

"This is ridiculous," the archbishop said to her and then added, "I refuse to believe this."

"You already do," she said of his own faith and nodded to the icon on wall. "You just find it easier to believe it happened back then than you do that it still happens now."

He scoffed and sputtered and, though he did not spit on her, sprayed a bit of spittle in his fluster. Some tarnished the gilded necklace that lay upon his turquoise vestments, adding weird concave and convex effects to the vestments and necklaces themselves. He turned, as if for the first time, and said, "What is a man doing here? Why two?"

Lance didn't hesitate to say, "We were about to ask you the same thing, father."

"Who are you! I demand you tell me why you are here?"

"Honestly?" Lance asked.

He nodded. His chains shook.

Alex said, "Mr. Cobbler's Son and I are insurance adjustors for a metaphysical insurance company. We're here to investigate the report of a claim against an accidental virgin birth insurance policy."

The archbishop said, "You actually sell insurance against this sort of thing happening?"

"Exclusively," Lance said.

More than the presence of a potential miracle, it seemed that his shook the faith of the father further. "How can you verify?"

"That's our job. You'll need to grant us exclusive rights to bring in the proper personelle trained in this sort of thing to verify. But yes, if we can verify it's truly happening, that the child is born alive, and so forth..."

"What if we want to terminate the child?" The archbishop asked.

The room went very, very still.

The young girl, who had been silent as other men decided her fate, said, "Oh like hell. You will NOT take my baby." It almost sounded like a growl.

"Uh, right," the archbishop said. "Of course not. Forgot myself." And he looked up to Lance and Alex awkwardly.

The other nuns stared that the man: his vestments seemed to have desaturated in the evening light.

The archbishop said, "Why would I want to help you verify? Why not hide the child so that he can grow up here?"

Alex said, "Sort of a raised by wolves story?"

Lance laughed and then said, "Easy."

The archbishop ignored this and stamped his foot and said, "Well? Why should Oracle Hill help?"

"Because," Lance said, "Oracle Hill is the beneficiary of this policy."

The archbishop said, "What do you mean?"

"If this poor nun—" he pointed to the gorgeous

young girl in pain ”—is indeed pregnant, a virgin, and delivers her baby, the full and no adjustments to that effect can be assessed, the full amount of the payout goes to Oracle Hill?”

The archbishop said, “If word of this gets out, it could damage us ten times over. How much we talking?”

“About an order of magnitude.”

“Order of magnitude of what?” The archbishop said.

“Oracle Hills.”

He stopped dead.

The room went rather still.

The nuns looked at one another, him, he them, they all looked at the two insurance adjustors.

He said, “Excuse me, but do you expect me to believe you’ll pay out *ten* full values of the city state of Oracle Hill, a city state several millennia in the making and preserving?”

“Correct,” Alex said.

“How?”

“Whatever currency you prefer,” Lance said. “We pay in dollars, euro, plumbum, narrative arcs—“

“No, I mean, how could you possibly have that much money? That’s inconceivable?”

“We have a rather large float,” Lance said simply.

That a payout of that size meant absolutely nothing to this insurance man shook his faith further. Or perhaps — perhaps — even expanded it. He looked out the window to where a mysterious starling landed. The bird, extinct in almost every timeline and habitat in The Vale or the Stations, startled him. He looked back and said, “Who do you need?”

They didn’t wait to answer the man, Lance simply went to work opening a tunnel in the floor with a cobblestone compass while Alex did a similar thing getting the nuns to agree — in faith — that a portal existed in the middle air of the room. Lance's elemental tunnel brought forth a South Korean OBGYN from his hometown. Alex's brought another from Columbia University. Together the women agreed that yes, in fact, the hymen was intact — a miracle in itself when they found out the other piece. For the Columbia doctor had brought along an ultrasound having been prepared for this particular contingency. Before they could apply the ultrasound, however, the poor girl started to shout out in the pangs of late stage labor. No anesthetic. Nothing but breathing and squatting around the room. It freaked the lot of them out, but it carried on.

And it didn't last long compared to Lance's own bride, whose labor had lasted three days. It went quick as a pistol shot.

The baby didn't cry though.

The archbishop gasped, worried that it had died.

But it clicked instead.

They all looked down to realize the nun had given birth to an infant dolphin.

"James," Alex said back at the docks. The nun was with them, holding her dolphin baby in swimming clothes. "What happened?"

"Remember the prophecy you gave us?" The pirate-turned dolphin asked. He was surrounded by roughly a hundred pirates-turned-dolphins.

Alex sighed and said, "Vaguely?"

The dolphin's eyes went green and hazy and the waters turned to ink as he said, *"The Oracle Hill virgin shall be with child and it shall be a dolphin savior, the dead pirate captain reborn through wombroving. On his return the dolphins shall become the pirates again."*

Lance said, "You didn't. That dead guy in the Lamentation Station was really the same dead pirate captain?"

"Mayhap," Alex said.

"So he just had to learn to wombrove to a virgin? To conceive of himself in a virgin womb?"

"Mayhap," Alex said again.

Lance sighed. "So who took out the policy?"

"I did," James said.

"Wait, what?"

"Well you know," James said, "if our only real shot of being pirates again was this virgin born dolphin, I didn't want some religious system screwing it up."

Lance laughed.

"You know they could have aborted the baby or something, once they found out what it was. So I took out a policy that would benefit them directly through the preservation of the baby. Only had to wait then for our Captain to get it right."

The baby dolphin, having wombroved, was already growing to full size.

"Fine," Alex said. "Count it fulfilled."

A hundred dolphins turned, at once, into naked pirates. Some of them weighed down with their absurdist gaudy jewlrey and neckwear and hats and boots and pantaloons tried — very hard — not to drown immediately.

Alex looked at Lance and said, "What?"

"I just can't believe you went with the virgin birth prophecy."

Alex said, "I mean, how was I supposed to know it'd work? There's virgin birth stories in like every culture ever."

Lance said, "People forget that myths are arts. That myths are the art of imaginative symbols, combined. We have entered more deeply than they into the Eleusinian Mysteries and have passed a higher grade, where gate within gate guarded the wisdom of Orpheus. We know the meaning of all the myths. We know the last secret revealed to the perfect initiate. And it is not the voice of a priest or a prophet saying 'These things are.' It is the voice of a dreamer and an idealist crying, 'Why cannot these things be?' The place that the shepherds found was not an academy or an abstract republic, it was not a place of myths allegorised or dissected or explained or explained away. It was a place of dreams come true. Since that hour no mythologies have been made in the world. Mythology is a search. Myths came with the pirates, philosophy with the philosophers, prophecy with the prophets. All that remains is for all three to merge here in an actual, historical event: mythology, philosophy, prophecy are all sad. But when they merge and all come true, what happens?"

They looked at the pirates.

The pirates were happy, throwing gold around and dancing in and out of the water with the otherwise baffled nun, now holding the captain to whom she'd given birth.

The delphic pirate named James walked up to the nun.

"James?!" the new mother asked in half horror and half delight. "We thought you died!"

"Hey cous."

"Women give birth every year to the lineage of mankind," Lance said. "The moment we short circuit that process in the history of our world, something else happens entirely to those caught up inside the story. The philosophers and prophets and mythologists suddenly agree on the high story of history."

"SEE THERE?" Alex asked, "Consensus? Totally a thing. All the pirates *agreed* the prophecy was true, believed in it so much that they manifested it into the world somehow."

"Oh come on," Lance said. "You're the narrator of their world. The moment you gave them a final cause and said that this would happen, it was bound to happen one way or another. In fact, had I been a character in your story, I totally would have bet on it happening because the over-under on it would make it probably the most undervalued surefire bet in that entire story. Whatever else would happen, *it was almost guaranteed* a pirate-dolphin would be born of a virgin. All the friends were there to witness it, see?"

The pirates all nodded their heads, coin and teeth necklaces clattering and clanging with the nodding. They acted, to be honest, much more like a class of toddlers than they did like a crowd of pirates.

"Could it be either?" Alex said. "Consensus of characters or the authorial intention?"

"Only insofar as authorial intention happens higher than my utmost heights and deeper than my inmost depths: at the finest motes of the being of any given character, their consensus depends on the author."

"That's not fair, you cheated," Alex said.

"How?"

"You wrapped my idea *into* your idea."

"Well it's that or the other way around. I like mine better."

And so forth.

Notes

23. The Delphic Oracle

1. Alex having donned his kerchief, and Lance his cap.
2. Apologies. Once again, it seems like I — Lance — forgot to take my pill for this bout of Theodor Seuss Geisellschaft Syndrome. Symptoms include random bursts of anapestic tetrameter and spontaneous fuzzy red and white striped hats, as well as occasional inflammation of anti-communist arms race sentiments.
3. Further apologies, once more again - being of a suprametaphysical nature our substance inheres in a pataphysical substratum, and we are accordingly prone to seasonal and existential allergies. These attacks are generally mild and manageable, but we will on occasion have a need to clear our minds; we hope you will not be offended by the concept of the sound of throat clearing.
4. That is to say: despite other indications or beliefs it's just the real thing you bought, not a forgery at all - particularly helpful in complicated capers.
5. Don't ask me about raccoon-on-ship insurance, please. For the love of all that is good and holy. Trash panda payout is the worst, particularly in a space station.
6. Mid-descent from our final hop, falling at terminal velocity from a very great height, just as we caught a particularly lovely sunrise over the hill and a thermal on descent. Only time either of us could be properly described as "hawkish"
7. Now you'll need to listen carefully to how "withed" is pronounced in your mind while reading, for clarity's sake.*
     *And for the love of all that is good Scotch.^
     ^And the claret.
8. Obviously, there was no convenient place to put it while dropping towards Oracle Hill from thousands of miles up in the air. Would you prefer your coffee spilled all over nondescript white room ether? *We*, at least, try to keep that our white room ether clean for the incoming dead and dreamers.
9. We should specify here: this is *Oracle* hill, not *Auricle* hill. The Auricle lived on a very small hill and showed up in another adjustment report of ours. He's a frat bro type — sort of the universal receiver to the universal stater of most oracles. The Auricle tends to listen to providentially keystone statements of others, how others prophecy accidentally about their own fu-

tures, and then tends to say something like, "Totally" or "Bro" or "I know, man, right?"
10. It's a magic number.

CONTRIBUTORS:

Chuck Boeheim brings his career in science and technology to tales of science fiction and fantasy while leaning into the "sufficiently advanced technology" trope. He's prone to filling his notebook with celestial mechanics calculations and other research for accuracy before telling the human stories set against that background. (Don't worry, the math doesn't end up in the stories.) His debut novel Sellenria has appeared on the Amazon top Hard Science Fiction list, while Knots is an exploration of a magical world based on topology. Visit Chuck online at https://lamp.works

Benjamin Brinks (he/him) has authored fiction and non-fiction under many names. He lives in the Pacific Northwest with his wife and two children.

Benjamin Chandler is an American expat living in Slovakia where he teaches fine art and English literature. His original plan was to be there for ten months, but that has been extended into twelve years, with a wife and two sons gained along the way. In addition to writing, he also enjoys drawing, cooking, and playing card games.

Anthony G. Cirilla is an Associate Professor of English at College of the Ozarks, a lecturer at the Davenant Institue, the Associate Editor of the International Boethius Society, and serves as a deacon in the United Episcopal Church. He lives with his wife, Camarie, in Missouri.

Artemis Crow lives in the northeast with a tolerant husband, two senior Dobermans, and a Frisbee-obsessed German Shepherd. When Artemis isn't gazing at the stars and thinking about infinite possibilities, she's busy writing the next book in the Zodiac Assassins urban fantasy series.

Chris Edwards has written plot for multiple LARP systems (most notably Profound Decisions and Shadow Factories), but has no real-world achievements of any note, aside from amassing an (arguably) impressive collection of roleplaying books. He lives in continual hope that someday his creative talents will allow him to escape wage slavery and do something he actually enjoys for a living. He has had a few stories published. He also co-writes an audio-drama podcast (Tales from the Aletheian Society) which has run to three seasons.

Evangeline Giaconia is a queer writer, artist, and world traveler. Her writing is driven by her love for queerness, myth, and social transformation. She currently resides in Gainesville, Florida, where she works in a library and is often found knitting and reading interesting books turned in by patrons. She is on Instagram and Twitter @evgiaconia.

Teel James Glenn has killed hundreds and been killed more times — on stage and screen, as he has traveled the world for forty-plus years as a stuntman, swordmaster, storyteller, bodyguard, actor, and haunted house barker. His poetry and short stories have been printed in over two hundred magazines including Weird Tales, Mystery Weekly, Pulp Adventures, Space & Time, Mad, Cirsova, Silverblade, and Sherlock Holmes Mystery. His novel A Cowboy in Carpathia: A Bob Howard Adventure won best novel 2021 in the Pulp Factory Award. He is also the winner of the 2012 Pulp Ark Award for Best Author.And he was a finalist for the Derringer short mystery award in 2022.

Michaele Jordan was born in LA, educated in New York, and lives in Cincinnati. She's worked at a kennel, a Hebrew School and AT&T. Now she writes, supervised by a long-suffering husband and two domineering cats. She has written two novels — *Blade Light* and *Mirror Maze* — and has numerous stories scattered around the web. Her website, http://www.michaelejordan.com/ is undergoing reconstruction, but just grab a hard hat, and come on in.

Based in Dharwad and Pune, Bharat, **Shashi Kadapa** is the managing editor of ActiveMuse, a journal of literature. An engineer/MBA, his stories across multiple genres are published in more than 45 US and UK based web and print anthologies. He was the International Fellow 2021 for IHRAF, NY. Nominated thrice for the Pushcart award he won the IHRAF short story prize twice.. His works:

http://www.activemuse.org/Shashi/Shashi_Pubs.html

Zoe Kaplan (she/her) has been making up stories for as long as she can remember. She has a bachelor's in creative writing from Appalachian State University and no less than four different swords. Her work has appeared in Tree and Stone Magazine, Hidden Realms, and the Horror Library anthology series, among many others, and her story "The Test" was nominated for the 2022 Brave New Weird award. You can find her on twitter @the_z_part or on her website, zoekaplanwrites.com.

Gabriel Kellman is a recent graduate of The University of St Thomas, where he majored in creative writing. He lives in Minnesota. He writes primarily fantasy and works on board and card games in his free time. He's a longtime martial artist and lifelong cat lover. "The Visions of a Single Eye" is his first published short story.

Gordon Linzner is founder and former editor of Space and Time Magazine, and author of three published novels and scores of short stories in F&SF, Twilight Zone, Sherlock Holmes Mystery Magazine, and numerous other magazines and anthologies. He is a full member of the Horror Writers Association and a lifetime member of the Science Fiction & Fantasy Writers Association.

Juliet Marillier was born and raised in Aotearoa New Zealand, and now lives in Western Australia. Her historical fantasy novels and short stories are published internationally and have won numerous awards. She is the author of twenty-four novels and two collections of short fiction. Her most recent series is Warrior Bards. Juliet loves mythology, folklore and strong, complex characters. She is currently working on a fantasy duology with a conservation theme. When not writing—and sometimes when writing— Juliet is kept busy by a small crew of rescue dogs.

Donna J. W. Munro teaches high schoolers the slippery truths of government and history at her day job. Her students are her greatest inspiration. She lives with five cats, a fur covered husband, and an encyclopedia son. Her daughter is off saving the world. Writing is Donna's painful passion. Her pieces are published in Corvid Queen, Enter the Apocalypse (2017), Beautiful Lies, Painful Truths II (2018), It Calls from the Forest (2020), Borderlands Vol 7 (2020), Pseudopod 752 (2021), and many more. Check out her novel, Revelation: Poppet Cycle Book 1, and her website for a complete list of works at https://www.donnajwmunro.com/

Andrew Najberg is the author of the speculative horror novel Gollitok (Cactus Moon Press, 2023), the collection of poems The Goats Have Taken Over the Barracks (Finishing Line Press, 2021), and the chapbook Easy to Lose (Finishing Line Press 2007). Among others, his short fiction has appeared in Prose Online, Psychopomp Review, Bookends Review, and Utopia Science Fiction. His poems have appeared in dozens of journals online and in print, including North American Review, Asheville Poetry Review, Cimarron Review, Another Chicago Magazine, and Good River Review.

Carol Ryles is an Australian writer of science fiction, fantasy and horror. She is a graduate of Clarion West

2008, and her stories have appeared in over a dozen Australian anthologies. Her debut steampunk fantasy novel, THE ETERNAL MACHINE, was independently published in 2022. She blogs at https://carol ryles.net

Alexander Sirkman was ripped timely from his mother's womb at a foretold c-section, venturing forth once his elder brother Aaron had cleared the way. Existence has proven a questionable decision since then, but the balance of desserts and true friends has thus far outweighed the despair of loss and people who say "expresso". If you encounter Alex in the wild, do not make any sudden movements or loud noises, and approach slowly without making direct eye contact. Feign interest in a nearby magazine rack, perhaps. Once he is at ease, use your net to grab him and voilà, there you have him.

F.C. Shultz is an author and poet whose work has appeared in Ekstasis Magazine, Every Day Fiction, and the Of Gods and Globes anthologies. He's the poetry editor for The Joplin Toad and lives in the Midwest with his wife and two kids. He's trying to cultivate a deep appreciation for the simple pleasures, which means writing a lot of poems about birds (and novels about dragons). You can find free books and poems at fcshultz.com

Helen Venn began writing literary short stories and poems. Now, no matter how she tries, she ends up writing speculative fiction. A She attended Clarion South in 2007 and was an Emerging Writer in Residence at Tom Collins house in 2009. She is currently working on a novel. She lives with her husband and cat in Western Australia.

Victory Witherkeigh is a female Filipino/PI author originally from Los Angeles, CA, currently living in the Las Vegas area. Victory was a finalist for Wingless Dreamer's 2020 Overcoming Fear Short Story award and a 2021 winner of the Two Sisters Writing and Publishing Short Story Contest. She has print publications in the horror anthologies Supernatural Drabbles of Dread through Macabre Ladies Publishing, Bodies Full of Burning through Sliced Up Press, and In Filth It Shall Be Found through OutCast Press. Her first novel, set to debut in December 2022 with Cinnabar Moth Publishing, has been a finalist for Killer Nashville's 2020 Claymore Award, a 2020 Cinnamon Press Literature Award Honoree, and long-listed in the 2021 Voyage YA Book Pitch Contest.

EDITORS:

Emily Munro is pretty sure she'll get the hang of this whole author thing any-day-now. In the meantime she reads anything that sits still long enough, knits her own socks, and drinks far too much tea. She can be spotted scribbling away in a variety of Brooklyn and Manhattan coffee shops with the Starlings Writers Group and on twitter @thatEmilyMunro. She has short stories published in the two previous Of Gods and Globes anthologies, Scott's Planet, and Alternative Holidays.

Lancelot Schaubert penned the novel Bell Hammers, which Publisher's Weekly called "a hoot." He narrated it for audiobook. He has edited three of these anthologies as well as the 500 pieces from some 400 academics, artists, and authors over at The Showbear Family Circus. He's working on a documentary in Alaska and another in NYC, has produced photo novels and his own indie rock albums, helped judge the Brooklyn Film Festival, and has sold work to places as diverse as The New Haven Review (Yale's Institute Library) and Poker Pro, The Anglican Theological Review and Nonbinary Review, Writer's Digest and Space and Time.

At his monthly open house salons for artists, he has cooked over three thousand eggs Benedict to order for everyone from the person experiencing homelessness downstairs, a fashion stylist of Elle and The Met Gala, a professional drag queen, and a Chinese underground pastor.

His life used to be an adventure wrongly considered and therefore an inconvenience. Now it's an inconvenience rightly considered and therefore an adventure.

Ring out the music of the spheres, folks.

Showbear Family Circus, resources for your own creative work, as well as ongoing serialized work by Lancelot.

Thanks for buying, reading, and sharing the work of living authors.

www.ingramcontent.com/pod-product-compliance
Lightning Source LLC
Chambersburg PA
CBHW030836190726
48285CB00004B/1241